A Fanged and Bitter Thing

A Fanged and Bitter Thing

Sherlock Holmes and
His London
Through the Eyes
of Scotland Yard

by Marcia Wilson

Edited by David Marcum

MX Publishing

ISBN Paperback 978-1-80424-659-7
ISBN AUK ePub 978-1-80424-660-3
ISBN AUK PDF 978-1-80424-661-0

Published by
MX Publishing
335 Princess Park Manor, Royal Drive,
London, N11 3GX
www.mxpublishing.co.uk

David Marcum can be reached at:
thepapersofsherlockholmes@gmail.com

Cover Design by Awan
Illustration of The Yarders by Marcia Wilson

Sherlock Holmes and the Scotland Yarders
by Marcia Wilson

Further adventures forthcoming . . . .

Author Foreword
by Marcia Wilson

Looking back, it was a strange time. High school in the late 1980's meant Tolkien, King, Christie, and Poe were always checked out of the school library, but we had multiple copies of Sherlock Holmes on the shelf. If students were going to apply for English-oriented scholarships, by gosh, we were going to read the good stuff, and that meant short stories with murder and mayhem. In emulation of the masters, our choices were usually ACD or . . . Hemingway. It wasn't much of a contest. Hemingway didn't have a demon glowing Death Hound on the moors.

High school segued into college, but we had *Mystery!* re-runs on PBS, even if we had to visit people to watch it, and besides Jeremy Brett, we had Christopher Plummer's compassionate Holmes against Jack the Ripper, a role that shattered the domination of Rathbone and Bruce. Our classmates swore it was necessary for our sincerity as fans of Sir Arthur to see it.

If that sounds like pithy stuff for high schoolers, my generation had a flexible relationship with media – or even power grids. Even if they existed, they weren't exactly as reliable as the sun coming up every morning. The further into the West Virginia panhandle you got, the bigger the library room in the house. Even the poorest of houses, be they on blocks or wheels, had at least one shelf of sanity to rely on when the power was out, or the brownouts made hash of anything but AM radio. When a flood took out the local libraries, it was devastation.

There was media, but there wasn't enough – there's never enough – but as far as the books printed in the wake of Sir Arthur . . . it really was never enough. You were lucky to find something in a thrift store or library sale, and your odds were no worse than combing the bookstores in the mall. Oh, for the days when there was more than one bookstore in a mall. If something was found, readers had to buy it on faith that it wasn't a waste of their time.

Look, our standards weren't low, they were desperate. We made a lot of poor book-buying choices, which were hastily returned to the ecosystem of flea market sales for some other poor shmuck to buy up. One girl, bless her, would donate the books after carefully penciling in every sin the authors made against Canon, history, plot contrivance,

1

and attempts to pair Holmes up with a romantic partner. I like to think she cackled as she returned the much-improved dreck to the public. She always cited her sources . . . .

It shouldn't be a surprise when we wound up obsessing, ever so slightly, with what little we could find that wasn't terrible, and (*Hooray!*) didn't go against The Canon. I wonder if anyone has ever tried to list all the knockoffs and illicit print runs out there. Probably not – I'd like to think nobody could be that crazy.

Fan fiction was the outlet for a crying need that had hit breaking point. Paper fanzines of decent quality were even harder to find than a decent paperback on the shelf – you have never bought a pig in a poke until you've combed through a hand-printed zine catalog, squinted at the type, and decided to spend your allowance on what sounded the most promising – and too bad the cover art was rarely as good on the inside.

Fanzine editors lived in the twilight, trying to put out their passion projects between the obligations of home, family, and keeping a roof over their head, as well as hanging on to entire drawers of receipts to make sure a rival 'ziner didn't get spiteful and report them to the IRS. (That actually happened.) Zines were non-profit only, which is partly why the zines we could afford were always shipped Media Mail on whatever paper was on sale. If you were very lucky, you got your order in three weeks.

Maybe we shouldn't talk about the pastichery in animation . . . .

The Internet found its feet and bloomed with forums and places to hide and talk about the lack of stories, and that led to posting paper zines online, and people began writing fresh stuff, online, and showing it for reading and/or critiquing. Almost overnight there were clubs, groups, and social organizations that could get their fix on the stories between the boom-and-bust world of conventions and newsletters.

There were friendships made that I miss to this very day. The sheer power of a small number of people who were intelligent, thoughtful, and mindful of Canon encouraged so many of us. They helped with research, knew how to spell, and learned different languages in this world. They reviewed books, scrounged supplies, and let us know if someone was copying our plots just a little too much for comfort. Plagiarism and how to address it was a real eye-opener when it came to intellectual property that wasn't yours to begin with, but you could claim the OC's (Original Characters) were yours, and debatably, your unique perspective on the people, places, and things created under the pen of Sir Arthur.

I was a fan of these fans. They were amazing and – honestly – damn good writers. *Damn* good. They were role models. They read the whole Canon, and they kept track of everything, and they led us to places like *fanfiction.net*, where we could post with a minimum of fussing.

I could write about anyone I wanted, but it was partially out of respect for these writers that I began to veer away from making just one more story about Sherlock Holmes and Dr. Watson. I loved the stories, but part of their appeal was their world. And there was a lot to that world that was relevant today. Methods may alter crime, but motives rarely do.

At the time, there was a pretty well-represented group that was pro-Watson, and they wrote some of those "damn good stories" with Watson as the protagonist – or at least, a powerful, equal voice. The Granada series was a huge influence, as well as the Russian series, and throw in some of "the radio show" for good measure.

These fan writers may have loved the tight scripts and drama of the Rathbone and Bruce approach, but as they grew up, they said, collectively, "Man, that was bad for Watson!" There were other words, much less polite. Burke and Hardwicke were a positive force for the shift in the thinking that pointed out Watson was *not* an idiot and we couldn't do a decent job showing how smart Holmes was by surrounding him by idiots. This had already been tried, during Classic Dr Who, and nobody had been left happy about it. Nobody blamed the actors for doing their job too well.

Fine, I thought, *there are a lot of really good writers writing for Watson. I can do that.* But I also caught on that if Watson illuminated Holmes by writing of the man from his point-of-view, *maybe I could write about Watson through other people's eyes.* The question was: *Who?*

Enter a re-visit to the Granada Series, and "The Norwood Builder".

I make no secret of the fact that I am heavily synesthetic. Face blindedness comes with its own challenge, and I have to train myself to recognize people. With an irony that approaches opera-grade comedy, I literally could not tell Holmes from Lestrade in Granada's "The Norwood Builder". Also, Lestrade made me angry when I was a hero-worshipping teenager watching the show with other hero-worshipping teenagers. *How dare Lestrade challenge Holmes? Couldn't anyone see Holmes was the smartest man in the room?*

Older adult me revisited that part of my life and went *Oops!* because there were some of those Fanfiction Demigods that rather liked Lestrade and had plenty of backup reasons. I wish I could remember the name of the one who mused, *"Colin Jeavons is the only actor who could be bulldog-like and also ferrety."* I was doing a lot of research at my job, and that included the Victorian era and law enforcement. Somehow it all started clicking together, piece by piece.

A writer whom I regret losing (her entire message board went the way of LiveJournal – only, it vanished for good. Poof. No trace) challenged me on whether or not Lestrade was stupid. He knew more than he let on, she said, and I . . . kind of said, *"Oh? Prove it."*

Ouch. She did, lining out events in "The Boscombe Valley Mystery" and "The Second Stain" and a few other bits and pieces, and I ate crow. A lot of it. I was wrong. Still, I could at least write with this new perspective. Bad as it was to be wrong, it would be worse to stay with it.

Add to this a sleep disorder that can politely be called *insomnia*, and a marriage turning into a nightmare of violence, and no health insurance – but writing was the cheapest therapy out there . . . Lestrade slowly woke up and came to life. I'll blame Colin Jeavons for knowing what the writers wanted out of the scripts. It's on him.

"Trust your characters," my old English teacher would say, sternly, so I did. I wrote short stories that could connect with others to make a fuller piece. A necklace is made one bead at a time. I wrote at night. I had to. I needed to stay awake, listening to any sounds that might be my ex-husband's return to stalk us – tampering with my car, crawling under the house, draining the well his own children needed to drink from, and taunts to the police that tried their best, but could only work within the limits of the system. They failed, but it was the system that failed. They cared, and they shared my rage that when the ex was finally brought to justice, it was too late for one of his victims.

There is only so much a policeman can do against so much collective injustice out there. If Sherlock Holmes had existed on that force, they would have begged for his help against my ex-husband. They knew he could go where they couldn't, and they would know when not to ask the awkward questions about how information was collected. They would have sniffed and said, "Well, that's a pity," and shrugged and did things according to the law – *their* law – but not expecting civilians to follow the same oaths they swore.

I empathized with Gregson's ability to buck the rules, and I empathized for Lestrade's inability to do so. The Yarders took on their own lives and, without knowing it, the job had changed. I was now sitting back and watching the stories unfold, writing them as fast as they told them. They had a lot to say. They still do, but the stories are whispering now. We are safer, there is no need to listen for danger. I am learning how to sleep.

More years ago than I'd like to recollect, I received an email so startling I forwarded it to my sister before a family dinner at the pizza parlour. It wasn't a fantastic day. Before long I would be needing their help to flee across the country in the middle of a winter snowstorm. The mood was glum. We were subdued.

My sister looked at me over the table and said with uncharacteristic bluntness, "You impressed that man."

That man was David Marcum.

Marcia Wilson
February 2025

Scotland Yard's Story
Editor Foreword
by David Marcum

Back in 2008, it was still a different Sherlockian world from today.

In those days, the quest for more excellent Holmes adventures beyond the pitifully few sixty Canonical adventures was still quite difficult. Each year, only a few slipped through the needle's-eye clutch of the moribund major publisher model. (In fact, if one is still publishing by that route, then this fact remains true.) But there were many Holmes adventures waiting to be revealed, and they just needed an outlet. Is it any wonder that the Internet was that path?

Holmes pastiches have been around since William Gillette's 1899 play, *Sherlock Holmes*, showing that Our Heroes' adventures did *not* have to pass across the first Literary Agent's desk. Some amazing and accurate adventures appeared on the radio in the 1930's, courtesy of visionary Edith Meiser. And the door kept getting wider, with more radio shows, films, and the occasional book giving us more traditional, authentic, and Canonical Holmes.

But it was not enough.

In 1998, *fanfiction.net* was created, allowing another outlet for sharing Holmes's adventures, wherein those who had discovered them could get them directly to starving readers immediately, without facing the impossible discouragement of the faceless soul-dead major publishing model. I was fortunate to discover the site a few years after that, and began to visit regularly to read and print and archive stories about the True Holmes. There are thousands of Holmes stories located there, but many are parodies, or anachronistic, or related to modernized and offensive simulacrums, or with incorrect ghost-busting leanings. Others were clearly written by individuals who have no clue about Sherlock Holmes, or have hijacked him for their own agendas. These stories may be ignored, even if they have to be waded through – for buried in the muck of this backyard goose lot, for those who take time to look, are some true and rare jewels.

And in April 2008, the beginning of a couple of stories were posted, "An Ordinary Meeting" on the tenth, and "Truth is the Critic" the next day, both as written by an author going under the curious sobriquet of *aragonite*.

"An Ordinary Meeting" gives details of Lestrade's first consultation with Sherlock Holmes, and "Truth is the Critic" is written from the perspective of the Scotland Yard inspectors as they read *A Study in Scarlet* – and providing their reactions when see how Watson has described them. These were well written and interesting, and this approach really hadn't been attempted before.

(To be accurate, there had been some stories about the Yarders, but they were inconsistent. For instance, M.J. Trow's long Lestrade series veers wildly from legitimate mysteries to unreadable parodies, with particularly bogus attacks on Sherlock Holmes, and Trow inexplicably gives Inspector G. Lestrade the first name of "Sholto".

In "Truth is the Critic", *aragonite* was already painting the Yarders – Inspectors Lestrade, Gregson, Bradstreet, and Hopkins in particular – in well-rounded and respectful ways that hadn't been seen before. They had their own life stories beyond The Canon, and weren't just the inspector *du jour* appearing in this-or-that Canonical tale. Who knew then that this new author, slipping quietly onto the scene, had such an overall vision for these individuals, with fully realized details about their personal lives, their backgrounds and histories . . . and a plan for a massive overarching adventure that would span decades in their lives?

Over the next few months, more stories quickly followed – "A Cookout in Cornwall", "Route to Madness", and "Just Inspector Will Do" (my all-time favorite of these works, relating the events on the Paddington platform when Mary Watson awaits her husband's return from the Continent in mid-May 1891. I re-read it every year on Reichenbach Day.) But on April 17th, 2008, *aragonite* raised the stakes, publishing the first chapter of a novel, *A Sword for Defense*, the first of a massive story arc relating what Watson and Lestrade and the other Yarders faced in the months after Holmes's supposed death at the Reichenbach Falls.

While keeping one story going would overwhelm many authors, *aragonite* – whomever he or she was – had even greater ambitions. New stories and chapters began to be posted at a feverish pace. A week after *Sword* started, another serialized novel began, *You Buy Bones*, telling how Watson, in early 1882 and fresh from his first year living with Holmes in Baker Street, comes across a monstrous crime that directly and personally affects the Scotland Yard inspectors. And a few months after that, *aragonite* started another novel that served as a prequel leading to *Sword* called *The MoonCursers*, telling of Lestrade's own terrifying adventures in late April and early May 1891, occurring at the same time Holmes and Watson were playing cat-and-mouse with Moriarty, on their way to a fateful encounter in Meiringen.

Over the course of that summer, nearly every day brought some new chapter: Sometimes another episode in *A Sword for Defense* or *You Buy Bones* or *The MoonCursers*, and at other times a seemingly stand-alone story that that filled in some crucial and interesting aspect about the Scotland Yarders that only made the overall painting richer and deeper.

Imagine if Charles Dickens were writing and publishing three serialized novels at once, and adding in short stories too. And they were going straight from being written to being posted for public consumption as soon as they were complete. And clearly the overall storyline wasn't being generated along the way – there was a *plan*, for little threads mentioned here and there about Lestrade's boyhood or Bradstreet's family had massive importance much later.

Over many months during this time, *aragonite* was also constructing another massive work, *Test of the Professionals*, which related the events after *You Buy Bones* and served as a set-up for *A Sword for Defense*, telling us much more about Lestrade's past, his unfortunate and dangerous life-long connection with Professor Moriarty's agent, the truly evil Jethro Quimper, and the escalating and terrifying events surrounding his courtship with Clea Cheatham.

In August 2008, with all of this going on, *aragonite* started another brilliant novella, *A Secondary Stain*, the *other* events of "The Second Stain", in which Lestrade was not as clueless as he appears in Watson's manuscript, actually working behind the scenes to assist Holmes's investigation. It was the brilliance of this story that finally prompted me to write a fan letter.

Using the fan fiction website's messenger feature, I emailed an extensive message to *aragonite* in October 2008, and soon received a wonderful and informative reply.

First, I learned that *aragonite* was really Marcia Wilson. In subsequent communications, I learned that *aragonite* – which curiously I'd never looked up before then – is calcium carbonate used by marine organisms to build their shells and skeletons. Since aragonite can be found in cave formations, and since Marcy is a caver – the evidence of which can be found in some of her stories brilliantly dealing with caverns and London's Lost Rivers – I suspect that's why she chose the unusual pen-name.

Over many emails over many years, Marcy has explained to me that she wrote so prolifically in those early years because she had insomnia, and that was a very productive time to write. She also could *see* all of these scenes, and almost couldn't write fast enough to convey them. In her very first reply to me in October 2008, she explained, how she approached telling the Yarders' story, and why she named Inspector G. Lestrade *Geoffrey:*

> *I've never liked the playing down of characters. It's a lazy way to pump up the character in your mind. I have to be very careful not to wander into the Fangirlyverse. Usually I deal with it by giving a character a name I dislike, and for some reason, I dislike Geoffrey so naturally I stuck it on the poor guy.*

She also explained that:

> *I was so bleeding tired of writing against another person's notions on Holmes and Watson that I just went to another character that I rather liked. (When I was younger, I hated Lestrade. He should have been kowtowing to Holmes' genius like all of us!) Later on, I realized that it took a pretty remarkable man to refuse to see Holmes in a reverent light. [The] clues about Lestrade were subtle and interesting. There had to be a reason for someone who was supposed to be such a good cop to stay a police inspector after his initial promotion. I made him a Celtic Breton out of a half-thought. I was seeing Colin Jeavons in my head, and he's so Welsh he's probably half-Neanderthal! Being a Breton or a Channel Islander would have made [Lestrade] an English citizen, but he would not have been accepted as an equal in race or status by many people.*

Our communications continued, as did her writing. By early 2009, *A Sword for Defense* was complete, and the next book in the ongoing saga, *The Narrow Path* had commenced. Those were great days to be a Sherlockian and to be reading *fanfiction.net*, as there were other great authors there as well – *Westron Wynde* and *KCS* among them, all with powerful and correct understandings of the *True Holmes*. These authors were writing for the fans, and also for each other, and I was privileged to be in contact with many of them. In a few years, Marcy and *Westron*

Wynde – who turned out to be amazing pasticheur Sarah Bennett, whose works are slowly being made available from Belanger Books – began to take down their online works and publish them in real books. (It was at this time that I let Marcy and Sarah read my first Sherlock Holmes pastiches, written in 2008 and at that point seen by no one but my wife, and with their encouragement I started publicly publishing my stories too.)

Marcy initially published *You Buy Bones*, along with some related short stories, in 2010 (from Lulu Publishing. That version is now out of print.) Next came *Test of the Professionals: Leap Year* (2013, also from Lulu and out of print), also collecting the original online novel and working in some supplementary material.

In 2015, I came up with the idea of *The MX Book of New Sherlock Holmes Stories*, and of course Marcy was in the initial list of invitees. Since then, much of her writing has been turned to contributing stories to these anthologies, having submitted nearly two-dozen. Through these books, she became associated with MX Publishing, who issued a new edition of *You Buy Bones* in 2015, as well as splitting *Test of the Professionals: Leap Year* into three planned smaller volumes. The first two, *The Adventure of the Flying Blue Pidgeon* and *The Peaceful Night Poisonings*, were published by MX in 2016 and 2017, respectively. Unfortunately, due to a combination of events, the third part of *Test* – the much larger piece called *Leap Year* that relates the exciting conclusion to that narrative – was not published.

So for the wider public, those who were never able to read Marcy's massive *ouvré* on *fanfiction.net*, her available works consisted of these three novels, and her well-respected stories in the MX anthologies. (Unfortunately, Marcy, Sarah Bennett, and several others were forced to pull their Sherlockian content from *fanfiction.net* several years ago after some of their works were stolen – copied-and-pasted and then republished under other author names by way of Amazon's self-publishing program.)

In late 2024, I was in the process of working toward assembling and editing the final volumes, Parts 49, 50, 51, and 52 of the MX anthologies, a process which would continue into early 2025. While looking around in my computer files, I found something I'd forgotten: Years earlier, I had saved and formatted the files for five of Marcy's novels – those relating to Watson and Lestrade's adventures during The Great Hiatus. Since the late 1990's, I've printed and archived every traditional Canonical Holmes adventure that I've found online –

thousands of them – and I have over 175 binders of pure Holmes adventures – including all of Marcy's now-withdrawn stories. But luckily I had these novels as Word files. And I had an idea . . . .

I contacted Marcy, who hadn't had time in several years to think about publishing more of her works, and asked if I could shepherd these five novels to publication – *pro-bono*, just because I was passionate about other people reading these incredible stories. Marcy was willing, and so I started editing with great enthusiasm – even as I was supposed to be editing the final MX volumes, stories for which were rolling in every day.

It soon became apparent to me that to publish these five novels without readers knowing the events of the missing *Leap Year* would be a confusing mess. Too much happened in these books that continued from what happened in *Leap Year*. Clearly, that missing volume would need to be edited and published too. And while I was at it, why not re-edit the previously published three books – *You Buy Bones*, *The Adventure of the Flying Blue Pidgeon*, and *The Peaceful Night Poisonings* – into an overall cohesive narrative?

MX Publisher Extraordinaire Steve Emecz, THE Sherlockian publisher and the Sherlockian Gutenberg – the man who made Sherlockian publishing accessible to real people instead of guarding a narrow doorway, or deciding that Sherlockian publishing should only be available for a very narrow cadre of self-described elites – was enthusiastic, and ready to proceed immediately. But I needed to actually finish editing the nine books first. It was a joy, and a labor of love to do so.

I had read all of these books serially as published, hopping from story to story as new chapters appeared, back in 2008-2011. But to read the story now, in one place, in order and available in its entirety, made it even more amazing – and exciting for the thought of new readers able to discover this magnificent world: *Sherlock Holmes's London, as seen through the eyes of the Scotland Yarders*.

Even as I dug deeper into Marcy's Scotland Yard adventures, I was remembering the other stories – the previously mentioned *A Secondary Stain*. Her Yarder's Christmas novels, *Gunnysack Goose for Christmas* and *A Mouth of Ivy*. Short-story collections like *Devilry* and *It's All in a Name*. Other novels and novellas like *The Muse of History*, *Ghosts in the Making*, *Courage Rises*, *The Kings and Queens of London*, and the World War I narrative, *The Days of Our Years*. I had amazing fun editing the first nine books that are being published in

2025, and with any luck, I hope to be able to edit the rest of these, along with a collection of Marcy's MX anthology contributions, over the next year or so, in order to fill in Marcy's *Great Scotland Yard Tapestry*.

There are certain authors who "own" other Canonical characters by taking hold of them and defining them. The late Carole Nelson Douglas was Irene Adler's chronicler. Michael Kurland gives us the best portrait of Professor Moriarty. Will Thomas has absolutely defined Barker, Holmes's hated rival on the Surrey Side. The late Gerard Williams claimed Dr. Mortimer (even if only for two books), and Susan Knight is easily becoming the definitive voice of Mrs. Hudson.

But Marcia Wilson tells the True Story of the Scotland Yarders – and presents an amazing viewpoint of Holmes and Watson along the way.

I've said it many times before, and can't say it any better now:

Marcia Wilson has found Scotland Yard's Tin Dispatch Box.

David Marcum
January 2025

A Fanged and
Bitter Thing

Feud:
Their hate, a fanged and bitter thing
Lulled by a mutual grief, had slept
Like a long dormant serpent now
It writhed within their hearts and crept
Reluctantly, a little stiff
And cold, to its accustomed place.
Where quickened by old fire, each saw
It coil upon the other's face.

– Edith Mirick

Chapter I – The Return

It was a wonder Lestrade didn't have an accident himself. He pushed the growler to the limit against the London crowds.

Bradstreet was waiting at the steps of New Scotland Yard, surrounded by a pile of finished tobacco butts. He was smoking a new one as Lestrade fell out.

"What happened?"

"There was a witness," Bradstreet said gruffly. "Passenger. Family friend. Mrs. Whitney." He flicked a heavy rain of ash on the wet concrete. "Mrs. Watson had promised a friend photographs of the baby, and they had time to go have it done and get back before the storm."

Lestrade fidgeted. He put his hands deep inside his coat pockets and twisted in his heels as Bradstreet continued. The storm in question was grumbling over their heads like wrath. Wind and flecks of soggy snow struck London from all directions.

"Their cab driver's a solid sort. Father to the maid who works for them. He was good at what he does, but that early in the morning, who expects to run into a drunk?"

"One of the all-nighters?" Lestrade guessed.

"The very same. You might know him . . . Jas. Newton. Does the rides for half the criminals off the Gate. Because the fool was going too fast, he slipped on the only patch of ice on the entire road and the horse couldn't stop. Plowed right into them. Mrs. Whitney is in Barts – she missed getting killed by the grace of God's hair."

"But they didn't," Lestrade said hoarsely.

"No." Bradstreet cleared his throat. Then he did it again.

"This is awful." Lestrade leaned against the rail, unmindful of the soot that had collected during the night.

"A bunch of the men are at the train station, ready to meet the doctor when he comes in," Bradstreet said at last. "There'd be all of us if it weren't for the time, but Hopkins got the best growler, and Patterson somehow pulled Roanoke back to the job – don't ask me how he managed that with the new round of influenza victims. Gregson got a party of men at each of the stations in case Watson gets irrational in his grief and tries to hop another line thinkin' he'll get here sooner . . . ." Bradstreet held the now-forgotten cigarette in his fingers.

19

"Any idea when he's coming in?" Lestrade ran his fingers through his hair and too late, remembered he had little luck getting it back in shape. He jammed his hat back down with a snarl.

"Not much. *Bradshaw* lists three possible times, and that's the best we can do. He got to the mainland a few hours ago."

"You are joking," Lestrade stared. "He got from Streat to Scotland on a steamship that quickly?"

"Seems the captain likes his stories." Bradstreet smiled without humour. "Watson wrote up a bit on coastal fishing and the old man's loved him ever since, because he was scolding foreign fishermen who take too much from the sea and leave the home-fishers to go hungry."

Despite himself, Lestrade had to smile. He could easily see the image. How like Watson to make a friend without knowing it.

The smile melted with the snow. "The drunken driver . . . where is he?"

"Patched up with a few broken bones and a vow to change," Bradstreet answered flatly. "He's probably sincere, but it's still too late. It's up to the jury to decide his fate."

"It won't take them long," Lestrade answered. It was not his duty to feel sympathy. The best the man could hope for was the end of his license, which was likely his only livelihood, and a view of the bars for several long, unproductive years.

Duty . . . . "Roger, I have to get to work. Let me know when he gets here . . . He is coming here?"

"We brought them here, so he'll be following," Roger agreed gently. "I'll let you know as soon as I know something. I'm stuck here all day anyway." Bradstreet always was a terrible liar.

But Roger did not call for hours.

The day crept.

Lestrade finished enough of his paperwork in time to send a wire to Clea, and returned back to his more pressing cases with a heavy heart. By the time Bradstreet returned, the hour was late, his stomach was empty, and his head was full of a throbbing pain.

"Let's go," Bradstreet said simply. "I put Monty in charge of the reporters."

"The reporters?" Lestrade repeated, slack-jawed. "Those vultures made it here? They had the gall – !" He rose to his feet, fury adding to the hammers in his skull. "Those – "

"They'll be sorry they had the initiative," Bradstreet said calmly. "Especially when Montgomery is finished with them."

"I can't imagine they'd stick around. One look at him and . . . ." Lestrade allowed someone else the right to be a holy terror reluctantly.

20

With tight lips he shrugged into his coat, one sleeve at a time while Bradstreet found his bowler. His voice trailed off. No need to start babbling. "Damn," he said at last. "Damn."

"I know," Bradstreet whispered. There were tears in the stout man's eyes. Who could see what happened to Dr. Watson and not remember their own losses?

"I feel worthless." Lestrade muttered.

Gregson was there with Dr. Anstruther. Hopkins was nodding as he turned away to some errand. The young man met their eyes for a moment, all silent sorrow, and then his face dropped back to its usual professional mask. Lestrade felt a stab of pride for the youth. He always tried to hard to do the right thing – and he nearly always did. *His record's cleaner than mine was at that age . . . .*

"He's with – " Anstruther visibly checked himself, and the policemen appreciated his respect for their office, that he would remain calm and professional. "Forgive me, gentlemen, Dr. Watson is with his wife's remains now." His composure quivered for a moment. "And that of his son's."

The words made it true. Lestrade's soul reflected soundlessly on Mary Watson *née* Morstan, and the warmth she carried inside her. Without her, the world was truly as cold as it felt.

And Arthur . . . .

Gregson was pulling his hat off his head, strange tears spilling at his eyes down his face. "Not his son too," the big man whispered. "That sweet little boy."

Lestrade remembered how Gregson had been the terror of the naming-pool over Christmas, insisting the Watsons would name their child "something impossible to pronounce" and harassing anyone who disagreed. He had enjoyed himself immensely over Arthur's incoming birth.

Anstruther swallowed hard. "I would rather give any other news," he said huskily. "But it would not be true." His own eyes gleamed, and he lowered his face, so the Yard would not say they had seen his disgrace. "It was quick, sirs. So quick. They only had time to be startled . . . that was all." He wrapped his arms about him with a shiver. "It's Watson I'm worried about. He'd gotten straight off that train and come here. That's no place for a man to linger. He's already been there a half-hour."

"I doubt he's aware of the time." Bradstreet spoke from quiet experience.

"No."

"Can't we get him out of there?" Gregson asked.

"He won't leave."

In the silence that followed that announcement, Lestrade sighed. "I'll try."

"I'm going with you," Gregson answered. "He might swing a punch."

The inspectors shivered in the chill of the room. It was cold. New frost was gathering over the old broken crust against the stone walls and spreading up the corners, glazing ice in sullen patches. Outside it was hardly better. People were scrabbling for warmth, trying to survive one night after the other even though they must have known it was only a matter of time.

Before they were all stiff and cold like the poor wretches underneath the sheets in the room.

Behind him, Gregson shifted awkwardly, and Lestrade realized that for all his gifts, his superior intellect and strength and his ability to solve cases, the bigger man was afraid to go any further.

Lestrade made up his mind quickly. "Tobias," he whispered, forcing the other to bend his head closer, "can you make certain we are not disturbed?"

Gregson did not hide his relief. "You needn't worry, I promise you." He nodded and backed soundlessly up the stairs. Lestrade could well imagine him sitting at the top and glaring at anyone approaching.

Lestrade turned back to the business at hand. He braced himself. His breath plumed in the air.

The man sitting by the edge of a shrouded table did not react to the click of Lestrade's footsteps on the brittle stone. He was badly underdressed for a vigil. No heavy winter coat, just a suit and light scarf around his neck. No hat, even. Lestrade's chest ached at the sight. This man, so military to the core, had forgotten himself in his loss.

No sense fearing what would happen. Lestrade stopped and silently rested his hand on the other's broad shoulder. Through the cloth the strength of the man was palpable. Lestrade knew that if he so chose, he would be picked up and thrown straight up the stairs like a hurley ball.

But he wouldn't.

John H. Watson never forgot his strength.

"John," Lestrade said simply.

No true reaction, but Lestrade knew he had been heard. His own expertise with grief had taught him that no matter how deeply a man mourned, they would still hear the words that pattered at their ears. It was just a matter of finding the words that would go through the haze of grief.

"John, Scotland Yard has a message for you."

Grief was not impervious to the unexpected. Very slowly, John lifted his head. The frozen snowlight caught the first threads of silver at his temples. Silver that Lestrade was positive had not existed a week ago. The eyes were still the same hazel, but not the usual gentle sparkle. John was wearing his "Battle-scar" expression, waiting for the next calamity.

"The Yard is here. We're all here for you. Just tell us what to do." As Lestrade spoke, he realized Watson's confusion was developing. On some level, it was understandable: Why all this concern for one tragedy in the midst of the winter epidemics?

But on the other, deeper level . . . Lestrade realized he was seeing something he did not like.

"John, where can we take them?" He swallowed hard. "What are your orders?"

John slowly roused himself, a bear coming out of hibernation. His muscles shuddered, and he managed to stand, a flash of pain running across his face for a moment as his leg sent a bolt of fire up his back. "Where?" he repeated slowly. "That . . . that is an excellent question, Inspector . . . ."

"There's St. Mary's. It's closest to the Strand . . . ." Lestrade put his mind to all the churches and chapels the Watsons might have frequented.

"No," Watson said heavily. "No church."

Lestrade was horrified. "No church, John?"

"With the influenza cases rising? In the middle of an epidemic?" John's head swiveled down. He stared hopelessly at the white sheet – a larger form curled against a tiny one. "How could I do that to them?"

Lestrade wondered for a moment if John's senses had taken leave. "John . . . ."

"You saw the churchyards," Watson choked hoarsely. "You saw what happens to the dead. Geoffrey, *how* could I do that to them?" He gulped hard, and for the first time, the shine of tears brightened the dull glaze in the hazel eyes. "How could I do that?"

For a moment, Lestrade was flabbergasted. Somewhere along the line, he and the other men at the Yard had imagined Watson had financially benefited from his partnership with Sherlock Holmes. Perhaps he had. But if so, Mary's illness had surely dried up whatever funds they'd possessed. And Watson's own nature couldn't keep a tuppence in his pocket when there was a starving child selling violets on the street corner. The more he thought about it, the worse he felt. John's sense of honor would have *never* requested help. All those extra hours, partnering with Roanoke and Anstruther and agreeing to serve as a Police Surgeon and writing on top of everything else . . . John couldn't afford a plot that was typical of better class burials. It would be the common churchyard or no other . . .

. . . and he was afraid of something. Lestrade almost recognized it, like hearing the echo without the original voice, but Watson was honestly afraid of taking his family to the open churchyard.

"Tell us what to do, John," Lestrade said firmly. "Tell us what you want done."

John had been staring at the sheet again. The words seemed to snap him back to reality for a moment. His spine stiffened and his hands slowly clasped behind his back.

"There's a crematorium attached to St. Bartholomew's," he said tightly. "Ostensive purpose . . . for the disposal of certain . . . elements . . . but also used for the rare humans who see no appeal in preserving the sanctity of the course . . . I need to make arrangements."

"No, you don't." Lestrade had made up his mind, and he could do so quickly. "We'll do that." Watson blinked at him. "May I have a moment?"

Puzzled, Watson nodded slowly. He was still staring at Lestrade when the small man hurried back up the stairs.

"You lot, listen up!" Lestrade bellowed at the top of his lungs. A shocked silence collapsed into the station house. Even the clerks had stopped in the middle of their filing reports, and Constable Nalan, teacup frozen halfway to his lips, stared goggle-eyed.

"Now I don't think I need to tell any of you what's happened with Dr. Watson." Lestrade was still using a volume far above his normal length, but when he was worked up he could keep it indefinitely. "And I don't think I need remind you what he's done for us in the past and now as one of our surgeons. God forbid I remind you the times he's gotten himself out of bed at owl-hours and treated one of us because we were injured in the line of duty and we didn't trust anyone else for the job." Lestrade narrowed his eyes and lips at this point. "Well, we've done wrong by him, and Scotland Yard needs to make amends for this. He's never asked us for a tuppence out of turn, and he's never asked us to turn in our debts to him even though his poor wife's illness took everything he owned. I put it to you to tell me a single time he ever made a complaint before us."

Lestrade read the red, downcast faces and shuffling bodies in his statement and felt his heart sink. It was worse than he'd thought. Watson's sense of honor was too high to allow him to move forward when another was falling back. At the same time, that very honor could not permit him to ask for help, even when that help was justified.

The Yard really didn't know how to deal with him. It certainly didn't know how to show that it knew what their sense of purpose meant to him. Only a man like Sherlock Holmes could keep a man like Watson engaged. And now Holmes was gone, and his family had just followed. The entire staff at New Scotland Yard wasn't enough of a replacement.

24

"This is how it is," Lestrade snapped. "If the doctor won't be asking for what is owed him, it isn't my place to tell his debtees what to do. But right now, he needs a bit of help and I *think* we're capable of giving it to him. Now after the horrors we've been witness to in the churchyards, I don't expect to hear any criticism of his decision to have his loved ones cremated." By increments, he saw agreement settle over their features. Nalan set his teacup down, his expressive face mournful.

"Bradstreet, Constable Hawkins . . . Briggs. Can you spare some time of Barts and see if a cremation can be arranged? Gregson, your talent lies in finding the unusual folk in life. Surely there's a priest from some church out there who doesn't believe cremation is the way to hellfire. Pevensey, Lucas, Jonathan . . . your wives have been an example in their ability to see to the widows and widowers of the Yard in the past. I trust their cleverness can be put to use again – get Mrs. Gregson on their army. She could organize the Beefeaters if she had to. My wife already knows the news. She's just waiting for the word to start cooking. Someone give her the word." Lestrade lifted his volume and his outrage. "And I don't care if you have to lie to the world. If you have to tell them some god-forbidden disease has forced the necessity of a cremation, then you do it!" Lestrade roared. *"Am I understood!"*

They scattered like rats.

Lestrade was left with the skeleton staff in the room, and they were duty-bound to their desks. He paused though, and gave each one a pointed stare as he turned his back and made his way downstairs.

Chapter II – Skeletons Emerging

The days blurred. Watson could not remember all of one day to the next. Only pieces survived, the way a shattered window only survives in fragments.

He remembered Theresa and her father trying to shoulder the burden of the tragedy on their shoulders. The old cabman had aged ten years. His horse had been fatally injured in the collision and he'd watched with a terrible, sad pride as her carcass went to the factory. His livelihood was gone. So was an old friend.

He remembered telling father and daughter not to be ridiculous. That it hadn't been Theresa's fault for not forcing Mary to stay inside, nor the old cabbie his fault for not being in possession of supernatural awareness.

No, no, I insist . . . take the end of the month's wages and have yourself a rest . . . you're both in shock . . . .

Finally, they complied. Perhaps only to ease his mind.

He remembered visiting Kate Whitney in her hospital room. Flowers were there, and sugared fruits . . . but the people who sent them, her own flesh and blood . . . were absent. She was completely alone in her expensive, privately purchased room with its double window and the bit of stained glass on top.

Poor little Kate, Mary had often said. *A bird kept in a cage out of callousness, because they think a bird belongs in a cage.*

She had wept to see him. She was awkward and in pain from the broken and dislocated arm bound to her waist. The floor doctor was insisting on morphine and she was terrified.

She has a right to be.

Watson sat and talked with her, but afterward he had no memory of anything he'd said . . . just a vague impression it had been about her treatment in the hospital, and were they being good to her? If morphine was not agreeable, then they could slowly wean her off it, but it couldn't be too quickly or her body would not let her rest and rest she needed . . .

He remembered Mrs. Hudson on the street. She made him come back to Baker Street. She brewed him tea and they sat in her small sitting room . . . He'd rarely been in her rooms. It would have felt like a peculiar invasion of her privacy in his mind, for she had been forced by penury to allot a portion of her house to himself and Mr. Holmes.

"You're welcome to stay here as long as it takes, Doctor. No fretting with the rent. That's been taken care of."

He had not known what that meant, but it was too much effort to ask. So he merely refused, insisted he wouldn't feel right leaving his home, when all he could really think of was how his choices were still haunted rooms. He could pick between his old rooms and the spectre of Holmes . . . or return to the ghosts that awaited him at home.

Of course he would choose home. Much as he was fond of Holmes and his memory . . . to spend even a night here would be to live in too many memories. Holmes had been most of his life before his marriage.

Holmes in life had been content with solitude . . . Watson did not think he would grudge him the time to mourn in his own house.

Telegrams assaulted him at his own doorstep. The messenger boy had waited in the weather for his return. Watson made out the slim dark shape, slumped over his satchel with his head bowed over in exhaustion. Watson mentally kicked himself for letting the child shiver in the cold and had him come inside for a cup of tea laced with treacle. It wasn't until he caught the sound of a once-familiar sniffling that he realized he was serving tea to one of the old Irregulars.

He gave the former urchin a heavy tip and a stern admonishment to get out of the cold. A moment later he remembered he was still talking to one of Holmes's boy detectives, and changed his dictum: The boy should curl up by the kitchen fireplace tonight. There was a pallet he kept rolled in the back store room for the purpose . . .

Young George was asleep before his head had finished settling on his folded coat pillow.

Watson went back to his sitting room in a daze, picked up his letter opener, and began reading the correspondence. He selected Mrs. Forrester's telegram first, and was instantly heartsick at the contents. For a long moment he simply stared at the black print before him, wondering how the poor woman had managed to avoid the chicken-pox for this long, and would she even survive it at her age?

It was a terrible thought, but a natural one. He was as fond of the woman as he could be – she reminded him of a combination of Mrs. Hudson and his own mother. What he could remember of her . . . .

He wrote out his response with mechanical concern, thinking ahead to the protective offense of her own physician – the man was so fresh out of school he squeaked and was anxious to take upon himself the patients under his father's care – but Mary would have asked him his opinion anyway. His last salient memory was setting the sealed envelope on top of George's satchel with the money required for the return wire, and going to bed.

Yelling – no, *screaming* – woke him up.

27

Blurred with confusion, Watson was halfway out the bedroom with his dressing gown unbelted before he realised it was all outside his practice. Shaken, he hurried back and dressed as swiftly as efficiency allowed.

It wasn't until he had the door unlocked and tugged open that he remembered his face still wanted a shave, but he soon realised no one was noticing him. They were too busy running from the constables that had taken charge of his doorstep.

"Oh. Beggin' your pardon, Doctor." A constable that Watson didn't recognize tapped his folded-over fingers to the brim of his helmet in the more countrified style that marked a transplant from the outlying districts. *They never do stop trying to tug a forelock . . . .* "I hope we didn't wake you up, sir."

"Not . . . not at all . . ." Watson heard himself stammering. The other constable he knew. "Briggs? I didn't know that was you. Where's your usual shadow?"

Briggs grinned, showing a lower tooth missing with pride – it was probably knocked right out of his jawline in some awful mulligan by the canals. "Phillips? That lush is off celebratin' his new baby, the lout. I don't know what my cousin sees in him . . . He's been written up once already for being late."

"He has? That's unlike him."

Briggs shrugged. "He knows better," he said calmly. "The Home Office doesn't take kindly to making exceptions."

Watson remembered hearing about the constable who was suspended from duty for being late. He'd been delayed at the funeral of his only son.

I could not be a policeman. Not ever.

But he respected those that took the duty.

"What's going on?"

"Oh, nothing to worry yourself over, Doctor. A few of the pests from the newspapers . . . can't mind their own business. They took off fast enough when all we did was glare!" Briggs' toothy grin was overly bright. He didn't want Watson to worry.

"Thank you, Constables," Watson told them quietly.

"No, sir. Thank you."

He returned to his upstairs rooms in a silent fog and shaved without even noticing himself in the mirror. His hands did their task while his mind was elsewhere, thinking to the past. He remembered watching Mary and Arthur holding each other in the warm covers as they slept. Both faces had been exhausted from the effort of birth, but both were also completely content with each other.

In those moments, John had truly experienced what love meant. He had been content to do nothing more than to put his arms around both and sleep with them, or lie awake for hours and listen to the softness of their breath, amazed at their fragility.

Mrs. Gregson's small regiment of volunteers descended upon his house without asking permission. John realized too late that the woman used her muteness as a weapon. While she was pretending not to understand him, her brigands were scouring the house from top to bottom, seeing to the laundry, and attacking the library with lavender-water against the paper lice.

Gregson himself came about with Lestrade later. They carried a kettle between them.

Times changed, and people changed with them.

Watson could only look upon these two men who had been such bitter rivals they never saw they were food for parody – when? Nearly eleven years ago.

"It's almost time," Gregson said simply. "Ought to have some strengthening before we go."

They ate the thick vegetable stew and Lestrade pulled out his flask to place them all against the growing chill in the evening. Together they escorted him to the crematorium and sat, one on each side, as the flames glowed and Mary and Arthur came back to him hours later in the form of innocuous ash.

He would remember the small ceremony in the graveyard's little chapel later, and the name of the soft-spoken little priest who blinked like a timid little owl behind his thick reading glasses but betrayed a fierce intelligence and an even fiercer love for his people when he spoke.

"I'll see to things on your end." Gregson closed his visit as quickly as he'd arrived, and never waved as he walked out of the graveyard. The door creaked shut on its hinge in his passing.

"I apologize, John," Lestrade said softly. It was warm in the stone building. Perhaps the wooden floor was the reason, or perhaps the warmth from the memorial candles. There had to be over a hundred. "They deserved better than we could give them."

"Don't be absurd." It was the first time Watson had turned sharp. "Mary would scold you for such words, and she'd be right to do so." He looked at the smaller man full in the face. "Mary never expected a reward for the good she did in this world," he said. "But nothing pleased her more than to be taken for granted. To be seen as someone reliable enough to be of help . . . ." His voice cracked like thin glass. "She would be well pleased, even though she would have told you not to bother."

Lestrade snorted, shocked into realizing the truth. "You are most likely right."

"I am no Sherlock Holmes. But I am right in matters of my wife." Watson paused and stared at the ground. "It's just as well," he said softly.

"I – pardon?" Lestrade wondered if he had heard right.

"Mary and Arthur were a part of each other," the doctor whispered. "She was frail, but her spirit had a strength like no other. No one else had her strength. I do not believe she would have let our son enter the next world without her hand to guide him."

Lestrade had seen many things in his life, and he could see why Watson would say such a thing. It still broke his heart to see the soldier facing his life alone.

Lestrade had lived alone or isolated for much of his own life. Now that he had known what matrimony could be . . . he couldn't remember what those pointless nights were like. Looking back on those complacent days was a horror. At the time he had been satisfied. Now he did not know if he could survive Clea's absence. *I would have to for the boys . . . but it would be hard . . . .*

"How is Dr. Mortimer?" Lestrade asked at last.

"I made him return home," Watson said without regret. "He needed to see to his family."

Their thoughts grew self-directed. Neither man spoke much as the vigil of the night continued. The owl-eyed priest lit fresh candles and vanished just as easily. A metal creak betrayed the door again. Gregson was coming back. Watson felt Lestrade stiffen next to him. Something was happening.

Gregson lifted his hand in greeting, but his gaze was serious as he neared.

"What is it, Inspector?" Watson asked wearily.

"Er . . . some news for Lestrade." Gregson looked down at the chapel floor to his polished shoetips. "It ah . . . it might be . . . bad news, Lestrade."

"You can say it here." Lestrade was almost as tired as Watson. He wasn't certain he could leave the room for a private conversation. And how bad could it be in comparison?

"Very well." Gregson toyed with his hat. "We got a message from Browning. Encrypted message, if you know what I mean. It's about the estate your family came from – down in Plymouth."

Lestrade fought the gravity of fatigue as he climbed to his feet, Watson regarding him with silent curiosity. "Gregson, spit it out, man. Nothing can be as bad as you stringing it out." He was terrified. Completely terrified. They all relied on Gregson to be a cold, unfeeling machine in bad times. Not like this.

"Browning and Jacobs are still looking for proofs of Ivo Quimper's murder." Gregson dropped his hat down and rubbed at his forehead. "It would appear there was more than one unexplained death in that house." Gregson sighed. "They found the skeleton of an infant inside the walls."

Watson sat upright at the news. Lestrade dropped his hat to the floor.

"Luke," the little man whispered. "They found Luke Quimper."

Chapter III – Vigil

Watson was taken aback at how the normally steady Lestrade had reacted to the news of this strange, grisly event. He bent forward and buried his face in his hands, trying to control his breathing as he stared at the floor.

Gregson sighed, not pleased with his news. He passed the smaller man a folded small square of paper with writing all over its surface. "I felt you ought to know," he added, "that it is clearly an older crime – much older . . . but there were some . . . papers found with the skeleton. My apologies, Doctor," he added carefully.

"Not at all," Watson assured him.

"And some of the boys chipped in for the vigil." Gregson pulled a string bag from over his shoulder and lowered it with a glassy clink upon the floorboards. "I already checked with the little friar . . . or whatever you call the men of god in this church."

(Watson paused to wonder what kind of church it was. There were little ornaments to clue it) . . .

"He's used to people eating and drinking to stay up a night, but he does ask no card or dice games for money."

"Most kind of you, Gregson . . . ." Watson reached for his money pocket, but Gregson cleared his throat.

"Boys already took care of that," he said firmly. "And if you need anything, just poke a head outside. Murcher is walking the beat at ten, and Barrett is following after. They know to swing by and see how things are going, but if I were you, I'd not linger outside." The pale man shrugged awkwardly. "Newspapers, you know."

"Are they out there now?" Watson asked in alarm. He started to rise up.

"No, no . . . not at all. When it looked like we couldn't keep them from looking for trouble, we gave 'em plenty to choose from. A bunch of us sent tips to every rag we could think of, tellin' them you'd be mourning in about twenty different cemeteries. MacDonald even told 'em you were going to Edinburgh . . . and did you know there's more'n one church over in the Orkneys?"

Watson's face twisted as it failed to decide on the proper reaction: Laughter simmered close to the surface, but he tried his best to look disapproving. At last he only smiled.

"No, I did not know that. What denomination?"

Minutes passed in silence once they had the chapel to themselves again. Watson now understood why it was just they two and the occasional visit by the man of the church. Everyone else was out shielding him from the public eye.

He tried not to dwell on his gratitude for the emotions it sponsored. It was like that terrible night on his way home to Mary from Switzerland . . . looking out of the train to see her surrounded by countless policemen. Half the plainclothes had even donned their uniforms in a show of respect. All had held a bull's-eye lantern against the darkness.

Watson thought of Holmes as a bright light in the dark and, like a bull's-eye, he was focused in his light. He did not merely shine. He looked out and peered through the world with purpose.

The candles fluttered in a tiny draught, taking his attention. Mary and Arthur's ceremonial urn rested in the centre of it all. The tiny chapel was humble, and of the three pews, theirs was the only one stable enough to linger in. It was heartbreaking to see how loving hands had done what it could to prevent the effects of time upon the wood and glass.

"Remind me to give that poor clergyman a donation," Watson said to himself.

"Already done." Lestrade had finally lifted his head. He was openly shaken, but more like his old self. "Rather a nice donation was made in your name."

"Really, I didn't want anyone to keep spending money on – "

"S'not. The donation was made in repairs. Ought to look like a different house of worship by the end of the month. I just hope my wife didn't volunteer me for more than the paint mixing. This time of year, I can't set mortar worth a hang."

Watson felt his emotions threaten to get the better of him. Lestrade smoothed over the moment by leaning over and picking up the bag Gregson had left. "A-ha! Thought I smelled garlic."

"Garlic?"

"I took the liberty of the local butcher's." The little detective held up a very familiar looking object. "I suggest an evening with liver sausage and strong ale."

"That sounds like a very real plan." Watson realized he actually had an appetite. "So long as you don't ruin my reputation as a Northumbrian." He took the loaf of bread meant to go with the sausage. "As I recall, all the proper Scots monasteries eschew both garlic and tomatoes as unhealthy foods."

"Well, I do attend the Anglican church. When I'm not on duty." Lestrade broke the bread apart with his strong hands. "Which is most of the time . . . I don't think I've been in a church during its usual hours more than eight times in . . . good Lord . . . since I started up as a lowly constable. That's . . . ." He screwed up his face in concentration as he did the math. "Thirty years. Soon to be thirty-one. No wonder I'm so ignorant."

Watson did a fair job with dividing the sausage with the bread. They agreed to leave a third aside for the kind old churchman should he come by again during the night.

He was so tired. Sleep was out of the question, but his eyes blurred until the row of candles became a single, shimmering curtain of light.

"I suppose I ought to explain what just happened."

Watson opened his eyes, grateful for the distraction. Lestrade was staring at the floor again. Gregson's paper had been read and was slowly turning into tiny scraps on the floor.

"You needn't if it upsets you."

"Oh, you might find it interesting." Lestrade made a hollow sort of laugh, like a man would if trapped in a dry well. "A case with interesting points to it, as Mr. Holmes would say."

Lestrade needed to talk. "Go on," Watson encouraged.

"Back in the mid-eighteenth century . . . it was the year the calendar changed over [1] . . . a wealthy man lost his only son and his wife with the baby." Lestrade wordlessly picked up one of the ales and flipped the stopper off. "This led to a problem, because the baby had already been promised in marriage to a cousin within the family . . . a cousin who wanted the name of the family joined with a ridiculous amount of the wealth. What to do? The father chose to hide the death of his son and went to one of the servants. They'd just had a son themselves."

"They took the son?" Watson guessed.

"Not as simply as all that . . . but you might as well say that's what happened." Lestrade drank and leaned his head into his hand. "The servants had once been quite prosperous. Times had fallen hard upon them, so they had the memory of being well-to-do, but they certainly didn't have the means. And then the master offers them . . . a deal. He takes their son and raises him as one of his own . . . and that will be one son they needn't ever worry about. Correct? All they need to do is terminate their rights to the boy." He let the bottle hang in his hand. "Happened a lot back then, from what I understand. You know, I even found some records where men and women legally turned their own illegitimate children into their bondsmen. Legally. The court turned the children over, and they worked like the slaves they were to their own flesh and blood, until they came of age and were thrust straight out into the world." Lestrade flipped his free hand. "Just like that."

"It was common," Watson agreed quietly. "I can't imagine it today . . . but I suppose in those days it was nothing to think of."

34

"Well, I am not used to it. I think it's awful."

"As do I."

Lestrade sighed. "The boy who died . . . his name was Luke Quimper . . . was replaced by the new Luke Quimper. But there was no legal way to bury the child in a Christian burial. So what happened to him? You wouldn't believe the stories I grew up with. We would terrify ourselves creating ghost stories about a child trapped in the walls. We didn't know the whole story of course . . . but we heard the handed-down bits of rumours . . . Mostly we didn't believe what we were saying . . . but at night time it was harder not to believe."

Watson shivered inside his coat.

"There was one thing the servants did correctly: They were told to give over the page of their Bible that marked their son's birth. They did. *But they kept the bill of sale.* It's been passed down father to son ever since then. It's been the secret no one knows about until they come of age. I suppose this means I've come of age now." He swallowed dryly. "I inherited the mantle of horror. But I suppose that's nothing compared to what happened when Jethro Quimper learnt we were blood-kin to each other after all."

"What happened?" Watson felt no exhaustion now, just a strange thrill at this "mantle of horror" as Lestrade put it.

"The knowledge drove him mad. He beat his own father to death and left my father to take the blame – *and he would have.* My father would have taken the blame rather than let the word escape. But that was taken out of his hands. And . . . *he* might be mad now, but he had enough presence of mind to pass on the proof of the sale. I went ahead and sent an encrypted wire to Browning and Jacobs . . . They were dealing with the Plymouth murder after all . . . and that inspired them to start looking harder in the house of the crime."

Lestrade shook his head. "They tracked Quimper's movements in that house somehow . . . somehow . . . to an old room mostly used for storage. Quimper had struck a panel, looked inside the wall when it fell off, and then he put the panel back and went on. That inspired them to look." His hands still hung lifelessly at his knees. "They found a carefully wrapped skeleton of an infant."

Watson didn't know what to say.

"Funny," Lestrade continued. "We weren't allowed in the house much as children, especially me – but we always thought the haunted wall was the one up against the master fireplace."

"I am sorry your family has to be enduring this," Watson said at last.

"I am trying to understand . . . but I just can't," Lestrade admitted. "For what it's worth, it hasn't driven me mad, so I suppose I'm made of sterner stuff than Quimper is."

"As if *that* would have ever been in doubt." Watson smiled at half-a-hundred incidences in the past – and half of those had Holmes complaining about the little detective at the top of his lungs. "Lestrade, the very notion of you being mentally weak is enough to make the stone dog laugh," Lestrade snorted. "I'm quite serious. You're most tenacious, and you're quite stubborn, but I've seen you back down from your stance after no more than a moment's thought when you realized you were wrong."

"I've had plenty of practice," Lestrade joked half-seriously.

The candles nearly guttered. They fell silent as they watched, but the tiny flames survived.

It was awkward to return to talking once they stopped. Thoughts crowded their heads, but they wanted out in no particular order. It was easier to concentrate on eating.

"That's a western wind," Watson said suddenly – it was like a blurt after so much silence. "The storm's breaking."

"Good." Lestrade thought of the poor people in the eastern end of London. There would be fewer corpses to pick up once the cold stopped killing them. "I am ready for spring."

God, you are a fool, he thought just a moment later. Spring would be the anniversary of Mr. Holmes's death. Less than two months . . .

"It is over."

Lestrade felt a chill as he looked at the doctor. The man was leaning on his knees, head slightly down as he stared at the floor in a fixed manner. In the candlelight his skin was newly bronzed, as if he'd returned from another jaunt to the desert.

Something made Lestrade sit up and take notice. Careful notice.

"It's passed now," Watson was saying, as if to himself. Lestrade had been a confessor many a time, but usually for guilty men.

The doctor rose to his feet slowly, and seemed to stretch within his clothing. He stepped forward to the ceramic urn that housed his family and as Lestrade watched, he rested a fingertip on the lid, thoughtful and reverent.

And strangely peaceful, as if he had just turned a cornerstone . . . .

"He can't hurt them any longer, so I feel I may return your courtesy, Inspector."

Lestrade remembered almost too late that when Watson was utterly at his tether, he hid inside a more formal and stiff language. Probably how he was taught. He rested his hands under his hat and nodded.

"Whatever you feel is best, Doctor."

36

"I know what is best. But I've been trapped of it." Watson was silent for nearly half-a-minute – Lestrade counted – while he watched the sea of words rise to tidal levels.

"Can you imagine what it is like to know of a terrible crime, and yet be completely lacking in proof?" he wanted to know. "To have not one shred of evidence because it was all taken from you?"

"Stolen?" Lestrade guessed.

"That too."

Lestrade felt a black well open up between them. Watson was listening hard for what he would say, and he was listening for the right response. If he missed, he would miss the moment.

"I fear we're used to that, Doctor. I'm not saying that to excuse it, or to have you think we're callous and cold to tragedy. We're not. But we cannot move outside the boundaries of the law . . . and if we break a law to seize evidence . . . the courts will find us as poorly as the very criminals we have exposed. Perhaps more, for we are in a position of trust and we daren't break it."

Watson nodded. "I understand," he said. He looked up to the ceiling for a moment, and sighed at the small, understated little cross resting in the niche.

"I knew Colonel Moriarty once I was sent to the Berkshires. But my brother knew him the longer. He'd chosen that regiment. I wanted . . . I wanted the stronger medical training and the allure of India. So I went to the Fusiliers." He looked at his hands for a moment. "I was soon-enough sent to join my brother, for there was need of me."

Lestrade heard the way that was said, and the bitter tang in Watson's voice, but said nothing.

"Afghanistan is rich in gemstones. Did you know that?"

"Something of it," Lestrade admitted. "I always thought it was like the way Cornwall is supposed to be rich in Baltic Amber . . . you have to go out and find it first."

Watson laughed softly. "And there's no guarantee if you will. Very good. And it's true. The people value water over gold. But rulers enjoy wealth, and rulers have wealth." His lips tightened. He was quiet again while Lestrade waited.

The doctor leaned his head back. "I was twenty-eight years old when we first met, you know."

"So young?" Lestrade recalled in surprise. "You seemed much older."

"The lot of Nor'eastern Englishman, raised as a Colonial," Watson said simply.

"Do tell me about it."

"I was born in 1852. I grew up some in Australia, reading of the American Civil War in newspapers while watching the world change around me in the sub-continent. By the time we returned to the north-country, I thought of myself as a grown man. Just as any good Scottish family would think. By the time you met me, I had been a surgeon for several years – years in which I devoured my own sense of self in the blood and vessels and muscles and tendons and bones and ligaments and nerves of the human race." Watson's eyes had gone inward, surprised at the confusion of life. "I had no other future, you know. I was the second son, and received no property." Watson's face showed no bitterness, only a faint sense of wonder. "And while commissions were no longer purchased, my family was considered well enough to approve of my future rank as a Major."

"You worked hard for your rewards, Doctor."

"It is not something I'm proud of speaking of," Watson said heavily, "for I wished to believe I was in a good, solid world. I knew there would be crime wherever I went, but I was not completely prepared for what I saw in Afghanistan." A cloud passed over his face and he looked down. "And as a medical man, I was uniquely qualified to observe men who were not at their best behavior."

"I assure you," Lestrade said, "I have no desire to ask for names."

Watson relaxed slightly at that. "It is not in the best interests of the bereaved to give full details." He rubbed his head. "But there was a time when myself and a few of the others noted that some of the remains of the dead soldiers were being . . . tampered with." Watson swallowed harshly. "Even now, it is difficult to speak of."

"Doctor, I am fully aware of your discretion." Lestrade was privately wondering what had happened for someone like Watson to be so traumatized. Watson said his nerve had been shattered after Maiwand, but looking at him it was hard to imagine Watson afraid of anything.

"I'll be brief," Watson said curtly. "As long as we understand it goes no further than this room." The Yarder nodded his agreement. Watson's shoulders slumped. "Valuables were being smuggled back home in the corpses of soldiers who had died."

Lestrade gulped hard. "That is monstrous – !" His arms unlocked from their position. He straightened up in his horror. "Watson, are you sure?" he whispered.

"I examined the bodies myself," Watson said heavily. "And some of us were able to band together and . . . stop this travesty in a way that prevented scandal. It was all we wanted. The idea of the grieving families to know the true purpose of why their loved ones were shipped back for burial . . . ." The doctor shook his head violently. "We could not bear the thought that they would learn the truth."

"And you are seeing parallels to this case, the one Hopkins is working on?"

"Not . . . exact ones," Watson said very slowly, sifting through the possible answers. "The funeral homes in question were involved with Colonel Moriarty's scheme to smuggle out the gems. But as far as I can see, the similarity ends there . . . It's as if . . . forgive me if this makes no sense . . . but it is if someone else heard of this . . . escapade and took inspiration from it." Watson rubbed his forehead, looking every inch his age at that moment. "Colonel Moriarty was the man in charge of this horror. Colonel Hayter caught wind of it . . . and he and my brother arranged a . . . way of cheating him from his foul treasure. I wasn't there, so I can't say what all the details were. But Hamish found it necessary to don my uniform on occasion and give a false impression of his own whereabouts."

"If you were alike enough in appearance, I can see how that would work."

"Moriarty suspected, but couldn't prove anything. My brother fell to drink and nearly ruined the entire effort." Watson sighed heavily. "But I could not entirely blame him. He was . . . wrecked inside. A woman he wished to court had chosen another and he did not take the news well."

Lestrade thought of his own misery when he convinced himself Clea was an impossible dream. He hadn't torn up a tavern, but he had answered the call to a fight with ungodly enthusiasm.

"I would not be surprised that Hopkins has found proofs in the trail of part of Moriarty's old schemes. It's the strangeness of some of these cases, though. I can't *completely* pin it all down. It eludes me." His hand made a fist. "I need to examine the rest of those remains . . . ."

"We'll see that you get your chance." Lestrade pulled out his pipe and set up a smoke, purely for his hands to stay busy. "How is it you ended Moriarty's scheme?"

"We could not expose him, but we could take his treasure away. Hamish did that. He took care of things while I was raving with enteric fever. To this day I am not certain if I imagined our conversations or not. I desperately wished to speak to him, but we were already growing apart." The flatness of his voice was terrible. "We had been growing apart. I wished to be my own man, not his. He saw me as an extension of his own life, and he used me as thoughtlessly as a man uses his own hand." Watson clasped his hands behind his back. "I tell you this to explain my inability to supply all the information. Hamish left clues behind . . . and I was left mute."

Lestrade heard him swallow.

"Colonel Moriarty did not know which was which. And he knew we were not . . . amicable. He is a patient man, and he watched us carefully, I am certain, for signs of wealth. I had no money that could be explained by a pawned gemstone here and there. Hamish slowly died of drink. When he did die . . . Moriarty still waited. I was beginning to work more closely with Holmes, and looking back, I believe that Holmes was already collecting the Professor's attention. He would not have wanted Holmes to know of him before he was ready."

"You're saying the Moriarty brothers were hand-in-hand with the Professor's Empire."

"I think it goes more than that, simply from what I know of the Colonel. I think he followed his brother to the extent that was required because he expected to take over the crime family. The Professor was enough of a calculating machine that he failed to turn his reins over to someone just because they were family. Someone else must be his witness."

"Dear God." Lestrade breathed as it all hit him at once. "Watson! When the Professor died, his brother wanted to take over, but someone is standing in his way . . . Gregson said this all sounds like a private war going on between rivals in the old gang . . . Moriarty needs the money those gemstones could raise!"

"Neither of us could completely attack the other," Watson agreed. "He has a horror of exposing his family name. I had my brother, then Holmes . . . and then my wife and child." He swallowed hard. "Now . . . now I have very little left to lose. And I can tell you what little I know."

"But . . . Colonel Hayter was involved. Doesn't he know anything?"

"Hamish hid the gemstones from both of us. It was safer that way. He played chess with Moriarty . . . he knew how the man thought. Moriarty knew how Hamish thought. As long as we were ignorant, we were fairly worthless to his schemes . . . but Hamish died and I took his sword . . . ." He sighed. "Moriarty knows by now that it must have been Hamish. All possibilities are discounted."

"Doctor Watson," Lestrade whispered, "you are in danger."

NOTE

1.   1752 is when the calendar switched from Julian to Gregorian.

Chapter IV – Waiting for Montpellier

The vigil continued.

They talked. Eventually it turned into Watson talking with Lestrade listening.

It was a strange moment for the little man. Watson's ability to make friends was natural as breathing, but he couldn't imagine this man confiding in him in anything if Holmes were still alive.

Then again, Holmes would probably know what to do. He wouldn't have to think about it . . . He'd say something and Watson would answer to it . . . .

Watson's knowledge of the gem smuggling wasn't extensive – not by a long shot – but it was enough to raise the hair on the back of his neck. Lestrade soon felt utterly out of his depth, and Watson was now – finally – given a chance to speak to someone about what must have been a heavy burden in his life for the past ten years.

Pieces of this are going to come back and haunt me. I just know it.

Watson finished with his palms against his thighs. Spots of red were in his cheeks. "And that is all I can think of . . . I am sorry to bring this to you, Inspector."

"No. Not at all," Lestrade whispered. "You did the right thing, not saying anything."

Watson was completely shocked, if temporarily, out of his grief. "You're joking," he blurted.

"Certainly not. The law must be upheld, but as you said, there was no physical evidence and . . . it wasn't safe to press the issue. No one cares for a dead informant, Doctor – which," he added as sternly as he could, "you may very well be if you don't have a caution. Consider the source if you please. Within the past handful of months I've been drugged by a turncoat inspector, fallen to food poisoning, encountered a knot of thugs who were paying far too much attention to *you*, fallen into an open grave and . . . Well, we can leave it there. It's been an unusually busy winter, and Gregson feels the remnants of the Professor's gang are involved in most of this. He's usually right about large crimes, even if he doesn't know a decent tobacco from street sweepings. The final line is the fact that I wasn't taking care of myself and when I finally fell to the latest epidemic, it was because I had no strength to fight it off. Try not to make my mistakes, Doctor – make your own!"

Watson's response was interrupted by the creaking of the little door in the corner. The little priest came out for the third or fourth time to replenish the candles. Watson offered him part of the meal a little shyly, and the old man brightened as easily as a child. He took the bread and sausage with a blessing to them both and held the food gently in his hands as he left again.

"I wonder how often he gets to eat," Lestrade whispered Watson's very thoughts.

"Does part of the donation include something for the priest?"

"It ought," Lestrade answered flatly. "It isn't just a charming phrase to say 'as poor as a church-mouse'." He tapped his glass bottle. "Perhaps he isn't from a popular church? Would that explain the state of this place?"

"It might," but Watson answered doubtfully. "But I do not know what sect he would be from."

"There's a Catholic emblem over by the doorway . . ." Lestrade mused. "I *think* it's Catholic . . . ."

"I thought *you* were Catholic."

"Me? I don't think I'm even baptized." Lestrade tried to make it into a joke. He failed miserably. He got up and went over to the wall to cover their mutual embarrassment. "He's killing a dragon, whatever he's doing. St. George?"

"The Archangel Michael was also a dragon slayer."

Lestrade ran his finger over the wooden carving. The angel – he could see the wings now – was serene and fierce at the same time. His halo had been painted with a thin gold at one time. Fixed to the earth was a gape-jawed serpent that looked like some nightmare of a legged snake with batwings. The angel stood upon the body, a final comment to the battle.

"I probably am baptized somewhere," he said. "I don't think my mother would have put up with any neglect like that. But I never learned anything outside of a few prayers, and I've picked up the habit of naming my children on the nearest Saint's Day. If I'm a Catholic, I'm a very bad one. I don't have a single word of Latin in my head outside of the nonsense Latin . . . and now that my boys are starting to learn it for their schooling, I'm realizing just how very ignorant I am in it."

"Nonsense Latin? You mean Pig Latin?"

"No, it's when a song breaks and you have to have something important-sounding to fill the space – *dominum dininum tinimun mun* – that sort of thing."

Watson laughed thinly.

"What now?"

"I cannot tell you." Watson stared at the wall of glowing candles. "I wish I could."

Lestrade found himself walking around the tiny chapel, looking at the near-invisible murals that popped up here and there. Age and neglect had caused a great deal of harm to the images.

"How is Colonel Hayter? Will he be in danger now?"

Watson breathed through his nose. "The Colonel is off the board, to use one of Moriarty's terms," he answered heavily. *His daughter is married to Moriarty's favourite ally . . .* "I sent him a wire, but he is tending to a very ill friend. I told him I understood and not to trouble himself."

"From what I understand, he'll come as soon as he's able," Lestrade spoke confidently.

Watson approached the candles glowing about the urn. "How bad are the newspaper hounds?"

"That lot? Not nearly as bad as the celebrity hounds," Lestrade said with utter contempt. "They'll all be looking about for you so they can take one of their sickening photographs or write up something horrible."

"The use of English language and English initiative at its worst." Watson rubbed at a tight spot between his eyes. "I don't know we'll avoid them."

"Oh . . . I think that's taken care of." Lestrade spoke so casually, Watson knew something was up.

"Did you make another 'donation' of something, Lestrade?"

"Me? No. It's just that we were given an offer of help from someone who is an expert in avoiding unwanted attention."

"Langdale Pike?"

"My word, *no.*" Lestrade briefly wondered what tragic accident would befall him if he tried to even step foot in that man's club. "Some folk you impressed once upon a time . . . They were rather desirous of returning a kindness with a kindness, so to speak."

Watson had no idea what Lestrade was talking about, but in that admirable way of his, he restrained from pressing the issue.

Gregson felt the lack of sleep catching up with him. A cup of tea right now would be the wrong idea . . . Best to just stick it out. Bed would be soon enough.

Hopkins cleared his throat from behind him. The younger man drifted forward, lowering a folder full of paper down on his desk.

"It doesn't look good," he said. "I've gone over it twenty times. The Blakes are deep in a funeral home scandal, but the fact that they're the only names that keep coming up . . . ."

"You think they were being paid extra money for the risk?"

"Why else? Bradstreet's work had it nailed spot-on. They've lifted their standard of living but all this time, they were being paid well to take the blame when the truth came out." Hopkins nearly collapsed into Gregson's guest chair. "I'm a fool, Gregson. I should have seen this from the start. It's so . . . so *obvious* when you look at it backwards! Now look at all the time I've wasted in chasing after all those dead ends." The young man rubbed his fist into his tired eyes. "Time wasted while they covered their tracks even better."

"We still have Dr. Watson. He wanted to take another hard look at those bog bodies at the museum," Gregson reminded him gruffly. "I'm not certain what he's looking for . . . but – "

"The man's got good instincts," Hopkins said at last. "These bog bodies are from Streat, and Streat was Inspector Loseth's origin . . . and Loseth was in the gang pockets . . . ." He groaned. "Just like Pennywraith."

"Just like Pennywraith," Gregson agreed. "Which reminds me . . . I do believe I'm going to have a little talk with him on the morrow. Do you want to come along?"

France:

The man known by the hotel as Sigerson was in a foul mood shared by the rest of France at the moment. The only difference was that his temper had nothing to do with the weather. Weather was a trifle.

Not so for the French, who had expected at least permeable skies for the beginning of March. The closer one got to Good Friday and Easter, the more festive and optimistic the atmosphere. This year Easter would be past the Ides of April – too far away to begin celebration in his mind, but not to his companions. Sigerson eyed the looming clouds above his head, and was grimly amused at the way such worthy hopes could be dashed to the rocks, as easily as a drop in the glass. [1]

Weekends were meant for a quick rest before the actual holidays, and they faced their allotted days with a joy that would puzzle an Englishman. But interfere with the quiet celebration the humble labourer planned with his family? One break in the unrelenting rain, and all of France appeared to be as crowded as East London during a fish sale . . . and while there were markedly less examples of ripe language, there were plenty of high feelings. Twice he'd witnessed the birth of two ill-advised duels.

"Look out!" The cart boy cried out in Provencal French. "*Excusez-moi!*"

"*Pardon,*" he answered hastily, and barely missed a gout of dirty water from the spin of the wagon wheels. The load of laundry continued on its way (annoyed curses trailing in its wake by less-agile pedestrians), and the man known as Sigerson was left wondering what amazing business dealt with the weekly wash by the cartload.

He shook his head at himself, fondly amused. The country pulled at him. Perhaps it was merely the force as strong as his Vernet blood. Perhaps it was the intriguing similarities and differences in the law. All trace of his English accent was lost now, worn down by the daily practice in the street.

"Another one?" someone was asking up ahead. "Can they not find the killer?"

"Of course not. This time of year? We're clotted with visitors."

"I'd say it was one of the visitors."

"Too simple. One of us. Using the travelers as a smokescreen. Why would a guest to our country feel the urge to knife a hotel maid?"

He sighed, low in spirit at the conversation.

The French were an admirable people. He might be a patriot, and England would ever come first, but that did not mean he would have to walk blinkered throughout the world. There were a few things the French could teach the English . . . .

And, surprisingly, a few things the English could teach the French.

It was difficult not to be one of the hangers-on when a murder or cause of death came across his life. Revealing himself or drawing suspicion would be a certain death sentence . . . but still . . . .

Watching the way the police went about some things was *maddening*.

It was worse when he heard them complaining amongst themselves, and wishing for a system as organised as Scotland Yard.

Another killing. Another apparently pointless killing, as the authorities would say. He was frustrated at the shrug the government appeared to be giving the matter. A madman, they said. His victims were all at random, there was no pattern . . . no way by which to solve it . . . .

And it would appear they had found another victim up ahead . . .

The crowd slowed. Sigerson used his stick to gently increase the space between himself and a troupe of house painters. Glimpses in the crowd opened up here and there. A man in uniform was bending over a shrouded form too small to be anything but a human head. Another man, younger and tall, was poising an expensive-looking portable camera into the top of a wine barrel . . .

The flash of a bulb shocked him. A moment later his every nerve was on cold fire. The photographer was too far away, he reminded himself. Inside his coat his free hand was clenched to white bone. *There is no sense in jumping at every shadow that shows . . . you will betray yourself for certain.*

Even if the photograph was developed and his face was in it . . . the image would not be conclusive. While he flattered himself on his features, he was still not the sort of man who stood out in a crowd of hundreds.

His nerves hung in tatters. His heart still pounded in his ears at the closeness of his call. A moment of carelessness, nearly compounded by a panic!

Why had he even gone outside? What had been so important that he'd needed to leave his rooms? In the harsh light of logic . . . nothing justified carelessness. Nothing justified an indulgence of boredom.

He needed cocaine. A small dose to let his mind rest tonight. This tooth-edged, raw sensation of always running, never being at peace, was eating his foundations to sand. If he did not recover his sense of self there would be no point.

He would slip, and Moran would use his time wisely.

Waiting had never been so hard.

Cocaine. There was an apothecary shop not far from the riverbank. An attractive little place, one of those tiny businesses he'd always meant to visit while in France but never managed to get 'round to. Now he was grateful for never having the time back then. The odds of his being recognized were much lower.

He would have to grow a beard again. He disliked it but had to face the facts. Beards chafed. The tints to make it the ridiculous dishwater-blonde itched too. Beards were unsanitary, unseemly, and never worth the trouble of making them. And yet they were an effective disguise . . .

The first clammy drops of rain began to fall. The crowd, if anything, grew even more sulky and the policemen were cursing at the looming destruction of evidence.

Your own stupidity if you think there's something to be had on the sidewalk, he thought in a sudden fury. *A blind man could tell you she was killed elsewhere . . . Did you not see the stamp on the barrel? The Desmarais Winery has been out of business for nearly thirty years! Imbeciles and fools, men who are hired not to think! At least Scotland Yard had the sense to consult me when they were out of their depth!*

He forced his anger to cool. It would do no good. He was not hired to solve this case, and there were no clients. There was nothing but the passage of time until Mycroft sent for him again.

Cocaine, he thought firmly. *Get the cocaine, and have the food sent up to the room every day . . . Read the newspapers and travel mentally, but otherwise stay put and vegetate while the horrid beard grows.* He would have to be careful in his trip west.

Montpellier, he reminded himself. He must stay strong until next winter. *Until Montpellier.*

Then, he could finally rest.

NOTE

1. Barometer.

Chapter V – Time Keeping

Lestrade had been asleep. He woke up from the change in the air. It was warm inside his coat. Even his feet were warm in their thin shoes.

The first conclusion was he was still dreaming, but a sharp, painful squeak sliced through his eardrums and sent him upright faster than his bedstead alarm clock.

Watson was pressing the door open in its frame. The wood against the slightly damp stone had been the source of the sound. Light flooded the small chapel, turning it into a badly illuminated cave in comparison to the outside. The air smelled sweet and . . . clean.

"I can scarcely believe my eyes," the doctor was saying in a reverent voice.

Lestrade got up before completely ensuring his balance, and blinked sleepily as he staggered his way to the door.

It had warmed up during the night. Warmed up to the point where one last snowfall had struck the world. It had hit so hard and so fast the particles barely had the time to catch the flying smuts from the stacks. It was about the whitest snow Lestrade had seen in years.

White . . . and blue.

"It's . . . *blue*." Lestrade stared. "Doctor, the snow is *blue*."

"Yes and no." Watson's voice was muffled. *Was he smiling?* "The snow is so wet, it reflects the blue spectrum. I used to see it every so often when I was young . . . but it was still . . . still something to notice."

He is smiling.

Lestrade didn't know what to say. He couldn't stop staring either.

Watson caught his gaze, and cleared his throat. He was still smiling despite the watery quality of his eyes. "She loved light blue. It was her favourite colour . . . I used to tease that it was because her eyes shone that shade in the light . . . ." He pulled his handkerchief out of his sleeve and sniffed in it.

Lestrade reminded himself as sternly as possible that he wasn't the tender-hearted sort. He found it easier to look elsewhere.

It was all blue-white. Everywhere he looked. The snow creaked under his shoes and stuck to the cuffs of his trousers. That poor little priest had swept the walkways several times during the night.

Beyond the overgrown gate, he could hear the cursing of the cabbies as they plied their morning trade. The wind was rising. Already the snow was melting. *More work for the Water Police today*, he thought. He imagined the coming floods and how it would make the influenza worse.

A dark, bear-like figure was shambling up to the gate, mounds of snow falling on his broad shoulders as he crossed beneath the snow-bowed trees. *Bradstreet.* Here to let him go home and rest a bit before heading back to work. Lestrade lifted his hand, glad to be distracted from his troubling thoughts. He was happy that Watson's mood had abruptly salved . . . but a policeman's work was never done, and even in grief they were expected to work. No excuses were permitted.

The Runner's eyes were circled with lack of rest. Lestrade knew he'd slept – nothing could keep that man from his six hours – but it hadn't been quality sleep. Things must still be happening at the station . . . .

"Hold on a mo, Lestrade," Bradstreet said under his breath. "The doctor might want a wire sent back." He was holding a square of paper in his hands. "Came all the way from Reigate . . . ."

"Not at all." Lestrade rubbed the back of his neck. The sun was trying to shine through the remnants of pearl-grey cloud, tinted with the light brown smears that promised the snows were still waiting.

He would have to see how Clea was doing . . . The boys would be coming home sometime today . . . .

Knowing his wife, she would have set the cooking school on her ear and was creating mountains of food.

Lestrade wrenched his thoughts aside for the moment. Watson was opening up the paper with a frown of concern. That frown deepened as he read the contents.

"Not bad news, I hope," Bradstreet murmured.

"Colonel Hayter's falling ill," Watson told him. "He won't be able to come in . . . it's probably the influenza." He rubbed at his chin. "He is usually so careful, but . . . I should like to send a wire back to him."

"I'll send it," Lestrade assured him.

"When you get back to the New," Bradstreet said on his way out, "there're some papers I left on your desk. Ought to help you with your other investigation."

Lestrade didn't know what Bradstreet meant by "other" but nodded all the same and pretended he did. He went on home where Clea nearly cut him in two with the force of her arms thrown around him. He cleaned up quickly and took fifteen minutes on the settee before it was time to get to New Scotland Yard.

Bradstreet's paper was sitting on his desk. Lestrade read it, his heart pounding as he absorbed the news.

Baldwin's case had been expedited from his longstanding case history and positive identification for his role in the Aton Bank Robbery years ago. At the same time, there were three cases of murder against him put forth by reliable witnesses.

49

Bradstreet's information between the lines, which had been provided by a friendly barrister, was clear.

Baldwin would be sentenced to death unless the hard-headed English jury decided otherwise.

The sentencing would be soon.

Lestrade swallowed a mouth full of ash.

No, not ash. Sand.

The sand's running out of the glass.

And I'm running out of time.

Somewhere in France:

At dawn, the fire burnt out.

The last of its warmth died out with it an hour later while the remnants of the passing storm rattled the small window of his room.

At noon, the servant-boy left the luncheon tray in the hallway and took the uneaten breakfast tray.

In the afternoon that followed, he managed to leave the bed long enough to find the extra blanket kept in the chest at the foot of the bed. He felt as though he barely made it back under the sheets in time. His teeth chattered and his skin trembled all the way to his very skeleton.

At supper, the more experienced boy for the hotel knocked and came inside when there was no answer. With a poise better suited to an adult, he asked politely if M. Sigerson would prefer to have a cup of broth while he built the fire back up. Impressed at the young man's calm (and obvious experience), he gave consent. The boy set up the pillows for his comfort before dirtying his hands at the ashes, and warm broth was placed in his hands mere moments later.

"It is good you will take the broth, yes?" There was a slight German accent in the youth's voice, just as there was a slight Teutonic cast in his chiseled face. "For my mistress will be certain to send for our physician if her boarders are ill. But if you are taking broth and sleep . . . she is less likely to harass your sensibilities."

He talked as though he learned most of his language by reading books. Well, it wasn't the most unlikely thing he'd encountered. "I shall be fine once the chill of this rain leaves me," he explained. "I was caught in the wet on my way back."

The boy's light blue eyes were thoughtful on his mistresses' client. "There is a bad sickness about, Monsieur. I would be careful. It turns to something worse very quickly. The first stage is intolerable enough."

"Am I not in the first stage now?" Sigerson asked dryly.

"Not yet, sir. The first stage lasts a week. If this is what you have, you will be very tired and weak . . . You should eat whatever attracts you, for keeping your strength up is very important."

Sigerson thought about pointing out that tired and weak was already his current state, but chose to set it aside. Clearly he had a choice: Try to hole up and ignore his condition in the relative mental comfort of being ignored until the door was kicked down (and the damage added to his bill), or he could accept a slight bit of coddling and offstay an intolerable level of concern from strangers.

The boy reminded him of Watson. Calm, suggestive of treatment, but in a way that let him make the only choice.

Alone again, he closed his eyes and thought of the last time he'd been so ill in France. Watson had dropped everything to come to his Lyons rooms. A complete week he'd stayed, waiting on him practically hand and foot until he was well enough to get to England. To this day, he remembered nothing but the crushing blackness that kept him in bed. In the wake of his renowned success and Europe's maddening praises, he could not even eat or drink. Watson might have saved his life, for Holmes had not endured a depression so severe in years.

Not an overall bad experience, for it had led to an interesting case and the introduction of Watson's friend Hayter.

An interesting man, to be sure. He was all proper military, but he had without a doubt the least-trained butler in all of Holmes's experience. The way the old man carried himself, Holmes suspected he had been part of Hayter's military entourage before his retirement. He kept the household up with military neatness and no woman could have kept the décor cleaner . . . but his *faux pas* of coming in to tell his master the news of the murder was something no brought-up butler would have done.

This suggested to Holmes while he recuperated that Hayter's eyes were still on law and order. He made an earnest effort to keep watch on his part of the world. The guns on display were hardly the stuff to frighten a burglar . . . save close range . . . but Holmes had every faith the Colonel had better upstairs.

It was enjoyable to watch the closeness between Hayter and Watson. Long conversations had carried on with Holmes falling silent in periods as he took in the sight. Hayter's honest appreciation of Watson was refreshing, as Watson (in Holmes's opinion) rarely got the attention he deserved.

Hayter honestly cared about Watson, and in the rare moments they were together and Watson was absent, they had the chance to talk about him.

51

"Brilliant man," he said. "I didn't really meet him until Afghanistan. A shame. He's the sort of man we can always use in the Army. Never lost his head once. That's hard enough to train into a man, but he had it natural." Hayter glanced upstairs to where Watson was now sleeping the sleep of the exhausted . . . taking care of Holmes had not been a light task. He produced a box of thin cigars and Holmes smiled. A fellow conspirator.

They plucked the bands off and started smoking without pause.

"Sounds terrible to say, but I trusted him as my doctor over some codger who had twenty more years' experience."

Holmes was hardly surprised. Watson demonstrated a lack of confidence in the abilities he knew he lacked in – it was not in him to bear a false sense of accomplishment. If he knew something, he acted on it. If the procedure was unfamiliar, he went by what he did know.

Even now, it seemed wrong not to have Watson here taking care of him.

He always knew what to say, and didn't care if his reluctant patient was recalcitrant about medical health.

If Watson were here right now, Holmes could well imagine the tongue lashing that would result.

"How many days has it been since your last decent meal, Holmes? I mean decent meal, not something you purchase on a whim after you've already dulled your appetite with tobacco!"

Holmes smiled at the memories.

"For that matter, how often have you been sleeping? Not even as much as six hours a night, for that would be unacceptable for your behaviors. You have clearly been without for as long as you have been without proper nourishment!"

Holmes chuckled in the growing darkness.

"Confound it all, Holmes! Can you not treat yourself with more respect?"

"Why should I? It is just housing for the clock, Watson. The clock is what is valued, not the housing."

"A clock only exists when it is working. A broken clock is a broken clock. And Holmes, how does a clock break? It is wound too tightly, or run too long. How often have you been at the fringes of health since Reichenbach? Tell me if you have enough rationale in your brain to recall."

"I can recall quite clearly." When Watson was right, Holmes dealt with the matter by being unconcerned. *"I have been ill three times since last April. Not an unusual statistic for a man who lives in London."*

"But you aren't living in London, Holmes. You are living alone. And I am not here to save you from yourself."

"I need no saving."

"You do."

The Watson in his head was even more obstinate than the Watson he once lived with. It was one reason why he could not regret his friend's pursuit of matrimonial happiness. Gibe and sneer about love how he may, Holmes had to concede that Watson's energies would be better off directed at his own house and home.

Holmes smiled at himself, for even the cocaine could give him a brief flight of fancy. Watson was better off worrying about his remarkable little wife and new son. He had accomplished that much. Pulling away had been necessary. Watson would not have left his side otherwise.

And on that assurance, Holmes slept.

Chapter VI – March 1892

February 29th*:*

The newspapers being less than perfect entities, only four mentioned the phenomena of Leap Year marriages and the proper social context of the following wedding anniversaries. This was possibly because no one paid attention to the workman's class when the gentlemen were making news, and very few gentlemen would be married on Leap Year. The Lestrades were relieved that their own example was given less than twenty-five words. It falling on a Monday for that year, it was for the most part another workday celebrated quietly at home over supper. That and another explanation to the children as to why it would not be a particularly good idea to tell everyone at school their parents had been married for two years now.

March 4th*:*

Inspector Gregson visited the disgraced Dr. Pennywraith in his cell. His visit was less-than-twelve minutes in length, and the abrupt manner of his departure implied to all that the doctor was less-than-helpful with his information.

Thanks to a well-paid messenger boy, the Yard knew that Mrs. Forrester, the wealthy friend of the late Mrs. Watson, was recovering. Colonel Hayter was on the mend as well, and it was a relief. Watson was not safe in the world without a close circle of kith and kin. Watson slipped away when his new schedule permitted and saw to each one individually. His work with the Yard was about to progress at last, for Dr. Mortimer had pulled many connections to permit his attendance at the London Museum where the bog bodies rested.

March 8th*:*

Inspector Hopkins' pursuit of clues led to a mysterious fire at the old Bank of Thames-backed funeral home. Enough was destroyed that the young man went home that night in a spate of utter dejection. He ignored all the kind entreaties from his fellow detectives. That night he felt as though all his efforts in the case had ended, and he was now worthless to the search. Gregson told him he was being an idiot, but Gregson was not known for his successful bedside manner.

His feelings would have been understood (if never admitted) to the man known as Sigerson lying in a working-class hotel room in France. There was no question the gentleman with the grey Nordic eyes had fallen victim to the miasma clinging to the earth. He shared the honour with enough of the guests, but at least they were all paying guests and not likely to get into too much trouble with politics or women! So said the proprietrix as she scheduled another round of clothing, warm teas and soups, and a light bread rich with beaten eggs.

Of all her ill guests, she had to confess Sigerson had her concerns. The man insisted on daily newspapers sent up to his rooms, but he was not even well enough to read them. It was a shame, but perhaps it was just as well that he could not read. The papers were only full of the disastrous murders . . . not suitable material for one who was trying to recover.

March 9ᵗʰ:

Inspector Patterson had been pressing himself too close to the bone in his efforts to return to his old informants. His efforts were finally rewarded when he at last came across positive proof that his murdered assistant, "The Wardrobe Man", had been a former excavator for Sir Niles on the Isle of Streat.

Upon hearing the news, Gregson's response was to curse loudly and at length before explaining himself: Questioning Dr. Pennywraith, was no longer a possibility as the Home Office did not sanction the use of a spiritualist in investigations. The doctor's poor heart had been a closely kept secret, and he had been found dead without a single glimmer of regret or surprise on his face.

Watson took the closure of the news with barely a blink. He was finally allowed to view the remains at the museum, and he planned to clean his schedule out of all other cases so he could concentrate on the ancient bodies. Whatever led to the Wardrobe Man's murder, it had to be influenced with his work on Streat.

Watson was a busy man by nature, and he was keeping busy for a good reason. That he had not the time to look through Sir Niles' notebook spoke of just how busy he was.

March 10ᵗʰ:

Little Kate Whitney was allowed to come home. She was meant to be picked up by her husband, but when Isa never showed, Watson escorted her back to her house along with cold, forceful instructions to the suddenly attentive maid. He left Kate with one of her school friends, tracked Isa into an opium-infested den, and packed him out into the open air where he promptly forgot his manners as a gentleman and gave the wreck of a man the thrashing of his life.

PC Grover was the unfortunate witness, but he was sage enough to quietly avoid a report and simply pass the information on to Inspector Hopkins instead. Hopkins all but swallowed his teeth and took steps to ensure no rumours would be coming from *their* quarter.

Hopkins might have been more astonished had he known that Watson had gone to Whitney's older brother and informed him it was high time he dismissed the maid as worthless and subserving, and the rest of the staff was callous to the lady chosen by their master. He told Brother Whitney where to find a decent, hardworking young woman who would have poor Kate's best interests at heart.

March 12th:

Sigerson's publishing agent was unpleasantly surprised at the delay in his promised dissertation on European hunting. The explanation of long extended illness satisfied them only because the epidemic was a fact and not something one would be capable of fabricating.

Watson's publishers were much more understanding. So much so that he was quite astonished to find an advance cheque in the mail from *The Strand* for two more of his contracted stories, "The Beryl Coronet" and "The Copper Beeches", and "Silver Blaze" was only an approved outline and a fistful of notes.

He decided to start working on "The Beryl Coronet" first. It was due for a May publishing date. "The Copper Beeches" would follow in June.

March 15th:

Lestrade's request to see "Bold Tarby" Baldwin at the prison was approved. His surprise expanded to that evening when his wife told him Dr. Watson had dismissed his Theresa for better lodgings and applied for a new maid of all work directly from her school. His surprise compounded unpleasantly the following morning at the steps of Newgate: Baldwin had been struck down with the influenza. Visits were inadvisable until the condemned man had recovered.

March 27th:

Kate Whitney was soon fast friends with her new maid, Theresa. That she had been Mary's maid beforehand made it even better. For his part,

Watson had no ill feelings for Theresa. She was a face he associated with Mary and Arthur, and to live that close to the memories threatened to crush him. He needed to breathe, and space was at a premium in a city of millions.

March 28th:

On Monday, John Watson woke up from the sunlight on his eyes and realized the planet was actually turning. Spring had gone from being a cruel promise to a soft reality. The surprise was enough to pull him out of bed for a stare at the window overlooking Mary's little garden. The snowdrops were in bloom against the chill of the building's shade.

He stood watching the sunlight's beams cast delicate shadows across the set brickwork of the path . . . and when he finally turned his head, it was to prepare for work. It was a morning like any other since the funeral, for time and responsibilities took no mourning days. But there was one difference about today.

The doctor went to his closet and pulled out his black suit, black cravat, black waistcoat, black gloves. His jet cufflinks and jet-hung watchchain followed suit.

Today he was ready to find answers.

Chapter VII – A Bell from the Past

Newgate was a bitterly cold place to be, even in the first week of April.

Inspector Lestrade made his way across the soggy mess of the courtyard with his hands clutched up at his collar. PC Cooper followed suit, drafted for the duty by nothing more than a quick word from the little man.

Cooper needed no invitation.

"Wait here," the inspector directed him once they were inside. "I have no idea how long any of this will take."

Cooper took in the small room, replete with a tiny stove and teapot with a long line of polished cups hanging on the wall. A prison guard was settling himself down at the small table and stirring something into his cup with gross enthusiasm. The guard caught their gaze and cheerfully waved to the newcomers. "Yes, sir."

"Tea's good un' hot, gents!" he exclaimed. "Shall I make you a cup?"

"I'll save mine for when I get back, thank you, Jake," Lestrade said with automatic courtesy. Without a further word he shut the door.

The guard chuckled lightly. "That's old Lamps for you," he said with relish. "Broke his own mold, he did. You must be Cooper's boy."

Cooper jumped a little. "Yes . . . yes, sir," he said.

"Are you Grasshopper or Tadpole?"

"Ah . . . I'm Tadpole."

"Thought so. You didn't look like a grasshopper." The guard sucked his tea loudly. "Never saw either of you boys when you earned those nicknames . . . but I guessed. Sit down there, lad. I was pleased to call your old father a friend."

"Thank you, sir." Cooper awkwardly pulled his helmet off and loosened the buttons of his coat.

"Name's Joseph Tincher. Didn't know your father long, but you didn't have to. Got exactly what you saw with him. Not a bit of deceit in his nature. I was with him an' Lamps during the Hyde Park Riot . . . By the time I got out of the hospital, I thought I should try another line of work, so I joined up with the prison." Tincher slurped his tea again. "Boiling hot," he explained. "But if I don't get it in me right now, I'm going to be worth nothing on the ride home."

Cooper busied himself with a half-cup and agreed it was hot. "I don't know too much about my father, except I'm supposed to favour him."

"Well, you do at that. Gave me a start when I saw you walking behind Lestrade. Thought to myself, "There's something to angels, because there's Lamps' guardian right there." He chuckled at himself. "Those two were tight, like brothers. Lamps saved your dad's life during the riot, but he took an awful pounding for it. I'll never forget the sight."

"I don't know anything about it." Cooper said softly, but he leaned forward in his eagerness. "Can you tell me?"

"Course I can. They'd ripped your papa's helmet right off – we never did find it, I suppose it was taken home as a souvenir or a chamber pot – and a piece of brick got him on the chin. He went down and fast as that, Lestrade was yanking his own helmet off and stickin' it on Pacer – that's what we called him. Stood over him and kept 'im from getting trampled by the mob until the rest of us could close around him. I tell you, twenty seconds can be a lifetime. I got myself a broken arm for my troubles, but at least I wasn't left a cripple. Enough of us were though. There were vacant posts in the Met when the dust settled." Tincher chuckled again, ruefully. "Bradstreet was there too . . . I remember thinking how glad I was to see that man. Takes up a lot of space in a room – like having a bloody wall against your back in a scrum!"

Cooper risked smiling at the scandalous thought. "I don't think he's gotten any smaller."

"No, he has not. Has a presence, doesn't he? I forget there are folks out there bigger than he when he comes into a room." Tincher slapped his palm on the table and held out his hand for a shake. "Good to see a Cooper back at the Met."

"I never liked you, though I respected nearly everyone else in your family." Lestrade gave Tarby Baldwin the chill he deserved. It wasn't easy. In the wake of his illness, Baldwin looked as though he'd already crossed the line between the living and the dead. His skin was grey and dry upon his sharp bones. His small black eyes burned like polished stones under a sunken browline. Lestrade hadn't known it was possible to make the man more unpleasant to look it. "But I promise you it will all go better if you are forthcoming with your information."

"Oh, it will go better for me?" Baldwin wanted to know. "I like that, dear Geoffrey!" Contempt warped the snake-like face in the wiry little man. His broken teeth gleamed little glints of light at the points. "Go better for me in what way, *Ermine*? I'll still be dead when the door drops. How's it going to be better for me?" He paced against the limits of his cell as he spoke.

Lestrade never said a word through Baldwin's mocking rant. He concentrated on cleaning his fingernails with the end of his little penknife.

The entire gesture was discourteous in the extreme, and almost an invitation to get a swing in the face.

"I'm taking," he said in the silence of the prison, "that you've managed to live for years without knowing what the consequences of your actions would be." He looked up then, and held Baldwin's gaze with his own.

"You can pick your last meal, and what you want to drink. For some reason, dark beer is the preferred, even when they can get a tot of good whisky . . . I can't say why. Could be because nearly everyone who drops blames their actions on the drink. You don't have that luxury.

"James Berry just stepped down as Hangman . . . I can't say why to that either. From what I hear he's lost a bit of his skill with the death-drop, but while some of them were messy . . . they were swiftly dead and no mistake." [1]

Lestrade appeared to think for a moment, and in the stone room, a chill had settled.

"He's got his queerness, and I'm not saying that because he used to be a policeman. He has this insistence of coming to meet the condemned before they go out, have a talk with 'em and the like. He measures 'em and gets their height and weight, because that's what it means to do his job proper. He puts straps on their arms, and he picks a rope that's good for the weight and height of the condemned man. He always walked with the men he was about hang. He put the white cap on their faces so they don't see the scaffold that's about to kill them. After the priest gives his words, and the man has his last ones, the lever is pulled." Lestrade made a thoughtful expression. "I wonder how his replacement will do? New executioners . . . those first few months of work are *always* at risk . . . ."

Baldwin's face was cut of the same stone in his cell. "You're a hard man, Lestrade," he said evenly. "Always was. I could see you had it in you, even if your brothers didn't."

Lestrade appreciated the man's nerve. "Perhaps we could have all saved a lot of trouble if you'd persuaded them otherwise."

"Might have at that." Baldwin admitted. His awful teeth glinted whenever his lips moved. "But it wasn't my place to tell my employer what to do."

"Don't pretty a pig, Baldwin. You advised Quimper, and he listened to you. You advised Armoricus, and he listened to you. Quimper told you to guide that robbery. You put the gun in my brother's hand. You told him to pull the trigger. Cooper died. Are you saying that was ultimately Quimper's plan? To kill a policeman so you would all hang for it?"

Baldwin shrugged lightly. "Not any policeman, Geoffrey. Just the one. It was Cooper's fault he got in the way."

60

Lestrade's face stopped all expression.

Baldwin grinned. "Found that last piece of the puzzle, did we?"

Lestrade coldly struck a match to his cigarette. "Didn't think you'd take that tactic," he said. "You've surprised me a bit, that's all."

That was received like a red flag to the bull. "Oh, I surprised you? And you weren't surprised that you were going to be killed by your own flesh and blood?"

Lestrade shrugged again. "He tried for years upon years. I never quite knew why, but that was what he did."

Baldwin laughed. "You don't know why?" The little killer clipped his hands behind his back and leaned his shoulder to the wall. Lestrade offered a cigarette. After a moment it was taken. "Quimper wasn't *allowed* to kill you, you fool. You really are as stupid as Holmes said you were."

"I've heard better, and from experts, Baldwin." Lestrade was still using that faintly bored tone of voice. "Unless you have something new to add to this pot – "

"Oh, the truth is worth a good smoke." Baldwin puffed to underscore his point. "Not bad," he admitted. "Would they give me a pack of these instead of the last meal?"

"You get the option of the smoke of your choice with your meal. The warden keeps Spanish cigars on standby, but there's a box of *specials* he has in his drawer."

"Well, now, that's fair enough." Baldwin concentrated on his first infusion of tobacco since his illness. "Armoricus hated you from the start. Said you looked too much like the Seagull for his liking. Seems the Seagull didn't care for Armoricus. Called him a spoiled boy. Armoricus wanted to join the family . . . trade . . . you see."

"Smuggling with the MoonCursers?"

"The very. And Potier thrashed him within an inch of his life for having that urge. Gave him a speech that his family's trade was to take care of his parents. Well, that didn't go over so well. Old Seagull made an enemy then, and here you came about."

"Offhand, I'd say he didn't want Armoricus in the trade because he was so tight with Quimper. Potier hated anything with the last name Quimper."

"He was probably right to do so. As tight as Armoricus was with Master Quimper, it would have been a part of Quimper's own empire soon enough. Bottom line was, Potier made it clear that Armoricus and Paul weren't going to have anything to do with *his* empire, and that must have gone down a bit bitter . . . ." Baldwin *tch-tch*'d in mock sadness. "But he was still good friends with the master's son, wasn't he?"

Lestrade blew a smoke ring. "Doesn't explain why Quimper wasn't allowed to kill me. He's did as he pleased to just about everyone else."

Baldwin's shrug this time was heavier. He didn't know and that bothered him. "Some sort of agreement hatched between your father and his . . . Your father could be a stone fool, but he must have known something that Quimper didn't like. Ivo laid the law down after that Wild Hunt went bad in Plymouth."

"Which probably made them both hate me even more." Lestrade shook his head. Despite himself, he laughed. There was little choice in the matter.

"Quimper wasn't allowed to kill you, but there wasn't any sort of restriction on your brother. And Armoricus was happy to make Quimper happy." Baldwin grinned, knowing just how unsettling his broken teeth were – it was like seeing a shark lurking behind a human face. "The Aton Robbery . . . well, when that was suggested – "

"By whom?" Lestrade asked coldly. "Armoricus or Quimper?"

Baldwin grinned. "Not much point in my saying, is there?"

In other words, Quimper. Armoricus is already dead and Quimper is now come into full power with his father dead too . . . .

"Go on."

"Aton was your area back then. Armoricus figured, seeing as how you'd been such a good boy with your parents . . . ." Baldwin paused to let the knife twist just a bit deeper, "there was a good enough chance you'd bow to the rules. It was a quick plan, I'll allow. But everyone figured you'd do what you always did and let Armoricus have his way. Now, the boss of the gang – no idea who that would be – " Baldwin lied through his shattered teeth, "said fine then, but if things get out of hand, you know what to do."

"And when you saw things get out of hand," Lestrade said evenly, "you gave the gun to Armoricus and told him to take care of matters."

"See, I *knew* it was going to happen." Baldwin paused to preen in his own cleverness. "Everyone else thought you'd bow to them because you always obeyed them in the past. I saw you growing up, boy. I knew that look in your eye. As soon as you were away from Plymouth, you were going to be your own man. They didn't see what I did."

"Good for you."

"Well, it all went to rot anyway. Rot and then some. Bank robbery went to Hades, Armoricus dropped, Paul in Dartmoor – "

"And Quimper without his trusted bodyguards."

Baldwin shrugged. "You set him back a bit, that's all. His father sent him to the Continent to avoid all the attention . . . and he came back smarter than ever." Baldwin was laughing now, without a sound. "And somewhere along the tracks, you must have gotten smarter too . . . or luckier . . . Old Davids believed in you enough to push for your promotion, who would have thought? And then you go and steal Quimper's woman right from under his nose."

Lestrade didn't remember moving. He was just standing up with Baldwin's throat inside his hand with the greasy little killer's back smashed against the wall.

Neither of them spoke. The room felt as small as a closet . . . and hot.

A thousand words crowded Lestrade's mind, beating desperately at his teeth to get out. If he opened his mouth, they would escape.

He wants me to say something.

Lestrade never claimed to be a genius. But there was something amiss, and it rang like a tiny bell through the roar of blood in his ears.

That bell had rung in his ears before, when his brothers were pretending to be kind to him, to like him, because they were plotting something behind his back.

It had rung when his father suddenly broke all patterns and opened a conversation with him one day, telling him he'd make a good jockey and it was time to train him for a respectable livelihood.

It had rung when the Master suddenly noticed him one day and observed that it was a shame he had grown too much to be a jockey for one of his stables . . . but there was *always* the need for a good horsemaster.

"I don't think I'll be as good a horseman as my father, sir," he'd said properly, aware of the heat of his father's body behind him, and that of the pony on his other side.

"Oh, there aren't many choices for a man in this world. What would you be?"

Sweat had nettled his face, for Ivo Quimper never spoke lightly to the help. Behind him his father was radiating fear.

The fear had forced him into honesty, for there was no good lie to be dredged up so quickly.

"I want to be a policeman."

And the silence had grown white and thick. At the time, he'd only thought of his betrayal in going against the plans of the elders. He hadn't known of the true depths of the Quimper's illegal empire. They'd ensured him ignorant.

"Well, there's always a need for a good policeman." Jethro Quimper smiled at his father. "Isn't that so, Father?"

"Very much so."

The bell had rung loudly then, and he'd left that very night. To this day he could not explain the fear clawing his heart and the sensation of a trap, sprung and whistling past his ear. He'd packed what he had and borrowed money from his mother and ridden to the train with a much-younger Donasian. He did not breathe until he set foot in London. His mother's money had been enough to start a stake as a cabman, and that held him in place while he applied for the policeman's exams.

And then you go and steal Quimper's woman right from under his nose.

The bell was ringing.

Lestrade grimly had to admit that despite a lifetime of wishful thinking, his entire being was an interesting topic among many, many people that he found despicable.

"I can hardly fault myself for Quimper's bad manners." Lestrade had to force himself to speak exactly those words, and not the ached-for shout that was struggling to escape. "You can always say, 'Like father, like son', and leave it at that."

A flicker of disappointment struck Baldwin's small eyes. Lestrade had won the round, but he did not know how or why.

It was maddening.

NOTE

1. A disastrous hanging that led to a near-decapitation in 1891 inspired the Home Office to decide not to continue Berry's employment, In March of 1892 Berry tendered his resignation, but unsuccessfully reapplied a few years later.

Chapter VIII – Hidden in Plain Sight

France:

Madame Gerard caught the quick movement of a very familiar-looking boy in the corner of her eye. "Adrien!"

Adrien jumped like a frightened – and guilty – cat. "Yes, Madame?"

"Are you going up to the explorer's room again?" She stared pointedly at the rolled-up newspaper tucked under the boy's arm. "Adrien, you little cabbage. Is he paying you enough for your troubles?"

"*Oui*, Madame." Adrien said quickly.

"I do not understand this . . . a sick man should be convalescing with a good glass of wine or sweet milk and a book of philosophy, not gory murders."

"Everyone is concerned, Madame," Adrien pointed out respectfully. "I believe he wants to know as much as anyone else."

"God love the poor man," she answered with feeling. "Have you neglected your boots?"

"All done."

"Scraps for the pigs?"

"Done."

"Did you put the lavender water down in the library?"

"Yes, Madame."

"Then see to your lucrative guest. However," she added sternly as Adrien made to bolt, "you are to escort Michelle and Angelique to their homes when they leave their duties." She chuckled at the boy's manful repression of distaste. "That has been your task since the killings began, my boy. That is not likely to change. The girls are nice, but too countrified for my liking. Still chickens in this world of foxes. Keep your eyes and ears out for anything amiss. I will not see their names in the death tolls!"

Adrien swallowed hard. Unable to speak for a moment as the gravity of the murders came upon him, he nodded.

"And you," the proprietrix added with an even sterner voice, "never think that because you are a boy, someone will not murder you. I tapped you for your quick thinking and your even quicker feet! The gendarmes are slow this time of year, for they have far too much to do. Keep your whistle about you and your lungs in good working order."

Adrien noted the half-eaten tray by the door and felt some of his hard efforts were about to be satisfied. The explorer was undoubtedly recovering. It was a shame in a way. He was full of stories that made one feel as though the teeth of the Alps were upon one's skin, or the bitterness of a tropical rain swamping the villages.

But how the man chafed at his inability to read!

"Enter, Adrien," the familiar voice commanded.

Adrien obeyed, and quickly put the paper on the pile at the table and saw to the fire. That was always his first task.

The explorer was sitting up in bed, with some of what could pass for natural colour on his thin face. He hadn't been fat before his arrival. Now he was even less.

"What news, Adrien?"

"I fear nothing new, but there have been no new murders – at least, sir, none discovered at the time of the print or by the speed of the gossips." Adrien sat up from the flames and poured more water in the carafe. "Supper will be brought up before the bells. The cook, she is anxious to try a new soup with chicken and leeks and thyme."

"It sounds tolerable enough. Did you – Ah!" Sigerson's grey eyes lit like lamplights as the boy pulled a small parcel out of his pocket. "Give it here, my boy, and thank you." His long fingers took apart the brown paper wrapping and a familiar gesture told Adrien to bring the little black case. The boy politely went to the "newspaper table" and neatly unfolded the day's offering on top of the stack while the explorer took his dose of cocaine.

Unlike most men under the drug, the explorer appeared to be calmed by it. Adrien had heard of a few who were made that way by nature, and had nothing but pity for those who were cursed into being contrary. His own witness in the riff-raff areas of the coast had at least taught him that cocaine was far safer than the morphine.

"So, no newsprint, and no useful gossip." Sigerson sighed heavily and set the black case back in its drawer. His grey eyes fluttered shut for a moment. "There must be some method of relieving my *ennui*, but even the violin has lost its charms, for lifting the bow takes more strength that what I have upon me." His lips twitched. "And I already promised on the grave of my parents to your outstanding mistress to save my strength for meals."

"It is best you not anger her." Adrien supplied. "She is not afraid to send for the physician, nor for the police."

"By all means, we shall do neither."

Sigerson slid into his usual state under the cocaine, and Adrien used the time to tidy up about the room. By the time he'd finished the man's eyes were opening with a fresh thought.

"Adrien, how well can you read?"

"Well enough, sir, to know if you are being cheated at the chemist's."

"An excellent answer. Would it tax your nerves to read to me in the evening?"

"My only duties are to escort two of the maids home at night. Then I would be free for an hour or two."

"Very well. There is much to read, and I feel I am running out of time." Sigerson thought for a moment. "There is a great deal of paper there, is there not?"

"Several inches, sir."

"No time." He sighed. "Take it upon yourself to censor my reading then. If it is about affairs outside of France, I do not wish to know of them. I'll learn about it soon enough. Just for now . . . read to me everything that is happening with the murders, with France itself, and everything that is to do with the eastern side of the country."

"The eastern side, sir?"

"There is nothing of interest on the western side, my boy."

" . . . and that was that," Lestrade finished.

"Good God," Bradstreet said. "I go away on an extradition to Ireland, and you hit me with this?"

"Good God is right." Lestrade rubbed the back of his aching neck. "So how was Ireland?"

"The weather was horrendous, the food terrible, the lodging matched the food, and there were mobs of angry Ulstermen waiting to spit on me for taking one of their own back to the hated Englishman's land."

"Sounds like you got off lightly, Roger."

"I know. I can't imagine what I did right. Didn't even get a rock thrown at me." Bradstreet tapped his cigar ash into its tray. "Even better news, I cleaned up that case with the Aldgate thieves at the same time. Right on my way back to the boat, who'd be in front of me at the dock but Mr. Lewis Hartley himself."

"Oh, you blooming idiot. You would save the best for last . . . ." Lestrade was laughing at the image. "Six years of weaving in and out of the eye of the law and sending us all those nicely written taunts . . . and he never looked behind him?" Lestrade half-turned and signaled wildly. "Hopkins! Come here! You need to listen to this! Bradstreet nicked the Haversham Forger by accident!"

"It wasn't an accident, Geoffrey . . . ."

"It was to him!"

Bradstreet rolled his eyes and, with a martyred air, began relating his story to the expectant Hopkins. By the time he'd finished, Hopkins was hanging on to the self-invited Gregson. Patterson had emerged just in time for the punchline, and his dour face crossed to complete and bewildered miscomprehension at Bradstreet's line about the double-lined suitcases, sending Hopkins into deeper realms of mirth.

"It doesn't translate well," Gregson explained. "It's a joke about Haversham's alternate respectable lifestyle as a designer for women's luggage. You almost have to have been there."

"Women's luggage?" Patterson repeated. "Someone makes a living out of designing luggage for women?"

"It would seem to not be a very good living, if one is inspired to a life of criminal cleverness."

"Clever but not endlessly lucky . . . ." Hopkins looked over Bradstreet's shoulder and his entire countenance changed. All eyes went forward to the front door.

Dr. Watson was allowing the door to shut after him. The doctor had dropped a bit of weight since his bereavement, but so far it was not poignantly obvious on his neat clothing and perfectly trimmed mousatche. Lestrade made a note to ask Clea how her new maid was getting along at his practice. Was she doing enough to see that the man was eating correctly?

"Dr. Watson, would you like a cup of tea?" Patterson cleared his throat. "Don't worry. I think Hopkins brewed it." That earned a quick frown from Gregson.

"I should welcome it," Watson said softly. A thick bundle of papers kept in a sterile manila folder was tucked firmly under his arm. "And I should also like to discuss some of my findings with the Yard."

That meaning private.

"Good enough." Gregson made a quick decision. "Gentlemen, since this case may or may not involve all of us, shall we go to the downstairs meeting room?"

By now, Watson knew that meant a barely airless basement room with a large table, rickety chairs and a massive blackboard that comprised most of one wall. He joined the little cluster of plainclothes men as Lestrade held open the door to the back stairs.

"I'm afraid you haven't missed much," Hopkins apologized. "We've been working on tying up our own loose ends with some of Moriarty's old gang."

"Anything of note?" Watson asked as he took an offered cup of tea in a cheap cup.

"Well . . . not much except Patterson found a tie to a lot of the dead men," Gregson admitted. "Or something in common. They were patrons of the local fighting pits. The problem is you can't prove anything. *All* the pits are frankly swamped with illegal activities. You might as well say a criminal has been known to use a bullet, and therefore we can track the crime down if we go visit the bullet factories."

"Why am I not surprised?" Watson said wryly.

"But you might have found something at the museum?"

"I found something, but it is . . . ." He took a deep breath. "Perhaps this should not leave the room until this information has been . . . dealt with."

That was enough to frighten a dead man. Lestrade saw Hopkins lower his tea and set it gently to the tabletop. Patterson's skeletal features melted to waiting neutrality. Gregson silently took a chair. He was the first. Bradstreet followed, but everyone else remained standing against the wall.

"It is the Yard's usual policy to delay release of information, if the information is of a sensitive nature." Gregson spoke in a way that advised everyone else not to argue with that point just now.

"Then . . . ." Watson's voice slurred faintly. He stopped and paused to run his hand through his hair. It was possible no one at Scotland Yard had ever seen the sober and dignified physician make such an unkempt motion. "Inspector, I . . . I'm afraid I have some news the Museum will not welcome."

"Watson?" Lestrade broke his stare and cast his eyes about. "Someone find a chair!"

"If I sit I won't be able to stand again," Watson snapped. "Inspectors, I've spent two days with those bog bodies. I bore in mind Patterson's informant had originally hailed from Streat . . . and that Lestrade's attacker had been from Streat as well. It was Hopkins' work with the funeral home scandals that led me to begin thinking along the lines of the bog-dead as . . . well, as cadavers."

He smiled faintly as a tiny spark of hope lit in the youngest inspector's eyes at this comment.

"I've been through and over every possibility, every nuance, I have investigated each option and I'm afraid it's all been for naught." Watson took a deep, shuddering breath. "With the exception – and the sole exception – of the first remains excavated on Streat – that of the warrior-king, these are not Neolithic sacrificial victims, nor are they Bronze Age or third-century burials."

Gregson had leant forward and was folding his arms, brows knit to one single line of worry as he watched the doctor. "Well, then, what are they, Watson?" he asked.

"Murder victims," Watson said heavily. "And quite recent at that too."

Gregson began patting down his pockets. It was just as well, Lestrade thought, that one of them was able to move. Patterson looked ready to fall down and Hopkins would be the next to go. "We'll be asked to submit proof that these are modern murder victims, and not ancient remains." Gregson had found a pipe from somewhere. He filled it with fingers that did not quite obey his mental commands. Lestrade felt no calmer, but managed to strike a match without burning himself and held it over the other man's bowl.

"I have the damned proof!" Watson snarled. He struck the table with his folder. Gregson jumped. "D'you want to see it all? Here it is. First of all, and most telling, we can use the Warrior-prince in comparison: This corpse holds a simple meal in the stomach. The Curator's report said so:

"'A fire-scorched bannock, or rather, a cake made of barley, coarsely ground using a stone quern, for fragments of that stone were mixed in with the cake. The cake was sweetened by honey and there was presence of a strong type of wine – not grape. It was too early in our history for grape and it couldn't grow up there anyway. [We needed the Romans to bring the grapes in.] *The fragments of peel indicated an alcohol made from blackhaw, or hawthorne, mixed with blackcurrant, a fruit suitable to the climate and soil conditions of the island at the time.'*

"The prince was not bound, but he clearly died after the result of his injuries, and it is universally agreed he died in some sort of battle. His arms bear fractures from heavy blows, and a sword-point went partially into his abdomen which granted him death but not instantaneously. He had time for some care, and a meal and a drink full of medicinal herbs to ease his passing. The weapons he was found with were heavily scarred and dented. There's even a chip in the edge of his gladius." Watson paused and cleared his throat. "The Ogham about his waggon has not yet been translated, but a few words here and there suggest the prince's last words were in the nature of a curse against the foes who killed him. That is beside the point, but I'm mentioning it for comparison."

"Go on, Doctor," Hopkins murmured.

"Yes. Well. The *other* victims were bound with a rope made of stinging nettle fibres and a tough fibre made from beaten willow and oak. Now that *isn't* the strongest cordage in the world, but it is enough to do the job if it is well done and the victim is drugged. The clothing the victims wore was well-woven wool, but if you want me to say these victims are ancient sacrifices from the pre-Roman days, I'm afraid I can't. These are modern people, and they were selected for sacrifice."

"How stridently can that be proven?" Gregson wondered. "If we were up against a . . . a hard-headed English jury?"

"Fairly well, if the jury has two active brains between them." Watson spoke with flat confidence. "The stomach contents alone are enough and never mind the teeth, but I'm getting ahead of myself . . . ." He took a deep breath through his nose and held it.

"The stomach contents of the bodies was not conclusively examined like the Warrior Prince. I took the liberty of examining a few samples taken from the gut and intestine of the other corpses. Now, they had eaten a bannock cake, that is true. But this barley was ground by a machine, gentlemen! Or a faced millstone. There are no stone particles inside the cake! Also, there was a great deal of wine traces in the stomach and root vegetables. There were carrots . . . and potatoes in two of the stomachs."

That sunk in slowly, like a heavy stone on its way to the bottom of the sea.

"Potatoes didn't hit us until Queen Elizabeth!" Patterson had gone white as chalk. He sought a chair and took it, leaning his head into his hands. "My God," he whispered. "We've got citizens of the Crown under glass, on display as pagans . . . to hide an act of murder . . . ."

Chapter IX – Anniversary

It was all obvious . . . and terrifying.

Watson fell into a brown study as the others silently digested the ramifications of what he was saying.

Patterson lifted his head first. His glittering eyes were hard as nailheads. "Doctor, what else did you learn about the bodies besides the fact that they are obviously modern?"

"They all had something in common. They were all to a man crippled in the leg or arm somewhere. And there were signs of recent injuries on their bodies. Broken bones for the most part, but overall, brutal signs of murder. They were bound, beaten, drugged, and finally their throats were all slashed before they were thrown into the bog. I'm afraid that is consistent with the precious little we know about the bog people." He remembered the tea in his hands and drunk it. "This is a fiendish mind at work here, gentlemen."

"Why would men of today be killed in imitation of the past?" Hopkins mumbled.

"A cult." Patterson said it slowly. That hard look had intensified, and with his gaunt, tall frame he resembled a more frightening version of the late Sherlock Holmes in the room, the way Mary Shelley's Frankenstein's Monster resembled a more frightening version of a human being. "We've always known Moriarty's gangs used people in all sorts of filthy activities. But how did they maintain control? A cult is easy. Clubs are popular! Men gathering isn't a thing worth noticing . . . and we know that there are rival factions splitting off and adding to the fire."

"Moriarty's men were deep in the fighting rings and pits and sportsman circles." Bradstreet rubbed his knuckles against his jaw. "We've already caught on that the gang is getting rid of their worst members by sending them after us."

"Yes . . . they're killing two birds with one stone while we slowly whittle down to twigs," Gregson grunted. "They're winning on that score."

"Another Hellfire Club!" Patterson suddenly snapped. His voice cracked like a whip in the room. "Bloody Hell, it's just another Hellfire Club." He slammed his hand on the table and stood on its force. The skin over his face had melted to paper over the hard bones. "Right in front of us. In front of me. I ought to have known better."

Watson had grimaced at the sharp sound, but remained silent.

"It's the best way to keep mum, you know. Share in something shameful. If one cracks, you have to make damn sure no one's brought down with you, or your end won't be any at all neat." Patterson finished his garbled sentence by fishing for a slender little pipe. "I saw it over and over in my work in disguise." He swallowed thickly. "It's how they recruited people. They *create* blackmail."

Watson was feeling an ache between his eyes. Patterson's grisly revelation was as bad as the one he'd just given. Recruitment. Moriarty's gang had been vast . . . too vast to merely crumble with the death of the king. All men from all walks of life had been affected from the man's careful, mathematically precise calculations.

Recruitment.

Watson's considerable powers of imagination could see it easily, despite his sincere wishes against it.

Someone who needed to be cultivated for Moriarty's work could easily be set up for a lifetime of blackmail. All one had to do was invite them over on the false pretense of a "social event" – only what kind of social event would greet them?

Lestrade had half-risen out of his folding chair and was chafing at his hands. His face was drawn. Years suddenly rolled backwards, making him look as unwell and sallow as he had before his marriage.

"He had the resources for it," the small man admitted. "Look at how the Quimpers kept control of their allies for years – generations – by having those Wild Hunts. People were hunted down and killed like animals, and anyone who joined the hunt was culpable with the crime. It makes me wonder just how long the Quimpers have been the agents for Moriarty's people!"

"We may never know, but at least we're starting to get the picture," Bradstreet pointed out. He looked faintly ill.

France:

"Adrien?"

Adrien was confused. Surely it was not time to get up yet. His day began with the dawn and it was still dark outside.

"Adrien, my cabbage, are you awake yet? The doctor says you must take this."

Madame was there? In the dark? And why was the doctor here? Was it M. Sigerson? Adrien opened his mouth to ask questions and felt the pull of gauze and sticking plaster against his face. The pull stretched to his eyes.

"Do not try to speak, *cher*. You need to drink."

73

The drink was bitter, like all medicines. Adrien felt the softness of the pillow beneath his head and sighed. A pain he hadn't been aware of was beginning to fade.

"What is happening?" he asked faintly.

"You will be well, my boy." It was the explorer's voice in his ear now. "And thanks to you, Angelique and Michelle are too."

It all came back to him and he yelped. A large hand pressed gently at his chest and he stopped trying to move.

"There, now see? Stop flopping like a flounder. You have nothing more than a broken arm and a crack on the head. You are also the Hero of the Rue, you fine young fool." But Sigerson did not sound angry at him despite his words. He sounded proud.

"They are all right?" Adrien pressed. "The man, he was . . . ." Words dried in his throat. "He meant . . . ."

"I said they are all right, did I not? You are working yourself up over nothing." Sigerson patted his unbruised shoulder lightly. "You're a fine *gallant*, are you not?"

Adrien thought that over as he heard the *click-click* of Madame's heels walking out of the room. A metal tray clinked in the hallway. "Are you angry at me, sir?"

"Angry at you? No. Not at all." Sigerson's voice hushed. "I am . . . well, you remind me of a good friend of mine. At first I told myself it was because you loved my stories of the world, and then I thought it was because you were like him in that you could trick me into taking care of myself . . . but now I see you are also like him in that you run to danger without a moment's thought or a regret. It would have been just like him to put himself between a killer and two frightened girls . . . If you must emulate him, my young friend, you must do it all the way and learn the art of the pistol." Sigerson chuckled. "It would be in the interest of your health."

Adrien hadn't meant to doze, but the medicine was more powerful than the questions in his head. He had a sense of the passage of time, but little else.

And Sigerson was speaking.

"Clever old Shikari . . . What sort of bait for a detective but a murder?"

Adrien's mind closed for the rest of the night.

When he next opened his eyes, the Explorer was gone.

April 24th – Kensington Street Practice:

74

Watson had slept late, as was his usual custom after the strain of Saturday. The well-to-do preferred to visit during what they called "appropriate hours", but those who worked for a living had fewer luxuries. He also felt for the poorest of the poor, who knew Sunday as a working day and church as a vague myth. As a result, Saturday was one of the most hectic and trialsome days of any week, and Sunday evening would be little better. At the same time, the poor had fewer complaints about what the doctor said to them, and they were certainly slower to quarrel with him.

He dressed himself and employed the hot water for a strict shave and headed down the stairs. The silence of the house pressed on him and, despite the growing strength of the daylight, he wanted to go back upstairs and burrow under his bedcovers.

You'll survive today, you fool. He chided himself weakly. This time last year, he had found Holmes in his consulting room and asking if he could draw the blinds.

One year ago. Three-hundred-and-sixty-six days – he did not forget Leap Day, meaning the literal "year and a day" of the poets.

Watson tracked his despair with the old grief piled upon the new. In the solitude of his kitchen, he made breakfast of last night's cold beef and mustard between bread and ate carefully. The first of his patients should have been knocking at the door by now. It was almost noon.

He tried to think of any celebrations that would have explained the unusual quiet. None came to mind. By the time he finished and the final cup of tea was drunk, he was pulling out his watch and measuring it up against the one on the wall. They both agreed.

Passing strange, he thought. Not that he was against a quiet day . . . but this was out of the ordinary.

He brushed himself down, set his watch back, and went to the foyer. No sign of anyone on the step. He was unlocking the door just as a hurried rustle of paper caught his ear.

"Oh! Hello there, Doctor." Inspector Lestrade was sweeping something behind his back. In concession to the brightening April weather, he was wearing a light coat and hat. "I stopped by to see if you were doing anything today."

"Today?" Watson wondered if it was actually worth it to ask the little man what the devil he had behind his back and what was it doing on *his* door. "I seem to be having a bit of a slow day, if that's what you mean."

"Well, that's a shame," Lestrade answered with patently false sincerity. "On the other hand, do you think you could stand to see some friends of mine? They were most grateful of a favour you did them in the past – you and Mr. Holmes too, to be truthful, but his favour was a bit different from yours."

Watson let that sink in. "If they're friends of yours, they're welcome enough to come here. I could bring in a luncheon . . . ."

Lestrade cleared his throat over Watson's suggestion. "Might not be good for your business," he said succinctly.

"Oh." Watson caught on. "That sort of friend?"

"That sort of friend."

"Allow me a moment to get my stick."

Lestrade waited until they were in the cab Lestrade had whistled up from around the corner before talking. "Watch the bag," he cautioned. "It weighs a ton and you might actually hurt yourself if you kick it."

"I won't even try," Watson vowed. Lestrade grunted and – carefully – slid the gripsack to the end. He sat down with relief.

"Ferrying bricks, Lestrade?" Watson meant it as a joke, but Lestrade's mouth dropped open and his eyes turned as large as table-tennis balls. "Lestrade, I wasn't serious! Truly!"

Lestrade breathed out in his relief. "Don't scare an old copper like that," he said reproachfully. "For a minute there . . . ."

"I can imagine," Watson supplied quickly. "You *really* have bricks in there?"

"Well, not too many . . . but enough for a sampling." Lestrade made a face and rubbed at his stiff shoulder. "My friends are quite the accomplished kiln workers. The good landlady is looking for a particular quality of brick, that we've been told isn't made any more."

"And you think your friends may have some in stock?"

"I hope not. They're colourful enough without adding brick thievery to their repertoire . . . but they're excellent emulators, and I'd say they can find a way to create a creditable imitation . . . or even a forgery."

"I'm already curious, Lestrade," Watson assured him mildly. "You needn't try to convince me any further."

Lestrade chuckled lightly under his breath. "I hope your week was quieter than mine . . . We had to put down an entire gang of robbers off the Serpentine."

"That would explain, perhaps, the unusually high number of bruises I had to treat."

"No doubt." Lestrade's overall demeanor was that of a man who is mostly content with life, but something sober lurked inside his dark eyes.

Watson commented that the man appeared distracted.

"Oh. Well, there's no getting past a doctor. I'm just a little unwilling to admit April's here, you know? I keep feeling that we're going to get more bad weather." Completely sober now, he looked down at his hands. "I always hated this time of year to be truthful. Hated it worse than winter."

76

"I find that surprising. When I think of all the poor souls the winter months end or hamper – "

"But you expect it in winter. We put up with the misery, and people freezing to death in their own homes, and the crawlers struggling to keep warm with paper stuffed in their shoes or cooking rats *because we know it can't last.* Winter gives way to spring. But when spring comes, we've worked ourselves up into a pitch and next thing you know, *Bang!*" Lestrade clapped his hands together. "Three days of mild weather and everyone thinks they're immortal. Lions is down with the cough *again*, can you believe it? The big-hearted fool overdid it helping street-sweepers get to their homes on a rainy night after a bunch of evening toffs in opera suits wanted to have some fun at their expense."

Lestrade sighed at the end of his anecdote, and Watson asked what had happened.

"Well, he didn't do what I would have done," the little detective shot back crisply. "I would have arrested all of them so they could explain to the judge what they were doing with their respectable time on the next morn."

Watson stifled a smile, but he could imagine Lestrade's solution rather easily.

"A-ha! Here we are."

Watson looked out the window and nearly started. A row of tombstones met his eye, but they were like few stones he'd ever seen. They were tall . . . or they had been at one time. Vines climbed over the carvings, and thick beds of rose bush and hemlock marked the gates.

"Lestrade, what is this place? I confess I do not recognize it." He actually stammered. Lestrade had never seen the man so caught without his feet.

"We're in the old Gipsy part of the cemetery," Lestrade answered with a bland smile. "The Dooleys are back for the season, and they expressly requested the chance to pay their respects."

"But . . . I do not know them!" Watson whispered back. Frantic with ignorance. The shouts of playing children caught the ears of the men. Someone was cooking something over a fire . . . a stew rich with onions and watercress.

"Well . . . they know you," Lestrade answered reasonably.

"They do?"

"You treated one of the old man's grandchildren last winter. Bad case of croup. No one else wanted to get near a 'dirty Gip'." Lestrade repeated the phrase casually.

"That little girl?" Watson repeated. "I had no idea they were Tinkers."

"No idea at all?"

"W-well . . . I was puzzled when they paid me in a gold coin from King James' regime."

"That sounds like Padriac," Lestrade snickered. "He dances with the law, but never really goes over the line. My advice is get his thanks over with. The longer you protest, the longer he's going to think you're being coy."

Chapter X

"It's the only place. The only place . . . has to be . . . ."

When one thought of Scotland, they normally thought of the Highlands (a fact that upset the Lowlanders), whisky, Edinburgh, kilts, and bagpipes.

They did not often think of caves.

But if one was from a family of smugglers . . . .

Lestrade grimly hauled a thick folio of maps to one side with a grunt – must've weighed two stone – and started on another. Dust floated upward from the pages and soon swamped the little reading room. He hoped the library understood . . .

Well, they ought to be, as I certainly pay enough for the subscription service.

Cave of the Dead Druid.

That damned message on Hamish Watson's blade . . . it was a message inside a message inside a message, like one of those paper puzzles Martin was always playing with.

Watson said he had *not* been the smarter twin. Very well. But he also claimed to be simple-minded compared to Sherlock Holmes. There was nothing simple or stupid or idiotic about a man who could be the closest friend of that maddening, too-smart-for-his-own-good, private consulting detective. Watson was smart. Very, very smart. Unlike *some* people Lestrade could think of (if it wasn't uncouth to think ill of the dead), he didn't have much of an urge to show it off.

Uims. The old Gaelic for cave.

That word existed today in a *particular* surname in Scotland.

Weems.

Lestrade pored over index line and index line, column and charting code until tiny black characters danced before his eyes.

A Celtic surname wasn't "just" an identity. *It was your land. Where you were from. It was what you did. It was the index to an entire family tree and history of the country itself.*

He ought to know. The Lestrades had to change their name generations ago to avoid persecution.

And now look at us. One of the most uncommon names on the whole blessed island . . . plus France. More Lestrades out in the Missionary Lands than anywhere else. Wouldn't that be a joke to the old founders?

79

Weems. *There.*

Originally from Fife in Scotland (residents called Fifers), Lords of the Castle of Wymes, name derived from *Uamch*, cave, from the numerous caves in the land and on the shore . . . .

Fife was a *busy* little area – one constant source of trade and retail facing the North Sea. Coal, rich farming soils . . . salt panning . . . heavier trade since the 1870's when they suited up for the increasing demand for coal . . . .

Oh, dear Lord. There was a Wemyss Castle, and a Castle Wemyss . . . both on *opposite sides of Scotland!*

Lestrade stopped for a moment and wiped his face. Too fast, he reminded himself. *Slow down. Don't look for the* obvious *clues here. You aren't chasing a pickpocket going to ground, or a crooked pawnbroker.*

Weems Cave.

His fingertip stabbed the paper like a snake's head.

There!

Just off Smoo Cave in Durness, believed to be in the same limestone strata as Smoo, further down from the flow of the ocean which would be . . . to the northeast . . . Lestrade felt his heart batter his ribs from within. That was practically on top of the world! One might as well toss a ball from the coastline to the Isle of Streat! *Weems Cave* was redundant. It was the same as saying "*Cave-Cave.*" There had to be an older name. This was the English version. [1]

Scotland doesn't forget a damned thing if it doesn't want to. There's another name for Weems Cave . . . and it won't be translated to "Cave-Cave" . . . .

The bell chimed the hour. Lestrade shot up from the stack of books in shock. The day was gone.

"I need to find this place."

Dooley took in the sight of his ersatz kinsman. Galvin – as Lestrade was known to the Gipsies – was red-eyed from lack of sleep and thin about his face. He was further surprised when a piece of paper was put before him. Galvin knew as well as anyone that the written word was difficult for the old Tinker.

Drawing grey brows up like stockings, the old man sucked toothlessly on his pipe and obligingly spread the paper out. His grandsons and nephews clustered about him curiously. "Dearest, Galvin could use a cup of the good black tea."

"Not too black," Galvin/Lestrade answered hoarsely. "I've been drinking the stuff since Monday." He wiped at his eyes and sank into a folding chair.

80

"Hmm!" Padriac saw not the confusing tangle of words, but a carefully drafted chart. "Galvin, this is quite good. Did you do it?"

"No . . . my oldest did. Good draftsman."

"Best you keep an eye on your boy," Dooley's nephew Corvin whistled. "The plate engravers'd seize 'im up."

"Let's not think about that," Galvin breathed.

"Hmm." Dooley ran his tobacco-stained fingers over the paper. *"Uamh Nan Iarann- Iarmailt?"*

"Doesn't that mean 'Cave of Iron Sky' . . . I mean, 'Sky Iron'?"

"Hmm! This is one of the old sea caves to the north. Old homeland, eh?"

"I'm not certain it was copied down correctly. The author was severely Anglo-Saxon. He spent a lot of time complaining about the word orders in Celtic sentence structure. But, it seems to mean 'Cave of Sky Iron'."

Dooley puffed carefully. "A good chart, but old. Is this all you have?"

"No, I have this . . . ." Lestrade had pulled out his other piece of paper and smoothed it on his lap. "It was an account of the Cave in its history . . . during the Viking wars it must have been a bit of a temptation . . . ." He cleared his throat.

" . . . *But the cold Northmen did seek to trick Hamish into giving up the secret of his treasure, and forced him upon swordpoint to the Cavern of the Sky Iron. Whereupon, Hamish took them by boat into the first pool of the cavern, where the streams from above fell into a roar . . . ."*

Lestrade stopped and cleared his throat again, hoarsely. *"Hamish, being a strong swimmer, led his boat with his captors across the end of the pool, where the roar of the downflowing water and the darkness of the cave itself hid the waterfall that drained to the second pool until it was too late. To the terror of the Northmen, he lept from his boat and plunged to the safety of the far shore. The Northmen, weighed by their armor, drowned at the bottom of the pool and were never seen again."*

"That's quite a story!" Corvin exclaimed. "I'd like to hear the rest of it."

"That's all there is!" Lestrade slapped the paper down. "It was a fragment out of a book . . . *A huge bloody chunk was torn out*, perhaps on purpose . . . and this is the only thing left. Now, a shooting star can be a meteorite. Meteorites are full of iron. If someone says a 'Cavern of Sky Iron', I'm going to think it's a cave that got slapped by a chunk of some very precious iron falling from the sky from back when the Vikings were sailing and rampaging the coast for a good deal less!" He took a deep breath. "I could not care less about the iron – I get the inkling this Hamish

81

fellow got rich off it and retired to his country villa of choice. But I need to know where this cave this might possibly could be."

Padriac looked at his nearest grandson, who was a few years older than Lestrade. 'The Cave of the Druid'," he said.

"Ah." Little Ron nodded wisely. He looked at Lestrade. "In the old days, they called it 'The Cave of the *Dead* Druid'. I merely thought there was a Druid buried in it somewhere."

"I think we all did . . . ." Tinkers throughout the large tent were looking at each other and nodding as the truth was resurrected. Not a little chagrin was present in the pipe smoke. Garrow looked skyward. "How many times have we watched a shooting star and pointed, shouting, 'Another one!'"

"So do you know where it is? How can I get there?"

"Just a moment." Old Padriac lifted a gnarled hand. "If you're going to want to go to a place like that . . . ." He let the silence drag out a moment. "Are you in disguise?"

"There are some people that shouldn't be told where I am."

"I see. Then we have to make certain you just aren't noticed." Padriac smoked a bit in thought. "It is now Thursday . . . ."

Kensington Practice:

Watson was frustrated. The red lamp that advertised his practice had been broken by a fortuitous hoof and a loose cobblestone. It would take a full day to see its replacement. In the meantime, it put an unprofessional light (pun nonexistent) on his practice.

At least something is going to be done, he reminded himself. It was a poor tactic, but one he could do little about.

The post had sent him a letter thanking him for producing two months of writing so quickly. That brought a faint smile to his lips, but no further.

He felt tired.

It was the wearing-down of grief, and the closer he grew to the anniversary of Holmes's Death, the worse he felt. It loomed in his mind, the Fourth of May.

It was only the next Wednesday.

He and Mary had still been in mourning for Holmes when she was taken away. And Arthur too . . . Now his emotions were confused and murky. He missed all three with equal force. Sometimes the individual grief stood apart and sharp: The missing corner that housed Arthur's crib. The pile of brightly coloured toy blocks given them by the Lestrades. That had been returned with a sense of relief. That was a simple solution.

82

A glass jar of vanilla sugar given to Mary by little Kate . . . (He wondered how she was doing but wasn't certain he had the effort to ask.)

Mary's dresses were gone. Her shoes. Even her jewelry. After some thought, he sent it to Mrs. Forrester (who was still housebound but recovering). His reasoning was that Mrs. Forrester had been the most important woman in his wife's life. She deserved to have some of her own kindnesses returned.

He could not rid himself of all her sewing. After weeks of anguish, he forced himself to pick up her basket and send it to Kate. Kate's needle was as good as Mary's, and she would take the honour of finishing Mary's work.

Finished things he kept. He didn't know what else to do.

When his mother died, it was simple. She had scores of relatives and her things were simply sent to them. Mary had no family outside of the Forresters . . .

At night in his worst moments, he felt all his griefs combining into one amalgamated mire of sorrow. The sorrow of his lost brother. The rift between them. (No choice there. That was the tragedy.) Colonel Hayter's hopes for his daughter and Hamish – cruelly dashed . . . It only went on from there.

Feeling the weight of Atlas upon his shoulders, John picked up the next letter. It gave him a start to see the very Forresters of his thoughts on the paper.

Opening brought no illumination. It was a bland request for his presence at the Forrester estate in Kent "*the next time he felt free,*" and the final sentence was downright opaque:

" *. . . to pass on some things to you that Mary would have wished . . .* ."

What could that mean?

Watson's growing depression paused in the strangeness of this innocuous missive.

Before he could change his mind, he drafted out his response and leaned out the door for one of the boys that liked to hover close by for a tip.

He felt better for doing it. Going to Kent would be painful, but it would not be half as painful as lurking in his own rooms with the drapes pulled.

There was one letter left. He felt the ease growing as he picked it up to read.

His struggle to combat the black mood had been all for naught. It all came back upon him, and then some, at the too-familiar name on the paper.

Colonel Moriarty, West Station.

His mouth comprised of dust. He swallowed hard, and did it again. At last he set his lips into a thin line and slashed the flap open with a vicious sword stroke.

From one of the bereaved to another,

Colonel James Moriarty

John thought of the bone-deep cruelty of the note, and how well it could be disguised as a facetious condolence. His heart pounded in his chest until the air grew grey and dim. He sank to his chair and almost missed it. The polished wood of the arms anchored him in and he pushed the offending paper with the flat of his hand until it fluttered to the floor. Without a single sound he buried his head in his arms and let the tide of grief crash over.

NOTE

1. Smoo Cave is real. Weems Cave is fictitious, but not wholly. Consider it a conglomeration of cave lore and actual caves.

Chapter XI – Shooting Star

The rains had finally broken. France had an air to it that was indubitably much better than what it had been.

Sigerson carried a single bag of his possessions in his left hand. Sigerson was supposed to be left-handed for this persona, and it had become an amazingly believable aspect of his character to his reading public. Every once in a while he would inject a complaint about the difficulty of his *gauche* handedness in a right-hand society, especially travelling to foreign countries where the customs might be very different. He was still astonished at how popular that small decoration had made his accounts.

If people were wholly predictable, then I would have never been a detective, he reminded himself with a faint smile.

He was already tiring. The roads at least had transformed from thin soup to a medium the tint and consistency of bitter chocolate sauce. The horses were less-than-enthusiastic about travelling, but the cabman was eager to oblige when he heard his fare wanted to leave the city proper and head for the stopover depot for Nîmes. Such a jaunt would pay well and do his horse a world of good.

Holmes closed his eyes when the cab took off again, and rested his head against the back. His beard prickled abominably – Really, how did Watson stand a mustache? False beards and wigs made sense to him. If it were good enough for the Pharaohs of old, surely it was worth considering here?

The cab jolted slightly, and the man above swore in Oil dialect. Holmes smiled wearily to himself. The French were never without their little dramas.

He was well advised to leave this one.

In stages his humour dissolved. He had little cause to be cheerful at anything. Nothing should be droll now. Not when he knew that Moran had been sponsoring these hideous acts of murder on his behalf.

If that boy had acted less impulsively . . . .

The near miss for all of them caused his heart to pound anew.

Moran was a hunter of men. It was only a matter of time before he tracked him down to this city. The difficulty was in where to go *now*. Montpellier would be safe in the winter, but not now. Mycroft was still shoring up his defenses and ensuring his boltholes.

Young women murdered to bring him out of hiding. Moran knew his quarry well . . . knew he could not resist the unknown and was compelled

85

to follow each case to its end. Knew that the case of Saucy Jack had not gone well with him and left sourness in his mouth.

Had decided to replicate some of the aspects of that bitter failure and wait for him to come.

He would have, too. He would have gone to that abandoned winery in search of clues . . . and what fate would have awaited him? All for a fever and the local miasma, he would have walked into Moran's trap.

He had to flee again.

Neither Watson nor his remarkable young *doppelganger* at the hotel would approve his getting up and about so soon, but to linger would be to open permission for Moran to directly attack the Madame's girls.

Nîmes.

Nîmes would have to do.

I began my flight on this day. Fitting that I begin another one for the same reasons.

His lips set as the old resolve settled.

He could not prove Moran of murder . . . not yet. But murder was Moran's livelihood, as intractable from his being as his card cheating.

And murder, God willing, will be the means by which to trap him.

He watched the city streets dissolve to country roads in silence.

And he wondered how Watson was doing.

If Holmes had asked that question of Inspector Lestrade, the little professional would have responded that Watson was doing well . . . but he usually did when faced with a completely unexpected situation.

Thrifty folk that they were, the Dooleys conserved food as much as possible by turning it all into stew. This particular mixture was full of emerging spring greens, a bit of bacon, and enough squirrels to warm the cockles of Colonel Hayter's heart. In concession to the returning weather, they served it all up with ash cakes and a thin, lightly sweetened syrup that Watson couldn't quite place.

"They make it out of milkweed flowers," Lestrade explained to Watson's quiet question. "Don't ask me how they learnt the trick. They hang the flowerheads over a steambath and get the sweetening out of it that way."

"That's remarkable," Watson confessed. "Milkweed?"

"Whatever you do, don't be down on milkweeds around Tinkers. They absolutely adore the stuff, and they're quite grateful it came over here from America." Lestrade nodded at a boy wearing a quilted jacket in concession to his sickly pallor. "Chances are his coat's stuffed with milkweed fluff – or cattail. It doesn't make a person sneeze like feathers can."

Watson thought the Dooleys might be living in the open air, but they looked only marginally healthier than the city folk of London. Lestrade commented that certain diseases were common among the clans. Mostly cataracts, jaundice, and the failure to thrive with infants. For about every ten children born, three died in the first months. Death was something they faced casually, for to make too much attention to grief was to say it was more important than living itself. Every spring they settled in the old graveyard and spent the week cleaning it out. Out of courtesy to the rest of the graveyard, they also did their best with the other sections. It gave the old sextons a much-needed rest and sponsored good will. In trade, the Dooleys always had a quiet place to shelter with their children. It was close but not too close to the loud thunder of London.

They talked about it freely, and how they combated their health problems by remaining on the road and in the free air. Watson found his notebook filling up with notes and quotations as they explained their life to him, and what they did to remain as independent as possible. They were a far cry from the idealized notion of Gipsies, and were rather strict on the differences between themselves and "the other Folk". They even emphasized it by demonstrating the differences in their languages.

Watson took what he was seeing and indeed, could not line it up with the band that lived by Roylott's estate.

It surprised and pleased him that they read and liked "The Speckled Band". They knew about Roylott, and explained no one of any sense would have settled on that one's land. Word travelled like the people themselves, and the band who sheltered with that unlamented man had been declared unclean for their social habits some years past.

"A tragedy all around." one of Dooley's sons, a strapping board-thick man called Corvin announced. "He taught his daughters to be afraid of everything. He may be dead now, but that poor girl will be afraid for much of her life. And she'll think of fear when she sees or hears of Gipsies. That's the legacy he'll leave behind. And it makes it all the harder for the housefolk to see us as God's Creatures."

"Hard enough to get them to admit we are God's Creatures," his brother Ronny pointed out. "It was our folk who made the nails for the Crucifixion, and for that we wander."

"That best not be a complaint from your lips, baby."

"Ha!" Ronny tossed a balled-up dock leaf at the bigger man. To Watson he explained: "Sure, we made the nails for the Cross. But do you hear us complaining about our part in His death? Why would we deny it? Wandering the earth is fair enough for what we did."

"You shoulder the blame for your ancestors?" Watson was utterly fascinated.

"They were *our* ancestors, weren't they? And why shouldn't we attest to the world?" Corvin looked thoughtful through his left eye – the right had a developing cataract for which he was treating with an herbal soak. "Are we any different from the Crusaders who marched for their faith? Can you see any of us pretending there was no Christ? Any of us knows better! Give us the credit for owning up to our part, and we give you folk the credit for seeing us as we are. Not pentitents, but living reminders."

This led to an explanation of how Tinkers saw the law, and he found it no different from the general attitudes of London: The law existed, and would be adhered to, but why bother the police if nothing was happening?

Lestrade rolled his eyes skyward and added a few comments of his own to that, which sent the Tinkers within earshot to howling. It was clear the little professional was a source of affection and trust.

"Just don't use my name," Lestrade cautioned. "I travel with them *in mufti* on occasion."

"I can always change everyone's name," Watson assured with a growing grin. "Mr. Arthur Doyle does the same thing . . . I may as well follow the footsteps of the master."

"So long as it doesn't sound *anything* like Dooley . . . These folks can riddle a rusty needle out of a rye field."

Constant gibes over the cooking aside, it was soon time to start up a game of road bowling.

Lestrade gave out at the third round, pleading the need to save his strength for tomorrow's charity banquet at the Lancashire Rose school. "I'll stand by and keep the points," he added and held up the score card – the slate off an old roof and the spine of a sea urchin for a pencil.

"You needn't bother," Watson responded cheerfully. "It's clear I can't stand a candle to Mr. Dooley here."

Padriac Dooley's grandson – Well, one of them. Watson thought that might be Liam, but he wasn't fully certain – grinned through a mouth of shockingly large teeth. "Not at all. You're learning quick, Doctor. Tell you what, we'll bowl for words." He picked up the cannon ball and tossed it gently in his large, work-scarred hands.

"How does one play for words?"

"Easy 'nuff. If I win, you have to teach me a useful word, and if I lose I give you a word in the Shelta. What say?"

Watson's thin face flushed with the heady mix of a challenge mixed with vocabulary. "I say, *sconce*."

"There you are, then!"

Lestrade shook his head and trotted over to the old log where Padriac was sitting with a few of his large dogs. "You've done it now, you lot. He'll bowl until the owls wake up."

Old Dooley's bright black eyes twinkled at the thanks, like blackberries inside a grey winter hedgerow. "Do you think he'll write about us?"

"Will he? Yes. Will it see print? Hard to say. Publishers are a strange sort from what my inlaws tell me." The two men chuckled. With the incentive of gaining *mink'er tāral*, Watson had already taken the lead in the game.

"The doctor was always a fair man, but we didn't really know him as much as we did his friend. He was a good enough boy." Dooley smoked his pipe a moment. "A good boy."

Lestrade had never thought of *Mr. Holmes* as a boy. Perhaps a too-clever rascal at times who clearly hadn't known the end of a hazel whip in school . . . but *boy* . . .

That was the difference between his world and that of the Tinkers. Men were men when they married and took upon the responsibility of family.

Lestrade wondered how Mr. Holmes would have felt at that. He had the regard of kings and queens . . . people Lestrade would have never been allowed to see. At their most charitable, Lestrade would be an unfinished product to their eyes . . . someone who was only fulfilled by his station in life and that was to serve.

But ask the Tinkers, and *he* was the adult of the two, and by that reasoning, he was the most accomplished. What cared a Tinker for kings and queens?

It was all very unsettling. For the most part, Lestrade didn't care about the way things operated between the gentlemen and the working class. He generally saw both as advantageous and crippled, each side needing the other in some way and not being the least bit grateful for it either. His sourness to his betters he calmly attributed to being raised in the corrupt estate of the Quimpers. It was a struggle to overlook the obstacles in justice when a crime struck upwards. Too often the police shouldered the blame for finding a criminal who had been popular.

"You look a-weary. Galvin."

"A little tired," Lestrade smiled thinly. "I could use a cup of tea. Even Gregson's."

"Don't say that," Dooley scolded. "I've better." He shuffled to the steaming little pot by the coals and hooked the handle off the heat. "Fresh sweetmint," he declared. "Wake you up and a dash of the cham to chase away the bad thoughts."

"I'll take that prescription."

Dusk rose, and Watson had gained enough of the Tinker's language to say *Hello. Goodbye. I am a doctor. Yes, I take credit. I do not speak*

Shelta. And *Can you help me?* The lessons were a success. Out of fairness, he traded Liam with descriptive adjectives that were a source of hilarity to the troupe.

They parted ways not long after: Watson rode back with some of the younger men who had to drop off a wagon to the fitters. Lestrade lingered, admitting that Clea had sort of "given him the boot" while she was cleaning up for tomorrow's guests.

"She might let me back in tomorrow night," he finished with a wry shrug. "We'll see. It depends on who shows up."

"Women need some time away from their men once in a while," Dooley agreed. "Makes them forget some of our faults." They resettled to an open section of the old graveyard. The Dooleys who had drawn the lots for the job had cleared the undergrowth and thick vines away from the oldest tombstones. "Anyway, it feels good to be out in the open, doesn't it?"

"Feels . . . pleasant, actually," Lestrade agreed. It always surprised him to feel calm out in anything like the open country. London's murky lights shone on the other side of the world from the clearing. *Delayed reaction,* he decided. *There's little to love about wide open spaces with no places to hide in . . .*

The old Tinker leaned his rickety back against a stump, and puffed his pipe with a deep relish of life. Lestrade was glad to see it kept the insects away. Gipsy children giggled as they settled down for the night while their elders shushed them. Phorp limped heavily over, his fur bristling with the rising dew. With a grunt that sounded like an armload of bagpipes he collapsed in stages, his wolfshound head bigger than a full-grown chicken resting on Lestrade's lap. Dark brown eyes looked up at him through a light fringe.

"My legs are going to sleep," Lestrade protested.

No reaction.

"Padriac . . . ."

"Oh, that's just Phorp . . . Has no attention span worth a hiccup. You'll be free soon enough."

Lestrade gave up. Phorp had attacked Jethro Quimper with severe prejudice almost a year ago. He could stand a little coddling. Without a word he reached up and stroked the large head. Phorp made a happy sigh. The dog was warm against the night's chill. Behind them started a bout of what appeared to be a contest on who was the most outrageous storyteller.

He slowly relaxed enough to yawn.

A shooting star melted like a candle before their eyes. Lestrade brightened in a moment's interest from his fatigue.

"There goes another Druid," Padriac commented fondly.

90

"Eh?"

"That's what we call 'em." Padriac nodded. "Something the old folks would say . . . When you saw a shooting star, you knew a Druid somewhere had died. *Druidhe-eng*. Death of a Druid."

Lestrade sat up, his tiredness a memory as something walked ice water feet up and down his spine. "Death of a Druid . . ." he repeated softly.

"Something wrong, *kam a'kena*?"

"No . . . no, nothing's wrong, Padriac . . . ." Slowly, Lestrade sank back to his place but his eyes were wide and he could feel every nerve tingling. "Nothing's wrong . . . ."

Something was finally beginning to be right.

Chapter XII – Secret Values

May 4th, Kent:

Watson hoped his reaction did not show upon the sight of Mrs. Forrester. The older woman smiled. Her beauty was still very much apparent, but it was a beauty diluted. The strain of her illness had left her pocked with dry, red scars over her face and hands. One old boil had been very close to her left eye. He tried not to look at it. The maids had put up her hair in a loose bun. It had paled.

"I look a fright, don't I?" she said faintly.

To hear a voice as thinned down and dilute as her body . . . Watson collected himself and took the guest chair by her convalescing bed. "Not at all, Mrs. Forrester. Not at all."

"You're a polite liar, you rascal." She smiled gently. Her lips cracked. "My doctor . . . said I wouldn't have much chance. I did my best to . . . survive."

"I am pleased you did." Watson reminded himself there was no point in acting maudlin. He leaned forward and took up the dry wrinkled hand. It was *too* dry. It didn't feel like it belonged on a human. "You have been getting enough rest?"

"And broth. I'm so very sick of broth. Nothing with salt, or sugar . . . or nitrates. Very boring, John. So boring . . . ." She sighed, and her breath sounded through her nose.

"Are you forbidden tannins?"

"Tannins?"

John reached into his bag with one hand and pulled up a slender bottle of pale red wine. "Mary meant you to have this for your birthday," he explained.

"Bless that girl." The widow's filmy green eyes shone with tears. "Shall we have a glass over supper? You *will* have supper with me, won't you?"

"Of course I will, Mrs. Forrester."

"Will you stay the night? I wish to talk with you . . . but it is very tiring to stay awake."

"You needn't worry. I promise I shall stay." He would have promised her anything.

"Thank you." Her weary eyes closed, but she continued talking as they rested. "I need to know something, John. Please be honest with me."

"Of course."

"Did Mr. Holmes ever speak to you of the problem he solved for me?"

"No. Not at all," John said a bit defensively. "I wouldn't have pried, I assure you."

"Peace, John . . . ." Mrs. Forresters' hot, dry hand lifted shakily upon the bed covers. "I merely wanted to . . . make certain . . . I was not repeating a tale already told." She paused to take a breath. "I must rest now . . . please join me for supper. You know . . . where your old rooms are . . . ."

Northern coast of Scotland:

Lestrade watched, his hand lifted as the small boat of friendly (and well paid) fisher guides made their way out of the small cove. Little Ron grinned and instead of waving, held up a frighteningly sized fish with bulging eyes. No doubt they'd be eating well tonight. Knowing the Dooleys, they'd settle into a crackling fire in a Tinker-friendly inn and offer up the fish as a gift to the owner. That would lead into a nightlong escapade of drinking, lying, and earnest pledges of goodwill – some of which might even be remembered in the head-achingly cold light of dawn when the returned to pick him up.

Lestrade sighed and turned to crunch his way up the sloped beach – it was more sea-ground rock and pebble here than shingle – there was enough daylight to settle in a camp and get that depot of safety going before he went to work.

And he'd best show *something* for his efforts. Gregson, Patterson, and Bradstreet had all gone out on a limb for him in this. Hopkins had carefully been left ignorant of this law-stretching game of hooky. Best they not all risk their badges, and Hopkins hadn't been in the service a quarter as long as any one of them.

Lestrade wouldn't have even asked this sort of favour for himself, but it was for Dr. Watson, and indirectly, for Sherlock Holmes. That echoed in all their eyes. Watson had proven himself as one of them, as well as he was capable, and a man who would follow his own rigid ethics before a narrow-minded concept of the law. The signs were clear that Watson had pulled favours for all of them at one time, and probably more than once. It was high time the man started getting some of his own back.

Wind blew up and died just as swiftly. Lestrade found a few handfuls of dry driftwood here and there – the salts would make it go in a flash – and enough coal to make a few days' fire if he were unlucky enough to be stranded. He carried it all to the mouth of the cave and tried to ignore the utter chill that hung in the blackened air from within. This wasn't his grandfather's caves. Not by a chalk.

To think I became a policeman to get away from the family smuggling business . . . .

He caught up fresh dulse in the tidal pools and lucked out on a large crab, stabbed it dead with his penknife, and wrapped it up in the seaweed as he looked for more lumps of coal. Crabs weren't the most filling meat . . . You stopped eating them because you were worn out from picking out the tiny bits, not because you were full. But it would add to the dehydrated mix Clea had thought up.

The wind rose with the tide. Sea spray mixed with the sporadic swirl of rainfall. Hard to say which was colder. Lestrade watched as day fled over his head and left him behind. The first pale lights of the stars were out. He'd known their names once. He'd forgotten most of them in a land without stars. London didn't even have the sun half the time. His life was concrete now. Cobblestone and muddy ditches, the smell of horse dung miles outside the city limits. The city itself was a fume that poisoned, and yet he stayed.

It was more *honest* to stay in London. People who lived where they never had to think of clean air or water or schools forgot such problems existed. They didn't know injustice because they never lived with it.

He took the stones piled loose at the cave mouth and drystacked a windshear wall to protect the fire. His face was taut from unease as he worked to get the flames going with a hot lump of charcoal. At least it wasn't the country. He *hated* the country. It was annoying to try to explain that to his oversized brothers-in-law, but he just didn't feel safe out there in the wide open sweeps.

That was something he agreed with by Mr. Holmes. Countrysides were horrors untold. Watson enjoyed the pastoral peace and quiet of the countryside without any of the terror – which indicated that either Watson was oblivious, or he was originally from a place where everyone knew everybody's business and you couldn't sneeze without the entire district saying "God bless you." Lestrade suspected the latter.

Clea's mixture of powdered milk and potato, salt, and lemon went into the small cook pot with the crab and seaweed. He burrowed deeper into the folds of his heavy coat and thought about what was to come while supper cooked.

Going into a cave alone. If that didn't take the candle . . . .

He fed the fire and kept his back to the heavy bedroll. Outside the ocean was turning into a smooth grey curtain, darker than the sky. Blackness rolled in from his right. The cave must face nearly pure north. He could see why this Hamish person – from whatever point in antiquity – would be able to hoarde a treasure in iron ore all to himself. This place was not only difficult to get into, it looked like the stuff a schoolboy's

94

graveyard tales were made of. It was a rotten fishing spot, the locals said, but Lestrade knew better. Superstitions get you every time.

Superstitions. They were a prey to nearly every mind. Lestrade didn't like to think about them. Most days he didn't have to. But a policeman had his superstitions, like anyone else (he supposed). If their church was in support of it, they carried crosses like shields. Created a pattern of lucky behavior, and hung their charms on watch chains.

They spoke of the shades of dead loved ones (especially those who had also been policemen) who appeared in their dreams and counseled their behaviors. More to the point. They also saw loved ones who had disapproved of their chosen profession.

Probably *gentlemen* didn't have any beliefs or fears like that. They were better fed, better clothed, could send their children to whichever school of their choice and travel. Bottom line: They were a good example and a model of behavior to their less-fortunate brethren. They had the leisure to attend chapel every Sunday. Now there was a luxury. Lestrade was forced to make a detour on his way home after work more often than not.

A model of good behavior *wouldn't* be superstitious, would they? They understood it. They used superstitions, the way Quimpers used the fear of the Wild Hunt and the Devil to control the countryside. Well . . . there was that Stapleton fellow, who tried to do the same thing . . . .

For long moments, Lestrade gnawed his lip as he muddled through a disturbing series of thoughts. This usually happened when he was by himself. He was outside of procedure. He should be working with a constable or three. He *shouldn't be doing this alone*. Going it alone was the sort of thing that would shatter the Metro from within. It popped the cork on corruption and error and made bad examples. It disabused trust.

And yet . . . .

He'd known when he cracked Watson's crib last autumn and invaded his attic and found that damned sword that led him to this mess . . . he'd known he'd turned the corner. What was it about the man – and his late friend – that could force him to bend the rules for justice? God as witness, no one else could.

He ate half the stew mechanically, topped the lid and set it in the coals to keep warm while the small tinker's teapot steeped a handful of litchee and hawthorne. Time to go in. The bedroll was carefully pulled open in the rockledge behind the fire. A moment's fishing pulled out the large ball of twine and two oil lamps. He still wasn't certain if he'd made the right choice, but the light they put out was clearer and less likely to confuse his eyes. Hopefully it would be worth the extra effort to bring it down.

The cave was warmer and without a doubt drier than the worsening sea cove. But he had no relish for stepping out of that biting wind. Once he went inside, it would be like going inside Watson's house. Another corner. And this was a larger corner. He could feel it. Things weren't going to be the same.

A smart man would turn around and go back to the village for a constable's assistance.

Smart men didn't go into caves alone, anyway.

"At least I *am* an imbecile," he said aloud, and tied the end of the twine to a rockspur jutting out of the cave wall.

Kent:

A barn owl swept across the clipped field, screaming to frighten up the field mice. John watched its ghostly shape pass his window without an expression on his own face. Less than a year ago he had jumped at that sound. He was too numb to do anything at this point. Mrs. Forrester's strong, vital personality had been crushed by both her illness and Mary's death. It shook him to his very centre to face this, for she could be a mirror for what was in his own soul.

She sat up in her bed and took French Onion soup with small pieces of toasted cheese floating on top. He was grateful to see she was taking something with substance. His own dinner came with a spinach quiche and spring mushrooms of a light, pleasant texture.

In concession to her weakened state, he kept his conversation as pleasant and minimal as possible. Gradually as the dishes cleared and he opened that promised bottle of wine, she began to speak.

"Did Mr. Holmes ever intimate to you the reasons for my consulting his services?"

Watson thought carefully, but knew the answer was no. He shook his head. "He said it was a trifle, and it must have been to him. I thought to more about it." He tried not to smile, but it was difficult. "I confess, my mind was not completely on Holmes when . . . when I saw Mary."

Some of the widow's old spark returned to her eyes as she took the half-filled glass. "I can imagine. She was a remarkable girl. I was fortunate to have her as long as I did." She paused and took a breath as if her lungs had pained her.

"Mrs. Forrester?"

"I beg your pardon. It does still hurt at times . . . ." Those weary green eyes opened. "I wanted you to know something about Mary, John. Know it and keep it, for when it is my own day, there will be no one else left to remember."

John was shocked into the oblique manners of putting down half his wine before he could speak. "I beg your pardon?" he stammered.

"My dear John – It was to find Mary in the first place that I hired Mr. Holmes."

It was a small, fleshy white face with a too-wide mouth and too-small pink eyes. In the cachement of his lamplight, the head was no larger than a chipmunk, but being seen by *something* after fording two active pools and falling into only one was enough to make the salamander look like a flesheating, subterranean Komodo dragon.

Lestrade fell backwards, and only missed getting another bath in the meltwater by an accident of balance. He hit a boulder instead, which was harder but indefinitely warmer. The lantern rattled on its wire bale in his chilled hand, and he held it over his head.

Man and troglodyte regarded each other while the waterfall babbled behind the detective. Lestrade's heart gradually stopped trying to slither its way out from between his ribs. The thing was blind. It gradually turned its head and dropped into the pool a yard from his wet feet. It was surprisingly long and lean, and slipped through the water like a *brollachan* in Bradstreet's stories. Its whiteness glimmered through the crystalline water like something beyond design.

Brollachan. Shapeless, senseless, deformed creature.

Lestrade took a deep breath and slumped against another, drier rock for a brief rest. Should he ever go (completely) mad and accept Roger's offer to buy up some of his Scottish land . . . it would be a different fate indeed. Roger had fond fantasies of growing old and grouchy together, plaguing the crofters while they fished for salmon. By God, no. If he was going to pack up and move to Scotland, he would show his so-called best friend the parts of Scotland even the *Revisionists* didn't know about.

All right then. Two pools, one of which holding the bones of two unwary Vikings and probably the splinters of their boat . . . and there's an old runoff passage just ahead . . . .

Lestrade knew by now that caves operated under simple rules: Water went down unless it didn't have a choice. Over the centuries, the original underground streambed had failed to keep up with the dissolution of the rock by water in the pool, and was now higher than the pool by at least five feet. Another, smaller channel was pulling the water off in another direction, but it was far too narrow for a human to enter it. In resignation did Lestrade stick the lantern on the higher rock ledge and climb up after it.

Water-slickened stone met his eyes. The passage curved instantly and went down. Lestrade gnashed his teeth in a moment of self-loathing and checked the dwindling ball of twine secured in his pocket. Physical effort made freezing an impossibility now, but he was ravenous. Just see the end of this, he promised himself, and leaned on his knees to peer further into the gloom.

Footprints.

Lestrade's heart leaped up into his jaw for the second time in ten minutes. Footprints leading down . . . and coming back. His breath steamed in the air. He crept forward and examined them, but he was no tracker, not like Mr. Holmes. *He made his way down, and he got back . . . I'll take that as a good sign . . .*

Was he tracking the dead Hamish Watson? Or someone else? Footprints could last for ages inside a cave with no atmosphere to disturb them. He knew that now.

He sat there for a moment, thinking this over. Hamish Watson's eyes were going bad, and slowly ended some time before his death by drink in – '87? But that didn't mean he couldn't explore a cave. Lestrade now knew from his experience that eyesight wasn't the only quality needed to walk underground.

He didn't see any other footprints . . . but there was a strangeness where he'd stuck his lamp. It was sitting right in the centre of a heavy, square depression.

A square. *A box.* A chest.

Lestrade paused only to check the amount of oil in the lamp – still good, but he would need to switch on the way out – and hurried as well as caution permitted. The rock suddenly opened up, parted like the pages of a book, and he found himself inside a blind alley.

Lestrade had been in the bottom of a doline before, and he prided himself on knowing he was looking up a sinkhole, but it still gave him an uneasy feeling to think that floodwaters could go all the way to the top . . . wherever that was. His lamplight could not go far enough.

It was a little bigger than his own sitting room, and warmish. He smelled the outside air, and something sweet, like fresh soils.

And there was a chest. Made of metal and about the size of a suitcase, it had been chained to a bolt fastened inside the wall. Lestrade took in the fact that the masonry hammer was still propped up against the wall. Hamish Watson had only meant to hide the box here, and bolt it against any floodwaters.

Nothing for it. He picked up the hammer. One good swing and the hinges split. Even smart men made that mistake. Why break a lock when the hinges were small and on the other side?

His lamplight spilled into the chest. Its contents threw the light back in colours: Gold. Silver. Coins. Gemstones.

Lestrade swallowed around a throat that had just gone stiff, and reached into the chest. He recognized the coins from the veterans on the Force: The Arabs loved their Fatima's Hand, and hammered the emblem of Mohammad's daughter into everything. These coins were linked together with silver, and the links depended with mineral rainbows.

"*The caves of Afghanistan* . . . [Watson had said that night in the chapel] . . . *a place the stuff of legends are made of, you know. I can easily believe Thieves' Cave from Sinbad and the cave of treasures from Aladdin were based on those caverns. They were easy to be lost in. It must have been a simple matter to hide things.*"

Watson's words flurried up and swept past his mind like dry leaves:

"*The dead were being used to smuggle treasures back to England.*" "*It is not in the best interests of the bereaved to give full details.*" "*But there was a time when myself and a few of the others noted that some of the remains of the dead soldiers were being . . . tampered with.*" "*Even now, it is difficult to speak of.*"

No doubt. Bodies as human boxes to smuggle treasures out of the East . . . *Stolen* treasures. How much planning had gone before this? Finding the dead, secreting the gems inside the cavities of the bodies . . . it would have to be the skull, for the nostrils would be plugged up against contamination . . . Arranging for the bodies' shipment home . . . probably even with the recovering men like poor Watson, half-dead with fever himself.

Hopkins' research made new sense. The funeral homes had been part of the smuggling ring. The funeral directors had seen to the corpses, removing the contraband and disposing of them quickly, pretending to be a charity in order to get all of this accomplished. Their commission must have been dreadfully high to take this risk.

The bereaved never caught on, did they? They only knew that their lost loved one had paid into some burial fund that they hadn't known about. Who *didn't* want to believe the one they grieved for had tried to think ahead for the future? Even a lush could think ahead, and every parent or spouse or sibling wanted to think the best of their relative.

A burial club. Like a good club or an Easter club. It was so easy to believe.

It made him sick.

Lestrade leaned back on his heels, wiping at his forehead. The colours shimmered. He had no idea how much wealth he was looking at. For a man who was lucky to survive on a policeman's pay . . . the amount went beyond the realistic and into the fantastic.

Lestrade didn't even fathom the value of what he was looking at. It was simply too much. And too alien.

Give him an oak desk and he could say how much money was needed to keep one in cab fare for a year. Which train cost 4d a mile. A month's potatoes. How much it cost to keep his informants happy and helpful. Schooling for his sons. A life free of debt. How much he had yet to save before he could buy the building from Mrs. Collins and create some property for his sons' future.

Gregson once half-killed himself to bring a murderer to justice in a tiny Sussex village. The people had chipped in to buy him the watch he wore today. *That* was value. Lestrade's family's health and safety was value. He didn't understand what he was looking at.

Peterson had taken a ridiculous reward for finding that silly blue carbuncle in the goose given him by circumstance, and supported by Mr. Holmes – proof the man hadn't been a complete irritant. Peterson had shared it with that poor old man who'd lost the goose in the first place. That was value too.

But Lestrade still didn't understand how a mineral could be worth something. Or why people killed for them. He looked at the box at his feet, and he knew full well why Watson had left the box here.

Value. He'd seen the poorest urchin in London band with his mates and steal springwater from ten miles away to give to an old street crawler with a sore foot because spring water was healthier for her sickness. To him that was value.

A carnelian cameo, no matter how pretty, couldn't do that.

Lestrade found the light was trembling. It was his own arm. The horror of the situation leant upon him. A condensed and more terrible dread than what he'd felt when he held the blooming sabre in his hands.

Value.

Who did it belong to? Afghanistan? The people who had carved their name in the blood of Watson's friends? No. If the gems were being smuggled out using the dead, then these things were stolen from someone who had rights to them. Rights the British government would have to recognize.

It didn't belong to Moriarty. If it belonged to *anyone*, it would be the unknowing relatives of those violated corpses. Tell them what happened, and they would all be willing to trade knowledge for poverty and ignorance. A necklace wouldn't wash the stain away. It would pay for their house mortgage, but it wouldn't pay for the end of horror.

No mother or father or wife deserved to know what had happened to their fine young man that went to battle. *The dead were sacred.* Call him superstitious and call him a fool again. But the dead were not the playthings of madmen.

"Bloody Hell," he whispered. "Now what?"

100

Chapter XIII – Future Thoughts are Troubling

"**D**id Mary ever speak of her family?"

Watson had no need to think backwards. "No," he said simply. "That is, not in any remarkable way. She retained a longing for her father for years, but when she knew the proof of his death . . . she was able to accept it." He leaned forward, setting his wineglass on the small table beside them both. "We both felt a peculiar longing for our pasts abroad. I suppose it was because we both miss . . . missed . . . something of our childhoods."

"I have not that experience, but I imagine I have some small comprehension." Mrs. Forrester sighed and closed her eyes for a moment. She sipped at her wine and rallied herself.

"It was very difficult for the children of Colonials . . . but harder for the women. That ought to go without saying . . . ." The widow shifted restlessly on her sitting bed. "Forgive me," she murmured. "Even the softest sheets chafe, and I declare it makes me say pointless things."

"You just need to get your rest up, and you'll be fine before you know it." The assurance rang flat between them, to John's shame. Mrs. Forrester would not be "fine" for some time. He frantically sought to deflect the subject. "How are your children?"

"They are well." A thin eyebrow perched skyward, warning him of his transparency. "I wish to speak of Mary. And why I had sought Mr. Holmes's advice for what he called a minor domestic incident, or some such . . . he called it a trifle, and I am certain it was to his intelligence. But it was hardly that for myself."

"He had that ability," John agreed in a voice barely above a whisper.

"It was to find Mary . . . and also to end the mystery of her mother that I consulted our late friend."

John swallowed hard. "I had no idea," was his hoarse answer.

"Mary's mother did not die after her birth. It was merely the kindest thing to tell the child."

John needed a moment to collect his voice. "I confess I am a little afraid of what you have to tell me."

"You needn't be . . . ." The widow's cracked lips threatened to bleed again as she tried to smile. John wordlessly produced the small pot of balm and she carefully daubed her lips with a fingertip. Her eyes closed in relief before opening them again. John's eyes were upon her as tight as nails into wood.

He was searching for signs of Mary in the older woman's face. Was it the shape of her eye? The pattern of hair swept from her forehead? He sought answers in the shape of her bones, thinking of Holmes with Baskerville's painting and discerning Stapleton's true motive to it all.

"I have something to give you, John." Mrs. Forrester gestured with her hand to the dresser at her right. "Top drawer, if you please. A brown, ordinary-looking packet with a pale yellow ribbon."

John's sense of puzzlement grew as he did what he was told. It was not bound, but he had no urge yet to open the thick pasteboard cover that held the papers within.

"Morstan is an unusual name, is it not?" Mrs. Forrester asked in the voice of a wraith. "I entrust these papers to you, John."

The soft rustle of padded feet moving from polished floor to carpet pulled Watson out of his withdrawn thoughts. He dropped his hands from his half-undone tie and peered out the door. The aging spaniel of one of the Forrester children was slowly settling itself down into a sisal mat underneath the sweeping green fronds of some sort of exotic plant. It sighed and lifted its dark eyes up to regard the newcomer.

Mary would have known the name of the dog. Who it preferred. Why it was sitting in the hallway waiting for someone who was not there.

He returned to removing his dinnerwear and set it out carefully, unsure if he would stay another night. London was already pulling him from Kent. His mind was back in his practice and his lonely rooms. In a way, he felt as though he were intruding on a part of Mary's life that needed her presence. This house was hers. He was the guest.

He was changed, and he felt completely alone in this large, spacious house.

In the privacy of the room, John chafed within himself. He began to pace. His fingers dovetailed together until even water would not be able to slip between the crevices. He stared out the window and watched fruitlessly for a sign of something to prove there was another sign of life upon the Kentish lawn.

There was only the sound of the owls, and a few bold frogs. At last he gave up the hope of distracting his thoughts upon such means, and turned to the library shelf. He expected to see something appropriately distracting. (Mrs. Forrester shared his occasional foray into the yellow-backed novels, though Holmes would protest the offerings were pure *galimatia*.) [1]

The Sign of the Four.

Mrs. Forrester had loved the story enough to collect and bind it in a leather folio. John regarded that large book in the deepening silence of the night before he finally picked it up and set it in his lap. The edge of the bed creaked softly beneath the extra weight, for it was not a light thing when caught up in leather.

Here it was. In all his writings, John had never exposed so much of himself – not since the events of *A Study in Scarlet*. He thought briefly of the circumstances that had led him to connive Holmes and Colonel Hayter into the same room together . . . in a way that had been very personal for him and very nerve-wracking but to do anything less would have been to demean the story itself.

He brushed through the soft paper pages gently, allowing his eyes to linger here and there on a particular sentence or an illustration. They had not known Mary's visage, nor had they deigned to copy a person exactly. He felt they had overdrawn themselves on that one showing of her with that large, wide smile. But they had caught something of her warmth and heart, and that had been the important thing.

The day had been a dreary one, and a dense drizzly fog lay low upon the great city. Mud-coloured clouds drooped sadly over the muddy streets. Down the Strand the lamps were but misty splotches of diffused light which threw a feeble circular glimmer upon the slimy pavement. The yellow glare from the shop windows streamed out into the steamy, vaporous air and threw a murky, shifting radiance across the crowded thoroughfare. There was, to my mind, something eerie and ghostlike in the endless procession of faces which flitted across these narrow bars of light – sad faces and glad, haggard and merry. Like all humankind, they flitted from the gloom into the light and so back into the gloom once more. I am not subject to impressions, but the dull, heavy evening, with the strange business upon which we were engaged, combined to make me nervous and depressed. I could see from Miss Morstan's manner that she was suffering from the same feeling.

John slid his fingertips over the page, feeling his heart quicken. It had been a powerful moment for him. A single event trapped in time like an insect to amber . . . he remembered it yet.

But of that sterling moment, there had been a codicil of memory that stood apart within that:

Holmes alone could rise superior to petty influences. He held his open notebook upon his knee, and from time to time he jotted down figures and memoranda in the light of his pocket lantern.

He was glad of that moment. Few men could be a Sherlock Holmes. Few could ignore atmosphere for the important. It was how he preferred to be remembered.

He liked Mary, too. He called her an exemplary client for her attention to detail, and he enjoyed her wonderful composure. He never

103

noticed how beautiful she was, but he did notice her mind. And how could he not notice her deeper qualities? I've seen few women so young with such an ability to control oneself in such a situation.

He rested the book in his lap until the circulation to his feet threatened to stop. Mary's world. So much of his life had become hers . . . so much of her life had become his. Like two trees slowly growing together, they had gently shifted and begun the process of metamorphosis into a common whole – the ideal of the long-established married couple. And now . . . she was sifting away from him.

The initial shock had passed. It had felt like the mindless cruelty of a bullet passing through a beautiful cathedral window. Now there was nothing to do but watch the shards of glass and glazing and colours that were the fitted pieces of that window to finish its fall through gravity. It felt like a pain that would never go away to witness such an end to grace and beauty . . . but gravity could not be fought.

Inspector Gregson admitted to very few mistakes. He made a substantial one just then when he pushed the cracked door to Lestrade's office and frightened Patterson out of a decade.

"Sorry," he apologized inadequately.

Patterson's face was still pale as narcissus against his darker hair as he staggered backwards against Lestrade's desk. His skin shone thin as rice paper over his age-sharpened cheekbones. "Quite all right," he answered in a strained voice, and there was no doubt he was lying. "I was . . . I was just leaving."

"Now you've done it," Lestrade said when they were alone. "It'll be a month of Sundays before he comes back here." He leaned back in his chair with a supercilious eyebrow. "I had to promise him my personal notes on the Leeds Garroter to even get him to walk into my doorway."

"He's a jumpy one, and there's no lie. Man's about to crack under his own strain." Gregson carefully handed the filing forms over to a grave Lestrade. "I take it your trip was successful?" he wanted to know.

"Yes and no." Lestrade flicked his dark eyes to the turning Patterson out in the main office (He was searching for a pen to write with.) "I'll tell you about it once the madness settles down in here."

"Huh. That'll be a hundred years from now." Gregson flicked another look to the tall, skeletal man outside and carefully shut the door. "Lestrade, that man's about to lose his presence. He was a CID operative full time. As long as he's staying here in our boring old offices and pushing papers, he'll be rotting on the inside out."

"I know." Lestrade rubbed at a tiny spot on his cufflink. "That was actually why I was trying to get him in my office. I may have convinced him to go back underground."

Gregson blew out his cheeks. "It's what he's good at. Better at that than staying here."

"He's like a soldier, isn't he?" Lestrade mused. "The war's not over for him, so he needs to go find another war and settle it out."

Gregson nodded. They were silent for a moment. "What did you find out?"

"There was a cave Hamish Watson was using to cache the stolen gemstones Moriarty's gang was smuggling through those corpses." Lestrade waited for Gregson to finish shutting the door tight before he started speaking again. "Wretched place, let me tell you. I'll take a nice sewer next time."

Gregson snorted. "Go on."

Lestrade took a deep breath, and then: "There's not much to tell. The box was opened – smashed open – and the contents were gone – save for this one piece of evidence."

Gregson gave Lestrade a long stare, and an understanding seemed to pass between them. Then, Lestrade repeated, "Save for one piece of evidence." He reached into his pocket and dropped something small and shining on his desk.

Gregson picked it up with a scowl. "What the devil is a carnelian sculpture of Qwan Yin doing in a box of Afghanistan loot?" [2]

"Leave it to you, Euclid, to know whoever this Quan Yin is."

Gregson sniffed but did not stop examination of the tiny, translucent orange and gold sculpture. "Qwan Yin was the Chinese Goddess of Mercy. She's loved as seriously among the Chinese as you Catholics love the Virgin Mary."

Lestrade overlooked yet again Gregson's accusation that he was knowledgeable enough to even *pass* for a member of the Church. (The last time he checked, superstitions alone did not count as actual experience and catechism. Needless to say, his personal *post-mortem* plans involved a nondenominational cemetery where excommunication was unlikely.)

"People collect things," he said instead. Arguing with Gregson was about as smart as arguing with the late Mr. Holmes – either way, you were guaranteed to end up bleeding and broken, though Gregson was all too willing to have you bleed for real – preferably on your own papers. "Perhaps it's just that simple, Gregson."

Gregson glared at him, as if Lestrade had just offered him a bouquet of stinging nettles. "Afghanistan was a trading route crossroads, Lestrade. I'm thinking there's more to this than meets the eye." His frosty eyes settled into his smaller opponent, who kept his features schooled and cautious.

"The Afghanis *wouldn't* keep a heathen object on them," he said. "They're true to their faith."

"Gregson, it's just a single emblem. I'm not certain much more than this should be construed . . . ."

Oil to the flames. Gregson started pacing back and forth within Lestrade's small office. Lestrade watched him, patient.

"The cave you found," The bigger man said at last. "That account was based on one of the old Viking attacks up north, and a Scot named Hamish tricked them."

"More than trick them," Lestrade agreed slowly. *Here it is, Gregson . . . think it through.* "They went straight up to their Maker."

"Actually, they went straight down, if your account was correct," Gregson corrected. "If they drowned, they went to Ran, some sort of sea witch." He caught that Lestrade's jaw was hanging open. "Lestrade, do you never read anything?"

"Who has time to read?" Lestrade huffed. "Well, besides yourself. *Some* of us have work to do."

"Tsk." Gregson ran roughshod over that. "The point is . . . well, I'll back up a bit. Do you know any twins?"

"A few." Lestrade didn't need to think about it.

"How would you describe their relationship within each other?"

"Close, of course . . . but not always friendly. And they tend to have their own language. Seems like . . . well . . . seems like a lot of their little ciphers are in the nature of . . . well . . . ." He hesitated. "Jokes."

"Exactly. It's a joke to them that the world doesn't understand." Gregson pulled out one of his awful cigarettes. "Now, to all accounts, Hamish was a clever man. Much more clever than our Watson – poor man. He's clever enough. Sounded like another version of Holmes. But have you ever met a clever man who couldn't resist being clever?"

"God, no," Lestrade groaned. "They can't help it. It's like telling Lord Nelson to stop squinting."

"Right." Gregson grinned, no doubt thinking of all the times Lestrade had been raked over the coals kept a-burning on Holmes's tongue. "*Why a cave,* Ratty? Why a cave out in the middle of nowhere pinned to the bloody great abyss? Why not just bury the junk under a dung heap in some farm, or brick it up below his house, or even stuff it in a place like Cox?"

Lestrade stared at him without blinking. "Gregson, I'm beginning to be a little afraid of where this is headed."

"You see it, don't you?" Gregson leaned forward on the table. "It's another clue. Hamish couldn't resist being clever."

"Clever enough to stick it where he did!" Lestrade protested. "Gregson, I'm afraid I don't see where you're going with this. What sort of message was Hamish leaving behind just by leaving a bag of ill-gotten swag inside a cave darker and colder than the Chief Inspector's heart on Boxing Day?"

Gregson leaned forward, mouth open . . . and Lestrade saw his face change. The big man pulled back, a thoughtful look (downright sly, actually) crossed his white face and he tapped his chin with a finger.

"I'm going to think this through," he said, and so slowly it was like pulling the words out with a floss.

"That's reassuring." Lestrade gave that statement the skepticism it deserved. "This isn't going to be like the time you 'thought it through' with the stolen cave bear bones, is it?"

Gregson's expression wobbled like one of those sand-weighted dolls before settling into scorn. "Mistakes can happen to anyone," he pointed out loftily. "It only proves I'm born of woman."

"Dear Heaven," Lestrade prayed. "If I was an educated man, I'd say something at that – probably in French. But I'm not. I'm a workman, thank you, and I'll continue to solve my cases in a workmanlike manner."

Gregson shook his head with that damned smile still on his face. "That's always been your biggest mistake, Ratty. Think of the time you'd save if you tried to solve crimes in your head, instead of on your feet."

"I'll stick to what I know, sir. That way I'll know they're actually solved." Lestrade's answer was as serenely arrogant as Gregson's bid for brainwork.

The late Mr. Holmes, they were certain, would have been greatly entertained.

NOTES

1. Gibberish.
2. Oddly enough, "loot" was an old word even then, an Anglo-Indian version of the Hindi *lut*, for stolen property.

Chapter XIV – Defection?

Lestrade came home appreciating the slightly lengthening days in London's notion of daylight. And with summer came a slightly lowered chance of dealing with London Particulars. Amen.

"Mr. Lestrade, you have a rather strange-looking message." His landlady met him at the front steps. She then went back to instructing the little urchin on his deliveries while the inspector waited patiently. Once the child scurried off she pulled a folded-over square of butcher's paper out of her apron pocket. "I was about to give it to Mrs. Lestrade, but her hands are dirty with the back garden."

"She doesn't believe in wasting time, does she?" Lestrade smiled fondly. "I suppose a few days without rain have made us all a bit nervous."

"Yes, indeed. London isn't London if one isn't worrying about something falling from the sky." Mrs. Collins flicked her apron crisply and vanished inside. Her bark at the all-work maid followed in her wake.

"Oh, there you are." Clea was just emerging into the foyer. Her hair was loose over her shoulders and the strict way she scrubbed at her hands spoke of her examination in the old vegetable plot. "You missed the excitement of today, dear."

Lestrade paused while transferring his coat and hat to the coat tree. "No policeman that ever walked over 'missed' excitement, Clea-*bihan*," he reminded her. "And forgive my reaction, but the last time you referred to something as 'excitement', it was that wretched chess charity that sent half the Met to Barts with broken bones, sprained limbs – "

"Missing teeth . . ." Clea added. "Poor Roger."

"Oh, he doesn't count." Lestrade dismissed his best friend lightly. "He stuck *his* back in and got 'em to stay."

Clea shuddered. "And people say the Cheathams are a hardy lot. All that aside, we were assailed by a telephone salesman today. He insisted the progressive household simply must have the Ericsson Eiffel Tower telephone."

Lestrade snorted. "Did you tell him tabletop phones are disastrously impractical when one has two budding Thomas Alva Edisons in the house? No . . . wall-mounted. Wall-mounted and up high." He shook his head. "I even offered Nicholas a broken telephone so he could take it apart, and you know what he said? He said there wasn't any use because if it was broken, how was he supposed to know how it worked?"

"He did have a point," Clea pointed out with a smile.

"Our sons always have a point."

"Now that's an excellent point in itself." Clea gave him a friendly pat on the shoulder. "Upstairs, Inspector. I was about to have some tea before supper. If I know you, you've had a sausage roll off the street or oysters at the Keg."

"Where are your *childer*, woman?" Once in their own building, both slipped into a patois of workman's English mixed with partially palatable scraps of Breton and Lanky.

"Upstairs in the book room, where *we* shall be headed. I'm treating the sitting room against the spring miasmas."

Lestrade shuddered slightly. Clea would have filled a small, porous clay pot with some sort of fumigant oil and set it over the fire to evaporate into a fume. One year it was lemon oil. One very memorable spring it had been wintergreen – souring everyone on the subject of sweets and stomach ache remedies for weeks.

Clea caught his look. "Cedar."

"Ah. Good." He yanked off his grimy collar and sighed. "Give me a moment, would you? I need to call your brother Myron on a business question."

"Do I wish to know whose business?"

"Mine." He sighed. "In the course of an investigation."

"I'll stay well out of it!" she exclaimed.

Lestrade had once seen a fully operative clock made out of wood. Since that moment, he had thought of his oldest brother-in-law as a wooden clock: A rather extraordinary man who was content to perform a rather ordinary function with his life. Numbers contented him as much as his homelife, and he was childishly unaware that his mind easily performed the tasks of several men at once with books, numbers, and statistics. Lestrade had the unpleasantness of many accountants in his life, but Myron was actually enjoyable.

He answered the telephone on the second ring.

"A bit of a thorny question, I'm afraid," Lestrade explained after the pleasantries. "It's about the world of fighting."

"Fighting, did you say?" Myron was bemused and small wonder. He was roughly three times Lestrade's size, but not, it was worth saying, the "fighter" of the family. "Wouldn't Bartram or Andrew – or rather, anyone else in the family – be better qualified for this?"

"No, and you'll see why in a moment. You keep the books for Bartram's career. You keep a record on his injuries?"

"Well, of course I do." Myron was horrified at any other possibility. "It's good business to know where he gets hurt and how often."

"And he's not the only fighter you keep books for."

109

"Well, no. Being the brother of Bartram of Lancashire, not to mention the son of 'Chokehold' Cheatham, has made my name a bit indispensible. Fighters like honest reputations, you know."

Lestrade hoped Myron meant the honest reputation of the bookkeeper, for Bartram's ethics in the ring were a bit flexible.

"What sort of fighters do you cover?"

"Take your pick. Boxers are rising in popularity, and a few savate . . . three singlestick professionals . . . ."

"Interesting." Lestrade was scribbling notes one-handed as fast as he could. "What about the ah . . . unprofessional athletes? People who just get into the ring or mat or whatever and whale at each other for a purse?"

"Never in short supply." Myron's voice was heavy with disapproval. "You want to talk injuries, I can give you far more than you want to know."

"Really? You mean that?"

There was a tiny pause on the line. "Is there something you are looking for, Geoffrey?"

"I don't know yet. We came across a few bodies . . . ." Lestrade wisely did not say how old they were, or how old they were *supposed* to be. "There were broken bones and signs of other injuries, looked to me like they were fighting injuries. Like people who were whaling at each other, as you just said."

Myron was silent for a long time. "Geoffrey, you best be careful."

"Am I on to something?"

"I hope not, and you'd best hope not as well. Mr. Quimper's *modus operandi* was to organize such fights. It was how he got rid of his more troublesome people, if I'm to believe the rumours. Quimper wasn't the only one out there, either. If someone is causing trouble or getting too expensive . . . well, there were always ways of solving the problem. One last chance to redeem oneself, if you get my meaning." Myron made a sound that sounded like teeth worrying at a pencil. "There isn't a single fighting club that doesn't have some sort of dealings, however shallow, with a criminal gentleman or three. The work is dirty, but they joke the money washes up clean."

"Well, I'm hoping it is nothing." Lestrade wondered if anyone was listening on the line. "I promised your sister I'd leave off the dramatics. What I'm just looking for is say . . . typical injuries in sport fighting."

"Check the forearms first." Myron answered. "Joint injuries are legion. Broken fingers are common as well, and missing teeth. Jaws can be a good clue . . . but be careful if you're checking any injuries below the belt. Sometimes a cab wreck can make similar injuries . . . and gin."

"Gin?"

110

"It isn't just a cheap joy. It'll clean out just about any wound as well as give a man the urge to pick up the fight again. Some of those fighters even brew their own gin – leaves, berries, whatever bits they toss in . . . Oh. Check around the eyesockets. That must be one of the most common ways of getting hurt. The bone around the sockets can get fractured, or even warped out of true."

"*Ech.*" Lestrade thanked Myron for his time and hung up the phone with a pensive expression.

The boys looked up from their books at the sight of their parents. Father was cleaner at the edges with a new collar and cuffs. "Hello," Martin piped up. "*Tad*, can you help me with my Latin?"

"Latin?" Their father looked to the ceiling. "The most to Latin I get is when I'm trying to get change from the shaved iceman in the summer."
1

"I'm not certain that's Latin, *Tad* . . . ." Nicholas, ever literal, started to say with a worried expression.

"*Flavia est puella*," Martin broke in quickly. "Flavia is a girl. *Flavia est puella Romani*. Flavia is a girl Roman."

"Roman girl." Nicholas corrected stubbornly.

"It's how it translates!"

"But you've got to translate it so's it's right English too!"

"'*So's*' isn't right English, Nick. Nor's *right Eng*lish – it's *good English*!"

"Do you know how Uncle Bartram speaks '*good English*'?" Nicholas pointed to his fist.

"*Diwall!*" Their father snapped. "As usual, you're bickering because you're both right!" He paused to glare at each. "You've got to translate the words as they come out if you're going to understand them, and then you've got to turn that into good English! I declare, the two of you spend more time arguing when you could just as easily get along and – What?" He had caught Clea trying not to smile.

"I was just thinking," Clea said demurely. As demure never worked with his little wife, he merely lifted another eyebrow. "Our sons sound like two inspectors I know."

"You're being overly harsh again, dear." With one last look that carried Biblical imprecations against any more disturbers of the peace, he found the newspaper and settled down with it. Clea was still smiling as she set up the tea.

"You won't be filling your bellies up on tea," she warned. "There's a good supper waiting for everyone tonight."

"What is it, Mum?" Nicholas would never have to worry about his belly filling up.

"Pigeons and forcement [2] with apple snow balls."

"Pigeons!" Nicholas exclaimed with delight.

"Nicholas, I'm fairly certain they're all dead," their father said without looking up from his tea.

"I should like to have a few pigeons," his youngest son countered. "They would be a good way to start up a business, wouldn't they?"

Caught by this unexpected bit of cleverness on Nicholas' part, Lestrade stopped stirring his tea. "So long as you didn't eat the profits and didn't get too attached to them," he admitted.

"You mean like the rabbits?" Martin asked with a glint in his too-dark eyes. "I thought Nick was doing rather well until the Hinkle's dog got too attached to his rabbits and 'ate the profits'."

"There's a word and a place for too-clever imps."

Nicholas sighed at the tragedy. "We could keep the pigeons on the roof."

Lestrade knew where this was all going. "I'm not going to build you anything resembling a coop or a dovecote until you decide what sort of pigeons you want. Take your time," he added firmly.

"I should like a large bird." Nicholas was already daydreaming. "We could sell them."

"We?" Martin repeated in alarm.

"But I like messenger pigeons too." He brightened. "Can you use them, *Tad*?"

Lestrade narrowly missed choking on his pekoe. "What, you mean for work?"

"Yes," Nicholas answered serenely. "I should think they would be useful."

Clea pondered the scene before her: Her hard-to-flap husband staring across the table to his youngest son while his forgotten cup hovered dangerously over the cloth. She doubted the boys knew their father's regular forays into the underworld of London, but he was getting a bit paranoid of discovery of late. Being CID (and that was common record) was enough of a risk for the organised "families".

"I think that's a fine idea, Love." Clea smiled. "You know, there was a dovecote at Lttle Venice. I wonder if your grandfather would enjoy starting up some birds. You could trade messages back and forth."

"Messages," Geoffrey blurted, and rose from the table. "Pardon." He hurried out of the room. Clea could hear him muttering about "stupidity" and "no head" as he went.

He returned a few minutes later, looking much relieved. "That was from Padriac. They can make the bricks for your walk the next time they're in London – weather permitting of course."

"I look forward to it!"

Martin and Nicholas were discussing the finer points of breeding "runt" pigeons, which was named from a French word for common and not their size as they could reach stupendous proportions. Martin was arguing the larger the bird, the slower the growth, and Nicholas was insisting that would make them worth even more on the market.

Geoffrey stared at them, then at his wife. "You know, when I was their age, I think I was caught up in fishing."

"Sounds harmless enough," Clea chuckled.

Martin had lit upon the aspect of messenger pigeons. He was now insisting they could expand this future venture with both kinds, and has anyone thought of selling a special paper for the job?

When the doorbell rang, Lestrade was grateful for the distraction.

He was surprised to see it was Gregson.

The big man pulled his hat off his head, face set and tight. "I was stopping by," he said by way of a polite excuse. "Have you a moment?"

"Of course . . . what is it?"

"Patterson's left."

Lestrade waited, but Gregson was saying nothing else. "Wait a moment . . . you mean . . . he left?"

"Packed his desk up again and took off about two hours ago. What the devil did you say to the man?" Gregson demanded.

"I . . ." Lestrade stammered. "Gregson, I'm as shocked as you are! All I said was . . . ." He stopped, thinking. "I said rather much what you said. That he needed to go back and get his feet wet again with undercover, because that was his element."

"Well, you must have hit the right note," Gregson opined. "For something."

"Something? Did he go back?"

"Not even that. He tendered his complete resignation. Took the train back to Exeter. It looks like he's retired *but good* this time."

"I don't know what to say," Lestrade confessed. "He didn't seem to have that idea in his head when we were talking . . . I mean, he was tired and discouraged from the fact that we're getting bloody nowhere with the remnants of Moriarty's gang." He scowled. "And he didn't look all that well when I first saw him, before Christmas."

"He'd best be careful," Gregson decreed soberly. "The Home Office is looking at all of us now. What if they decide Patterson isn't retiring, but defecting?"

NOTES

1. Italian ice men were London's "ice cream vendors" selling flavoured cups of shaved ice.
2. A type of vegetarian stuffing, with breadcrumbs standing for the meat and herbs and spices for flavour.

Chapter XV – Limousin

Limousin:

They had struggled against the powers of an unseasonably unforgiving winter, but the long sweeps of oak orchards were finally passing from first leaf to second leaf. In the farmlands, the dark red cattle named after the region grazed while field hands kept an eye out for predators. The calves were still young and awkward. They would be an easy meal for a wild animal like the occasional boar (not completely unheard of) . . . and an unscrupulous human being.

The traveller reviewed with studied weariness these pleasant bucolic sights. He was exhausted. At least here it was too underpopulated to be overtly noticed. Who bothered in the rush of springtime labours to make note of another idle wanderer trying to absorb the flavour of the wine oaks?

To be honest, Holmes had not quite known there was *so much* to wine making . . . nor had he dreamed that a harvest of oakwood for wine barrels could make or break a man's fortune, destroy a winery's reputation, and level a rival as surely as disease in the grapevines.

As the guest of the Luciens, he was free to stroll across the forested lands as much as he desired – to ask questions of anyone upon his way and see the rich world of wine and oak.

"The oak, she improves the wine," swore the wine man who was stained like wood himself, and who bore the most atrocious accent Holmes had ever heard in France. It had traces of German in it, and Polish. "The oak must hold the wine within her grip or it will not be a true wine."

Before he could politely decline, the oldster blissfully poured out a small glassful from a barrel that (judging by its absolute cleanliness), had been filled up just that autumn. "Try this. The glass is still young and harsh." He pressed a small bottle of olive oil into the hands of his guest. "Take a spoonful's worth," he scolded. "You must coat your stomach first or you will die too young."

Holmes had no particular plans to die in the near future, so he did as directed. Then there was no choice but to sip the gift.

"It is . . . vibrant," he said. It was a decent enough way to describe and apologize for the strength of the wine. It made him think of the chardonnay in his favourite establishments . . . but there was no mellowness, no gentle tones. It was pure and raw power upon the tongue, and thus the tongue was shocked.

115

The old man hooted. "The oak must age the wine, and soften it. The wood marries to the grape, producing the butter and vanilla overtones. The two are stronger together."

Stronger together. Holmes was seeing this partnership was appreciated in the land. It was the source and inspiration to many proverbs and wise sayings.

He was surprised to find he liked it here. It was the closest thing to restful he'd come to, and it was only in part due to the country. He was away from the presence of so many humans. He was beginning to see a complexity in the natural world around him that rivaled that of London itself.

There were crimes even in the animal kingdom, but there were also intricate puzzles and gigantic realms of the unknown and little-understood. His mind drank in the unknowns eagerly.

The old man – Holmes still did not know his name – sighed and settled his rinsed glass upon the scrubbed table. Surrounded by limitless supplies of drink, he was the last thing from a drunkard one might find. "That is that," he said. "We must take you back to the house, sir."

"So soon?" He looked out the square window to the strongly burning sunlight across the fields.

"There is a strange man in our parts, sir. We would not wish to see our guest harmed."

"A strange man?" Really, he ought to revise his conclusions if they have noted him after all.

"Yes, an Englishman. He travels alone, and they say he carries a rifle when he walks at night. He could be . . . ." The word was sought, lost, and finally expressed by a meaningful tap to the temple.

"A madman?"

"There are no shortages. Englishmen do not come to our land for amusement, sir. They come to hunt, or to examine the oak orchards, or to buy our cattle. But we are not an *amusing* land."

Holmes felt a small chill at the calm, matter-of-fact way the words had been uttered. "I see," he said. "Well, if he has a rifle, then he must be here to hunt."

"One would think so," was the grave response. "That is the problem with Limousin."

"Problem, sir?"

"There is never," he was told, "a shortage of things to hunt here."

"Good Lord, is that Watson?"

"I'm afraid so," Lestrade whispered back to Gregson.

"Poor fellow."

116

Watson stood just down the street from their conversation. He looked like the racehorse who knew its days were numbered before it was sold to pull cabs. Black from head to toe made him look unhealthy. Lack of sleep carved grey hollows in his cheeks. He was beginning to lose weight.

But he smiled to see them. "This is a surprise, inspectors," he said as if it were a pleasant occurrence to collide into two Yarders on a crowded street. "I thought you might be here, but not so early!"

"Hello, Doctor," Gregson puffed slightly. With the end of the cold weather came a bit more of his old mobility. "You wanted to see us?"

"Well, yes," Watson coloured a bit. "If you have the time."

"I lost a wager so I have to treat *him*," Gregson jerked a thumb sourly at a very smug Lestrade. "You may as well come along and witness the deed."

"You wouldn't have lost if you hadn't been cocky," Lestrade answered back.

"Does your wife know you eat in taverns?"

Watson chuckled lightly. "May I ask what the wager was?"

"He thought I didn't know how many pencils were in my desk."

"I say, Lestrade, I'd lose that wager myself!"

"See?" Gregson wanted to know. "You're a mistake against nature."

"Mistake, nothing. Bradstreet borrows without returning. I had to go buy another box last week and put a moratorium on his 'permanent loans'," Lestrade sniffed. "He's preying on poor Hopkins as we speak. Someone needs to do something."

Inside the tavern, Gregson shuddered and ordered oysters for all. Watson showed no upset at dining in a lower-class establishment, nor did he shy from the oysters. Gregson had the inkling Watson was less a gentleman and more a citizen of the world with his attitude.

"How can we help you, Doctor?" he asked as the platters of lightly fried seafood clattered on the plank. A bowl of dipping sauce and a plate of seaweed followed.

"I didn't order that!"

"They know what I like," Lestrade shot back, still smug.

Gregson stared. "You know, when I was a constable – a lowly constable – along the Thames, I had to round up a bunch of dead herons some fool had shot on the Isle of Dogs. The smell that came from their carcasses is muchly like I think you're going to be like soon."

"What were herons doing at the Isle of Dogs?" Lestrade wanted to know. "That place isn't fit for leeches, much less a bird."

"Don't change the subject. You're going to start smelling like sunburnt prawns caught in the tide by the end of the day – No, I do not want horseradish!" Gregson gagged slightly.

Lestrade shrugged and popped an oyster in his mouth.

"There's a lesson to be learned by this," Gregson said darkly to Watson. "Never gamble. It will all end in tears."

Lestrade, who had bitten down on a particularly juicy piece of fresh horseradishroot, sniffed loudly as tears came to his eyes. "I quite agree." He reached for a napkin.

"I'm afraid I must confess to an error on my part." Watson took his napkin with a polite nod to the girl and sipped carefully. "I made a mistake . . . a foolish one." He sighed. "Without meaning to, I brought back one of Sir Niles' notebooks on the bog bodies." Briefly he explained what had happened.

Lestrade and Gregson looked at each other when he finished. "It's nothing a man can be proud of, but at the same time, Watson, it's hardly grounds for sending you up to dig ditches a few years. It was an accident. You ought to be able to sneak the book back to Sir Niles with a bit of arrangement, correct?"

"That . . . ." Watson set his lips. "I do not think I can go back to Streat," he said. "My work is taking my attention, gentlemen. And as Sir Niles is a suspect if not an accessory to some of the strange goings at Streat . . . ." He shook his head.

"What, you mean you haven't looked at the book?" Lestrade blinked. This possibility had not hit him. Gregson was similarly affected.

"I've had no time," Watson said in a voice barely above a whisper.

They knew what that meant. The grief had demanded his time and soul.

"Here's what I say," Gregson said at last. "The procurement of the book many not be a problem in itself. Yes, if there's evidence that we need in a trial . . . but if we have this book leading us to the root evidence, like what really was Loseth's business on the island . . . then we can work backwards with a clear view."

"We just aren't going to make a habit of this," Lestrade said sternly – mostly to Gregson. "Although I'm beginning to suspect the success in Mr. Holmes's cases depended on such collecting of evidence."

"At least we never had to worry about him swiving the fair maids and getting the footmen drunk," Gregson pointed out. "I don't know about you, but me, I'm counting my blessings. With that said, just drop the book off – Oh. Thank you." Gregson tucked the small volume in his coat. "I hope your day was better than all this."

Watson felt the smile escape, and let it. He was relieved. His sense of honour had been caught in this thorny matter, but it took the recent exposure to the Yard to understand they were worthy of that sort of trust.

"I can't say my day was any more illuminating. Did anyone upstairs ever learn what that boy was doing with his pockets-full of opium pipes?"

"They must've missed you," Gregson said around a grateful swallow of beer. "Boy was a member of the Mudflats Gang. We got his sister to identify why was left of him, and she didn't seem surprised he'd been dead for a week underwater. They run all the way to Bethnel Green and sell whatever they steal from the dens."

"That is risky," Watson sighed. "I can't imagine a grown man getting away with that." He accepted Lestrade's offer of seaweed without a blink and tore a piece up to go with his oysters. "Was it the boy you feared?"

"No . . ." Gregson answered heavily. "It wasn't our Toby, but he's too old to be a cocksparrow or any of the other child-thieves now. His being mute was an asset when he was in the small gangs. Now it's turning him into someone who could easily be blamed for someone else's mischief."

"There's a good lad in there," Lestrade agreed with a tired nod. "And he's old enough to be put to useful work, whether or not he's fifteen or sixteen."

"I'm keeping my eyes out for that boy. Next time I collar his neck, he's marchin' straight home with *me*." Gregson had come to his decision with his usual speed and lack of second thoughts. "Just you watch him try to get something over my wife!"

Lestrade snickered at the thought, but kept his mouth shut of opinion in an act of willpower Watson admired. "All that aside, gentlemen . . . Are we still free for tonight?"

"Ugh! I'm afraid so," Gregson moaned.

"I wish you all the luck," Watson prayed earnestly. "It hardly sounds like an enjoyable evening. But perhaps a profitable one."

"It might be what we need to finish this case," Lestrade muttered. Weary hope flickered in his eyes. "I most certainly hope so. Staying up with paper and chalk would be a fair enough trade if we can prove a tie between Pennywraith and the Burial Charity."

"Who found out Pennywraith was a part of the Burial Board?" Watson wondered. "Hopkins?"

"Hopkins. That in itself isn't at all unusual, but it is when you think of his suspected activities."

"I'm pleased with Hopkins," Gregson said gruffly. "When his lead paid out, he went and found another one. Says Pennywraith's files that aren't adding up."

Watson's face twisted. "A revolting business," he decreed flatly. "I dislike few things as much as I dislike a corrupt physician."

"You're welcome to come along if you like," Lestrade offered.

"Thank you, but no." Watson smiled wearily. "I must rest if I am to function at all on the morrow."

"Oh? Something up?" Gregson passed the rest of his plate to Lestrade.

"I'm attending the rugby match over on the field," Watson explained. "Strange to say, there's a common belief – or should I say myth – that only a doctor who played rugby can understand the injuries on the field."

"Dear me," Lestrade stared. "Is there anything in London you do not do, Doctor?"

Watson shrugged slightly, a bit pleased at the off-handed remark. "It keeps one flexible."

"My eye."

Gregson looked up from a most wearisome stack of dry papers. "Something in it?"

"No. *My eye*. As in, *rot*. That bit about being flexible and getting it by staying obscenely busy. Man's just trying to work himself to death." Lestrade slapped another finished sheet of paper on top of the slowly growing pile and lifted his voice to Hopkins waiting at the chalkboard: "*Browne* with an '*E*', Christian name of *Zachariah*."

"Got it." Hopkins dutifully copied the name on the board with the rest. "That makes four."

"Six. God in his Heaven," Gregson swore and pulled back from his chair a bit, pushing the heels of his hands into his eyes to alleviate the aching soreness of peering through reams of Pennywraith's hand.

The set-up was simple enough: Hopkins gave Lestrade and Gregson a double list to sift through – the list of dead soldiers who had "benefited" from the burial charity, and the other list was the list of civilians Pennywraith had addressed within the timeframe of the war and the year following immediately after.

If Hopkins hadn't noticed a dresser by the unusual last name of Honeymaker on both lists, they never would have found this track.

"There are most likely many more names," was Lestrade's sober observation.

One hour, six names. Several hundred more files to go.

"Let's stop a moment," Gregson said, two more names later. He rose stiffly and began working his aching neck back and forth. Lestrade needed no further enticement. He leaned over the conference table in search of his cigarette case when one of the most baby-faced constables the inspectors had ever seen tapped briskly on the door with his gloved fist.

"Begging your pardon, sirs," the youth cleared his throat, "but there's a telephone call for Mr. Lestrade. Says it's urgent, sir."

"Urgent but no name," Lestrade grumbled as he got to his feet. "Probably has another stranded cat."

"You'd be so fortunate," Gregson jibed after him. He grinned at Hopkins. "Man's got his own following of eccentrics."

"Don't we all?" Hopkins wondered. "Mine are all in my family. That makes it a bit hard to hide from them."

"You have it there . . . ." They universally broke into the waiting teapot and chewed on sandwiches collected for the purpose. Gregson's wife was firm believer in hearty slabs of beef and cheese.

"Pennywraith must have been in the pockets of the gang for years," Hopkins said at last. "Does anyone know how old Moriarty's gang is – was?"

"Impossible to say for certain," Gregson grunted. "Gangs aren't made up like a new suit at the tailor's. It was likely a case of his taking over an existing organisation . . . in which case, we could trace 'em back to the Norman Invasion if we try hard enough!" He sniffed. "A lot of what we consider crime now used to be perfectly legal if you had Crown sponsorship, so what exactly constitutes a gang?"

"A group of unsavoury individuals who have no concern for their fellow man in their desire to acquire wealth," Hopkins said after a bit of thought.

"Nice, there, but you could argue that of half the Heads of State . . . at any given moment in our history." Gregson took a huge bite and chewed frantically. "Not to mention the minister my parents go to."

"That's unsettling," Hopkins noted.

"Isn't it."

Chapter XVI – A Role Call
for Murder

Gregson was pulling out another cup of tea from the sideboard when a grey-faced Lestrade returned. Gregson struck the sideboard with the pot. Hopkins tensed over the chalk.

"That was Patterson," the smaller man announced heavily. "He may be retired for all of six days, but it didn't stop him from asking a few questions for his own personal satisfaction."

"What is it?" Hopkins asked.

"He wanted to know more about those dead bog men that we know are recent murder victims." Lestrade went straight to the water jug and ignored the tea. "Had a hunch. Sent a photograph of their faces to a few people he knew." He took a large gulp of water. "They were all fighters." He slapped a sheet of paper down one-handed. "Names and descriptions of fighters on the graft who had reason to vanish . . . ."

"Fighters." Gregson chewed on the edge of his cigarette furiously.

"Low-rate, cut-interest fighters who, in his own words, made their keep when they started up the 'draw' fights – bringing the first of the crowd in and keeping the blood hot before the real attractions hit, like the famous fighters." Lestrade tried to think as he drank. "My brother-in-law said something about that once . . . in passing. I need to think back on what it was. The man doesn't exactly volunteer a conversation."

"You've got that right," Gregson agreed with a sigh. "Fighters. Well . . . isn't that what you were researching with your family anyway?"

"Yes, but I didn't expect to get this so soon." Lestrade returned to his seat. "I knew death fights were very illegal, but also very very well paying, but I did not know matches were used to set one's place aright within the Family." He suddenly rapped his knuckles on the veneer of wood. "And how some rival gangs settled their scores with fights."

"Makes sense." Hopkins was ready to accept it. "If two rival parties are at war with each other, it's a lot of risk and fuss to make it an outright war. What if they settled their differences with a sort of duel? Winner's side takes all."

"Mr. Holmes once said there was nothing new under the sun." Lestrade found his knife and sharpened another row of pencils. "Good for him, but his advice that we need to sit down and do nothing but read for a year . . . that's the worst advice I've ever gotten." Dissatisfaction tinted his voice as he shaved thin wood and lead. "I'm starting to understand why the man appeared to be half mad every time I saw him."

"Oh, a genius usually is mad to begin with." Gregson dismissed that with easy charity of the superior. "It's to balance out their being so smart."

"Comforting philosophy, Gregson."

"Let's take a rest." Hopkins had added Lestrade's little contribution to the corner of the board. "My hands are stiff, my back hurts, and I'm starting to see double letters."

"That's probably because the lamp wants trimming." But Gregson obligingly pulled a chair out for the youngest professional. "Let's see if we can't squeeze out five more cases, and call it a day." There was a grateful vote in unanimity.

"What are you doing with that?" Lestrade asked wearily as Gregson pulled out Sir Niles' little notebook.

"Now that I've got a moment to kill, I'm going to take a peek."

"I'd rather become the best professional in the Yard because I am the best, Gregson. Not by default because you topped from a heart attack."

Gregson whistled. "What was it I was just saying about genius and madness?"

"You're implying Sir Niles is a genius?"

"Positively tops." Gregson held up a sample page. It looked like mad spiders dancing over the paper. "This is . . . this really is mad." He turned a few pages. "He spends two pages talking about what he had for breakfast!"

"Quit complaining, Gregson. You took the bloomin' book. Now you have to go through it for anything useful."

"Wedlock is supposed to soften a man, Ratty," Gregson retorted without his usual wit.

"Well, skim over the breakfasts. See if you can find something about the bog bodies dug up over there – Will that make you feel better?"

"If he spends two pages on salmon with poached eggs, it'll take twenty to get to the middle of the day . . . ." But Gregson took the suggestion. A few minutes passed while Hopkins tried without success to flex the life back into his writing hand, and Lestrade sharpened everyone's pencils.

"Here we are. Subject Two . . . Full Moon. Full Moon? Male, six-foot-two inches, two-hundred pounds precisely, partially lamed from accident . . . blue eyes, single eyebrow, tightly curled blond hair, collected Last Quarter . . . ."

"That's disgusting," Lestrade grumbled through his teeth as he worked on his last pencil.

"Subject Three, male, five-foot-seven inches, brown eyes, roostertail eyebrows, clubfoot sinister, one-hundred-and-thirty-five pounds. . . ." Gregson kept reading. "Short black hair, terrier crop, scar across forehead going down to eye . . . missing right index finger . . . That's odd. It says 'last quarter' here too . . . ."

"Gregson!" Lestrade slapped his pencil down on the table. "Find something useful, would you? Not that bone-chilling list for Madame Tussauds, please."

"This could be useful."

"How? How does the eye colour for a bog victim count as useful? How the blazes did they know what colour the eyes were when they dug 'em out of the bog? They're all pickled like walnuts in that dark water!"

"I have no idea." Gregson was man enough to speak without chagrin as he paged forward, then backwards through the book. "But it's quite the extensive list. He's got them listed in months . . . years . . . ."

Hopkins' mouth fell open. His heart pounded, choking the words in his throat.

"Hopkins?" Lestrade frowned.

Hopkins struggled to speak. "Full moon," he croaked. "Last quarter. Moon phases . . . sacrifices."

Then it hit Lestrade.

"Dear Lord!" Lestrade's chair clattered to the floor. "There wouldn't be eye colour in a bog victim!"

Gregson stared at the book in his hands as if he'd suddenly been told it was made of human skin. "What kind of monster makes a role call of murder victims *before* they're disposed of?" He went to the wall chart against the desk and started paging. "Last quarters are the week before full moons . . . collected before the full moon but not killed until the damned moon is in the sky! WHAT kind of monster makes a list of this?"

"A man who makes lists," Hopkins strangled. "A man who makes lists, Gregson."

"When's the next last quarter moon?" Lestrade wet his lips.

"It's . . . ." Gregson looked up, his face stricken. "tomorrow night."

Everyone swallowed at that.

"How many?" Lestrade finally asked.

"I . . . I don't know . . ." Gregson stammered. In the lamplight his eyes had grown blue-white and round. "There's . . . there's three pages . . . four . . . six . . . six." He breathed out in the terrible silence. "About two men listed on each page . . . ."

The three men stared at each other. Neither knew quite what to say.

"This is a matter for the Home Office," Hopkins said at last.

"They'll want to know how we got the book," Lestrade protested.

"Call it a donation!" Gregson snapped. He peered across one page, then another. "Oh, my word. Look." They crowded behind his shoulders. "Look at the way he's set up the victims by numbers. And how he's got this here – " He pointed to a small, unmistakable symbol for mortality: A tiny cross in black ink. "Here, and here . . . but not all of them. Whoever No. Twelve is, and Twenty and Three and Seven . . . they don't have these marks."

"So they aren't dead?" Hopkins dared to guess.

"That's my inkling. But look at all of these who have the death mark! Of twenty men here, it looks like all but . . . five are dead!"

"We need to find these men." Lestrade yanked out a sheet of fresh paper. "Start listing their descriptions – Hold on a moment, read me back that description of the man with one eyebrow."

"Number 14." Gregson peered into the poisonous little book and dutifully re-read the description.

"That's him." Lestrade circled one of the names on his sheet. "George Blakely. Says he has three broken teeth in the bottom. Should be easy enough to find that out."

"Want to bet your men are all in here?" Gregson wanted to know.

"Not about to," Lestrade snarled. "Keep reading. Let's get this down and finish the reports before we all fall over."

"Try this one, then . . . ." Gregson turned the next page over while Lestrade waited impatiently. "Five-foot-nine, brown hair, brown eyes, brown moustache, thick neck, partially crippled in left arm. Right leg . . . ."

Lestrade's pencil snapped in twain.

Hopkins didn't pause to be mannerly. He ripped the door open and pelted up the steps for the nearest telephone and the emergency wire.

"Yes?" Watson found himself looking down at the unlikely image of a street urchin with a large basket of blooming bread seed poppies and lilies in his thin arms.

"Delivery from a friend, Doctor," the boy piped up. His face was all but hidden in his large red scarf, which was much finer than the rest of his dirt-ragged clothing. "Belated condolences, 'e said. No name."

Watson frowned as he traded the duce out of his pocket for the flowers. His weary mind was far away from the situation at hand, so as he moved to place them on the table he did not notice a subtle change in the air, emanating from the gift. He only thought he was tired, and the low crackle of the flames coming from the fireplace lulled him.

He sank into the low couch by the fire and straightened out his leg without thinking. His head lowered by degrees into his hand and his mind wandered. Something calmly dry and unemotional noted this was the first time in days he'd allowed himself to fall into such a state. It was a temporary relief to not feel anything but simple fatigue.

By the time the lock snapped on the front door, his reflexes had slowed enough that it was a simple matter to finish the job the drugged poppies had started. His body was slow but his mind was bright with the deepest fury he'd ever known as they pinned him down to the carpet with the weight of their bodies. The fury only built in him as he watched from over the gloved hand that silenced his shout for help, watched the tall one pull out a small bottle and a rag. They were careful, he noted. If he survived this he would remember how careful they were. These men had the knowledge and the nerve to dose him with three-and-a-half ounces on the spot. He watched without blinking as the rag drew over his face.

Chapter XVII – A Blind

Lestrade swore out loud. "We're too late!"

"*Hell!*" Gregson broke away from the cab and threw himself to the door hanging so slightly, horribly ajar. In the red lamp of the surgeon's practice, the bricks of Kensington threw bloody shadows into the facing. The black space was small between the door and the frame, but it was large enough to sink their hopes.

"*Ghah!*" Gregson snarled and brought up short as Lestrade tried not to collide into his broad back. "Chloroform and I don't know what else!" He whirled and threw the door back open. "I'm going to start opening the windows!"

"You do that!" Lestrade pulled his handkerchief over his face and stepped inside the consultation room. Signs of a fight were clear: A tipped-over chair, papers scattered over the floor, a spilled vase leaking water and crushed flowers into the carpet. *Mary's going to be upset,* Lestrade thought before he remembered she was dead. "Oh, God," he said aloud at the small glass object under the taboret.

"What is it?" Gregson snapped impatiently.

Lestrade picked it up in his gloved fingers. "Chloroform. Just enough to knock out a grown man. No more."

"Bloody Hell. *Experts.* Now what." Gregson turned as if he would like to punch the nearest person. He stopped. "Hell, look. The flowers are drugged too!"

"I didn't think anyone was still plying that trick," Lestrade confessed darkly. "Lions! Post a guard by the door! No one in or out without our authority, and that includes the Prime Minister!" He muttered to himself as he scurried throughout the room, keeping to the side away from Gregson. "Drawer's open. He must have been reaching for his revolver . . . *Damn it!*" Lestrade swore.

"What is it?" Gregson was at his side instantly.

"Look," Lestrade pointed. Against the wine-red of the carpet was another, livid splotch. "Blood for certain." He dropped to his knees to examine it while Gregson drew an invisible line between the drawer and the bloodspot. His eyes lit up at a small hole in the wall. "Point for the doctor!" He hissed triumphantly. "He got a shot off. Look for the revolver."

"Ahead of you." Lestrade was reaching under the settee. He yanked the weapon up triumphantly. Gregson hovered while he opened the five-round chamber. "Three shots," Lestrade sniffed. "He must have fired all three – it smells strongly enough."

"Three shots, one bullet in the wall," Gregson whispered. "D'you think he got three of them off?"

"You've seen him shoot. If you waste a single bullet in the Queen's Army you have to answer for it out of your own pay! These things are at their best at thirty-five yards, but every Army man I've ever seen can fire just as well at a hundred . . . Let's keep looking." Lestrade dropped to the carpet again, squinting for some kind of difference in the floor.

Gregson hallowed from the doorway. "Ha!" He pointed at the dark wood of the frame. "That's where a slug connected with someone's shoulder. Look at the angle of the blood spray."

"Two, then. There's a third shot we need to account for." Lestrade jumped slightly at the sound of pounding feet outside. "That's Lions. Let's see what else he has to tell us."

"Inspectors," Lions was out of breath as he stopped at the doorway. "Some Kensington policemen."

"Let's go outside and not contaminate the crime scene," Gregson held the door open for Lestrade.

Constable Crane tapped his fingers to the brim of his helmet. "*Sirs*. We were on the Kensington beat when we heard a series of shots." He indicated his partner, a new man Lestrade recognized but could not name at the moment. "Brown and I came running, blowin' on our whistles the whole time." Sweat still stained Crane's face. "We were just two blocks away, but they were quick, sir. We could make out three men limping, carryin' a fourth slung over the first man's shoulder, piling into a growler. Looked like the doctor. Wearing mourning-black frock . . . They took off like the devil, but we followed as best as we could."

"Go on," Gregson encouraged. "Where did they head to?"

"That's just it, sir. Brown got a cart and we followed 'em to the trackline down past the Serpentine, but the carriage was empty. We found some of the Water Police and they said there was some kind of ruckus and they were kept on to see what that was. We told them what was going on at our end, and we made our way back here to report. The Water Police posted a guard by the growler. It was practically in the water and they said it was close enough for their jurisdiction."

The Serpentine had been a blind. It was a case of where they were intending to go after that. No doubt some place close to the Thames. It was on the other side of Hyde Park. "Not so bad," Gregson murmured. "Next time, lad, try to check in on the scene, even if one of you must stay behind."

Crane flinched as if struck. "My fault, sir. I was afraid we'd lose the doctor . . . and we did anyway," he finished miserably.

128

Lestrade sighed wearily. "You did good. If you hadn't been there when you had, we wouldn't have known where they were headed. Now we have the Water Police involved, and they're excellent at what they do." Like nearly everyone else at the Yard, Lestrade felt the Water Police, with their eternal dealings in drownings, corpses, and smugglers, worked harder and did more with the least amount of pay or thanks.

"We'll go talk to them now." Gregson clapped his hand on Lestrade's shoulder. "You two stick around and give Lions whatever assistance he needs. Are you up to that, after all that running?"

His concern was just what the policemen needed. The young men puffed up with a mixture of pride at being asked to do more and indignation that Gregson thought they needed the rest. Despite the worry crushing Lestrade, he had to admire Gregson's cleverness.

"Now." Gregson met his eyes. "The Serpentine Tracks."

He woke up by degrees in complete darkness, his empty stomach clenching from the effects of the drug. His mind was fogged more deeply than it should have been. A response to the strange element in the flowers?

Clever, he thought. *Nepenthe in the poppies. A vicious spider with a taste for literature.* Another spasm hit in his midsection and he instinctively tried to curl up, arms over his abdomen in protection. He couldn't move. He tried moving his head, but everything felt slow and stupid. Rough wood scraped the side of his face. He wasn't sure if he was lying on his side or sitting up. *Sense of direction wrong*, he noted coldly. *Small wonder I feel nauseous.*

Clockless moments passed as one by one, his senses retreated back to his brain. The throbbing sensation in his skull was explained when his sense of hearing returned. Smooth movement slid underneath him, like riding a serpent. He couldn't move because his body was restrained. It was dark because he was in something made of sanded plank wood. Crate? *Crate . . . large one . . .* He tried stretching to see what the dimensions of the crate were, but found himself frustrated. Whatever was preventing his mobility was doing a damn good job –

Something heaved, up and to the side, and his nausea doubled. He choked down the need to vomit. Cold sweat damped the air of his tomb. For several minutes his mind was quite empty of thought as he struggled not to retch. The pitching sensation was not a figment of his imagination . . . it slowly translated to the rock and yawl of a craft on water.

In God's name, where was he?

The doctor's mind thrust backwards, mentally shuffling through possibilities. Sensation was prickling its way back into his skin. Touch, the first sense. Dr. Thompson's first speech at Netley had been the use of

129

organoleptic means in analyzing one's situation – meaning patients, not kidnappings, but it worked just as well.

Faint stench of tar. Waterproofing. He couldn't feel any tar in the wood pressing against his face, but he could *smell* it. Tar in the layer beneath the wood, then. This was water-sealed. Storage space for something that couldn't get wet. That left out the usual sailing boats and sloops, where the crew merely kept their gear in waterproofed bags and saved themselves a few shillings on treating every inch of the craft –

Another heave. This time he saw stars, heard a wave slap not far from his head. Ocean water or the Thames. The Serpentine was fed by springs. She didn't carry that kind of force. He gulped for air. His ears rang in protest.

Think, John. Use those leftover brains your brother didn't want!

John willed his heart to calm again. The prickling sensation was growing worse. The opiates in the flowers were wearing off. It felt like ants were crawling on his face, trying to get under his eyelids. He tried moving again, now that he was developing some sense of his body. Legs still useless, but he couldn't tell if he was numb, paralysed, or simply bound.

Hands – simpler. *They* were bound. Wouldn't make much sense to bind a paraplegic. Had to assume his legs were restricted the same way. He moved his head slightly, trying to get a feel for what was holding him down. Rope. His fingers traced over the knots as best as he could, realised the untying was far beyond his abilities. *Bowline knot.* He recognized it as a knot normally used for rescuing people. There was still a faint trace of dampness to the cord. They had dipped it in seawater before lashing him. The fibres had shrunk as it dried, creating restraints as impervious as leather. This would have to be cut off.

All right. Hands bound in front, not back. No gag. That was really less encouraging than anything else. Whoever they were, they were making certain he could defend himself from choking on his own vomit, and they knew there was no need to silence him. He was out of range for a call to help.

Smell. Touch. Sight – nothing. Dark as midnight. It might even *be* midnight, but he doubted it. This particular prison was built watertight. Watson wasn't certain what kind of cargo this craft was used to hauling, but he had a terrible suspicion.

Sound. Nothing. The silence was thick in his ears. Another reason to suspect this prison was designed for humans.

Think, John. What kind of craft?

Cargo. Small cargo, if it were dealing with humans and things that couldn't get wet or exposed to air. The pitch and roll meant the craft couldn't be very large. Thames was a strong current. It could bear anything large and heavy enough to take a thirty-foot tidal drop. Thames wasn't a sporting river. It was freight and cargo and passengers and smuggling . . .

Another pitch. Realization came to Watson with the nausea. The dips of the craft were in one direction. He was in the centre of the boat, not the aft where cargo was often kept . . .

Keelboat. He was in the keel of the craft.

His heart hammered at the realization. Keelboats were built to navigate against obstacles. They were rowing sailboats, capable of going against or with the wind however need be, and they had a degree more resiliency than the light yachts. A keelboat needed a crew of anywhere from six to . . . ten? He was definitely outnumbered.

And Holmes thought all those seafaring novels a waste of time? To laugh at the irony.

Watson forced himself to swallow dryly and mentally re-inventoried his options. At this point, he had no idea who would be masterminding this. He just knew that there was absolutely no good to be had in this situation, and it would no doubt get worse. But Lestrade had promised to keep a close eye on him, and he very much doubted the inspector would observe the wreck of his living room and think anything but the worst.

He took a risk against the nausea and reached his hands above his head, although it was grounds for another dizzy spell. More wood like the sides and bottom met his fingers. No surprise. Everything was so tight he couldn't even tell where the opening was.

Oxygen must not be a problem. They have it tight against water, tight against air . . . there has to be a reason why they risk smothering their cargo . . . .

The answer came to him in a flash.

Holmes would be proud, if he wouldn't scold me for not realizing this sooner . . .

Watson rolled to his side inside the confines, the start of a plan germinating. He had to trust Lestrade to figure this out. He had to trust the man would understand the clues left behind . . .

Lestrade never leaves a single stone unturned, even if he has to track down each stone on foot . . . .

Only light could move faster than Scotland Yard's bad news. Lestrade groaned out loud as his wife stood on the bottom step for height and threw her arms about him in a tight embrace. His bones ached from defeat. When he tried to pull back she only held him tighter. For a full minute she held him that way, and then she was the one to pull back at arm's length.

"Dear – " he began, touching her face where a single tear tracked down.

"Are *you* all right, Love?" She asked in her blunt way.

"I . . . ." He began shaking his head, took the single step he needed to sink down to the staircase and put his head on his knees. "I feel like Dr. Watson must have when he was at Reichenbach Falls," he stammered. "A few minutes, that was *all* we would have needed . . . *just a few minutes . . .* ." he mumbled. "Just a few . . . ."

"You'll find him," Clea sank down next to him, her arm around his back. "The Yard isn't stupid."

"But can we find him in time?" Lestrade had never been so defeated before, but the words flashed between them in the still air. *Time.* "God," he said out loud. "We've lost Sherlock Holmes. Do we have to lose Watson too?"

Chapter XIII – For Want
of a Name

"Come upstairs," Clea said firmly. "You can't do anything for now. Trust your men." She squeezed his shoulders with her fingers. "Trust your men." She repeated. He made himself nod at her words, and she kissed him on the cheek, light as a girl with her lover. "Upstairs," she murmured. "You need to clean the coal off, and the boys want a hug from their father."

"Yes, dear." The memory of fresh pain spasmed his face for a moment. Watson no longer had his Mary, no Arthur to hold in his arms. The loss made his own life burn the brighter. If Clea was surprised at the sudden force in the way her husband suddenly held her, she could guess as to its cause. Clea had never been a dull woman.

She took his collar and cuffs without a word, stacked them neatly in the basket for the week's wash, and checked to see there were clean replacements for tomorrow. He dropped his cufflinks and tiepin into the dresser box wearily, and put up with her chiding murmurs as she despaired of the way the grime of London found its way into every crevice of his clothing. The boys heard him at this point, and pulled themselves out of bed to attack him in good-natured hugs from both directions. Their father managed to lift them up inside the crooks of his arms and he wondered, again, how much longer before they outgrew his strength. Their mother smiled at it all and sent them back to bed, reminding them that their father still hadn't cleaned London off.

"Gregson is taking the night shift," he whispered as soon as they were alone again – or hoped they were, but Nicholas had sharp ears. "I'll be taking up for him at eight."

Clea had known Dr. Watson almost as long as she had her husband. In the beginning, he had been no more than one of her customers, always polite and pleasant, but tolerant of no nonsense. Much later she'd come to know his wife. Their little boy had been a treasure. She missed them both. Her thoughts saddened her and she busied herself with brewing and setting up a pot of red tea off the fire. It would do Geoffrey good to get something hot in him before he fainted athwartships over the bed.

They'll find him, she told herself. *They will. Geoffrey never gives up. He doesn't know how to.* But she thought of anyone who wanted to harm that kind, strong man who had treated her decent and helped bring Nicholas into the world when the other doctors wanted to remove him from her in pieces . . . Clea stopped setting up the cups to wipe at her eyes.

Bother, I'm turning into a fussy old woman. Geoffrey's strong arms circled her from the back and pulled her against his chest. He smelled like hard scrubbing and steam. Clea didn't trust herself to speak at the moment and simply leaned back into his warmth.

Clea was a very strong woman. That strength was a source of mixed amusement and amazement at Scotland Yard. She took pride in that strength and her ability to handle whatever happened in life. In situations where most women would fall to pieces, she merely rose to the challenge.

But this was not a challenge. This was something terrible, and knowing it had happened was a reminder that nothing was truly safe in the world. Clea held on to her husband for all she was worth, not feeling very strong at the moment. He understood that, kissed her gently at her ear. She turned around and wrapped her arms around his ribs. Passion was and always would be a part of their relationship, and there would always be nights when one needed the other beyond the ability to speak.

It was their way of accepting the world outside was a living monster and while they could do little about that, they could create a haven in each other. He could make no apologies for the demands of his career, but there were too many times when it pulled them apart. These moments were the only way they could address that loss.

As so often, her husband was stretched out full-length in bed in the posture of sleep, but his eyes were open to the ceiling. Clea had tucked herself into his arm, using his shoulder as a pillow. There was no point in forcing him to get some rest. When a day troubled him, he relived it in his memory, brick by brick and step by step, trying to think his way through what had gone wrong and right. "Plodding through", he called it, but to her it was less plodding and more determination and patience.

After a time, she merely reached up and began stroking his dark hair. He was graying late. The mark of his age was showing one strand at a time and only at the temples. Considering his work, it was a wonder he wasn't whiter than her father. His French blood, he joked once to her during their "somewhat hectic courtship". The *joke* was that he was mostly Breton. His mother's people had immigrated across the Channel in the days of King Charles as bonded clothweavers, British in the eyes of the French, and French in the eyes of the British.

"So we both have our roots in weaving," she had laughed.

"The ties that bind," he smiled back.

Clea smiled to herself at that memory, and several others. They kept her awake as she continued to stroke her husband's hair, and she continued long after her touch lulled him unsuspectingly to sleep.

"The River men found a body." Gregson announced his arrival by blocking the small doorway of their dining room. The boys were long used to such announcements. Clea put the tray of bread down on the table before she could drop it, and her husband nearly broke his chair when he leapt to his feet.

"No, no, calm down!" Gregson looked shocked at himself. "It's not the doctor! But I think you should take a look at it all the same."

Lestrade managed to tug on his jacket one-armed while gulping coffee as Clea stuffed a handful of paper-wrapped rolls in the pockets. She knew better than to expect his return any time soon. With a single look to Gregson, she treated him the same. "Your tea-can," she demanded sternly, and filled it up with the same strong coffee that came out of the pot.

"Nice trick, that," Gregson admired as they stumbled out onto the street barely a moment later. He tore into the soft Egyptian wheat roll with strong teeth and chewed with a starving man's relish. "You could teach the fire brigade a thing or two about moving quick."

"We've gotten it down to a science." Lestrade let him discover for himself the bits of shived ham Clea wrapped inside each. "What am I to expect?"

"Do you remember James White, that little-time smuggler that's the joy of the River Patrol?" Gregson kept going while he gnawed.

"Oh, Good God, don't tell me he was part of kidnapping now!" Lestrade nearly dropped his alfresco breakfast on the pavement.

"He's not. I suppose there's a limit to his stupidity after all . . . ." Gregson pulled out his can and poured as he walked to the cab. "Back to it, lad!" he called up to the driver.

"Could've fooled me," Lestrade muttered cynically.

"He said he was perched under that little dock the children like to sit on, which isn't even a dock – it's barely above the water at high tide, but his missus can't see him with the flask over there. He was sneaking a nip in the night as it were, when the boards above his fat head rattled and a covey of men stampered to the edge. There was a flurry of talking, and he couldn't make it out an'way, with the slap of the water against the wood and stone, but he knew to keep his teeth shut when they tossed a dead man into the water right in front of him – " Gregson made a slapping motion with his fist against the flat of his palm. "He actually had the presence of mind not to move, if you can believe it."

"Maybe he was just frozen with fear," Lestrade offered. The man was not known for his presence of mind or anything resembling a spine.

"Could be . . . When that was done with, they went to the only boat that was moored there, and he could make out three men, acting like they were hurting, and they were carrying a third over the last man's

135

shoulders." Gregson grinned at the look on Lestrade's face. "I thought you might like to hear that."

"So don't quit now! *What the bloody blazes happened*?" Lestrade felt the urge to yank the driver off his seat and take over.

"He said they piled the limp one into the back of the boat and got in themselves. By that time he was tryin' to marry himself to the pillar stones, and thinking invisible thoughts." Gregson was still smiling. "Want to bet the dead man was the one what took that bullet in his uppers? They left two blood trails on the boards, and that carriage left behind . . . it was *swimming* in blood! They even tracked themselves all the way to the waterline!"

The dead man was not the usual water-bloated and clammed corpse that was stretched out for their inspection. Lestrade realized this was not a face conducive to assurance. It was a large, powerful man with the scars and thick musculature of a boxer.

"He seems familiar," the little detective frowned. "Is there a likeness of him anywhere?"

"Phillips made a good pencil of him, and we took a few photographs when the light cleared . . . and I sent it back to the Office so someone could look for a match among the photographs," Gregson answered. The end of his shift was in view. He was trying not to yawn now that he had fulfilled his duty of bringing Lestrade in to the case. "Are you in need of a copy?"

"It's my shift, isn't it? I would very much like one," Lestrade answered. He examined the man's hands, found them square and thick-skinned. "Good Lord." He took in the wound on the man's body. "That *has* to be Watson's bullet."

"It certainly wasn't any peashooter!" Gregson pointed a blunt finger at the water-leached hole of the bullet mark. "Left artery above the heart. He must have been grazed enough to stay on his feet, but enough left to leave a trail."

"Moving around might've torn open the vessel the rest of the way." Lestrade knew from experience how a wounded man could turn dead just for shifting around.

"Must have died in the cab on the way to the water. They threw him over to gain speed and put Watson in their boat for their journey."

"Does White know where they went?"

"He said they went across and downstream towards the old depot." Gregson smiled. "Already on it, you know. Betting you they moved him to the train."

"Then what?" Lestrade snapped. "A train to where?"

"That's what we're going to find out," Gregson promised. "Anyhow, this is your investigation for now. I'm to check in on Hopkins on my way out, and since he lives on the way over to Whitehall . . . ."

"I'll be sure to pass him any notes." Privately, Lestrade wondered what the results would be with that young man's boundless energy and clever thinking.

"I'm here to see Bartram of Cheatham."

The name of the era's most famous Lancashire-born wrestler – to Lestrade's mind he was the most infamous – was hardly unusual. The bodyguard at the door lounged slightly erect, looking down at the little man with hollow eyes, and kept chewing his quid. "Who wants to know?" he drawled.

Lestrade sighed. "You can take your pick. His brother-in-law, or Inspector Lestrade of Scotland Yard, seeking his expertise."

The man nearly swallowed his tobacco. Lestrade found himself wanting to watch the man closely in the off-chance he had swallowed something he shouldn't have. The muscular spasms would be a joy to watch.

"Come on in," was the drawled response. He had a Welsh accent, but his huge height suggested the hills of Cymry.

Inside, the drawing room showed the growing signs of taste and money. Lestrade didn't doubt it was due to the calming influence of Mrs. Louise Cheatham. He couldn't begin to imagine the circumstances that would lead Bartram to put up a framed portrait of a dog . . . Perhaps Bartram had taken a few too many illegal blows? His profile resembled Philip of Macedonia as it was.

"Ha." Bartram Cheatham emerged still in his dressing gown, which was tailored to fit his unique dimensions. For that matter, so was the doorway. He was tired of walking sideways to keep from hitting the frames. "As I live and breathe. My own brother-in-law. I'd about to accuse Jonesi of smoking the dragon." Bartram's single eyebrow went up, which re-defined ironic.

Bartram was always at his most vocal in the first few hours of his waking up. It was an unsettling phenomenon.

"I'm afraid I'm here to ask for your advice on something – not here as a social call," Lestrade said evenly.

"Ha," Bartram answered. "Well, now that I'm up, I'm going to eat. Might as well try the cook's attempt at lamb stew." He glowered. "Ain't Clea's. If I gotta eat it, you gotta too."

Lestrade sighed inwardly. Clea's cooking was a world apart of anyone else's. On a more primitive note, he couldn't blame the man for wanting to share the pain.

"So. What's th' historic occasion?" Bartram slammed bowls off the mantel-shelf and began dishing stew out of the smoking kettle hung over the fireplace. Lestrade in all honesty couldn't imagine the last time he'd seen real firepit cooking. The wrestler examined the half-loaf of stale bread on the shelf, broke it in half, and threw a piece into each bowl. "Ain't all that bad if you soak it," he advised.

If only Clea's breakfast hadn't been a memory and the coffee wearing off. Lestrade was a bundle of shredded nerves. He blew out his breath and picked up a spoon, practically threw the pencil drawing to his ersatz brother-in-law. "Do you know anything about this bloke?"

Bartram picked up the sketch as he stabbed the bread deep into the stew. It was as if the sun had left London. "What the *hell* are you doing with this bastard?" he growled.

"I just want to know who he is and what he's about."

"You don't want to know what he's about," Bartram snarled. "He's rotten, man. Tha' spend brass on him, by God I *swear* I'll pulp y'in front of my sister!"

"I take it you don't have a sterling recommendation on his company or character," Lestrade opined while blowing some of the heat off the pearl onion in his spoon.

Bartram frowned. It usually took him a while to catch on. Just as well Louise made the change for the books . . . . . "This a *real* criminal?"

Translation: *Has he been caught?*

Lestrade picked his words with great care. "He's a suspect in kidnapping the doctor who brought Nicholas into the world, Bartram."

"Damn tinker's woodscolt!" Bartram announced. "No better'n should be. Bloody Hell!" He snorted so hard Lestrade half expected the blood from last night's fight to fly out of his nose. "He's poison. You stay away. Saw him beat a man half-to-dead on the street once!"

"What happened?" Lestrade wondered. Considering Bartram was one of the finer thugs for hire, it shook him up to think that there was someone he eschewed.

"Sod tripped and spilled cigar ashes on the man's *dog!*" Bartram retorted. "Broke the man's ribs, collarbone, both shins . . . and that was just with his *bare hands!*"

Lestrade swallowed with difficulty. "I take it won't bother you then if I tell you that he's dead."

"Did you shoot him?" Bartram asked with an unholy eagerness.

"Not me. Dr. Watson did."

"Well, 'course. He's Northumbrian." Bartram shrugged that off – Why, Lestrade couldn't say. It wasn't the first time he'd noticed "Northumbrian" meant something special to Lancashire-borne. "Good for him. I should send him chocolates." He pushed the paper away as if the sight made him nauseous.

"So . . . who is this paragon of wickedness, Bartram?"

"Cole of Blackpool. That's a made-up title, by the way. Nothing to do with Blackpool. His agent thought it sounded good." Bartram still sounded upset at the sacrilege. "He's never lost a match, but that's 'cause he was better at cheating at any of us. I mark you, the moment the judge sneezed, he was there to kick you where it hurt."

"You didn't *fight* him, did you? Lestrade cringed at the thought. "Bartram, the man's a monadnock!"

"Doesn't matter in the pits." Bartram shrugged. "I had the strategy on my side, but he didn't take t'losing well. Hadda pack Louise off t'see her folks a fortnight for't die down." He shrugged at Lestrade's expression. "The pits pay a lot more than the legal fights." He took another bite of stew, with a spoon Clea would use as a ladle. "They even take care of your hurts. That's something a lot of those 'real' games wouldn't sponsor."

Lestrade rubbed his forehead.

"He grabbed the doc, huh?" Bartram looked into his bowl. "He worked for a tough'un. A toff. Not sure who he was, but I tell you, he'd scare you worse than the sight of Cole." He grunted. "Man's worse than an army of Quimpers."

"I find that hard to believe." Quimper was the gold standard of evil for Lestrade and his wife's family. Usually it was the only common ground he had with Bartram besides their love for Clea.

"I tell you what's hard to believe: His master's less than half the size of Cole. A ladylike man, as it were." Bartram shot back. "And he'd chill your blood with just a look. I mean that. One look at you through those cold eyes, and you'd be drawin' up your will that very night. A worse'n I hope to never meet. I don't think he's even human."

"Do you have a name?" Lestrade hoped against hope.

139

Chapter XIX – Oxygen

Bartram of Cheatham was less than vocal because he simply didn't like talking. Lestrade was one of the few people who knew this was rooted in Bartram's childhood stutter.

But when Bartram was silent because he was trying not to say something . . . well . . . .

Lestrade thought that was as bad as any sign.

"How far you want to go with this?" Bartram wanted to know.

"As far as this – !" Lestrade plucked his Guelphic Badge out of this breastpocket and held it up before putting it down on the table with a click.

Bartram stared at the piece of metal as if he'd never actually paid attention to it before. "You willin' to take on a grease spot in London?"

"If there's a murder within it," Lestrade answered back.

Bartram grumbled something. "I ain't callin' you a coward," he said. "You never were. But . . . You won't get 'em all," he added. "You think Jethro Quimper was slime to hold . . . You just try to get hold of the ones he was in charge of . . . someone like Barney Stockdale." Angry for a moment, Bartram's large face knotted like a washrag and he stood up, stamping to the window with his fists in his dressing gown.

"What about Barney Stockdale?" Lestrade asked.

"Worse'n Quimper cos he's a Thuggee," Bartram said sharply. "Not a single man'll stand up to him in court, won't even say boo against him after what happened to Steve Dixie." The big Lancashire man opened his large hands and curled the thick fingers into his leathery palms. "Best new fighter I ever saw come down th'pike. Thowld'folkes were slaves over in America. He got up enough brass on his fists to get 'em over'ere. Went up against him in the ring a few times. He boxin' an I was wrestlin' an' Stockdale was his man to speak for him."

"Steve Dixie . . . ." Lestrade remembered a dim name in a life crowded of detail. "He took that blow to the head back when . . . my God. That was the year I met you and Clea!"

Bartram nodded. "Good fighter. You ain't never saw a boy with so much talent. Guess they thought they'd be safe over here."

"What happened?" Lestrade already knew where this story was headed. He asked all the same.

"He was supposed to throw a fight . . . and he didn't. Now that wasn't his fault. Fool they put him up against . . . ." Bartram shook his head slowly, from side to side like a plough horse. "He wasn't as good as the information said. Steve won when he swung too hard, and he was on his way home when he got himself hammered. Man's a dunnelhead now. Simple as a Peter's Pence. He's good for roughin' up debtors or blackmail, but that's it. Now Barney's the *only* man who'll hire him, and he'll take whatever jobs there are . . . Ain't no justice to that, you know. Ain't nothing nobody can prove. We lost one of the best prizefighters you ever saw to a brick behint' th'ear."

Lestrade felt a strange sadness to see sincere loss on Bartram's face. He'd been friendly with Steve Dixie, but that had been made impossible with his loss of mind. Bartram was trying to warn him off a similar fate.

"I'll be careful, Bartram."

"No one called him by name," Bartram grunted at last. "Cole was a bad'un, but his people were even worse. Not even Stockdale was tight. They called him, 'Royal' behind his back."

"Royal?" Lestrade wondered if that was a powerful insult, or something laden with meaning. "I'll remember."

Bartram puffed his cheeks out. "Be careful," he glared. "I don't relish the thought of holding a weeping sister at your funeral."

"Believe me, Bartram, I don't relish the thought of being killed in the line of duty." The wrestler still looked doubtful. "Clea reminds me every night and every morning to be careful. If I didn't take that advice . . . Well, I don't think the Afterlife would be a big enough place to hide from her."

"Better you than me," Bartram snorted, but he was trying not to smile. "Got to admit, a part of me was a bit relieved when she transferred all that worry off me and on to you."

"Which you showed by threatening to toss me out a window every other day for the first year of my marriage."

"You never struck me as bein' a baby," Bartram protested. "I heard Clea threaten to toss you into a *wall*."

"Walls are different. They hurt less."

"They don't when I'm the one doin' the tossing."

Lestrade rolled his eyes. "You won't get sliced up by shard of wall, how's that?"

"That's better." Bartram finished his bowl and belched. "Serious. Anything happens to you, the Fancy'll be out on its ear."

"Pardon? What do boxers have to do with me?"

"Remember when Mad Jackson nearly killed you?"

"Which time?" Lestrade asked sarcastically.

Bartram was immune to sarcasm. "The second time."

"I had a concussion, Bartram. If something happened, I'll just take your word for it."

Bartram sighed. "Thowd'mon thought you might be killed, so he put a halt on the fights in London until you were found."

141

There were probably a few Israelites who faced the parting of the Red Sea with nothing more than a wordless stare and a refusal to move. Lestrade could certainly sympathize.

"Did he," he said. "I had no idea your father had that kind of pull."

"Jackson used to be one of us," Bartram answered back. "Good fighter, went bad. Would have reflected bad on us if we didn't do something." He sniffed loudly and stabbed up a piece of salted ham with his knife and chewed with rock-hard teeth.

From the Cheathams, Good Lord, protect us. Lestrade butchered the Irish prayer against Vikings with good cause.

"Twelve more dead men," Bradstreet said in wonder. "This is worse than a night in the East End."

"What have you found, Roger?" Lestrade rubbed eyes that were filled with glass sand.

Bradstreet looked very pale. "Blood all over the deck. Whoever did this was good. One bullet each, and then they got their cargo and lit like party snappers."

"Cargo . . ." Lestrade muttered.

"We found this." Gregson grinned and held up two familiar-looking objects. "Watson's cufflinks, or I'm a birch tree."

The silver monogrammed initials were clear enough. One was badly bent on the tip. "He was wearing those the other day," Lestrade bit his lip. "Where'd you find it?"

"In the cargo hold." Gregson was as gleeful as a child who had just won the school prize. "Here, I'll show you." He strode across the gore-smeared deck on his long legs. Lestrade hurried to keep up – Gregson had been as bad as Holmes when excited about something. "Or should I say, in the secret cargo hold? It's a hatch behind the usual spot where goods are kept."

"Is there some kind of registration on this ship?" Lestrade realized his error at the wince of Inspector Craddock. "I mean, keelboat?"

"Private deliveries," Craddock supplied, looking grateful for Lestrade's correction. The sun, wind, and water of the briny Thames had blackened his skin deeper than a Lascar's. "Small stuff, but it traveled a lot. You see her every day, like, on the Thames. She's tough, and her crew a singular lot." He nodded at the shrouded forms lying on deck. Most of them still leaked water from beneath. "Was a singular lot, I should say."

"How singular?"

Craddock opened the door to the cabin and Gregson went to the back of the wall where sacks of grain were still piled. He mashed his fist against the panels, and one fell open. Lestrade's chest clenched at the thought of

142

that small, tar-fouled darkness. It was large enough for a man, but only just.

"They were tougher than horseshoe nails." Craddock chewed on a toothpick. "But polite. Ever so polite. Their captain, he was most particular about their manners. Ran it all like a military drill . . . ." Craddock shuddered. "I've seen a few of these cubbies before, but I never get used to them," he said softly. "Hard to say how often they're used to make people vanish."

Lestrade felt sweat mushroom over his face. "Someone get a light," he snapped.

"Already looked, Ratty," Gregson protested. "That's how we found the cufflinks."

Lestrade looked at him pleadingly. "Tobias . . . Watson has no wife or child I can go home to and say that I've done everything I could. I have to see for myself."

Gregson flinched. "Yes," he grunted softly, and pulled out a small bull's-eye. "Try not to spill it," he advised.

"I'll go in first, you pass it to me." Lestrade held his breath and slipped feet first into the black space. "God, it's like a coffin," he said without thinking.

"I couldn't even fit in that," Gregson confessed. "Leastwise, I hope to never find out."

Lestrade did his best not to breathe on the small flame guttering inside the tiny glass globe. He laid flat but the darkness was crushing. How long had the doctor been in this godforsaken box? He was five-nine, but broad in bone and muscle. There couldn't have been more than an inch to spare on either side of him. With his Jezail wounds, that had to have been agony.

Jezail.

Watson was a soldier. If he had regained consciousness in this Hell Pit, then he would have reverted to the instincts of war. The enemy had captured him. What would be the next step? Lestrade set the lamp down as gently as he could and ran his fingers over the wood. Something had to have happened. Watson was smart, and he was *unbelievably* stubborn – more stubborn that Gregson or Holmes put together. He would have bitten his own blood out of his skin and written a message in it if that was what it took –

Something soft crushed under his fingers. "You missed something, Tobias!" Lestrade yelped. Gregson's big head filled the tiny space a breath later. "His cravat!" Lestrade panted, relieved to have some reward for putting himself through this hell.

"What the sodding – ?" Gregson said in wonder. "It's the same colour as the hold. Where did you find it?"

143

"It was in the very back, where his feet would have been. That's not right." Lestrade passed it to Gregson with relief and kept looking. "He was hiding it for some reason . . . Where would his stickpin be?"

"We didn't see anything shiny like that," Gregson didn't apologize. "But it was hard to look."

"Like you said, you'd hardly fit," Lestrade pointed out charitably. "This thing is watertight as a fishing float. It had to be somewhere . . . ." Lestrade's fingers stroked over something in the wood. "Hold on. There's . . . I think . . . Gregson, you or someone else with long arms pick up that lamp! I think there's writing in here!"

Gregson risked plugging all the oxygen out of the tiny space by leaning in and picking up the lamp himself.

"C . . . a . . . ." Lestrade fell silent, scowling. "It says . . . 'cargo, short trips. Not enough air for long journey .791 cubic feet per hour. Stopoffs.' What's a 'stopoff'?"

Craddock had been listening avidly. "It's our riverman's slang, sir. It's sort of like our own pet word for a water-based depot, I suppose. You stop at a stopoff, and dump your goods, pick up your new goods, and keep going."

"Would Watson know a word like that?" Gregson wondered.

"Watson? You've *got* to be joking. His bad leg and shoulder keep him land-locked, but let me tell you, he eats more fish than a seal!" Lestrade had satisfied himself the box was empty of clues. "Give me a hand, please, Tobias."

"Pleasure, Geoff." Gregson's meaty paw practically yanked the smaller man out. "Craddock, do you have a tape measure?"

"Er, ah . . . I think I can find one." Craddock took one look at Lestrade and hurried off, barking orders.

"What the devil are you thinking?"

"Just a moment, hold on to this . . . ." Lestrade yanked out his notebook and pencil, pushing them into the surprised Gregson's hands. "Get a clean page up, will you? I'm only going back in that pit one last time. When I call out the numbers, you write them down."

"What the hell are you measuring in there?"

"Oxygen!" Lestrade announced. Craddock had emerged with gratifying speed. He pushed a roll of tape into Lestrade's hands. "I'm going to call off the measurements, and you be sure to write them down. Length times width times height. Length is six feet. Width is two. Height is four."

"Forty-eight cubic feet, Gregson said softly. "Doesn't seem that large."

"It isn't." Lestrade was sweating. "I felt as claustrophobic as I could get." He wiped his face off with an already grey handkerchief. "All right. Forty-eight cubic feet. What's the weight of oxygen . . . 0.080 pounds-per-cubic-foot?"

"0.0807," Gregson corrected. "You took the same class I did, Ratty." He scribbled quickly. That comes to . . . 3.8736 pounds of oxygen. Any idea how much space Watson would take up in there?"

"There wouldn't be much room left over," Lestrade said soberly. "He's close to two-hundred pounds as it is . . . standard height, with an allowance for error."

Gregson scribbled quickly. "Must be why the box is so high. It's used to store oxygen." He chewed his bottom lip as he thought. "Damn, these are clever bastards, and *businessmen* to boot." He caught Lestrade's puzzled blink. "Won't risk the goods with brain damage," he said curtly. Lestrade looked sick. "Let's say there's one-and-a-half feet of height for the sake of breathing. That means we've got about . . . eighteen cubic feet. That's 1.4526 . . . ." He shook his head. "There's just a bit over three hours' air supply in there for someone his size."

"I think I'm going to be ill," Lestrade said faintly. He walked to the side of the boat and stared at the swirling brown water blankly.

"How many of our witnesses have vanished in this thing?" Gregson wondered. Lestrade had been praying he wouldn't say that. The big man rubbed his face. "Is this what happened to Jasper Townsend? Von Buren? Miss Regis . . . Gods, I can think of so many of our people who were willing to testify against the organized crime lords in London . . . all missing within a mile or two of the Thames and the Serpentine . . . ."

Craddock cleared his throat. "I've got a chart," he began. "Give me a moment, and I'll pinpoint some of the stopoffs we know of, and some we suspect."

Chapter XX – A Weapon

Scotland Yard:

"**H**old up!"

Lestrade turned to see Hopkins pelting through the lines. He waited, thinking patiently of the hot tea Youghal was brewing right now.

Hopkins panted lightly as he came to a stop. He looked as sleepless as the older man. "You wanted to know about the injuries," he managed.

"What did you find out?"

"I spoke to Dr. Mortimer." Hopkins ran his finger around his collar. "He agreed to help us keep this as quiet as possible until we have no choice." He smiled at Lestrade's nod of relief. "And he was quite useful. He said that the majority of sacrificial bog victims have some sort of physical problem beforehand. The most popular examples are lame, or have something similar-wrong with an arm." He took a deep breath, face sweating.

"Over-dressed again?" Lestrade guessed dryly. "You have to remember the weather is warming up, Hopkins."

"Warm weather is a theory until it actually happens. And where I live is proof of it," Hopkins shot back. "Anyway. The sacrifices . . . I should say, the real, genuine sacrifices, are usually drugged, struck on the head, cut across the throat, and finally pressed into the bog."

"Is there a reason why they'd insist on killing a man all over, and more than once?" Lestrade grimaced. "Oh. Right. The triple death. I'd forgotten. Well, Mortimer's just a fountain of awful information, isn't he?"

"Looks like it. When's the meeting?"

"You've got just enough time to take off that wool waistcoat and grab a cup of tea with me."

Inspector Craddock was one of the many policemen who had began his service work in Army uniform. He began by putting his own service revolver on the table next to Watson's.

"Adams .450's meant for quick fighting," he began. Around him the room (crowded with constables, sergeants, detective-sergeants, plainclothesmen and watermen) quieted. "I know it can look odd that we keep to a gun what was developed in our boyhood, but it was designed for its purpose. We're all drilled to fight until no thought at all is required, just reflex and instinct. Even with his reflexes slowed down by those poppies, he didn't have to think about what he was doing." Craddock looked haggard under his sun-beaten skin. "Maximum range is about thirty-five yards, but let me tell you, we were trained to hit just as well at a hundred yards. You got a feel for how low a bullet could drop per so many feet after enough practice. Not that there was any long-distance firing.

"They hit him hard and fast . . . those Berkshires can do more than twelve rounds a minute when they're in a fight. If he only had time to get three off, they had it planned out to the inch." He grinned. "But they didn't realize Watson was trained same as I was. When we come home of an evening, the first thing we do is unlock our gun drawer. It's how we were trained. And that drawer was right at arm's reach when they broke in."

Craddock's announcement was met with feral chuckles about the table, especially from the other veterans. To their thinking, the men had been responsible for their own deaths to be so stupid.

"I can tell you this," Constable Peake popped up. A tiny Army medal for bravery hung at his lapel. "These men weren't military, and I doubt they were led by someone who was military. They wouldn't have made that kind of mistake in judgment."

"There's a lot to what you say." Lestrade noted Gregson was chalking notes on the board as fast as his fingers would allow. "That would so far fit in to our suspicions that the cult is not military in nature. It's organized, but not to that point of efficiency."

"Cults are all about control," Bradstreet grunted. "I'm thinking they could easily don a militaresque aspect. They would have that ability if they bond their followers together on human sacrifice. But they haven't gotten that far yet. It would take the induction of someone who was already military in nature." He stroked his chin in thought. "I, for one, believe they wouldn't stand for the competition in discipline."

"Here's what I think happened." Lestrade stood in front of them. "Feel free to break in if you know I've gone off the tracks." He put his palms on the table by the Adams. "We know that Dr. Watson received a dubious gift of a drugged bouquet that, giving this time of year with cool evenings, had a good chance of slowing his reflexes inside a closed room with little ventilation. They waited, possibly peeping in the window until he appeared drowsy, and chose that moment to break in. They failed to realize that Dr. Watson is a light sleeper, a veteran of our worst war, and keeps a loaded Adams Mark within arm's reach. Three bullets were fired. One bullet was found in the wall, and judging from the bloodstains, that bullet went through one assailant. The other two bullets hit in non-vital but damaging areas but they were still able to finish what they started." Lestrade stopped to swallow bile down his throat. "There was a phial of chloroform on the scene – exactly 3½ ounces. I don't need to remind anyone *here* that carrying around a primed rag for drugging has led to errors that killed both the kidnapper and victim, so we can reasonably presume that these fellows were either operating under specific orders, or they were very good at what they did.

"Once they had Watson, they were under a ferocious timeline. He'd sounded the alarm with his bullets in a quiet residential neighborhood. They dashed to their cohort in the cab, and took off with our policemen arriving just in time to follow them to the Serpentine Tracks.

"The man with the piercing wound had been more deeply injured than he had first appeared. Watson's bullet nicked the artery at the clavicle – ironic, that – and he bled to death on the way to the river. They took the time to dump the corpse of their friend, tracking clear prints of their shoes in his blood on the dock and continued their mission, which was to deliver Watson under the cover of night to the little Thames riverport we all know as a smuggler's paradise . . . ." Lestrade rubbed his eyes again.

"Here is where things begin to be less clear. They switched him to the Thames somehow. It appears they had managed to drop Watson in that wretched coffin of a cargo hold, and he partially awakened from the drug at some point, because he took the time to pull off his cravat and cufflinks and leave the message on the inside of the wood – " Lestrade still felt slightly queasy at the memory of that tiny space. "But at the rendezvous, the kidnappers were set upon by a second party – a rival gang who for some reason had a great deal of objection to what was happening. The men were taken out systematically, bullet by bullet. Dropped like sheep at a slaughtering house. The blood was well spilled from their heads when the second gang boarded and found what they were looking for. This second gang was just as hasty as the first. They left all kinds of evidence in their wake, including a *second* dose of chloroform, but it was from a treated sponge. The bodies were then dumped aboard, and I'm sure they thought it would be at least twenty days before they rose up again, but they didn't think of random happenstance, and the loose net snagged their bodies long enough to pull them to the Limehouse nineteen days ahead of the usual floater schedule."

"It all *reeks*," Bradstreet snapped. "I can *get* that they were wanting to nab Watson because of his reports on those bodies. I can *get* that they wanted him for their cult because he has the same kind of wounding the other victims had – it would be no more than taking out two birds with the same stone – *but the second gang? What the Bloody Hell is that about?*"

Lestrade pulled in his breath. "I think we need to put Colonel Moriarty back on the list of suspects," he said tightly.

MacDonald flinched. "That's going into dangerous terrain," he said cautiously. "The Colonel is military as they come, and we've established this is not a military achievement."

148

"I know, but I'm not likely to forget his sally upon us." Lestrade slapped his hands together and got up to pace. "We're missing something here."

Gregson frowned. "Such as what?" he demanded.

"I'm not sure . . . the cravat . . . the stickpin . . . ." Lestrade ran his hand through his hair, upset as he could get. "Watson went to quite a bit of trouble to take off that cravat and hide it in the very back of that box where it wasn't likely to be seen. Gregson, where were the cufflinks found?"

"In the top, where his head'd be," Gregson supplied. "It had to have been a bother to get that done. There wasn't room for a man of his size to move around, but still, they were small and it was dark. Hard to see."

"He took off a cufflink, and used it to write that message in the wood," Lestrade said slowly. "His hands were bound, that's obvious. One cufflink snapped, so he removed the second cufflink, and finished his message. He couldn't bloody well put the cufflinks back on, so he concealed them as well as he could. *But what about the cravat*? He unknotted his cravat, did something with that stickpin, and somehow – don't ask me how – he managed to get that cravat all the way down to the bottom of that coffin." He paced. The room was thick and awkward with heavy thoughts.

Gregson slammed his fist on the wall, making the chalk fall off the tray. "Concealment!" He bellowed. "Goda'mighty! It was right there in front of us!" He was so excited he got to his feet, eyes gleaming at Lestrade from across the table. "He must have heard the fracas, figured out something even worse was happening. He ripped his cravat off and stuffed it in the back so the second group of kidnappers wouldn't notice his stickpin was missing!"

"I don't follow you, sir," Crane said timidly.

Gregson was so thrilled he didn't even snap. "You're John Watson. All you can think of is surviving long enough to see the bastards that did this to you meet justice. You figure out the possible length of the trip by the limited space and oxygen. You do everything Lestrade has described up to this point – then you hide the cufflinks as well as you can. Why not? These men moved very fast against you, but they shed evidence like feathers off a moulting duck! Their key is in moving quickly. But you hear something going on, something that tells you things are going from bad to worse. Maybe there's talking, threatening, shots being fired – whatever. *You have to take another chance*."

Gregson threw himself back into his chair, holding his hands out in his delight. "The second party is going to be looking for John Watson, *but they don't know what condition he's already in!* For all they know, he was grabbed while he was taking his cufflinks off – it was nightfall – so if his cufflinks are gone, why not his stickpin? The first group, as soon as they haul him out in the light of day, they're going to notice he has a stickpin and relieve him of it – it's a weapon, a lockpick, something that can cause harm! *But the second group isn't going to know any of that!*" Gregson yanked an invisible tiepin off his throat. "He's hidden his tiepin somewhere, but he can't let them see he has a cravat on. A cravat would remind him he might have a pin! So he stuffs that in the furthest corner of the hold. The second group will think that the first group has already searched him of weapons. If they notice anything, it'll be the cufflinks that are closer to the top, close to the opening! They'll be decoyed and not think of looking any deeper!"

"Just like you did!" Lestrade stared. "Gregson, that's brilliant."

"It'll be brilliant when we figure out *who* exactly has him," Gregson snorted.

"All right. Watson's been grabbed by organized, clever criminals. Where does this fit in with the rumors about Holmes?" Patterson spoke up for the first time. The lean man ignored the appalled hush in the room. "Come on, we're all thinking it. What if there's any truth to those rumors? *What if Holmes isn't really dead?*"

"Oh, that's a *simple* problem," Gregson said sarcastically. "Anyone got a three-hundred-foot salvaging hook?"

Lestrade glared, close to striking the other man in the mouth.

Patterson shrugged it off. "Or something even more clever," he continued. "We didn't get all of Moriarty's gang. His unknown second-in-command got away with him. But what's the first rule in organized crime? It's *hierarchical*. The king dies, the princes fall to pieces quarreling." He struck a match and lit up his pipe, aware he had a rapt audience. "If I was to take over Moriarty's empire, I'd want to stack my odds. And if I *really* wanted to stack my odds, I'd make it easy on myself and throw a royal scare into my competition." He sucked thoughtfully on his pipe and blew a smoke ring. "What would scare the Professor's men worse than the thought of Sherlock Holmes returning from the grave?"

"Hell, that would scare *anyone*," Bradstreet retorted.

"I'm not saying it would be easy," Patterson said wryly. "For all we know, it took this long to even find the right person and train him up!" He puffed again. "What if the other side believed it? They couldn't afford not to."

"Sherlock Holmes was immune to bribery, blackmail, jibes, and coercion of any kind," Lestrade agreed slowly, wincing as all eyes slid to him. "Taunts and mockery didn't affect him – it was a language he didn't understand. He didn't give a tuppence for anyone throwing his weight around. Although he followed the law, he wasn't a slave to it. You know as well as I do he turned a blind eye if it meant a higher justice was being served." He began pacing, the thoughts growing more and more worrisome as he spoke.

"No one could think to control Mr. Sherlock Holmes. Not the Home Office, not the Prime Minister, no gentry nor landed nobility." He stopped to wipe the sweat off his forehead. "But there was one person that had any kind of power over him, and that's John Watson."

"Are you certain?" Craddock asked doubtfully. "I mean, I barely worked in his circles . . . ."

"Lestrade's right," Gregson answered. "When Watson felt Holmes should take on a case, he'd cajole him right into doing it. He'd smooth the way, do the talking . . . Holmes listened to Watson more than any other person alive – probably because Watson was the only man on the planet Holmes *couldn't* frighten off. Lord knows he had plenty of reason to run screaming from the man. But he didn't. Holmes depended on him like no one else."

"If you are a high-ranking criminal with ambitions, and you think Sherlock Holmes is alive, then you're going to need a weapon on your side." Lestrade twisted his wedding ring in his hands. "Watson is the only weapon that would pierce *that* armour."

"If that's the case," Craddock cleared his throat, "would Watson be more useful dead or alive?"

"That," Lestrade sighed, "depends on just how personal the war is."

He was sick of being drugged.

Powerless or not, he was willing to at least kick out at the next fool who ripped open the crate for the next timed dose of chloroform. He was getting rather good at pretending to be groggier and less awake than he really was. They spent less time with the pad over his face each time. No doubt it helped that he probably looked as terrible as he felt. He no longer had any sense of time, save there was too much of it. He knew he needed food but the chloroform made that notion less than desirable. Water he needed more. If they didn't let have something to drink soon they might as well not keep him alive.

Thumping vibrations attacked the ear that was against the wood and nails shrieked as the top of the lid was pulled up. Lights burned his eyes and the world upturned as two blurry figures in dark, shabby clothing yanked him upright into the chill of the air. The sudden movement overtaxed his muscles and they held him in between to prevent his complete collapse, guiding his feet out of the crate and to the haven of an empty chair against a dining table.

"Major Watson," said a sickening voice from behind the wreath of smoke, "I'm so pleased you were able to join us tonight."

Watson caught the rank, and the pronoun, and wondered if it were possible to feel any more ill.

Chapter XXI – The Life
of a Soldier

"*Why* can't we head up to Streat?" Bradstreet all but roared.

"Dr. Mortimer was very clear – " Hopkins reached up and began rubbing at his temples against a forming pain. " – that if we get too close to the cult before we know where he is, they'll easily kill him and write off their losses." He met the reactions in exhausted agreement. "I know, I talked to him for hours – in person – and I went straight to the train as soon as I left Dartmoor, but I . . . he convinced me, gentlemen. We have a week to find him, for the sacrifices appear to be made during the full moon."

"How hard can it be to find a man on a place like Streat?" Youghal wanted to know.

Jones spat and fingered the watchchain at his waist. "Hard enough. They know the land. We don't. You saw how they hid him in that tiny keelboat."

"Chances are he isn't even on Streat, and won't in the near future," Patterson offered coolly. "These men take great pride in their cleverness. They brag about it at every opportunity."

As usual, Patterson's presence conspired an uneasy hush about the room. The man just looked unhealthy and half-dead, and his very coolness was starting to give the impression that he lacked enough life to have the warmer emotions.

And since he was retired, he pulled out his hip flask in front of everyone and took a drink.

"What are you suggesting, Patterson?"

"This is only a suggestion." Patterson's words were a ghostly echo of a year ago, when his arrogance had led to a disaster of a raid against the Professor's gang at the estuary. Back then, Patterson didn't 'suggest'. He demanded and assumed. "We sneak a party of men to Streat on the guise of being one of those tourists Sir Niles is bringing over. The weather's improved . . . people are coming in all the time . . . pass ourselves off as visitors and curious explorers . . . even a stranded fisherman would work! But we can't just openly show up and insist on searching the island. First we'd have to go through Scotland – no offense to MacDonald here – but we all know how delicate this is."

"The Queen's home!" Youghal moaned and struck himself. "She's over there *now*!"

"We mention anything like this and the Government will be swarming over this mess like flies over the marsh," Bradstreet snarled. "And they won't care about Watson either. They'll do as they please."

"Even if someone panics and kills him, they'll just see it as convenient proof of the crimes."

"Nor will they care how far Holyroodhouse is to the Isle of Streat." Lestrade watched as Patterson looked down at his hands. "They'll think 'Scotland' and they'll think of the past attempts on Her Majesty's life."

And the life of a grieving Army surgeon would mean very, very little in comparison.

It was a private car, stationary in some unknown locale. Watson didn't even try to look through the heavily curtained windows. It was nightfall anyway, and the air inside the car was thick and swirling from the fat cigar Moriarty held between his rough fingers.

The Colonel had changed little since their last meeting, but the hard light in his eyes gleamed far more brightly than ever. It was the look of a man on a campaign. He was at war. In a conflict. Dangerous stakes were playing. He could not possibly be more in his element.

It escaped neither man that each was wearing the mourning black of bereavement.

Moriarty's grey eyes paused over the tip of his cigar, a thoughtful expression resting on the other side of his moustaches. "Whatever the devil are those things?" he inquired mildly.

"Some sort of dried knotwork, Colonel." Despite laborer's clothing, their demeanor was hard and drilled. Men recruited from his soldiers, no doubt. "They'll have to be cut off."

"Do it," Moriarty ordered. "He won't be going anywhere." The thick eyebrows spidered up on his large forehead. Watson watched the knifework wearily, measuring his breath out in stages so he wouldn't faint. The rope separated from his skin in angry red grooves that beaded blood.

"Larkins," Moriarty nodded, and a valet bowed out with the silent understanding of a long-established manservant to miniscule signals. "Sit yourself down, Major," he grunted – the offer not being optional, as his men made certain of that. The cold grey eyes took in the long-dried smears of blood that made such a tack of his shirt and trousers. "How many men did you kill, Major?" he asked, mildly interested.

"One of my best boxers," a voice said behind Watson. It was a familiar voice, cool and fine. "And wounded the others . . . I believe, Colonel, you finished the job on the rest of my men."

Colonel Moriarty's shoulders shook with short laughter, amusement and a peculiar pride as he looked at Watson. "The fortunes of war, sir," he said with a growing leer of amusement. "The fortunes of war." He drew on his cigar again, which was a mercy to the doctor because as long as he was inhaling smoke, he couldn't speak.

"I am pleased that you can be so amused, Colonel." The cool, sibilant hiss again echoed in Watson's memory. *He knew that person.* If he didn't feel so half-dead . . . he forced his memory to relax and stop trying so hard. Light footsteps, almost feminine, trod their way across the carpet as the train rounded a curve. *Almost feminine . . . cool voice.* The realization came to him in a wave.

"Shall we, sir?" Moriarty smiled past Watson to his other guest. Watson had every faith this "guest" was not as restricted as himself. "There is an excellent port . . . and I would enjoy learning the truth of what I've heard on your skill in the battlefield." He swept his long fingers down to the arranged onyx chessboard at the small table.

"I'm not here for pleasure, Colonel."

Moriarty did not deign to protest. "You've never been more than a man of your work." He grunted softly to his companion. That appeared to be a statement with many layers. Around them the private car vibrated and rattled. Watson thought about the possibility of being sick. The bright lights burned his skull and the train's movements kept him feeling weak and disoriented after the chloroform.

It was almost unbelievable . . . he counted no less than four doses of the soaked rag, and he hadn't vomited once. If he had, he surely would be feeling better than he was now.

The other man stepped past him at last, returning to the empty booth-chair across from the Colonel. A deck of ornate playing cards slipped though his long, fine fingers as he shuffled – an incongruous movement against the heavy onyx chess set the Colonel had set up on the small table between the padded chairs. The hands were long and thin, womanly graceful. His body matched those hands, smooth skin wrapped around very gentle curves of muscle. The man had not been exposed to enough sunlight to create a look of health. He was corpse-pale, animated only by force of will and the feverish glow in his eyes, a glow as bright as his shock of red hair and the ghastly white scar on his face.

John Clay. Watson pulled his memory to everything he could remember of the man Holmes had called the fourth smartest man in London. Holmes had joked grimly that the ranking would make him a literal "one in a million" in a city of four-million.

"And now that we are all here," Moriarty paused, noting Clay's flare of nostrils as he looked at Watson. "does the sight of blood make you faint, Mr. Clay?" he asked with supreme gentleness.

"No sense being uncivilized," Clay answered, the sniff transferred to his voice.

Dear God in Heaven, let me show you uncivilized, Watson thought to himself.

"I am aware of the word, sir." The Colonel merely drew on his cigar again, but his lips curved behind the shield of his cigar. "And I acknowledge your . . . refined sensibilities as a man of the noble blood." Another sip of smoke. "Do not worry. We shall clean our soldier up and put cease to your offense."

Clay was either unaware or incapable of knowing he was being insulted. The only thing that mattered was the fulfillment of his desires. "That would be acceptable," he said shortly.

Moriarty picked up a black knight and examined a scratch in the stone as the valet returned with water and a towel. "Keep the water hot," he said absently. "There is a copious amount of battle on our guest."

If the hatred between these two grew any more palpable, I think I would choke on it. Watson busied himself with sponging the blood off his face as Clay and Moriarty traded looks at each other across the table. His dehydrated skin soaked the moisture right up. His wrists burned but, there wasn't enough blood on the rope burns to leave a trail for the police.

"Where was I?" Moriarty began again, most softly. "Ah, as I was saying, 'Now that we are all here' . . . ." He leaned back slightly, his half-consumed cigar balanced like a spirit level between his fingers, "it would be time to come to an amicable agreement, would it not?"

"This conflict is a waste of resources," John Clay said obscurely. "London is large enough for all of us."

"There is no 'all of us', sir. I am satisfied enough with my portion of the world. Your . . . master, however – " Moriarty chose his words with exquisite care while the smaller man slowly turned plum-purple, " – feels otherwise."

"There is no sense in disrupting a profitable balance of power," Clay retorted.

"I spent too much of my life being subordinate to my brother's wishes, Mr. Clay." The Colonel's voice was not to be mistaken for pleasant or timid. "His hold over me was that of familial bond. That is gone now, and I recognize no heir to my brother's work."

"Your interference could be seen as a declaration of war," Clay pointed out.

"Interference?" Moriarty smiled again. "Whatever do you mean?"

"I mean, *this*." Clay wrenched his cold gaze away, looked Watson up and down. "We had our own business with the doctor." His lips twisted, still displeased at the sight of blood and dirt and wood stain. "You waited

156

for *my* men to seize him, and as soon as he was secure, you killed them and took him for yourself. If the Yarders aren't fully incompetent, they will be after my men first."

"Merely being sensible in my resources." Moriarty was still using that calm, gentle tone of voice, and Watson would have rather heard anything else. "Call it a test, if it were."

"You are well known for your 'tests', Colonel," John Clay snapped. The color was beginning to rise in his narrow face again.

"Then I am surprised you did not think of it in the first place," Moriarty answered. He put down his cigar in trade for port. "I wanted to see how you fared. I must say, I wasn't at all disappointed in the Major . . . but . . . ." He shook his head slightly. "You are known for being a clever man. Did you not know what it is to attack a soldier in his own camp?"

Clay was trembling with rage. His ears flushed, leaving the tiny piercing scar on his lobe gleaming white. He stilled himself with an effort until he had returned to that cold, serpentine calm. "You let my men do the work."

"Again, it was a test." Moriarty sipped his port slowly. "From a warrior's standpoint, Mr. Clay, you were not at your peak."

"Is this what your aim was, then?" He tilted his head to one side, bird-like, his eyes bright with ghastly intelligence. "Was it *only* a test for you?"

"No, not only." But Moriarty did not elucidate further. He fell silent over his glass while his men traded glares with the rough-looking men on the other side of the wall – Clay's minions, Watson noted rather tiredly.

John Clay finally picked up his own glass. "I am under orders to bring the doctor back. I cannot disappoint."

"Mr. Clay," Moriarty murmured, "your reputation is not that of a man who seeks to disappoint. But if you may humor me . . . What is your interest in the Major?" Chill grey eyes slid lazily to the third party at the table. "It's not as if he's anything without Sherlock Holmes, is he?"

"I would argue that point, if we were not gentlemen and this was not your house." John Clay was beginning to catch on to how Moriarty wanted the game played. He took a drink. "We have use for the doctor."

"Hardly. His records and notes are locked up as safe as the Tower Jewels . . . even the most incriminating evidence cannot be applied for until the Vaults of Cox are opened and in lieu of the owner's death . . . the provisions writ for a ninety-year wait." He chuckled.

John Clay shook that off impatiently. "Perhaps you would be interested in a trade of information," he responded.

"Perhaps," the Colonel murmured, still in that polite voice. He snapped his fingers once, and Larkin resolved at his elbow with covered dishes. Watson felt yet another stab of nausea. "It would depend on the type of information, you see. And despite the fact that we seem not to avoid an overlap of interests . . . our armies are not in concordance with each other for the most part. Your master has his countries to conquer, and I have mine. We have little more than . . . border warfare between us."

"What is *your* interest in the doctor, then?" John Clay inquired. Watson was certain the man would rather pull a fish hook out of his own throat than apply for information, but he was playing by Moriarty's rules – and inquiring would be the closest thing he would get to being submissive.

"His part in my brother's death could be one," Moriarty answered. "For another, I told him not to continue in his way, and yet he did. He had every chance to recant. He did not. Would there need to be any further reason?"

And John Watson realized *Moriarty was lying through his teeth.*

Not a thing about Afghanistan, nor the missing dead, nor the gemstones. Not a word. Was he so adept at hiding his interests from his brother?

Incredibly, John Clay appeared to accept that reason. He nodded and set his glass down, proper manners, but he did not take his eyes off his host as Larkin lifted the lid off the steaming plate. "What if my . . . army, as you call it, had a stronger reason for him?"

"Would you? I would be curious at the very concept," Moriarty drawled.

John Clay paused for a heartbeat. "Sherlock Holmes is alive."

158

Chapter XXII – Negotiations

The core meeting had re-convened in private. With Gregson's wife caught up in what he himself admitted was "some kind of barmy church work", they settled for the "back room" at The Lancashire Rose. "If we're going to pay for a meal, we may as well make it a charity meal."

Over a kettle of beef-and-barley vegetable soup that was more like a thick stew with heavy slices of bread, the four ate while sorting out their thoughts.

"How many people do we let in on this?"

Gregson hesitated before answering Hopkins. He busied himself with another smoke. "As few people as possible. How are they taking the story?"

Without a word, Hopkins pulled a folded newspaper from within his coat and put it on the tabletop. Lestrade could read the headlines upside-down: *Local Surgeon Victim of Vicious Attack.*

"Well, about what I'd hoped for." Gregson skimmed the print quickly. "Part of me wanted to pretend his empty house had been vandalized while he was on vacation . . . ."

"We couldn't make it credible," Hopkins reminded him. "Too many witnesses, too many shots fired . . . and if we're caught lying to the papers *once* they'll hamstring us for the rest of our lives."

"The Chief Inspector is letting us keep the abduction quiet," Lestrade pointed out. "For now. The closer we get to the full moon, the worse it will be."

"Patterson." Gregson looked at the lean man. "How hard can it be to get on to Streat?"

Patterson shook his head. He'd eaten three bowls, which suggested his state of mind was doing his health no good. "I have friends . . . they owe me a favour or three." He met the skepticism with patience while buttering his bread. Lestrade found himself hoping the man took some of the supper home with him. "Two brothers. They . . . they lost their third brother to the machinations of the gang."

"Loseth?" Lestrade guessed.

Patterson nodded miserably. "They wanted him to get out of it . . . but he was determined to be anything but a fisherman." He drank his saffron in a reflective mood. "He went with his supporters . . . and they wanted him to be a policeman."

"A policemen for them," Lestrade answered with justifiable bitterness.

Patterson looked puzzled.

Gregson coughed. "Our friend Mr. Quimper tried to recruit Lestrade along the same lines." He left it at that.

The black parts of Patterson's eyes swelled up until there was little more to see. "I see." He busied himself with his drink. "I beg your pardon." He murmured with a genuine humility that was as startling as it was touching.

"Not at all."

Everyone pondered within their own thoughts for a moment. Hopkins spoke up next. "I beg your pardon, but there is a part of this I do not understand." He clinked his spoon within his tea as if to punctuate his thoughts. "Taking Dr. Watson . . . this is . . . very personal. I was under the impression that to take a personal issue in this particular gang was . . . well . . . dangerously unprofessional."

"It is and it isn't," Patterson explained. "What you or I would call unprofessional would be the only possible way to do things with the Moriarty crowd. They are hard-edged businessmen . . . harder than anything you will ever find. But fear and anticipation is an effective tool in controlling the gang – as well as the gang's victims."

The thin man wordlessly poured the contents of his flask into his table-drink. "Put it this way," he began. "Do you know how the London Zoo captured its elephants?"

"No idea," Lestrade said.

"Bet your youngest son knows," Gregson gibed.

"I'm sure he does . . . Go on, Patterson."

"The elephant is the largest land animal, and one of the most powerful. But once in a while, there's a need to actually grab an elephant from the wild. When that happens, they build a gigantic area out of poles, clothesline, and tarpaulins."

Patterson's audience stared at him.

"A tarpaulin isn't going to hold an elephant." Hopkins protested. "What's the trick?"

"They can't see through the tarpaulins." Patterson held up his hand flat and bent, to mime a wall. "Elephants are responsible for each other in the herd. They aren't going to risk their calves, mates, or other relatives on the unknown."

"Just like a victim of blackmail isn't going to risk the exposure and destruction to their family," Gregson mused. "It's simple when you look at it that way."

Lestrade cursed under his breath. The conversation was far too close to home, especially because this was a part of the world he usually tried not to think of. "These brothers of Loseth . . . You can trust them?"

160

"They've convinced me their motive is revenge against everyone who ruined their family."

"That could be taken more than one way," Lestrade muttered. He did so very quietly. Patterson was wearing his "*I am hanging by a thread*" look again. Against his better judgment, he nodded. "Very well, but if things begin to go wrong . . . we're going to stop taking this unhealthy level of initiative and go straight back to the book." He allowed concrete to enter his voice. "I mean it."

"It's a risk we'll have to take, you know," Gregson said after they were alone again. Patterson's leaving had been like watching a consumptive, and Hopkins' horror upon seeing the late hour, comedic.

"Look at him!" Lestrade blurted. "The man's a shivering ghost!"

"I agree, but that's not the whole point. He's worked in places for years that would have eaten us both alive. He didn't come out of it in one piece . . . but he did come out of it." Gregson poked at his fork. "You aren't normally afraid of taking risks."

"I don't like taking risks outside the rules, and you know why."

Gregson ignored the sharpness of his rival's answer. "I won't hesitate to give anyone a hand out of a horror like this . . . least of all a man like Watson."

"That isn't it." Lestrade got up and went to the miniscule window set into the wall. "This is about as dangerous as anything we've ever faced . . . dangerous and dirty. You saw what Watson looked like when he got back from Switzerland."

"Yes." Gregson didn't see his point.

"You know Watson as well as I do, Gregson. How do you think he felt when he realised Holmes sent him off on a wild goose chase . . . and that it led to his death?"

Gregson sighed like a leaking balloon. "I've got you. You think if anything happens to us, Watson will blame himself for our getting hurt or killed."

"He's a soldier," Lestrade reminded his prickly opponent. "He might be discharged, but you know damn well they see us as 'civilians'. They're the ones supposed to take the bullets and the risks, not us. Forget the fact that we're the police. He won't forgive himself if there are consequences."

"Bloody Hell," Gregson grumbled. "I never thought of it. Holmes was hard enough to work with . . . but Watson . . . the man's almost too supportive!"

"Had to be a balance somewhere," Lestrade joked without a whit of humour in his dark eyes.

Watson was already so weakened by the series of shocks that his mind delayed. Whatever his dubious hosts had expected his reaction to be, it had certainly not been a stone-walled silence.

The silence continued.

Until Moriarty began to smile.

His shoulders shook slightly. John Clay's growing bafflement and anger made it worse. A laugh bubbled up, slow and methodical like the man itself. It peaked to the surface like a geyser, until his very body shook with mirth. For Watson, something in his mind was refusing to function at all as he witnessed the panorama before him. He could only observe without thought or feeling.

"Ridiculous," the Colonel declared. "He's not alive. He can't be alive."

"Hardly," John Clay answered. "Would you like proof?"

"That I would."

The long fingers dipped into his breast-coat pocket and pulled out a small envelope. He placed it on the table between them, pulling his hands away before his opponent could reach for it.

Moriarty picked it up and let a series of photographs slide out. They appeared to be of crowds in various cities. He looked at one, then another, his lips making thoughtful moues here and there.

"Interesting," he decreed in a monotone. "But shall we ask the expert?" He lifted his eyebrows and selected a choice photograph from the lot, holding it up to Watson's face. "What do you think, Major? Friend or foe?"

Watson utterly froze. It was a street somewhere in France – the painted signs were clear enough. In the crowd was a single figure, just caught in the act of looking up. The long, lean aquiline face and short black hair with its steep hairline, nearly skeletal body clad in his usual black . . . was as if staring at proof that cameras could capture ghosts.

The distance between camera and subject was such that the smaller details could not be discerned – there was no way of knowing the tint of the eye, or the veins in the back of the hands. The ears were not defined.

"Well?" Moriarty pressed.

Watson coldly shut his mind off. He looked back at the Colonel.

"My good Major, there's no need to look like that." Still smiling, Moriarty returned the photograph to the stack. "Mr. Clay, I confess there's a resemblance . . . ."

"A resemblance? What more do you need?"

"What more do *you* need?" Moriarty shot back. In the stiff silence that followed, his eyebrows went back up. "Ah . . . what more *do* you need?" he asked softly. His gunmetal eyes went back to Watson. "Indeed."

162

He leaned his body completely back against his cushion, swirling his drink in the glass. "You don't really know for certain, do you?"

"Of course we're certain!" John Clay snarled, his first display of uncouth emotion. "It is Sherlock Holmes!"

"Without backup evidence, you really can't know for certain, can you? Not unless you put out the proper – " Another look at Watson. " – bait." Watson's dry throat tried to swallow.

"We're certain." John Clay spoke with absolute firmness.

It lifted another eyebrow on Moriarty.

Watson noticed the subtle electricity coming from the thugs supporting both men. They were preparing for a fight.

He hoped so. His hands were free. But he did need a distraction.

"Hmm. You have a cleverness in your tactics, Mr. Clay." The Colonel looked merely amused at the smaller man at the other side of the table. "Very good, you have a knack. But I am a tactician, and I have been one for a very long time."

"Obviously," John Clay grunted. "You are a Colonel, after all."

Moriarty grinned, leaning back. "How may we help you?"

Clay grimaced. "We wish to take your guest from your troubles."

"Who, John?" Moriarty drawled, looking Watson up and down. "Why, he's no trouble at all, Mr. Clay. No trouble at all."

Watson fantasized about what he could accomplish with fifteen seconds of freedom.

"That is, so long as he's cornered like a rat in a trap." Moriarty was grinning like a cat. "What makes you think I'd want to pass on my . . . 'troubles' Mr. Clay?"

"You would gain much from the transaction," John Clay answered.

His was such a soft voice. It almost failed to imply what Moriarty could lose if he refused the transaction.

"Really." Moriarty seemed to think that over for a few seconds. "Mr. Clay . . . you have tried on several occasions to lay your hands on the Major. That was your men, was it not, on that Christmas raid? I was and still am impressed by your unique and brilliant solution of ridding yourself of less than profitable workers. They actually did come close to taking him on occasion." Moriarty's grey eyes flickered in an obscene parody of Holmes's intelligence.

"I do believe he will kill you the moment he has the first opportunity," he mused. "You are an intelligent man, Mr. Clay. But you are not a *soldier*."

Somehow, he made it sound like it wasn't Clay's fault for being handicapped.

163

"I cannot return empty handed," John Clay answered. The original coolness was slipping back into his voice. Watson wondered what had just occurred to the man. "I am authorized to bargain."

"Are you?" Moriarty showed some surprise for the first time. "Well . . ."

The silence lengthened with unspoken expectations. John Clay's statement had been the last thing on Moriarty's mind.

The Colonel picked up a steaming roll and broke it in half in a crisp jerk. "Perhaps we can settle this like gentlemen. I propose we not allow this excellent dinner to go to waste. We have quite a few hours to go before we part ways. Shall we discuss our goals over dinner . . . and then move on to the actual negotiation?"

John Clay's boyish face flushed with the beginnings of triumph. "Most agreeable of you, Colonel."

Chapter XXIII – In the Darkness

Light rain freckled the chilly coast of the North Sea. In the half-light the boulders rising to the surface looked black as bottomless pits.

"You can just make it out," Lestrade clipped his spyglass shut against the weather and passed the brass tube over to Gregson. "Thank Heavens we don't have to worry about snow on top of everything else."

"I can live with that." Gregson looked quite miserable in the chill. "Seems like things are warmer now than they used to be. We don't have Frost Fairs any more."

"Can't say I mind," Lestrade said truthfully. He thrust his hands back in his pockets and went back to the small campfire for the teapot.

Gregson satisfied himself with Lestrade's instrument, and slowly turned in the packed sand and pebble to join him. The soles of his large boots ground particles loudly against crushed shell and stones.

"I'd be careful there," Lestrade had poured a tiny tin cup and was trying to balance it on a boulder to vent off some heat. "You don't know what you could be stepping on here."

"Nice to know." Gregson had to have the last word.

Lestrade let him have it. He concentrated on gently feeding softcoal into the flames in tiny fragments so the smoke would not rise too conspicuously. In his dark pea-jacket and muffler he looked like he belonged in someone's moonfleet, silently weighing contraband in with his ballast. The heavy cloth cap added to the impression.

"So where's John O' Groats?"

Lestrade obliged with a jerk of his thumb. Gregson naturally looked even though he couldn't see the legendary "most northerly village" in Scotland.

"Why don't they call Streat the most northerly? It's off the coast."

"It's lower than the Orkneys," Lestrade explained. "Bradstreet was kind enough to explain that."

"Dear Heaven . . . ."

"Look, Land's End isn't the most southerly point in England either. The mature part about growing up is knowing things are seldom what they seem."

"Especially if there are good advertisements in the world."

Lestrade answered by flicking dross over his shoulder.

"I hope Patterson doesn't take much longer," Gregson said at last. He found a niche between two armchair-sized stones and sank down to rest for the moment. They were going to be up half the night anyway.

"That makes two of us . . . Might as well try to get some rest."
Lestrade nursed his cup close to his lips. "And Hopkins *better* keep his eye
on him."

"Still looking for the worst? Good idea." He drank and looked
around. "What do you think those daft fools are doing?"

Lestrade barely glanced up at a tiny spit of land a quarter-mile
downcurrent. "Hunting for something off the shipwrecks . . . Something
they can sell."

Gregson shuddered. "This isn't like London. There can't be that much
out here."

"No . . . there isn't," Lestrade answered absently. "There never is.
That's why some people are tempted to make false lights and lure ships to
the rocks."

Gregson checked his hip flask and was reassured at its contents.
"They don't pay men enough . . . near enough . . . to guard the coasts and
rivers, do they?"

"Not near enough," Lestrade snorted. "I've heard them say the same
thing about us."

"I hate waiting," Gregson said five minutes later.

"Thank God we're off in CID business and not regular policework,"
Lestrade commiserated. "We'd be surrounded by miserable constables and
I'd be feeling sorry for them the whole time."

He stepped away from the warmth of the fire and leaned his back to
a rock not far from Gregson. Gregson saw him pull out a piece of paper
and slowly cut it open.

"You took your mail with you?"

"Not really . . . Clea said if I got bored – and she gave me five minutes
– I could catch up on the news at home."

"You were out for a day-and-a-half." Gregson protested with that
charming naivety common to men who never knew fatherhood or marriage
to wrestlers. "What can happen in a day-and-a-half?"

"Well, let's see . . . ." Lestrade skimmed the contents. "Your wife
won a friendly wager with Mrs. Bradstreet over the upcoming price of
gingham at the church supper, so I'm to warn you that you'll be seeing a
lot of gingham in your life when you get back . . . Looks like they let her
take the whole bolt home . . . I say, Euclid – shouldn't you be booking the
bets through her? She's *much* better at it than you."

Gregson growled. "What would I do with a bolt of gingham?"

"You're right . . . Tell her next time to go for a few yards of worsted.
Or some tie silk." Lestrade gave his rival a pointed, silent and judgmental
gaze right at his throat.

Gregson resisted the urge to examine his tie for the flaws Lestrade clearly saw. "Your wife can't have spent the whole letter talking about my necktie," he sniffed.

"No . . . she always gets the boring over with first . . . hmm . . . The Dooleys stopped by to 'drop off a few things' – Dear me, I know what that means."

"What does it mean?"

"Something I won't like and will have to live with." He sighed. "Including the hedgehog for Nicholas. The boy's in raptures, and his mother has promised him she has a recipe for it, baked in clay, if he doesn't take care of it and make certain it stays out of the way."

"Best watch what you're eating in the near future," Gregson advised.

"I'm the one who gave her that recipe . . . And Martin has taken over the pigeon project – so that's what the Dooleys were bringing over! Good Lord. He's building cotes on the roof."

"Aren't you supposed to build cotes on the roof?"

"This is Martin we're talking about. When he's done, poor Mrs. Collins will be counting an extra storey on her taxes." Lestrade sighed. "He's going to raise runts. I just know it. Martin can't do anything small or halfway."

"You mean those pigeons that are big as Cornish hens? You'll be set up for fancy suppers," Gregson taunted mildly.

"You're laughing now, but once Martin figures out how to make nitre from the droppings, you won't be. Manufacturing his own gunpowder and fireworks is only a step away."

"It must be stressful having a genius in the family." That was Gregson's version of sympathy, and it almost worked.

"You have no idea." Oddly enough, Lestrade grew quiet. The uncharacteristic silence grew so long that Gregson began to feel uneasy.

"He drove me mad, you know," the smaller man confessed as if no one else but King Neptune could hear. "Too clever . . . too sure of himself. Too . . . driven. I could get along with Watson just fine, but I couldn't . . . I couldn't be as strong as Watson."

"Watson's a unique fellow," Gregson pointed out. "Unique as Mr. Holmes was in his own way."

"Yes . . . ." Pensive and thoughtful, Lestrade was looking to the grey chop of the sea. On the other side of the visual world hung the grey smear of Streat.

Patterson signaled at dusk with a tiny lantern on cryption. Gregson tried to ignore that Lestrade huckled back in the shadows as if resting, his right hand loosely caught at his belt like a common worker. Keeping his hand close to his gun, the big man knew. Lestrade was getting itchy.

167

The lean CID man crunched forward on the drift of broken coal and shell. Someone's boot toe stobbed upon a piece of something metal and unwanted. A muffled curse was quickly swallowed. Two figures followed Patterson in the poor light. They were cutouts made of mourning crepe against the endless shadows of grey.

"Patterson, you look like a troupe of smugglers."

Patterson's long, frail-looking fingers spread helplessly. "Well, that's the impression I was going for." He dropped his hands to his sides. "Gentlemen, meet our guides to Streat: The Brothers Loseth."

"There's tea at the fire." Lestrade did not answer that directly. "Help yourself. A shame to waste the tea-leaves."

"You . . . eh . . . take tea with you everywhere?" one of the men asked gingerly.

"Cheaper than most vices."

Gregson stepped to the side and let the three men, chilled from the nonstop sea winds, refresh themselves. There was plenty to go around. Lestrade had drunk only his share, and used the rest for washing his gun.

"Wouldn't the acids and stuff in a bog keep the metal from rusting too?" Gregson had asked him. "We're about to go to a blessed island that's just rank with bogs."

"I don't intend on getting too close to those bogs," Lestrade had inarguably shot back. "They seem crowded."

Inspector Loseth's brothers barely looked like him. They went by the odd first names of Boggs and Hartley, and chewed tobacco as if it would be out of fashion by midnight.

If there were any two men who were more typical coastal labourers, Gregson had not met them, nor had he the imagination required to conjure them.

"There's a tin of biscuits over there too," Lestrade offered. "Help yourself."

"Ah'll cheust tak a nave-fil," the other brother said. His accent was far more Orkadian than his sibling. [1] It was Lallan Scot with a mix of Norse. Lestrade thought of the strange Norse tints in Quimper's henchman, Captain Wiltson of the Hyssop and the Athene.

"What time are we planning to head out?"

"Soon as the moon gets past the land spit," the taller and more Englishified Loseth responded. His gaze slipped to the older man who was trying not to wolf down his given meal. "Luck at him gavsin' intae his tea . . . Give us just enough light so we seems to be fishing for a bit of luck . . . any darker and it'll look as though we're hiding something."

"Heaven forbid," Gregson said to that. He pulled out an oiled paper map of Streat. "I want to know what's over on this side here."

168

"It's the channel where most of the ships go in." Patterson actually looked better in the camp light. Perhaps the advice to go back to what he was good at helped.

"The roost aroond back o' Streat's no safe fur iny boht." The second brother – a slight lisp around his stronger accent – slurped his tea loudly. He was making an effort to speak more like his hosts.

"He means the tidalway," the better-speaking Loseth answered. Lestrade's flesh prickled at the way the younger man was clearly bullying the older man around. "Our boat's too small to bother with that nonsense. We can head in no problem, so long as we look out for the rocks."

Lestrade had been putting his hand up to the sky, using his three middle fingers to measure the moon's projected rise in five-degree increments. "Almost three hours," he announced. "Time to pick up Hopkins' wire."

He had slept without artifice. There was no need to stay awake, and he was exhausted of usefulness.

For the moment.

He had to give them credit for tactics. It would be suicide to leap over the ship and swim.

Once, John had bet with Hamish they could swim around a small craft in the freezing water. That had been put to an end by an elderly neighbor – *What was his name?* – who caught wind of the contest. Hamish had been convinced he would win . . . John had been just as convinced that he could.

But that was back in the days before John saw the disaster on Hamish' countenance whenever he lost at anything. It wasn't even as childish as rage or jealousy . . . His brother had to win, or he meant nothing to himself.

It was before the days when John tempered anger with pity, and finally . . . compassion. The compassion had freed him, for Hamish had never been capable of feeling similar emotions for his younger brother . . . .

His only brother. Have you forgotten that too?

I have never forgotten anything.

How then do you explain walking away? Leaving him to die of the drink?

It was what he wanted.

I tried. I had no power.

A man has the right to choose his life, as he does his death.

If you were important enough to him . . . he would have lived for you.

But I was not. Another had that honour . . . and that one belonged to another.

You should have saved him. He was brilliant.

169

I did not have enough in me to save him. His brilliance outstripped my strength. And my strength was small after Maiwand.

He forced himself to breathe evenly. With it, his mind calmed.

The grey curtain of the ocean rested before his eyes in the tiny porthole – far too small to escape from.

Once upon a time, there were two boys who loved to play upon the shingles of the northern sea . . . .

One was a brilliant man, but the other was merely content with being alive and living in the company of his brother.

And both went to war, and were changed forever . . . .

Behind him was the cold voice from his nightmares.

"Your brother was a clever man." Colonel Moriarty was saying. In the silence of the cabin the largest sound was the slap of water on the other side of the hull.

But the war changed them in different ways . . . the brilliant brother was crushed by his enemies until he died.

Ash tipped softly into the tray on the table. A sound like snowfall against glass. The Colonel shifted his weight into his chair. Leather creaked. Watson could hear the breath in his lungs, coming out of his nostrils.

"Not that you were dull, Major, but it was always difficult to learn what he was thinking. You, however, are different."

And the second brother was left behind . . . to finish what was started . . . and to put an end to the corruption of his enemies as best as he could . . . one way or another.

NOTE

1.   I'll just take a handful.

Chapter XXIV – When Shall We Three Meet Again?

Watson said nothing. He existed in a mental plane away from this small cabin. They'd allowed him the luxury of cleaning up – more because the sight of him was offensive than the desire to grant him any decency.

"You are a very different study, Major," Moriarty mused. He trimmed his cigar neatly and held the edge to his lips. "Hamish was too busy. It was like trying to find a single bird in a flying flock. You . . . you're the lake the birds land in." He smiled to himself, expressing a thought unknown to Watson. "He was smart to tell you where the stones were. Very smart."

"I told you I don't know where they are."

"You have the key. That's the same thing." Moriarty's grizzled brow quirked up. "And if I know you, you didn't permit yourself to solve the riddle. That must have been maddening . . . I remember you were always playing with those little puzzles the soldiers made during their convalescence. Some of them were quite clever . . . ." His fingers, more muscular than his cerebral brother's, were long and strong. They gripped the cigar with overly necessary strength.

"How did he take my gems, Major? I wish to know many things, but that particular question has been . . . preying upon my vitals for quite some time."

"He never confided in me how he took away your *stolen* lucre."

"Confided?" Moriarty's lips went up. "In you, Major? You were his twin. They stationed you on the other side of the camp for a reason."

"The vaunted communication of twins is quite exaggerated." Watson hadn't meant to speak so sharply. His emotions always revealed more than he wanted.

"When he was in his moods, surly and uncommunicative, wouldn't it have been easier to imitate him?" Moriarty's mild, inoffensive voice was about control and confidence.

And he was not truly asking a question.

It was just as well. Watson had no urge to answer.

"History is laden with irony and the repetition," the Colonel mused as if idly, but the man was never idle, and Watson knew the tone of a superior officer about to strike down the inferior one. "You should carry a grain of sympathy for my cause, you know. You ought to."

Horror inspired Watson to turn on his heel, too astonished and appalled to even try to pretend otherwise. "You're mad if you think so," he answered coldly.

"No? Of all the people in the world, Major . . . do you not know what it is like to be a clever, resourceful man . . . a man who is above the head and shoulders of the common . . . who does well in school . . . does well in his athletics . . . is thought well of within his own circles . . . circles he must create himself . . . ." The taunting thread within the Colonel's tone was dark and twisted . . . and Watson felt his heart beat faster to hear it. "And yet due to the accident of birth, must still always be the second-best? Must *always* live within the shadow of the *first-born*, the *genius* . . . the *inheritor*?"

If the Colonel had stood, walked over, and struck Watson with an oak quarter-staff, it would not have been as sudden or painful than the verbal blow he'd just given. The doctor took a step backward from the force of it.

Those cold silvery eyes flared within the shadow of the brow line, for the blow had struck home.

"My brother's vast and vaunted empire of power and prestige?" Each wolfsbane word was a dart flying out of that thin, cruel mouth. "Nothing without my support. My connections. My *loyalty*, Major. And what did he do but give the title of Second to a man who is my inferior in every way? *Because it was an intellectual decision.* As if intellect is everything from the first spark of life on this planet to its last ray of sunshine!"

The Colonel still remained in his seat, but he felt as though he were standing chest-to-chest with Watson.

"Because I questioned his decisions when his intellectual decisions were the wrong ones. Because I knew something of the world more than he did with his numbers and ink. All my life I was his assistant. Is that so different from what you were to your brother?"

Watson's throat was dry. He had never seen the controlled Colonel so angry. Or so naked.

"Did you not try to help your brother when he, despite his remarkable genius, made his own mistakes? Were you enough when he fell victim to his own self-created vices? Did he ever truly thank you for the times you gave him aid? Did he even give you anything of your family's estate when he inherited everything just to drink it all away? The family pride fallen to the family humiliation. *You* wouldn't have done that, would you Major? *You* wouldn't have committed to such betrayal of the family's hopes and dreams, would you? No, *you* wouldn't . . . but *you* weren't the one entrusted to the family name and fortune. The second-born is always out

172

in the cold. The father kills the fatted calf for the prodigal son, while the good son at home waits forever at the door for his father's love."

"If you are expecting my help or sympathy for your own plight," Watson's voice was thick and glued up with the need to strike with his fists, "you are choosing poor tactics."

Moriarty laughed indulgently.

"I had a chance in Afghanistan to do something for myself. And I managed to do it. Not even he knew." The brief humour died. "But Colonel Hayter knew. And he sent his prized trustee, your brother. But your brother had need of you, because you were another weapon he could employ." The eyes snapped like grey fireworks. "Another tool. That's all you were to him. And yet, even now . . . you defend him." He shook his head. "You know that in some parts of Africa . . . in the case of twins, the first born is of divine origin, while the second twin is only human. How does it feel, Major, to be only human and living in the shadow of a god?"

Watson had fought hard all his life – for recognition, for his placement in life, for his rights and reputation. But staying silent and starving the Colonel's unholy need for attention was the hardest moment of them all.

The Colonel thought he knew Hamish. He did know about the brilliance of that mind . . . a brilliance like a diamond, hard and cold. There were *moods* inside Hamish. Bitter recriminations, and drinking . . . Hours and days passed in ignoring his brother for more "mentally equal company," and his taking the family estate without giving anything to John even though he knew John was as penniless as he'd ever been.

But Moriarty never knew that within those painful disasters there were other parts to Hamish. The times when his mind could come down from his lofty spire and notice his brother standing patiently on the ground, waiting for him to come down too.

For Hamish was not fully complete without the company of the human race, despite the gifts that astounded family and friend. University, colleague and acquaintance alike . . . Hamish could not define himself. For that he needed to see himself in another's eyes.

By the time they were old enough to understand, it was already too late. Hamish could not fill up his own hollowness. He needed their father for that, with his ready approval and praise and unquestioning love. When their father was gone . . . the hole within was larger . . . but there was still John. Hamish had never needed to question John's presence in his life. John had been there as rightfully as the colour of his eyes.

Some days it was easy. Hamish would be more like his old self from childhood. They could fish or visit the shingle and be content with doing nothing . . . or at least, John could do nothing, and they could pretend

173

Hamish wasn't counting the stones and shells or cataloguing the cloud formations. But those moments grew rarer with age, as Hamish' intellect grew with his body. Books, music, science, and clubbing did not do for him what a night of drink could do: Make his mind cease its frantic channering and let him be – if only for a few hours.

John had always known he would not be enough. He was the subordinate twin, after all, and it was natural to concede his identity within Hamish, just as it was Hamish' nature to speak for them both. It was a relationship neither could explain to the rest of the world.

And how could they? Twins might like or dislike each other, but they were still two people with overlapping lives. Hamish had always known what John was thinking or feeling . . . when he was not distracted by his own mental processes. And John had always known how to find him if need be. For all their differences, they comprehended alike. And they both knew Hamish needed assistance that was in proportion to his need. His need was as great as his intelligence.

There had been hope at first, that Miss Hayter could finalise the need and together they could be his supportive family. Colonel Hayter would have been honoured to welcome him into his family and supply the role as a father-figure – another hole within Hamish that needed filling.

But all that came to an end with Moriarty. When Moriarty inveigled his favourite creature to win her hand in marriage.

John had felt the death within Hamish when it happened. He'd also known that if Hamish had made the choice . . . he could have risen above his shattered heart and spirit and overcame his grief.

John had never given up on a fight in his life.

Had Mary her Agra treasure, he would have done something – possibly reckless and likely stupid – but he would have risked himself to create a fortune to place himself on equal level with her, in the hopes he might win her hand someday. He would have returned to Australia and the mines. He would have bought interests instead of racing tickets. He would have done something.

But Hamish did not. And so he died, one inch at a time, over the course of too many years while John could do nothing but let him.

Were John to attempt to explain and outline this to the insensate lump of evil sitting in that chair right now . . . it would take a lifetime, and there would still be no comprehension to brag about.

He shook inside himself, wanting more than anything to attack the Colonel for being rotten inside his skin . . . and for what he had done to ruin the first part of John's life . . . the lives of Hamish, Colonel Hayter . .
.

. . . and Miss Orpha Hayter . . . now Mrs. Jedidiah Harrison.

174

He hadn't thought of her name in years. The shock of it came over him then, as he realized he had buried so much of the past in his attempt to survive.

"Loyalty," he rasped at the Colonel. "You may not have been loyal to your brother at the end . . . but you can understand that I would choose to keep mine."

And the eyes flared again.

John's lips sewed shut in harsh triumph. Colonel Moriarty could kill him now or tomorrow or during the rise of the full moon . . . but John had won.

"There's no sense in politely asking you to tell me what form of news your brother left behind." Moriarty said at last in the growing smoke. "Your principals refuse, naturally, to give me what I want simply because I want it. I understand." There was a break in the speech as his lips communed with the cigar end. "You will be speaking soon enough anyway." That last was said as an afterthought, and sent the flesh prickling up Watson's arms all the way to his neck, where it refused to stand down.

"Fear is a potent weapon, is it not?"

It was very very easy for a man to get dizzy . . . and then deeply seasick as they watched the chessboard of waves fold eternally into each other. In the creaming wake of the slow-moving little fishing craft, nothing stayed the same. There was nothing like orderly regularity or anything resembling a straight line. The occasional gleam of the swelling moon and freckles of starlight made it much worse.

It was preferable to spending too much time in contemplation of the main sail, which to Gregson's thinking was a too-thin membrane of canvas and the only thing that provided locomotion across the waters. Ruin that thin, frail thing and they would be as helpless as bobbing eggshells.

Gregson had spent almost no time in the CID *in mufti*.

The northern coast was a harsh baptismal of truth. Prickly as the man was, Lestrade had to pity him. The stars gleamed like candles through a firmament of tissue paper. The tissue paper rolled and bent and twisted like a nightmare in a shadow-play, bringing tiny droplets of icy water past their faces and dampening everything on the small fishing craft. Miniscule silver beads gleamed on the dark wool of Lestrade's pea-jacket. Sometimes, Gregson saw him yank off his cloth cap and shake it, as fussily as a cat shaking water off its paw. Twice he witnessed a strange expression cross the little man's face upon the younger Loseth.

"I thought 'Scotch mist' was a myth," Gregson whispered in his ear.

"And you thought pea-soupers were memorable," Lestrade whispered back.

"What sort of tongue were they talking in?" Gregson persisted. "You were jawing with them like one of their own first born."

"I hadn't thought about it," Lestrade admitted. "They just sound like the Tinkers."

"The Dooleys? They don't sound half like this!"

"They do when they're alone."

Gregson rubbed his jaw, glaring. "If you tell me you've been slumming with vagrant, nomadic Picts – "

"I don't think Picts are still alive, Gregson," Lestrade retorted with a quality to his impatience that told Gregson that his rival didn't see the joke within the taunt, and was also . . . dead serious.

He blew out his breath in an uneasy sigh and watched Lestrade keep a scowling gaze on the single sail of the small boat. The three inspectors and two Loseth brothers were doing what they could to get the craft to the quieter side of the island and after nearly an hour of dealing with the wind, he guessed they were halfway across.

"Streat is one ugly island," Gregson said under his breath.

Lestrade heard anyway. "Won't argue with that." He watched the Loseth brothers quarrel amongst themselves as they cast down nets to go along with the appearance of fishermen. "Legend has it Streat was once connected to Scotland but the lands between sank into the sea. Rather like the Drowned Kingdom of Ys."

"That's lovely. Ys actually existed," Gregson pointed out. "Doesn't it give you a chill to think we're sailing over a drowned land?"

Lestrade was silent as he tied up the latest line of rope and thought out his response. Not far away, the older Loseth had pulled up a fish in triumph. His good-natured grin was spoiled by a short, curt comment in dialect on part of his younger brother. With the shy abasement of a meeker man before a bolder one, the bigger man put the fish (whatever it was) into the holding barrel.

"It isn't a cheerful idea," Lestrade said at last. "But give me a chill? The lands all came from the sea at one time. The ocean's been here longer than the land we walk on. Maybe the sea just took it back one day."

"Times like this," Gregson spoke slowly, and quite softly so no one else could hear, "where I realise you've got a smuggler in your blood."

Lestrade grimaced. "I can't say I'm proud of it," he confessed. "It's like a madness. I'm never content with things. Never resting when the moon is up . . . It's on the rise now, and I can *feel* it. London's at its most alive then . . . her most bloody."

Gregson blinked as a strange revelation came to him, for that small phrase, three tiny words: "Her most bloody" had just damned his rival as a Celt like nothing else. He hadn't known there were so many differences between them, and he'd prided himself on being not only smarter than Lestrade, but also more observant.

And he still was . . . so how had he missed that?

Lestrade had risen through the ranks because of his willingness to work the worst parts of London – and his not having much family to claim made him preferred for the dangerous work. Why had he thought it was something as simple as ambition? Lestrade must have taken the East Side of London for its oceanic development. On the sea, the moon brought the tides and the sailing. On the land, the moon brought crimes and madness. And in the East End, it all came together.

"Hand me that knife, would you?" Lestrade held out his hand absently to the left while he trained the spyglass with the other. "We're about to head into the current that flows about Streat. It looks like it'll be quick now."

"One can only hope," Gregson told him.

Chapter XXV – Judas

"Gregson?"

No answer.

The voice tried again.

"There's some ginger chews."

Gregson opened one blearing eye under the watery starlight, and spared Lestrade's professionally friendly advice with the withering look he felt the runt deserved.

"No," he gasped, "thank you."

"They really do help with the sea-sickness. It isn't just a superstition." Lestrade tried again. "It's kept me from disgracing the deck every time."

"Thank you . . . *no*."

"All right then." Lestrade shrugged as if a helpless assistant wasn't a problem. "What do you think?"

Privately, Gregson groaned bile into himself. He lifted his head up to peer over the top of the black sea-boulder resting into the soft sands overlooking the elaborate cluster of small buildings and supplies. Lamps gleamed the dull, fitful flame of oils that did not have their origin in anything as clean or efficient as coal oil. Probably burning parmacetti [1] or something worse.

"That boat house . . . well . . . is that what I'm looking at?"

"Just a moment." There was a quiet snick of brass metals as Lestrade pulled his tucked-in field glass out of his pocket. "Where?"

"Ten o'clock position." Gregson closed his eyes. Beneath his cheek gouged the agony of tiny barnacle shells and the salt-stench of the sea. Somewhere in the fuss of the sea spray, a flock of gulls whined and carried on. Gregson wondered what they were on about when there were no nearby lighthouses to keep them awake at night. His mumblings conveyed as such.

"They're already stirred up because we're not the only ones landing," Patterson said from overhead. The lean man's hollow face turned to the black lump in the distance that looked like the stone manor of the baronet. "Hartley says they've been getting visitors for the past week. A few guests at a time . . . all men."

"Well, I just wonder what that means," Gregson grumbled.

"Sarcasm," Lestrade said mildly. "How long will it take to walk out of this cove and into the fringe of things?"

"Not too long." The older Loseth-Hartley again made an effort to be understandable. "A half-hour perhaps."

178

"The last time I was here, they were in a foul temper." His younger brother added. "An important guest was invited, but he couldn't attend . . . something about on a big game hunt in France."

"Must be boar," Lestrade grunted. "Well, it's one less guest to worry about and we can think of it that way." He straightened the muffler about his neck and shook the dew from his cloth cap one last time.

"You don't look but a bit peaky," Gregson said when they fell in the end of the line, Patterson leading after the older Loseth.

"If there's something important going on, and it's about Moriarty's gang . . . then Moriarty's agent will be here too. You can take that wager." Lestrade put his hands deep into his pockets so he couldn't toy with them.

"I wouldn't take that wager if a roasted goose was offered with it," Gregson shot back. "Where there's rotting carcasses, there's vultures."

"Keep your eye on Patterson," Lestrade muttered. "I think he's ill."

"There's something wrong with him," Gregson agreed.

They all fell silent by consensus. It was not completely safe to be idly talking, even if they all appeared to be fish-laden workers trying to get home at the end of the day. Rope netting creaked between the brothers, and they were all beginning to smell like scales and offal.

Streat smelled odd. It reminisced of Dartmoor with the sea on all sides. Like a tiny moor, mist rose from the earth and caught wraiths in the patches of moonlight that escaped the strange cloud curtain. It gave Gregson the impression they were far from alone, or spied upon by the dead. That led to thoughts of the bog, and the grim secrets that could be hiding under their feet.

Gregson's imagination was far from poor. Still, he knew when it could be a handicap to his work. Lestrade's lack of imagination was probably an asset in times like this, he mused gloomily. The runt merely had on his usual dogged look. Did he even think ahead to the what-ifs? So far, he only pulled out his spyglass and gave the isle its quick pass-over every minute or so.

Hartley Loseth suddenly tripped, and that quickly he sank up to his ankle in something soft. Patterson was there to support his weight as he pulled out.

"I'm sorry," the bigger man looked as sheepish as a boy caught with flowers. "I always get a little clumsy on land."

"Clumsy by nature, brother," the younger Loseth butted in.

"No harm." Patterson finished the matter in a very quiet voice.

They slowed their pace. The bogs were not nearly as shallow as some places in Britain . . . but then, how were they to know how deep they truly were? Gregson was already wishing they were back on the mainland. He would have preferred to find work in the thick of a fish market than deal with much more than this.

"Look."

Lestrade had stopped to peer at a shape that looked about like any other boat shape on the waterline. Gregson hesitated for a moment as the small man passed over his glass. He took it, careful of the fact that the glass drew light to the eye.

"That's fancy enough for a man like Quimper. Just stops short of being a pleasure craft," Lestrade muttered.

"You're right." Gregson felt his heart skip. "It's a yacht of some sort . . . but who'd have cause to bring a yacht over here unless it was a gentleman?"

"I seem to recall that when Quimper wrecked the *Hyssop* to stage his death the first time . . . The crew joked he asked for a first-class lifeboat." Lestrade's eyes flashed sparks in the worsening darkness. "But that ship . . . that thing is a bit pricey for him. He likes his quality, but . . . that's flash. The man has too much pride to show off his possessions or his wealth like that."

Patterson said it first: "Military, d'you think?"

Still, Lestrade hesitated.

Gregson answered. "Military types are supposed to demonstrate their standing, and if they don't they're a disgrace."

"We need to be *very* careful then." Patterson dropped his voice, he was so rattled. "The military is *only* the first cousin to the Foreign Office."

"I know . . . ." Gregson nodded at the patiently waiting Loseths. "Gentlemen, instead of taking us straight to the tradesmen docks, can you take us over to the finer establishment?"

Mycroft Holmes was not pleased to see the missives on his desk. He ignored them for the moment – a single glance told him just how very unearthshattering they were – and settled into the precision of his late supper.

It was not until after the stolid simplicity of his roast beef with grain mustard that he felt obligated to tend to the small stack of papers.

He selected one seemingly at random.

A moment later his eyebrows were laddering up his forehead.

Alone and with no one to witness, the big man sighed, as if the Leviathan would make such a noise, should it rise out of the Biblical depths and obey the call of its stern maker.

"These are deep waters," he thought. *"Deep and turbid. And Sherlock is not fully aware of them yet."*

180

He took the paper (its brothers forgotten) and took to the padded chair between the fireplace and the book-rimmed corner of the sitting room. Behind his head, the Shelf Clock ticked the end of another day.

For a moment, the man looked indefinably weary. He certainly did feel it.

A madman pursuing one's brother in the forests of France might be a terrible prospect for any man . . . even though he had faith that Sherlock was more than a match for him on his own ground. The problem was . . . how much of it was his own ground?

He would feel gratitude . . . much gratitude . . . once Sherlock was able to return home. But for now it was a waiting game, and to wait until he would be able to ensconce himself safely in Montpellier.

Montpellier.

Once Sherlock came to that city . . . few powers would be able to approach him.

Montpellier.

"Look, sir." Boggs Loseth nodded. "That warehouse dock there. They seem a bit interested in getting that done quick."

"So they are," Gregson grumbled. He had to concede to Loseth's sharper night vision, as well as his familiarity with what felt like every half-inch of the isle.

On the other side of the comforting shield of piled-up sacks of corn, the party of five watched the human traffic flow in and out, up the gangplank and into the depths of the yacht.

Now that they were less than twenty yards from the craft, they could see many tiny pinpoints of light against the windows. Whoever was manning the yacht . . . they did appear to be alert, if not paranoid.

"All right. Patterson, you get off to the side behind those barrels." Gregson nodded to the barrels in question. They resembled a small seawall in the way they were piled half to the sky outside the sloping warehouse. "Lestrade, I want you to cover him." Lestrade made one of his strange little smiles and put his hand over his hip-pocket where his iron was kept.

"Hartley, Boggs – stick with me and circle the other side. We're not here to arrest anyone just yet. We need to know how dangerous it is first, before the reinforcements get here."

"Reinforcements, sir?" Hartley Loseth looked taken aback. He and Boggs Loseth looked at each other. "They've got reinforcements?"

"No, *we* do. Don't ask questions. Do as you're told – "

Lestrade was turning his head to mark the slim, dark shape of Patterson slipping through the maze of dark shapes. Something happened at the corner of his eye. Hartley was lifting a gun in his hand.

181

"*Judas!*" Lestrade had time to bark, and twisted back as he reached for his own gun. There was a shot at close range, an explosion at his head . . . and silence.

"*You bastard!*"

Gregson saw Patterson's body lurch forward, like a doll's yanked forward on strings – and fall into the sea with a graceless splash.

He did not surface.

In the slow-motion of a nightmare Lestrade collapsed on his back over the pounded grey sand of the wharf. His eyes were open and unseeing into the moonlight. Trickling black liquid ran across one open eye without blinking.

He's dead, Gregson decided coldly. All evidence pointed to the fact.

Boggs Loseth was lifting his own barrel and for a slender second, that tiny barrel hole with its bottomless black centre encompassed Gregson's entire world in the fitful moonlight.

But his hand was already rising on its own volition, and the world flared outward in the flame of gunpowder and lead. Boggs stared at him in the uncomprehending surprise of a dead man, and as the detective watched, the glassy-eyed corpse slowly tilted backwards

Men were screaming.

Gregson heard them.

Men were screaming.

They were coming this way.

NOTE

1. Sperm whale oil. A mangling of pronunciation that goes back to Shakespeare. The average Victorian would have deliberately preferred parmaceti to spermaceti

Chapter XXVI – History Repeats

Ask him about it later, and Gregson would be at a loss for a decent answer.

Patterson was gone. The Loseths were traitors. He simply understood in a flash that he could not abandon Lestrade because his children and his wife would want to know the truth.

Telling them the truth was what they deserved.

They didn't deserve to know their father's partner deserted him.

He merely paused long enough to hook his arm underneath that of his comrade's body and took off running into the darkness. With a speed and agility borne of desperation, he hoisted Lestrade over a shoulder and kept on running until the dark of the thin spaces between the buildings swallowed them up.

He stopped, completely lost with the sound of the ocean lapping against the ocean. He recognized the building against his back as the warehouse once sighted from a distance.

The damnable gulls were still fussing. He risked a peek around the corner (the smell instantly improved), and saw it was deserted. Everyone had run off to where they'd just been . . . and they were no doubt fishing poor Patterson out of the drink now and getting Hartley Loseth's story.

It was then he realized Lestrade was still breathing.

A strange flush washed over his body like a tide. And he lowered the smaller man (heavy for a runt) down to the cold earth. Dark metal gleamed in the thin light of the moon, and Gregson felt his heart pause for the third time that night as he realised Lestrade's hand was still wrapped around his iron.

And the smell of hot metal and a spent bullet still came from it.

He saved my life.

Gregson could only gape. Lestrade was a blank-eyed mannikin . . . but he'd had the ability and presence of mind to aim and pull the trigger and he'd been the one to send Boggs to the afterlife.

Numb with horror, Gregson looked at his own gun (still in his hand . . . *How?*). It was still fully loaded.

I'd thought I'd pulled the trigger . . . and while I was thinking of it . . . Lestrade went and did it.

I ran half-a-mile with a man on my back, with a loaded gun in his hand . . . it could have gone off any time . . .

Gregson pondered a moment, then as carefully as possible, stretched his big body on the planks to put his hand in the lapping seawater. He shuddered to think of what might happen if he found Patterson instead.

Lestrade groaned faintly. Blood painted half his face, but he was breathing and there was no shine of bone in the graze. The bullet that killed Patterson had nearly done him in. Gregson sighed and touched a seawater-dipped handkerchief to the wound. Comprehension struggled to take flame in the runt's eyes.

"Nice cut there," Gregson noted.

"They always . . . are." Lestrade glared. "Where do we stand?"

"Patterson is dead. Hartley and Boggs got to him first. You finished Boggs off," Gregson answered coolly. "We'll be next if we don't watch it. Hartley took off behind the warehouse, and you know he's getting help"

"Bloody Hell . . . ." Lestrade blinked back another wave of hot blood in his vision. "And I felt sorry for that webfoot . . . I'll be fine . . . Scalp wounds make you bleed like a pig anyway."

"You're the expert." Gregson found half-a-cigar in his pocket and gnawed on the end in thought. He looked around, his big body a liability in the room.

"Trapped like rats," Gregson summarized with a snarl. He yanked out his own iron and took a step to the side.

"Gregson, no!" Lestrade gasped out.

The big man was already gone.

Lestrade swore despite his fatigue. He leaned to the side of the barrel and peered out the open doorway. The wharf was a maze of dark shadow and shape, masking too many things.

Gregson never had time to aim his gun. A stick cracked him atop his head and he went down to his knees on the planks. A second blow, almost a tap, finished him.

Quimper.

Lestrade felt the blood chill in his face. The agent was striding around the wall, stick raised as a bludgeon as he walked to the fallen Gregson. The detective groaned once and was still. Blood trickled at his ear.

"*Quimper!*" Lestrade shouted. It stung his throat.

The agent was surprised enough to whirl, his face twisted in a look Lestrade never wanted to see again. It was every hot emotion in one pair of eyes, all directed at him.

"*L'estrade,*" he breathed out. The blue-diamond eyes burned. Gregson was forgotten. The weighted end of the stick swung through the air, barely an inch from Gregson's skull. "You keep fine company of late. I never thought you would attach yourself to your rival."

184

Lestrade pulled himself to his feet. The tall man smiled as he watched the effort. "Get . . . away from him," he panted. *Tobias, get up!* Panic scraped inside his ribs. He wiped blood out of his eyes. "Assault on a fallen man, now, Mr. Quimper? I thought your fortunes were better."

Quimper took two steps on his long legs, stick lifted. Lestrade pushed his hand against the low wall for leverage and committed himself to a *chausson* kick. He had no particular hope in it. Quimper had the physical advantage and a head unmuddled. But the surprise must have been enough. The agent's face blanked out in shock as the small man's foot drilled into his the spot below his ribs just before his stick could knock him out of the air. He rolled to take the impact on his back and crouched in a half-kneel, left hand suspended away from his body to use it as a shield for whatever blow Quimper would send at him. His head spun like one of Nick's tops. The world spun with it, a diagonal ellipse that made it nearly impossible to triangulate on his own position.

"*Goric!*" Quimper spat in the air. A strange exhilaration shone in his eyes. He moved to a stickfighter's initial stance, both men forgetting anyone else existed in that moment, before Quimper's men ploughed into the detective from both directions.

Oh, damn.

Lestrade fought for his life. There were far too many, but he'd been outnumbered before. And if he wanted to see Clea and Martin and Nick again . . . he had to.

Gregson had been bound in his own bracelets and thrown atop sacks of buckwheat. He was furious that Quimper had managed to knock the wind out of his sails so well.

They weren't watching him. Their attention was all on Lestrade – as well as they should, Gregson had to admit. He was fighting like the End Days. Gregson dearly wished he could kill him himself. He *could* have taken his chance and ran for his own skin instead of staying back and distracting Quimper's bloody great stick.

They were both dead. But he had to grin at the sight of Lestrade freeing his arm just long enough to uppercut an assailant. The stroke let him twist his body and kick another man in the guts just as he'd done that wretched Quimper. Lestrade never saw the point in "fighting fair" in a *real* situation. He had that in common with his in-laws, though he'd die to admit it.

"Enough, gentlemen!" Quimper lifted his voice wearily – a fight instructor who had hoped for better. "There are *four* of you, *Perhaps* if each man grabbed a limb?"

Gregson had to give the bastard points for being man enough to humiliate a pack of seedy garrotters like this. Chagrined, they moved to obey and Lestrade went under a pile of filthy men.

Jethro Quimper stopped a safe distance from it all to light one of his long cigarettes – they were expensive enough for Gregson to call them effete. There was a grunt as Lestrade scored one last point into someone's throat, and the agent exhaled pale smoke through his nostrils.

"Ask them if they know how to fight, and they always say yes," he commented under his breath. "At least when I bribe a policeman, I *know* what I'm getting in a battle." He adjusted the brim of his hat with fastidious attention.

It was an awful moment in his brain, but that neat-and-clean movement made Gregson think of Lestrade. Perhaps their common blood? What an unsavoury possibility.

Had Lestrade known in the beginning, Gregson doubted he would have ever applied for Clea's hand – her hatred of Quimper and everything he stood for knew no bounds. Just as well ignorance could do a man good . . . Lestrade was a man who would do nothing against the truth, and Quimper was the sort who'd find every drop of blood they had in common and personally carve it out of him.

Those light blue eyes lifted up, and the long hands closed again around his walking stick in a fighting motion. The fine mouth set in determination. He took a step to the dwindling scrum.

"Nice job," Gregson said with the unused sarcasm as he'd built up over the course of the week. He smirked as Quimper shot him a glare. "Just admiring your technique, Mr. Quimper. Or is that still your name?"

The agent was already cooling off. Holding the upper hand was the way he sat in the world. He bounced his stick on the floor, close to Lestrade's face.

"Pardon me for not swooning," Gregson mocked, "But I'm sure my astonishment knows no bounds to see Lestrade got the better of you like that – and so swiftly, too. Was that a mistake? Maybe you could duplicate the experiment?"

Almost . . . too far. Quimper's face was hot and white.

And then it smoothed over, cool and careful. A leer twisted his lips and he tapped the small man in the sternum with the point of his stick.

"Next time, Geoff, you need to take it easy on the poor man." Gregson twisted the knife.

"Gregson, stick a cork!" Lestrade strangled furiously. The stick shot out, slapping him in the face, very lightly. A clear warning. Blood slid across his eye and he blinked, trying to whip it out. He was hauled to his feet by the same fish-reeking hands and held immobile.

186

"Well, what are we going to do with you two?" Quimper had reverted to his old amused-at-the-world's-foibles guise. A single eyebrow went up and he took in his men. "Just when we were ordered not to kill anyone else," he marveled dryly. "The Almighty and His sense of timing. I never cease to be amazed." He leaned on his stick a moment, and paused, reached to his chest to rub it thoughtfully.

"Sod that, you *jangler!*" If Quimper could call Lestrade a changeling dwarf, Lestrade could call Quimper a court jester. "Where's Dr. Watson!"

Quimper's face slipped from its hard-earned control. Astonishment was beneath the mask. "Who told you about the doctor?" he retorted sharply. Ice-chip eyes slitted in anger that Lestrade only partially understood – Quimper was a showman as much as the late Sherlock Holmes, and Lestrade had accidentally upstaged his show.

Jangler indeed. Perhaps that was the right thing to call him after all . . .

"L'estrade . . . ." Quimper stamped to the detective. The end of his stick pushed his head up to stare into the taller man's eyes. "I asked you," he hissed, grabbing him by the hair to freeze his gaze in place, "a *question*. A *sensible, simple* question." Breathing hard, inches from Lestrade's own eyes, he was furious. Lestrade hadn't thought him capable of such an emotion.

"No one told us," Lestrade snapped back, as scornful as he could manage.

"You expect me to believe that?" Quimper tightened his grip.

"It isn't calculus, Mr. Quimper." Lestrade had never thought so quickly in his entire life. "You drown people. You're a part of the Professor's original gang. You chose Watson because he was an enemy, and his crippled leg would fit the profile of a bog man."

Astonishment wiped the agent's face clean before he recovered himself. He breathed heavily, eyes slowly shrinking back from their dilation of fury.

He grew terribly calm.

The calm, oily fox.

"Congratulations, L'estrade . . . Oh, you're mostly right." Quimper said softly. He stood practically against the smaller man, and his voice turned to a silken purr. "Dr. Watson is one of our enemies and needs to be taken care of, and he *does* fit the profile of being one of our bog men. Its true, and that may even be the fate chosen for him." He smiled and his hand, light as a caress, slipped against the back of Lestrade's neck. "But that was John Clay's idea to use Watson." Quimper gently pulled his head backwards, lowered his own head until his whispered breath rolled against

187

the detective's exposed throat. "But *I* didn't nominate him to be the crippled sacrifice, L'estrade. I named *you*."

The reek was terrible. It was so thick inside his nostrils it rang.

With the shifting of the tide, things were left behind on the shingle and the flat pools of the northern coast: Seawrack rotted with small sea-things – things with legs, and things that gasped pale and drawn in the moonlight. And he had no choice but to run over them, knowing that they would have all lived had they the choice . . . but that choice was gone. The boy who knew an aesthetic for a father with his prayers and his books was separate from the focused and hard-edged men he admired with the Guelphic Badge inside their breast pockets.

Inspector Hopkins had never ran so hard, nor so fast for so long in his entire life. Nor had his senses had ever been so sharpened by fear and necessity. The sea that roared about him was no louder than the ocean-pounding reef inside his ears. And yet it must have been the horror of the moment guiding him, for he never once stumbled upon the uneven ground that cast long black shadows under the flimsy moon.

"Hold on!" He shouted with what air was left in his lungs, and he kept running even though his lungs were drained and the wind cast his voice far behind his shoulders where it could do the least good. "I'm coming! Hold on!"

He got to the weakly floundering man in time, flipped him over with hands that began to numb as soon as it struck the cold of the sea. Salt water sprayed on his face as Patterson, who looked more like a dead man than half the corpses Hopkins had seen in the morgue, choked, and then spewed. As quickly as he'd pulled the man out of the shallow water, Hopkins turned him back over and let him relieve his lungs of the materials in his lungs. Blood gleamed on the man's large hands. He'd cut them to ribbons on the sharp rock and corals in his attempt to hang on to dry land.

Exhausted of strength, Patterson's eyes rolled back in his head. Hopkins saw the gleam of his whites like milk-glass marbles, and then he pitched into a dead faint.

"Thank God," Hopkins panted as the familiar shape blocked the nocturnal sun. "Give me a hand . . . please, Mr. Loseth. I don't think I can do this alone."

Chapter XXVII – Matched

They were thrown, still cuffed, into a frigid stone room that was all too clearly used as some sort of holding cell. Gregson sank against the loose pile of straw that had burst from a ticking-mattress by the wall across the door and grunted as he slowly moved his cuffed wrists down, and finally, over his feet. Once his hands were in front of him, he breathed a sigh of relief.

"What the sodding Sam Hill was all that about?" were Lestrade's first words after his head finally stopped spinning.

Gregson did not answer directly. "For the love of God, Lestrade. You've *got* to stop answering those letters to that Pinkerton Yank. He thinks he's bloody Mark Twain."

"Don't change the bloody question," Lestrade hissed. "What were you trying to do – *give him tips?*"

"Had to do it," Gregson whispered back in the darkness. "He was going to kill you right then and there, you dupe."

"And it is a *good thing* that you reminded him that he prefers to kill me slowly as possible?" Lestrade was furious enough to kill Gregson himself – if only one could be killed more than once – but he was wondering if there'd been something to the graze at his skull that led him to miss some important detail.

"We need *time*. It was the only thing I could do," Gregson grumbled. Or mumbled. He wouldn't look at him.

"You were very sure this would happen," Lestrade shot back. He was still furious – and afraid.

"He's a part of this cult, Geoffrey," Gregson grunted as he hefted his heavy body to an upright position. It was slightly less uncomfortable than before. "Seems to me they operate on fear and torture. It would be just like the bastard to add us to the list and get rid of two problems at once." He sighed in relief as his head rested against the wall. "If we can get back to the warehouse, we can get back to your gun. I put it down and it wound up in that corner by the corn sacks in the tussle . . . *Damn*, I want a drink."

Lestrade lowered his head, thinking. He didn't know what ached the worse: Their bodies or their defeat. Both felt capable of killing them.

Gregson's eyes had slipped half-shut. He heard the slight rustle as Lestrade climbed stiffly to his feet and went to the door. "Now what?" Paranoia coloured his voice. "Lestrade, don't do anything stupid."

"Years too late for that," the smaller man said. "Just . . . follow my lead. When you're better, *then* you can quarrel it out with me, but until

189

then . . . shut it." He faced the door and hammered it with his fist until it yanked open. Lestrade took a hasty step backwards out of the easy range of the truncheon. The owner was missing an eye. Over the dark brown eyepatch was painted an Eastern star symbol of some sort. Lestrade hoped dearly the man wasn't a Freemason. He already had enough of *them* angry at him.

"Tell Mr. Quimper if he wants information, we'll have to talk." The detective did not give him a chance to demand. "That's all you have to say."

The guard was rattled, but his automatic response – a sneer – was comforting. It meant he was confident and felt himself in control. That sort of man could be easy to goad. "What if I don't feel like tellin' him?" he shot back – the accent was pure smuggler. Even conglomeration of inflections and tones absorbed from all over the world. That meant he'd done a lot of work for Quimper. That meant he knew something of the man's mettle.

"Then I'll be a good lad and wait until I see him again," Lestrade shot back. "And I'll be sure to tell him his news was delayed."

The guard was not lacking sense. He narrowed the one eye he had left and took a cautious half-step backwards, nodding to someone in the hall Lestrade couldn't see. The results were faster than he'd expected. A wiry tall man built along the lines of a python grabbed him by the upper arm and propelled him out. The door clanged shut behind him.

Two of the men from the warehouse were playing a game of cards against a table when he was pushed in. Their guns were resting politely by the deck. An unspoken advertisement against making trouble. One was so thin he was unnerving to look at. Lestrade looked at Quimper instead.

Quimper was standing by the fire, warming his hands. He'd changed clothing and even had a fresh flower at his *boutonniere*. Lestrade's eyes were drawn to those hands.

They were the hands of an aging man.

The agent turned with casual interest, eyebrows sliding upwards to his re-combed hair. "Information, did you say?" The voice was as mild as ever, but it was the low glitter beneath that was as frightening as ever.

"An uninterrupted conversation might benefit both of us, Mr. Quimper." Privately, Lestrade wondered who he thought he was, to use words better suited to the gentleman's station than his own.

Surprisingly, Quimper dipped his head down at his shoetips, a smile lighting his face. The honesty of the humour startled and unsettled the detective, for in that moment the man was genuinely handsome and charismatic. Lestrade did not stomach such impressions from someone he hated so much. "We may as well sit, then," he said carefully. "Let your poor friend have his rest."

With a wary eye to the guard at the doorway, Lestrade complied.

"Now, let's get the initial greetings over with." Quimper crossed to the table, but remained standing for now, his stick again in his hands. "First we talk about how much we hate each other. I'll begin the process." He took a deep breath, still smiling. "You're an unintelligent, unimaginative, plodding fool, and your only nobility comes from your mother's blood. A shame it wasn't thicker."

Lestrade swallowed hard. "I'm set with being an unintelligent, unimaginative, plodding fool if it means I'm the unintelligent, unimaginative, plodding fool that's beaten you for so many years." Quimper's face flickered like heat lightning. "Did you think I would always speak to you discreetly?" the little man demanded. "Perhaps you should *use* your intelligent imagination to think of what I've been saving up on your behalf for forty years."

It took a long moment, but Quimper made a soft sound of amusement. "Very true," he said. The gleams in his eyes were back – that cold blue glacial lights – and Lestrade was glad for it. It meant the gloves were off and they could actually *begin*.

"I think you've sunk in the world," Lestrade gritted his teeth. "I never liked you, Quimper, but I could justify *respecting* a man who was a *professional*."

"I am still quite professional. I have merely learned to enjoy life more." The agent suddenly smiled, used his stick to push Lestrade's head back, exposing his neck. "Just as you have. You enjoy your lovely wife, and I enjoy attending to loose ends."

Lestrade's dark eyes turned black at the reference to Clea. They stared into each other's face. She hadn't been the cause of their enmity, but she had been the catalyst of their most personal conflict.

"*Where* is Dr. Watson?" Lestrade demanded, voice soft but intense. "What in God's name is your business with a man who is still *in mourning for his entire and only family*?"

"Ah." Quimper exaggerated a look of regret. "That *is* uncouth, I know. Not tasteful at all. But it isn't as though time and tide waits for a man . . . you should know that." He shook his head as if he was a school-master facing a promising but unfinished pupil. "I don't have him. It had been in our plans, and I'm impressed the Yard was able to divine that. But, no . . . ." The tall man shrugged, *ca va*. "We were unfortunately intercepted during a crucial moment in our project. He is currently out of our hands . . . but that should be changing very soon."

191

Lestrade felt his throat constrict. "So the rumor-mill was right for once." He managed not to talk through his teeth. Quimper would see that as weakness.

Quimper tilted his head. "A rather broad statement . . . In what way?"

"Trouble in paradise . . . 'The more cowherds, the worse the herd.'" Lestrade used the Breton quote. "Organized crime in London has grown . . . *unstable* of late. If that isn't an indication of restlessness among Moriarty's Empire, I wouldn't know what to call it."

Quimper pondered that, giving his due, and lifted a shoulder in a gesture that was not quite a shrug. It was almost an opinion. He lowered himself gracefully to the other side of the small table and poured out two tiny glasses.

"I'm afraid your friend has become an inadvertent symbol for the unification of the broken Family, L'estrade. We both need him, you see." He smiled very slightly and pushed the nearest glass to the other man. "For the part of my superiors, the presence of John Watson would confirm or deny the rumours of Mr. Sherlock Holmes's alleged death."

"'Alleged'?" Lestrade wasn't ashamed that his mouth had fallen open. "Are you certain you should be calling them your *superiors*? If Sherlock Holmes was alive, wouldn't we all know it?"

Quimper snickered, in agreement with Lestrade's assessment of his employers. "It all boils down to one particular fact, L'estrade: *The body was never discovered*. No body, no evidence of the crime, *nann?* Unusual amount of rainfall, very high volume of water . . . but the pool of water at the bottom is comparatively small. Did you know Dr. Watson searched the water personally and failed to find a thing?"

Lestrade hated to think of Watson scraping his hands raw in his increasingly desperate attempts.

"By that argument, the Professor could be alive too," he shot back.

"Possibly, but the two aren't completely parallel, *ma enebour*." Quimper knocked back his drink and set the empty glass on the scarred wood with a bang. "There is the world of the law, which you reside in – to all appearances sunny and well-lit for even and clean lines of behavior. And then there is the world outside it that all men and women of power reside in. This the world where much can be accomplished . . . so long as the world of Rules doesn't catch on to what is really going on. One can hide from the law, but it can be much more difficult to hide from that shadowy floating world. Frankly, the *only* lure to that world is the power that can be wielded inside it." The agent smiled in a self-contemplative fashion. "I shan't inflict my philosophy on you – suffice to say, unique men have the ability to live in both worlds. Sherlock Holmes was one of those men. He could have fit in with either, but he committed to the unforgivable choice of walking as he pleased on both sides. All for the sake of his Art, to be sure . . . but the consequences . . . ." He poured another glass for himself and tapped the untouched one. "I don't discourse sober in *this* day and age," he chided. "Nor do I recommend it to anyone."

Lestrade sighed. "Wouldn't it be easier just to tell me to drink?"

Quimper snorted. "Which just hammers home the differences between the two of us. If you didn't *look* a Potier, I'd *swear* you were Thomas Lestrade grown from a graft."

Lestrade could not hide his flinch at being compared to his father. *No less than what I deserve for challenging him* . . . He picked up the glass with his manacled hand and sardonically lifted it. "Yec'hed mat." It went down like a rusty razor. "Well, the plan's all well and good, but wouldn't Dr. Watson have been better lure several years ago? Such as . . . *before* he was married and was still lodging with Mr. Holmes?"

"*I'm* not the one who makes these policies." Quimper all but agreed with Lestrade. "The problem was a common one . . . One of the Professor's advisors was completely against it . . . held it would draw too many outside interests in." The agent leaned back in his chair, eyes gleaming. "Have you figured it out?"

"Other than certain parties must have underestimated him the way people tend to do?" Lestrade had only taken half the drink in the hopes that Quimper wouldn't instantly refill the glass.

"Very good." Quimper clapped. "Yes, they did. The only one who knew him on any level was the Professor's brother. And the Moriartys were that close sort of sibling that never felt the urge to confide in each other with any particular depth." The tall man smirked coldly. Armoricus floated between them. "I can't say I have any proof, but it does seem as though the Colonel Moriarty had unfinished business with your doctor-friend. He did refer to 'the War' with alarming frequently in my presence."

Lestrade could not hide his grimace. "I'd be disappointed if it were that simple," he said coolly. "Do you have *any* idea how many *dial-killings* from various wars we clean up after?"

"Probably more than I pay for," Quimper answered quickly. "But you see, they have need for him. And I have a few friendly obligations with Mr. Clay that needs returning."

John Clay. A name to the opposing forces against Moriarty. "Such as helping you get out of Plymouth after you beat your own father to death." Lestrade risked the same fate by even bringing it up.

The blue eyes sparkled without humour. "So you figured that out. You must be ripening in your old age."

"If you're going to kill someone, Quimper, get rid of your toothbrush as a gentleman ought to first."

Quimper blinked, momentarily puzzled, but Lestrade watched awareness fill up the blankness.

"Ah. I wondered . . . So where is your father now, Lestrade? I hear someone smuggled him out of Plymouth along unusual lines."

"He's as free as a man driven mad can be," Lestrade retorted. "And beyond your grip." He shook his head. "I knew you had a taste for cruelty, Quimper. I didn't know you'd indulged yourself so deeply."

"Indulge?" Quimper looked insulted. He tapped his stick against Lestrade's head, light as a feather, utterly controlled. Only Lestrade's stubbornness kept him from reaching up, yanking the stick out of his hands, and pounding him with it. "You wound me," he said softly. "This is no 'indulgence'. This is 'business that I happen to enjoy'." He smiled. "Those are hardly sacrificial victims, L'estrade. Those men dug out of the bog were members of our own cult."

"Your cult is only about control," Lestrade snapped.

"Of course. No one wants to admit they were involved in human sacrifice, does one? They're willing to do anything one requires in comparison."

"I can't see why it works."

"The contestants are each . . . shall we say . . . men who have failed their Family in some unfortunate way. They are given the option of salvaging their standing . . . not to mention their pitiful lives . . . by risking their necks one last time in the ring. If they win, their side wins the point we're debating over . . . and they remain in the gang with a higher status than before. But if they lose . . . well, most of them take the drink before they even see the bog."

"And somehow, Dr. Watson is the bone of contention between the two of you."

"Exactly. Ironically, he damaged our cause a bit when he shot one of our better fighters . . . Had he been whole, the brute would have been fighting for his behalf in the ring. It's come down to settling it with fists again . . . the two sides of the split factions, having it out like 'gentlemen'," Quimper's voice held worlds of sarcasm. "To solve the problem. The outcome's probably already decided on . . . but we must go through the formalities, mustn't we? And I must find a man to replace one of our best fighters."

"Set the match."

Quimper paused. "What did you just say?"

"You named your price," Lestrade said coldly. "You said you tapped me. Well?"

Quimper fell silent, but his eyes were active.

"You named your price," the detective repeated. "Set up your match."

194

"Why," Quimper said slowly, "Would you say such a thing to me, L'estrade?"

"Because all of us will die." Lestrade's heart was pounding so hard he wondered if Quimper could hear it from across the table. "Today to me, tomorrow to thee. Isn't that on enough of our tombstones?" He kept his hands still on the table's surface. "Or has it been too long, *Aotrou Kemper?*"

"Too long?" Quimper repeated softly. His eyes failed to blink. "And I am supposed to agree to your madness?"

"I think you will. You want Dr. Watson back."

"And you'd fight to see him come back into our hands? I'm not convinced."

Lestrade couldn't stand the blood anymore. He wiped it off on his shoulder. "*Enough.*" His eyes sank inside Quimper's as if he could kill him that way. "I'll fight for you, Mr. Quimper, if that means Gregson survives."

"He'll survive as long as you survive," Quimper pointed out, plainly skeptical. "Have you *actually* thought this through?"

"I'm wondering the same thing myself," Lestrade shot back. "It isn't like you to turn down an opportunity." Gregson wasn't the only one who could twist a knife. "How often do you get a policeman in your ring? I'm thinking it would be popular."

Quimper smirked. 'No, it isn't . . . ." The smirk became a grin. "As you say . . . popular. Plenty of my boys have a personal *kaz* against your kind."

"You once wanted me to be one of your boys," Lestrade taunted. "I wonder . . . is it worth the waiting?"

"It's too dangerous," the skeletal-thin man protested. "He's a copper! It's risking everything just for the pleasure of watching him get killed in the ring!"

"Dangerous?" Quimper repeated coldly. His eyes were hot. "You've never risked a thing in your life, Bosco. Has it ever occurred to you that risks are *worth* taking?" The cool blue-diamond eyes raked him up and down. "An end to it, L'estrade? Once and for all? Just to extend the life of your rival?" Quimper rested his arms across his chest. "That isn't much to my thinking."

"I'm willing to bargain for higher stakes," Lestrade pointed out. "I'll fight to keep him alive, but if you honestly want to see *something* for your blood-sport, then you promise me you'll leave Clea and her children alone, whether or not I win or lose."

195

And there it was. Lestrade had opened the chasm between them. He wouldn't refer to them as his wife and his children. He had to remind Quimper that Clea was a woman he had once fancied to love.

"And why should I?" Quimper answered calmly. 'Convince me why I would even want to."

"Because all your life, *you've wanted this.*" Lestrade slowly tapped the floor with his twisted foot. Drawing Quimper's eye to the once-broken bone. "You hunted me when we were both children, and I escaped. You pitted my own brothers against me – one is dead, the other worthless. I survived. You spent years on building an elaborate trap that would have forced me to work for you, and I never fell into it."

Lestrade stood up at that point, and took a single step to the agent, ignoring the way the other men stiffened up. It was only the two of them in the room now. Quimper ignored them just as exclusively. "1891, *Kemper.* You set the Wild Hunt on me again, and I *still* escaped you. How's your *hand*, I wonder? Dog bites can hurt like the devil and wound forever. I can sympathize . . . ."

Quimper was developing a dangerous flush, starting at the collarbone of his open collar and spreading upward like a water stain. Lestrade pushed one last time:

"We've been at this since childhood, Quimper. You've had a better life than I have. Policemen wear down, it's true. They burn out like matches. I don't have much longer before I'll be set out to pasture. But . . . for all your privilege . . . you *are* older than I am. How much longer do you think you can keep up your part?" Lestrade's smile was goading. It struck. It struck a nerve right there in front of him.

"Then you will fight." Quimper's face had stopped being human. Its features and calcified into something glass-eyed without expression. The look of a man who will not spook his quarry now that it had gotten close enough to grab it. "You will fight, and I will watch you die."

Chapter XXVIII – Fighting Chance

Patterson was like dragging out a man who was already dead. He hung limp in his soaking wet clothes as Hopkins pulled with all his considerable strength. The wool coat wasn't so bad while in the water, but once he was out it turned to lead.

The young man grunted, panic sweating his brow. *I can't get him out*, he realised, just as sand gave way like quicksand. A reek of black water and rotting plants filled the inspector's nostrils and he gagged, feeling them both sink into a chilly froth up to his waist.

"Hold on – ! Hold on, sair! Nereabouts there!"

Hartley Loseth tucked a large-looking gun into his coat pocket and pulled on the other side. Hopkins didn't catch on at first, but the big fisherman was trying to work with tears running down his face.

"Loseth? Where are the rest?"

"Na yit, sair." Loseth sniffed loudly. He looked too-ready to start bawling, but his face was turning numb and set.

Patterson's return to the land of the living was marked with a choked scream of agony as Hopkins tried to maneuver him by lifting him under the arms. Seawater wasn't as sticky as what was beneath his left hand. Hopkins gnashed his teeth and apologized as quickly as he could. Loseth pulled from the other end and Patterson tried to hold back a scream and fainted from the effort. His weight seemed to double.

"Dear Heaven, man, how did he get shot? He was right there with Gregson and Lestrade!"

"Caught by Sir Niles' mon," Loseth answered miserably. He added almost in an afterthought, "Boggs is dead." He sank down on the wet sand next to Patterson and put his head in his hands. "Me brither dead . . . I waar im not ta . . . Whitna steer we be in," the fisherman observed dully. "An hiddlc bc gin waar the night."

"Your brother is dead?" Hopkins' quick mind whirled. A mess they were in, indeed. Behind him a fourth figure lurched over the slim horizon. A large man with a peaked cap. *Finally!*

"Thought tae shoot the Inspector. But he was shot instead." Hartley nodded, the picture of biblical torment. "I waar im. Too mony deaths. I waar him."

"Hartley . . . if you're going to betray me and a wounded man, I advise you to think instead about getting up and taking a walk in – " Hopkins pulled back the hammer of his gun. " – that direction behind you, and staying put on the other side of this wretched isle until we've cleaned it all up!" He heard the shake of fury in his panting voice and hoped it stood for sincerity.

"He's telling the truth, Hopkins," Bradstreet answered heavily. "I saw the whole thing from the rendezvous. Boggs shot Patterson and I thought he'd gotten Lestrade too . . . but later I saw him and Gregson bein' marched to the stone warehouse under their own power." He shook his head. "It was a near thing. I didn't think Patterson would even be alive, the way he fell into the water."

He sank to one knee and put his hand on the man's cold, wet throat. "His pulse isn't too bad," was the confirmation. "We need to get him into a place where we can shine a light."

"There's a netting shack just up the cove." Hartley Loseth blew his nose, sailor-fashion into the sand. "Ha'f-sunk t'the sands."

"Are you certain about this?" Hopkins looked straight at the Runner and ignored Loseth.

"Na worry." Loseth answered in the voice of a man who is hurt too deeply to recover. "I wi' na stay." He climbed to his feet, the scraps of moonlight making silver in his cheeks and grizzled beard. "I waar im," he said. "But he noo listen. He the favor son."

Hopkins was upset, frightened for Patterson, terrified for Gregson and Lestrade as the case collapsed around his ears . . . but there was still room in his heart for pity to watch the broken-down old fisherman lurch across the rolling land to the far side of the shore.

"Damn," he whispered.

"Damn fathers who pick sides with their own offspring," Bradstreet answered without a pause. "I saw the shack in question . . . We can't even see about his bleeding until we get him to a safeway."

"Let's go."

"He's changed."

Gregson had nearly fallen asleep from that deadly mix of exhaustion, frustration, and boredom. Lestrade's low voice instantly snapped him out of it.

The big man sat up, the mattress crackling underneath. Lestrade hadn't moved a jot since sinking down into the corner by the moonlight.

Gregson watched, unsure if Lestrade had fallen asleep in his sitting position, he was so still. Steam from his breath coiled in the cool sea air.

"He was always a cruel man. He was a cruel boy." Lestrade began again metronomically, as if his thoughts could only be conjured in a neat order. "His father taught him well. They taught my brother how to be like they were." Silence. "They were teaching Paul. We weren't anything to them but manikins." More silence. "But he was always . . . he was the master of his desires, Gregson. *Always*. Business first, then pleasure." Lestrade lowered his head slightly. "Always."

"But he does seem to have changed," Gregson pointed out. "He's not the coldly controlled man he used to be."

"That night at Beckett's . . . ." Lestrade looked into his hands. "I saw his face when he was beating me . . . and then drowning me in that pond. I could see how much he enjoyed it . . . and . . . I could see that he was surprised at himself."

"It's a dark thing to learn." Gregson wished for a smoke. "Most men can't face that."

"I think he did face that," Lestrade murmured. "But I also think . . . that after so many years of only *controlling* his desires, he wasn't prepared for them to come out. It was like . . . he looked like a man in the grip of drink."

"And he's still drinking."

"Yes."

Gregson didn't think Lestrade had seen the way the agent had looked. The man hadn't seemed to be all that sane when he was at that unguarded first moment . . . then he buried that light of madness in his eyes, but still
. . . .

Gregson sought for something to snap Lestrade out of his mood. "Well, I suppose I shouldn't be surprised that you could get under his skin like that. Lord knows, you've got a talent."

"Ha." Lestrade made a fake laugh. "You'll have your chance, Tobias. It's not much but it's a chance. Get Watson while I'm keeping them busy."

Gregson nodded in the moonlight. Outside the wharf rats were running back and forth, barking orders and swearing at freight. "Looks like we're about to ride to the fancy side of Streat," he murmured.

"I'm going to get some sleep." Lestrade sank down into an acceptable spot. "Lord knows I'm going to need it."

"Before you do," Gregson cleared his throat. "Is there anything you might want to pass on to me about . . . the others?"

Lestrade was silent again, slowly thinking. "No . . . nothing comes to mind . . . yet."

"As you say." Gregson accepted it with a nod. Every man had their secrets. In the Yard, secrets weren't supposed to be kept. But they all did.

If things went too poorly, he knew Lestrade would pull out whatever card he was nursing close to his chest.

The shack was awful.

Small insects and not-so-small cousins scurried out of the light of the bull's eye Bradstreet half-buried in the sand to further hide the illumination. Patterson's own coat had to suffice for a wet tarpaulin.

Bradstreet took over like the much-experienced old officer he was. Hopkins wasn't ashamed to admit he was grateful. Only actual practice could give him the level of skill Bradstreet had.

"Bullet went through," he said. "But that's not the half of it. Looks like a rib's cracked through, and some of the threads in the hole . . . we need a surgeon to get them out. Inflammation's going to set in and I can't stop it other than – " He splashed his flask into the oozing dark spot in Patterson's white skin and the unconscious man moaned without waking up. "He's out because of the pain. That's a mercy."

Hopkins agonized over his uselessness. "I don't know what to do."

"Field work, Hopkins." Bradstreet did not scorn to call the much-younger man "lad". He'd made the grade and that made him equal. "As bad as he's hurt . . . ." He took a tiny sip for himself against the chill. "We've got less'n a week to get Watson, that's for sure. Patterson can't live for long like this."

"Now what?" Hopkins pulled out his own flask (his teeth were starting to clatter), and put his back up against a large drift of sand inside the shack. Sand was everywhere. It was no more than a shell of wood and disjointed, half-hearted attempts to do something against the wind and rains.

"We need to wait," Bradstreet chewed on his mouth. "Wait a bit further. Where they got the others . . . they'll be moving them soon enough." He shrugged out of his coat and made a blanket for the wounded man. "If they do anything, it'll be before dawn. So we need to just be patient."

Hopkins nodded in the darkness and breathed a bit easier as Bradstreet flipped the lid on the lantern, bathing them in gloom that would at least shelter them from prying eyes.

And Patterson was still breathing.

He was still breathing.

That was good.

Hopkins also sacrificed his damp coat to wrap about Patterson – it was wool and he would be unlikely to freeze with it – but now his own teeth chattered loudly over the sound of the surf, and if it were possible to curl against the soaking-wet inspector . . . well, he would have.

He even thought about it is a few times, but nothing could overwhelm the misery of being wet on a night on the rocky shores of Streat.

Bradstreet was at least dry . . . .

200

"Oh, no." Bradstreet was sitting up like an alert hound. Hopkins followed suit. "Get your glass," he hissed. "There's some people headin' down the surf."

Hopkins threw himself on his stomach and squeezed his vision between the eyepiece of his field glass and a crack in the shack boards. Bradstreet was already there, muttering under his breath.

The foggy night made it hard to see – damn near impossible – until the sound of crunching footfalls grew close. Hopkins counted three figures in the mist. Four. Four became six. A few of them were talking amongst each other. Disgruntled, complaining, and earnest. The last one had a voice that rang as clear as a bell in the night:

"You might at least recall the loan of a man's cigarette case, Georges."

Hopkins gasped. Bradstreet slapped his hand over his mouth.

"Sorry about that, sir." A thick-set man with a rough voice turned. The group paused and a long metallic object was passed forth.

"You're being paid well enough for this night, my good fellow. I would hope you remember that."

"Yes, sir, Mr. Holmes."

The tall, lean owner of the voice paused as he took his possession back, and lifted his head into the night sky . . . In the dark of the crevice, they could see his nostrils flaring as if caught upon a scent.

Stunned, the inspectors were quite incapable of movement.

Cigarette lit off a match, the tall man nodded in satisfaction, and the group continued on its way.

They waited without moving – and precious little breathing – as the men continued down the coastline to the small bastion of civilization for the Isle of Streat.

"Roger – " Hopkins licked his lips. " – am I going mad?"

"If so," Bradstreet answered hoarsely, "then it's catching."

"Is he under cover, like Patterson was?" A hundred questions were crowding in at once. A thousand. The young man swallowed hard, trying to sort at least one out. "Patterson survived undercover for years – What if Mr. Holmes was – "

"Easy off." Bradstreet spoke not ungently, but his manner was firm. "We don't know what we just saw, Hopkins. "We saw a tall, skinny man with a less-than-humble attitude in the worst possible light conditions, who appears to be going by the name of Mr. Holmes. We didn't hear 'Sherlock Holmes', nor did we hear or see anything else. And that's what we'd have to say in court."

"Dear God," Hopkins breathed. "We're in the middle of a snake pit. How are we going to rescue the doctor – and Lestrade and Gregson – and Patterson? It would take a Sherlock Holmes!"

"We can't say we've got one. What we've got is the two of us, and somewhere, not far from Dr. Watson, there's two more of us. That's four. And including Watson . . . we've all got a fighting chance. That's what we have to work with."

Chapter XXIX – Matchmaking

Someone dropped a metal *something* outside the locked door. The ringing aftershocks rivaled the Bow Street chimes in the stone walls.

Lestrade groaned and moved stiffly to an upright position as Gregson swore a series of choice opinions from the makeshift mattress. He felt as filthy as a night in Lambeth. Before the flood controls. His clothes hung on him with the damp, spiritless contagion of the night before, and the voiceless contempt of their stone walls had sunk into his very marrow.

He reached up and felt the blood from his head to his clothing had dried, which meant it would only be harder to get out.

Lovely. He blinked against the heavy pull of his lids and grudgingly admitted that he was in need of a shave.

Gregson had found uninvited sub-lettors. "Good night!" The tow-headed man exclaimed with a slap.

"Sleep tight?" Lestrade asked with enough sarcasm to corrode iron ore. For a pipe and a dare, he would have struck Gregson down at that moment. It was probably because what had been an impulsive act of charity in the dead of night now appeared to be a sign of incurable insanity in the light of day.

"And pleasant dreams to *you*," Gregson sniffed. He slapped at another offending insect.

"Don't do that. You'll kill the poor little things, and then they won't be able to jump on our hosts."

"You ninnyhammer, when we get out of this, I swear . . . ." Gregson shut his teeth at the sound of footsteps and took a prudent step back as the door rattled open.

It was the pilgarlic of last night, and his one good eye glared at them no less fiercely than the savage star painted over his missing eye's socket. He looked at Lestrade, then Gregson, and then back to Lestrade a second time, as if trying to calculate how much poundage in raw meat he'd get off both men if he took them to the butcher's before noon.

Already Tenderized.

Lestrade decided that he would give Gregson an easy go of it, and take up the one-eyed marvel instead . . . if he had the chance. The large, square-shaped men behind the pilgarlic reduced the odds of that quickly happening.

They were pulled outside. The encroaching dawn shocked them both for its abrupt change in air and temperature. The salt breeze caught the cobwebs in Lestrade's mind and pulled. A few even tore away. He lifted his head and breathed in, deeply, as if communing. There was precious little time for that during the false dawn. Someone with large, hard hands grabbed his upper arm and steered him off to the edge of the little fishing wall where they were completely ignored.

Lestrade caught on that their escorts were wearing constable uniforms. *Well, that just might have something to do with it . . . .*

"Move along, you."

"Watch yourself, Constable," Gregson snapped – purely in the interest of starting trouble, Lestrade decided.

"You deaf? I said move along."

"Hopkins, don't move."

Inspector Hopkins wouldn't have moved if his badge depended on it. Bradstreet's gravelly voice had slid into his fitfully dozing ear like a rockslide, rousing him to a state that was alert, pensive, and immobile.

When a voice like Bradstreet's came across a man like that, it behooved a man not to blink, open his eyes, or even think.

So there he lay, stiff as a board with his own blood pounding an orchestra of distraction in his eardrums as something was going on . . . something he was ignorant of.

The young inspector was forced by circumstance to seek information any way he could.

He was warm – uncommonly so for the weather and their makeshift shelter. Sand was beneath him, and his ears caught the faint whistle of wind scraping against narrow cracks in the drift-plank walls.

Below his ear, someone was breathing with heavy, strained lungs full of pain.

Patterson.

It sounded like the thin, sad pull of the tide rested inside his lungs.

Dear God, not this. Is there any mustard plaster to be had in this place?

Someone cleared his throat. *Bradstreet.*

He smelled the older man's perfume, a deep spicy fragrance like heather and borage. It mixed with the fear-sweat and scald of the ocean.

A gust of the morning wind came up, and the thin boards rattled. Hopkins shivered.

"Don't move," Bradstreet whispered again. "Wait till I tell you it's safe."

Hopkins heard a soft sound – a hand sliding over sand and pushing it away. Grains rolled away and rose up in fine dust. The young man held his breath against the swelling burn of a sneeze. Bradstreet repeated this sound, three, four times, and the warm, snug feeling about his shoulders began to lift.

He opened his eyes bit by bit. Bradstreet was patiently scooping a drift of sand off his body.

"Move slow," the Runner advised.

Hopkins took that as good advice. He lifted his head by degrees. Sand slipped into his collar like a waterfall.

"I had to bury you both to keep you warm," Bradstreet apologized and explained at the same time. "But I'm not certain I covered up his wound correctly. So . . . move slowly."

"Understood," Hopkins whispered with cracked, dry lips. He did one better, shifting his weight away from the unmoving Patterson. The bulk of the sand slid after him. "How is he?" he wheezed.

"No worse . . . but no better. I don't know what to think, but it probably isn't good."

Hopkins considered that, and had to agree. After a wounding like that, Patterson's health should be showing signs of something . . . If he was holding steady, then it could mean he was holding his own desperately, and losing valued strength. When the signs showed, it might be too late.

The sand had leached the wet off his body. Hopkins felt as though he'd been baked in the sand like a crab, but at least he was dry and . . . warm. He risked standing, and sand trickled through every crevice in his body to puddle around his ankles (and in his shoes).

He sighed in defeat and sank right back down to remove his shoes and socks.

Bradstreet grinned without a sound. "I had to do that not long ago," he assured.

"Now what?" Hopkins kept his voice down. "Any news?"

"They just took Lestrade and Gregson out of that stone fort they call a warehouse. There's too many of them, and they're wearing constable uniforms . . . I saw them get stuffed into a covered wagon with some crates before they were sent off to the manor." Bradstreet fished a piece of what looked like dried fish out of his pocket, brushed it off, and chewed absently. He was still chewing while he handed over a canteen of tepid and weak ginger water. Hopkins drank as much as he dared, knowing if he was thirsty Patterson would soon be in torment.

"I can barely see the hand before my nose, Roger. How is it you could see that?"

"If you aim a spyglass right, you can see more than people think. I suppose that's another trick we'll have to teach you along with tossing a truncheon."

"Oh, dear." Hopkins was quiet a moment. "Bradstreet . . . if that is . . . was . . . Mr. Holmes . . . then what's truly happening around here?"

Bradstreet did not answer at first. In the swelling dawn he was slowly transforming into a large, bear-like black form inside the poorness of the shack.

"I don't know, Stanley," he said finally. "Mr. Holmes was never one for confiding in one of us. And the man liked his dramas . . . but I can't believe he'd hide from Watson. What would be the sense in it?"

"I know. But . . . ." Hopkins struggled for words. "You know, the reason why we're not as good as Mr. Holmes was, is our ignorance. Criminals get away with what they do because they hide themselves well. That was Mr. Holmes's trick. He could see through them, while we couldn't."

"If only we could see through this," Bradstreet agreed.

"The body was never found." Hopkins hated himself for pointing it out.

"For all you know, someone hid the body to start up questions like this. You know what doubt does to a mind."

"I know . . . believe me, I know! I very much know!" Hopkins rubbed at his sleep-sore face. "And I'm full of doubts right now. For all the applications of his methods . . . for all the logic . . . there isn't a single scenario to this that I like!"

"We've decided not to use the doctor for the present."

Quimper nodded as if this was surprising news. It was a good idea to give the impression he could not anticipate outcomes.

About him, John Clay (acting leader) and the Colonel (whom Quimper liked more but respected less than the fearsome brother), were passing around drinks while Sir Niles orchestrated a complicated-looking series of orders to the butler.

Quimper was fairly certain he recognized the butler from a less-respectable and more-interesting past with the Kentish assassins.

Well . . . a man like Sir Niles could hardly have an ordinary man as a butler.

Not using Watson would have been his idea from the beginning. There were too many bones of contention about the whole matter. Better to ease back and work with what they had, and perhaps finish up a few matches (speaking of contention) before the case was settled.

"We still need a match," the Colonel grunted. He had grown a bit friendlier to Clay, which was a slight relief . . . Clay was unprepossessing in Moran's stead, but he was clever, could follow orders, and he could think on his own. One reason why the *Kelenner* did not tap his brother to

206

inherit was because the man looked to first impressions, and his dislike for "effete" men was well known.

The Colonel climbed to his feet with that unnerving ease of muscle and power and grace that marked him and Moran apart from the common herd. Quimper had seen the sight countless times, and it affected him each time.

"The men are restless and ready for their blood. While I'll tip my hat to Watson for knowing who to shoot first in the heat of battle – and at close range – the truth is we don't have a dramatic draw. We need a celebrity. Cole of Blackpool was a celebrity."

"We must have a celebrity, if we're to fully recruit the Mortons," John Clay agreed.

"We'll use Lestrade for the match," Quimper said quietly, looking at Clay as he did.

But the Colonel had overheard. "He's not a prepossessing character. Not physically."

"I assure you, Colonel, he is quite capable of fighting along with the best of your men." Quimper did not normally take initiative. John Clay was a suitable mouthpiece for his desires . . . for the most part. But John Clay did not fully own this situation. "It ought to be a popular fight, for how often has there been a policeman in the ring?"

Moriarty grunted that was true enough. "But can he fight?"

"He doesn't have enough sense to quit." *And if truer words were ever spoken, it was not in* this *room.*

Moriarty grinned at that. "A policeman *would* be a good draw."

Of course he would. "He'll fight to keep his partner alive . . . He knows they'll live as long as he finishes the fights."

"Gregson? They're rivals." John Clay risked dissent in the ranks, but he had to know.

"Bitter rivals, sir. Bitter as chocolate. Lestrade isn't going to give Gregson the satisfaction of saying he couldn't 'make the grade'."

Clay nodded his enlightenment and said no more on the subject. Rivalry was something everyone in the room understood. And the last word was a fact of life.

"This him?"

The man had no particular accent, no particular call to attention, and nothing to set him apart expect his face had been pummeled by so many fights he'd lost most of his character in the reshaping. Against the backdrop of what had to be the dankest, most miserable stone rooms that ever passed for a dungeon, he was the perfect accessory.

Except for his check coat. It was louder than a saint's festival in Ireland. Lestrade's sensibilities were nearly scorched by that coat, and the too-red scarf that went with it. He tried not to look at the bowler. It had a blood-stain on it.

"You aren't much, and that's a fact."

Lestrade lifted his head up – *All the better to look down at you, my dear!* – and cocked an eyebrow like the hammer going back on a gun. Gregson knew it meant the same thing, and braced himself for what he knew was about to follow.

"Why?" the runt wanted to know in a bored tone guaranteed to annoy whoever it was aimed to. "Are *you* going to be in the fight tonight? I'll try to stay awake."

Low chuckles rippled through the ugly looking crowd that was slowly forming. They were out of their bracelets . . . but there wasn't any point in causing trouble. They were outnumbered by far and by men who'd had a decent night's sleep and breakfast.

"He asked you a question, Davies," a lean man with pox scars pointed out.

Davies scowled, gun-shy at being teased. "I thought I'd be winnin' back some of me own tunnite. But there won't be much in the way of respect, I see. I could break you with one hand."

Another form of a low-class challenge.

There was no time like the present. Lestrade paused only to transfer his weight to his right foot and then he bashed the man's face in.

"Your kicks lost a bit of form there, Ratty," Gregson taunted as the scrum commenced. "Have you been getting enough practice?"

"And this isn't – practice – ?" Lestrade snarled as another fool's face got too close to him.

Gregson decided he might as well join in. Lestrade had probably done the right thing – a strong show was the only thing these fools understood – but a rockfight might be overdoing it a bit. He dropped as someone relaxed their hold on him in favour of the swelling "jump on Lestrade club" and picked up a rock of his own. It made a satisfying sound against a jaw.

"Fight!"
"Get him!"
"Kill him!"

Quimper sighed and paused to stub out his cigarette as he joined in the rush out the balcony door. It would appear Lestrade had been intending to keep his word on the bargain – not that Quimper had doubted otherwise. Dishonesty, like so many other talents, required imagination.

Quimper broke away from the block of Moriarty's broad shoulders and John Clay's narrow arm just in time to see Lestrade reduce a man's face to pulp.

On the other hand, imagination is required for some martial skill . . .

.

"He doesn't fight like a gentleman," Clay noted.

"I'm not sure there would be a point in that," Quimper pointed out. Really, Clay's grandfather did him no favours in his upbringing.

The Colonel liked it, though. He chuckled around his cigar. "Not bad," he decreed. "Gregson isn't shoddy either."

"We'll need something for later." Quimper signaled to the butler, who understood the situation and pulled out a whistle. It wasn't a policeman's shriller, but three blasts did the job. The mob grumbled as it fell back.

Lestrade paused to get one more sucker-punch in before he was relocked.

"You don't feel like making friends today, do you, Ratty?" Gregson wanted to know as they were yanked against the wall and held into place by the derbies again. Lestrade had come out of it surprisingly well, with only a split lip and a growing bruise on the chin to show for it – besides some tears in his clothing that the Mrs. Lestrade would screech about as soon as she saw them. His hat was gone forever – probably adorning someone else's head now, in which case Lestrade doubtless was willing to give it up.

"You know what I'm like before I've had my morning cup." He put up a token resistance as they were hustled up a flight of dangerous-looking stone stairs towards a sort of balcony crossed with bolt holes against invasion, and dropped his voice to the ground: *"Seen anything of Watson?"*

"Not yet," Gregson answered back in the same voice. He pretended to concentrate on the puffy swelling settling in just under his left eye. His shoulder ached like the blazes where someone's big boot had connected. *"They wouldn't be keeping him here."*

"So sure? This place is a stone fortress."

"It's tight all right . . . too tight."

Lestrade didn't follow, but he was used to that with Gregson.

"Button up, Euclid. Here come the gentry."

Chapter XXX – Kettle of Fish, Can of Worms

"**D**id they *truly* figure all this out by themselves?"

Gregson wondered just *how* stupid they thought the police were, to carry such frank skepticism in their eyes and voices.

Someone's been living above the earth just a bit too long, the big man thought to himself. He grunted a scowl at they were pushed forward to their knees – *Silly boys! They think it'll take something like this to demoralize us? They've never been hauled to the carpet in front of Miller!*

Judging from Lestrade's bland expression, he was thinking the same thing. Wouldn't it gall the Old Man to think all his abuse had come to some good somewhere?

"They had help, I fear," someone said behind them.

Lestrade risked twisting his head to look at the owner. Quimper again, he knew – but he couldn't help looking at the man.

All eyes were upon the agent as he strolled forward. Lestrade wondered if anyone else noticed he'd lost some of his original grace since last year. If the walking stick swung with a measure more control than before, and the steps were just slightly shorter in stride . . . who would notice?

"What sort of help would that be, Mr. Quimper?" the Colonel grunted.

Jethro Quimper shook his head with his lips appropriately pursed. "The late Inspector Patterson. He managed to kill Boggs Loseth, but not before his brother took care of him. There were no other survivors to the fight – he assured me on that score." The agent smiled diffidently at Sir Niles. "An excellent man you have, sir."

"Not at all." The baronet took the praise naturally. As the moment passed, the man stroked his beard back in place and picked up a pencil to write.

Quimper turned his gaze back to Lestrade, and his face was frozen. "A shame about the waste of his talents. He was the brightest man in the Yard."

"I'm more sorry about your pathetic gang than I am for Patterson." Lestrade looked *down* on Moriarty as he spoke. Gregson had seen that mannerism of Lestrade's countless times, and never failed to be impressed by it. Lestrade was far shorter than the Colonel, but you wouldn't know it by the way he somehow managed to look down his nose at the big man. "You gents really and truly stabbed your own backs when you killed him."

Moriarty slowly turned. He was a big man, so it did not happen too swiftly. His mourning-black clothes crinkled in the lamplight. Glacier-grey eyes slid like an avalanche over the smaller man. "And because of what, I ask you, Inspector?" he asked in a bored voice.

"Because," Lestrade answered in a mockingly identical tone, "of the gemstones, of course."

And the room went mad.

"He's feverish."

Bradstreet moaned softly at this pronouncement, but he didn't question Hopkins' judgment.

"We're going to have to keep him alive until we can get Dr. Watson out of there." The Runner sat up – he'd taken a short nap at Hopkins' insistence – and rubbed at his chin as he thought. "Hopkins, you're dressed for the part. Fake a limp and go beach combing. We need some containers for holding sea water, and something for a fire. This won't be pretty, and I'm certain it won't be very efficient, but we'll have to make do."

"Containers like discarded beef tins, bottles, things like that?" Hopkins pulled on his shoes as his quick mind thought ahead. "Not to worry."

"I'm not worried about *you*, Hopkins," Bradstreet smiled gruffly. "Don't be out too long, though. I've noticed there's enough people wandering around, but for some reason they aren't going close to the shack. I don't know why, but I'd like to."

"That's been worrying me too," Hopkins admitted. "I supposed we'll have to do as well as we can . . . ."

"Rinse any bottles out before you bring them back," Bradstreet cautioned.

Alone, the Runner settled upright and went through his pockets, one by one. He found what he was looking for in the third: A handful of change, various coins of differing values. Only two were made of silver. He shook his head in dissatisfaction. It would have to do, God help them.

He hoped Hopkins would have luck, and come back very soon. They had to work fast if Patterson was to survive . . . and they also had find the time to indulge in some low-class invasion at the telegraph station.

It's going to take the two of us to wire for help, and Patterson can't be left alone . . . not yet.

Bradstreet could have moaned his frustration as he stared through the warped boards out to the grey line of ocean. He'd thought once, at first in humour, to retire to this part of the world and to persuade Geoff to follow

211

him. Geoff had taken the silliness with the attention it deserved – nil – but over the years, the joking had grown just a little serious.

They were getting older – just watching Hopkins ought to be a reminder of that – and the world was slowly getting harder and colder against them. That they'd survived long enough to test up from constable had been enough of a miracle. One didn't ask for the lightning to strike twice in the same spot.

But he loved the cool, wild lands of his boyhood, and the feel of the salt on his face. He liked to be away from the blistering stink of London in summer, and to watch his children laugh in the freezing waves. Best of all, he liked the way his Hazel bloomed to the tall Amazon he remembered in their youth. Not that she was anything less than fierce now – but to take her here was to turn back the clock for a moment.

He hadn't wanted Geoff to see this part of the world under these conditions. Geoff and Tobias were most likely within the deepest troubles of their lives, and fighting to live just as hard as Patterson was fighting now.

"Just hold on," he said aloud, and he couldn't have said who he was talking to – Patterson, Geoff and Tobias . . . or himself.

Gregson had one split-second to take in the swelling volcano of the Colonel's face, and he lunged for Lestrade with his manacled hands. With desperate strength he yanked Lestrade backwards by the collar with the mad idea of shielding him from a brutal end. They both sprawled on the floor, Lestrade allowing a gasp of indignity – a second before the Colonel's heavy stick splintered its tip on the stone floor.

Lestrade's education was of lower quality than Gregson's, but that didn't keep him from noting the correct term for what was happening. It was a Gallimaufry of the first water, swiftly leading to abject pandemonium.

Sir Niles was shouting for order, and his men were hastening to obey. That they were also accustomed to obeying Colonel Moriarty made matters difficult – John Clay and Quimper were both pitting their bodies against the Colonel with all they were worth to keep him from unsanctioned murder, and their men were trying to help, but only causing interference.

Sir Niles was possibly the smartest man in the group at that moment. He barked something to his butler that Gregson couldn't make out a single word of in the hullabaloo, and the manservant nodded, circled the fray, and got behind the inspectors. A hand like cast iron gripped each man by the collar and hauled them up and away from the ring of confused shouting.

Gregson's ears finished ringing in the relative silence of a primitive stone gaol. Lestrade was lying flat on his back with his hands folded neatly over his waist, looking slightly startled at the whole mess that had just happened.

Part of Gregson understood two-hundred-per-cent, while the rest of him wanted to personally finish what Moriarty had started.

"Nice going there, Ratty. You've put out a fine kettle of fish and served it up with the worms."

"A bit of an extreme reaction if you ask me," Lestrade protested as he plucked a cobweb from his hair. "He's a Colonel, you know. I thought they had more self-control than *that*." He paused and muttered darkly: "I thought they had to. So much for British reserve."

"Yes, well, I have to agree with you there, but at the same time, I'm taking back everything I ever said about you that was good about your intelligence."

"*That* shouldn't take long . . . ." Lestrade neatly tossed Gregson's scathing comment into the proverbial dustbin and climbed to his feet. Gregson was still smarting from the destruction of his insult when he saw the butler was on the other side of the bars, glowering.

"Beg your pardon?" he asked with all due seriousness. Things weren't looking good – not that they had since Watson was taken.

A glare was his answer.

Lovely.

Lestrade had time to sigh – it was the kind of noise he usually exuded when faced with some new aspect of deskwork – and straightened warily as a long-distance door clanged on metal hinge.

Gregson took the cue, and joined in the wait.

It sounded like a small army, but it was in truth only the major players in the game.

"Leave us, Charter."

The butler nodded and did just that, leaving the detectives with what they were coming to think of as the two playing officers for each side of the split Family.

Moriarty appeared to be under control now, but his skin went from pale to beef-red to pale again from the intensity of his emotions.

He was leading the charge, but that might change before long. The way his ally Sir Niles was holding back from him a bit suggested as much.

"You, Inspector." The icy, composed eyes and voice struck at Lestrade. "Explain yourself. What are you meaning with this talk of gemstones?"

Lestrade played it cool as ice. He stared back at the larger man. "Well, that was why you sent me after Dr. Watson, isn't it? Because he knew where your rhino [1] was kept . . . ." Lestrade smiled. It was the kind of smile he kept on the shelf and dusted off whenever a big balloon wanted a nice, big pin.

"Enough of your pretending to be clever. You can talk now, or later." Sir Niles' voice was sharp as nettles in the cold air. "And later won't be nearly as comfortable as it is now." The baronet had folded his arms across his chest. "What's your link to Dr. Watson and stones he secreted?"

"Dr. Watson?" Lestrade examined his fingernails with impartial and studied poise. *"You think he has the stones."* He *tsked* under his breath in a near-pitying manner. "With you lot breathing upon him? Ah, wait a moment . . . This was the Colonel's little pet, wasn't it? The rest of the Family didn't know about it . . . well . . . *most* of the Family."

"What worries *me* is the whereabouts," Gregson butted in with a friendly clout on the surprised Lestrade's shoulder. (Lestrade was too used to Gregson's antics to display any shock.) "Grave robbing, are we? I know it's not supposed to be the same thing for Christians . . . but somehow I don't think the Afghanistan dignitaries think too kindly of an Englishman snooping around the graves of their ancestors." He made a chiding sound with his bottom lip and shook his head from side to side. "Really, rooting about in old caves like that . . . one would think there were safer ways to pass the time of day."

Moriarty's face was mottled a fast-changing red and white with his high emotions. His large head swung from side to side, like a great python's. "I don't know what game is being played here," he roared, "but I will not have any of it!" A thick finger leveled into the air before the detectives. "The two of you aren't going to go anywhere until this matter is settled!"

"For that matter, the doctor is staying where he is as well," Sir Niles answered in a voice harsh as reef rock.

The doctor. Watson's close by. He's alive – he's still alive, and he's going to stay that way until they're satisfied with this matter. Good show there, Lestrade. You played them and they were fools all the way. Gregson caught on like a grease fire. Lestrade had tossed soda into the vinegar, exposing Moriarty's lucrative secret in front of his so-called peers.

His peers were obviously not pleased with being kept out of the trust . . . .

Leave it to Lestrade to sow the seeds of dissent onto fertile ground. It was his best trick with interrogating criminals. Ten minutes in his company and the whole gang would be pitting against each other like terriers in the rat pit.

It would seem that a gang of gentlemen is just as bad as a gang off the clayfields . . . .

"This is too large a matter." Sir Niles glared at all of them. "You know as well as I our state of finances."

"It happened during the War," Moriarty snarled. "Watson's brother stole a cache I'd discovered in the desert. He kept its location a secret and left it to his brother."

"It may have started out a secret, but suddenly it has become something a great many people know about." Unspoken was John Clay's anger at not being one of those people at the beginning. His fellow gang masters felt the same way. "You are fortunate I am deciding the orders for our people, and not someone else, Colonel."

Someone else? Gregson's mind arrowed to that. John Clay wasn't the leader of his part of the gang . . . it was someone else and Clay was speaking for him.

Too much to hope for that they'd just up and mention him . . . .

"This matter happened before I even joined my brother." Moriarty's voice was sculpted and refrozen ice.

"We must take your word in that, as the Professor kept many memberships secret – even from those he confided in." Sir Niles nearly brutalized the Colonel with his response. "But as the treasurer who would like to see these squabbling factions come to terms with each other . . . I needn't tell you how much of our quarrels are involved with money."

"And these . . . policemen know something about this missing wealth?" John Clay spoke with a deceptive softness in his eyes.

"*Lestrade*? He couldn't *possibly* have this treasure!" Quimper exclaimed. Cold, mocking blue eyes sank into Lestrade's viscera. "If he had it, he would be finally giving his wife the attention she deserved!"

Quimper was just a hair too slow to escape Lestrade's grip.

This time, Gregson didn't try to pull Lestrade back. He watched, silently cheering his rival on as Quimper's head slammed into the bars, and then down into the stones. Lestrade's eyes were black as coal as he struck Quimper over and over, until someone thought to bring a rifle butt into the play.

Colonel Moriarty stared at Gregson as though he'd never seen him before in his life as Lestrade collapsed on the floor – as unconscious as Quimper. But for the interruption, the agent would now be dead. "You weren't going to try to stop your comrade?" he accused.

Gregson stared back at him.

A man could overlook the taunt of being remiss in his duties, but Quimper had done more than accuse Lestrade of beggaring Clea in poverty while he struggled to maintain his station.

All the money in the world couldn't change the fact that he was to rise no higher in life. Clea hadn't married him for money. She married him

215

because he *understood* her. Gregson had married his wife under the same umbrella, and wouldn't have it any other way.

Quimper had just insulted Clea Lestrade in the worst way by implying she had been foolish and irresponsible in her choice of suitors. For a woman who was smarter than most men, that was double the insult.

"Should I have?" he wanted to know coldly.

Moriarty thought that over, as the two antagonists were slowly separated.

He finally shook his head in agreement.

It was the least, Gregson thought, the greedy fool could do.

NOTE

1. Stolen loot, divided up between members of the thieving gang.

Chapter XXXI – Now What?

Gregson was taken out with the rest of the "chessmen", as Lestrade was starting to think of the *pro-tem* rulers of Moriarty's frozen empire. It made good sense. Criminals were separated all the time to keep their equilibrium off.

His head hurt, but it wasn't from the blow to the head so much as the overall punishment since getting the stuffings pounded out of him by Quimper. That, and the lack of anything decent to eat or drink since . . . .

He was still trying to remember that when something light clacked against one of the bars in his cell facing the ocean.

Now what?

Lestrade grimaced, putting his top teeth into his bottoms and took the easier option of going to that "window" on his hands and knees. He was flattering the architecture by even calling it that – the nook to the grey sunlight was flush against the floor, and was probably just used as a drain for the stormwater that ran in under a good solid helligan.

He pressed his face against the stones and saw a grey, aimless sweep of sand dunes and a few sea oats or whatever the broomlike things were.

And Hopkins.

Good Lord.

"Hopkins?" Lestrade could barely move, so he merely thought about giving the young man a good scolding. "What is going on? How'd you know to look here?"

Hopkins looked – honest to the Heavens above – hurt that Lestrade didn't give him credit for intelligence. "I listened to the guards," he explained in a voice that was barely louder than the surf just behind him. "I can't stay long. Onc't high tide comes about, I've got to hop to it . . . Where's Gregson?"

"They separated us." Lestrade sighed. "Poor fools." Wait till they found out Tobias could be annoying enough to make a Baptist weep. "Did you and Roger get to the wire?"

"The telegraph station's been destroyed!" Hopkins whispered back. His boyish features were too old in the fading light. "Utterly smashed to bits. Bradstreet found some things in the rubbish, and he's using it to fix up Patterson – "

"*He's alive?*" Lestrade caught his breath. "*How?*"

"Sheer luck, and it'll be running out if we don't find him a doctor *soon*. Bradstreet's fashioning up some colloidal silver, but he says the electricity in the seawater is are too weak for it to be very useful. Did you find Watson?"

"They've got him hidden up like the Mad Duke's Rubies," Lestrade answered gloomily. "And people are saying it's the ghost of bloody-all Sherlock Holmes!"

Hopkins didn't answer at first. "We saw the gent in question, Lestrade," he said. "Looks enough like him."

"Mr. Holmes might've danced with the law and led it astray, but I can't believe he would have committed to coarse sabotage and left Watson to languish in a frigid cemetery of a dungeon!"

"*I don't know!*" Hopkins looked helpless and ancient against the roar of the coast. "I don't know, Lestrade. He was a man of pure mind, and . . . Well, *wouldn't* he have held back on rescuing Watson if it meant he could get these damned parasites?"

Lestrade was rendered incapable of speech for a moment – and he knew it looked like he was caving in to Hopkins' point, but . . . he didn't know what to say.

He couldn't do this to Watson . . . He just couldn't . . . .

"Keep your eyes open," he rasped. "What's the problem with the seawater? Get it hot enough and it'd put out a charge."

"We can't get it hot enough. Bradstreet says we need batteries, but we can't get any batteries for making the colloidal."

"Hang on." Lestrade closed his eyes. "Bloomin' idiot . . ." he said under his breath. "Did you check the telegraph station for batteries?"

"I . . . no . . . ."

"They hit the station to ruin the wires, right? Well, fools like that, they don't think about anything past the equipment. They're thinking of the mechanisms and the cables. Did the cut the cables?"

"I'll say they did!" Hopkins exclaimed as quietly as humanly possible. "Cut it and then some!"

"Get back there, if you can. Look for the batteries. There's at least an entire volt in those little brutes. If you can salvage enough of 'em, you have the voltage you need for the colloidal." Lestrade fumbled in his pocket and awkwardly pulled out his watch. Wonder of wonders, they had not thought to take it. "Use this. The lid's got enough silver to plate a hospital." He had to let it drop on the rocks below. There was too much space between their hands.

"I'm off then." Hopkins actually sounded hard and professional in that moment. "You stay alive. Bradstreet will murder you and Gregson if you can't keep your wits about you another few hours."

"I promise you, we'd deserve it fully." Lestrade grinned. "They're just criminals, Hopkins. No system to them at all. Get that back to Roger, *and get those batteries!*"

Hopkins obeyed.

Lestrade watched him go, feeling a strange knot in his chest to see the man moving over the reef stones as if he were a part of the ocean himself. In the cold grey light, he possessed the same animation as the sea did.

He'll be all right.

Lestrade couldn't say *why* he knew that was so . . . no more than he could say why he doubted this stranger was Mr. Holmes. Sherlock Holmes had been a clever man, and he would have been able to explain it in a way that would make it all simple and juvenile to boot . . . .

Lestrade only had a feeling, and feelings were not what the jury – or the Chief Inspector – wanted to hear. He kept his feelings a secret as much as possible.

Still . . . .

There was something about the way Hopkins demonstrated his unthinking smarts by moving along the sea foam in pattern to the waves . . . If Lestrade hadn't known the boy was there . . . he would have just overlooked him.

Smart lad . . . smart man.

Why hasn't Miller taken him under his wing? He's from a good enough family . . . respectful . . . doesn't go above his station . . . .

He didn't know. He could only hope that Hopkins' bald honesty hadn't made an enemy of the Chief . . . just like it had with Lestrade years . . . decades ago.

Colloidal silver. Patterson was grievously injured if Bradstreet was making up a field kit of the stuff.

Not that he blamed Roger . . . Roger was a sharp man when he understood a risk to his children, and it was because of his children that he hammered and hammered and hammered into the medical field and then the chemists until he got the secret out for making the stuff.

Just hold on there . . . just hold on . . . .

He went to sleep on that thought.

There are few words that could do justice to the sensation of being on the other side of a set of bars while your worst enemy sits three inches out of range, reading your own wife's letter.

"I always enjoyed the lovely Miss Clea's sense of humour," Quimper smiled. "Hedgehog indeed. I wonder if I ever ate it in any of the charity suppers her school catered?"

Lestrade didn't know what was worse at that moment: Quimper reading his mail, the mail that his wife wrote to him, or knowing that Quimper had *been* at one of those suppers, eating his wife's cooking and parsing it down like a Frenchman with caviar.

"If you did, you obviously couldn't tell." Lestrade's mouth was civil only because there were too many uncivil things trying to come out. It was a verbal logjam threatening to choke him. "Adding a higher offense to your list, Quimper? Perjury, liability and murder not enough for the likes of you. You have to add crimes against the post now."

There was a silence as Quimper refolded the letter along its lines and Lestrade made himself stand. He knew he'd better. When a frozen-cold floor in the middle of a sodding dungeon against the North Sea in springtime started to feel as agreeable as a brass bed . . . it was time to get up.

"You never know when you ought to give up." Quimper commented with that sort of overdone patience one usually hears from the Home Office when they don't want to investigate too deeply into a case of a sensitive nature.

"I hope that's not a trait we share by blood," Lestrade spoke coldly.

Quimper's face congealed inside his skin. There had been a time when nothing would have interrupted his shockingly handsome features . . . but something unsavoury was beginning to emanate from him . . . and Lestrade had noticed it upon their last parlay.

"What blood we may have is too thin to measure without a dropper. A fact you ought to be just as grateful for, L'estrade."

"Well, you certainly proved the truth of that when you beat your own father to death." Lestrade sighed and went to the far wall where his back could rest. Distance was preferred right now. "Congratulations for finding *something else* to cause pain and misery. My own father's as mad as Paul now."

"I wouldn't know. I heard he'd vanished off the face of the earth with your mother." Quimper responded with something of his old, smug complacent ability, but it too was lacking some of his old strength. When he turned his head, the lamplight threw strange glints into his eyes, like Lestrade was trying to talk to something that was un-civilising itself by inches. "You wouldn't happen to know anything about that, I'm sure."

"Yes, odd, isn't it. Vanished as surely as if they'd . . . taken wings and flown."

Quimper went rigid. His hands shook over the knob of his wretched walking stick. Lestrade could see the silvery-grey marks where the Tinker's wolfhound had attacked him . . . only last spring. Only last spring, about Walpurgisnicht.

A hundred years ago.

"So the Seagull is still alive," the agent said at last. "I wondered about that. And he helped your parents flee . . . wherever to, I haven't the vaguest idea. The man has safeholdings all across this part of the hemisphere." He stood as well.

"Shouldn't you be getting your rest?" Lestrade mocked gently. Now that he'd learned he *could* stir Quimper up, it was fast becoming a low-class addiction. *No wonder he did it every chance he got . . . .*

Quimper ignored him, though the effort put a brick in his jaw where another man would have a quid of tobacco. He signaled to someone out the open doorway, and a beefy-looking man in worn togs came in, hand respectfully on his hatbrim by the forelock. Quimper wrote something quickly on a small piece of paper and passed it to the man with only a nod.

"Rest?" He resumed the conversation when they were alone again. "I don't think I need to tell you what an impressive sabot you threw in the machinery, L'estrade. There will be no match to settle any of the petty points arising between the sides."

The agent looked almost worried. "Dr. Watson will be safe – for the moment – until his role in the . . . missing gemstones is settled. On that score, you and Inspector Gregson will be safe – also for the moment – until the same. As you've managed to inform us by confounding the Colonel and causing the worst display of temper from him I have yet seen . . . the entire Board is in an uproar."

"You have a *Board*?" Lestrade gaped.

"Yes. On occasion, we also bathe," Quimper retorted frostily. He barked something, his accent suddenly turning Orkadian. A man who was even bigger than the last one came in with a set of bracelets. "Cuff them behind," the agent ordered. "*Always* cuff that one behind."

Lestrade didn't put up a fuss – he was trying to save what unbruised portions he had for the inevitable fight. But Quimper was right. He mostly needed his hands for balance with *savate.*

No word of Bradstreet or Hopkins. Not even a gloating, and he was positive Quimper would have been delighted at the chance.

Bad as one of his oversized inlaws, Quimper was.

Quimper led the way, his stick clanging metal teeth into the stonework as the guard propelled Lestrade from the shoulder. They hadn't cleared the end of the narrow hall when the first man Quimper had called was hurrying back. The note was still clutched in his hand.

"Sir, I'm sorry, sir," he panted lightly from having run back. "The telegraph station's out."

"*Out*?" Quimper demanded. "The weather's perfectly calm."

"Nothing wrong with the cable, sir. The set's been wrecked. Someone's come in and smashed everything to bits. *Then* they set the station on fire!"

Quimper became utterly motionless. "When?" he asked quietly.

"We're not certain when it started. Smoke was seen this morning by the fishermen wanting to wire in the latest prices on their shark. Big Loseth, he said he saw a gang of men hanging about . . . at least four of five of them." The man looked past Quimper straight to Lestrade.

Lestrade wondered what the devil for.

"Out with it, Joseph." Quimper barked.

"W-Well, sir . . . he said that one of them . . . went by the name of Sh-Sherlock Holmes . . . ." Joseph fidgeted. "And he looked like him. Just . . . like him."

Quimper regarded the squeaking man without a single change of expression. Lestrade was fairly certain *he* was staring like a pop-eyed corpse. His brain wasn't moving.

"One word of this to anyone, and I will personally slice your entrails out and feed you to the crabs while you still live."

Joseph wisely did not trust himself to speak. He nodded like a wind-up toy.

"Get back outside. Try to get a message out somehow, *even if you have to go back and swim.*"

Joseph fled.

Lestrade didn't fault him. Swimming to the mainland would be better than facing Quimper in a mood like that. The number of men he was supposed to have killed with his walking stick was proof of that.

"Not one thing, but another," the agent growled through a picket fence of gnashed teeth. "Nothing lasts forever, and dead men rise up never."

"Careful, Mr. Quimper. I know how the rest of that proverb goes." Lestrade spoke too gently to be seen as fully mocking, but Quimper's sharp, cobalt gaze was cold as a corpse candle.

"I can believe you'd know the old proverb . . . you didn't have to read a book to get it after all."

Quimper's sally was fairly mild, as far as that went. Lestrade was glad to start walking again.

Gregson was cuffed much like Lestrade, in a chair that was normally a little posh for their income. Lestrade thought of a glorified throne at the sight of all the stitched-up horsehair and mahogany. Judging by the condition of his face, his contributions to the conversation had not made anyone happy.

Moriarty was pacing back and forth, side to side, across a wall that was deep-set windows and double doors that were half window in themselves. The glass tax would have beggared everyone on Lestrade's street.

The Colonel was still furious. It came off like the fur off an angry cat. His left hand remained busy as it opened and shut the expensive watch at his waist.

Sir Niles and Mr. Clay were by default less of a worry. Sir Niles' butler – Charter – was lining up glasses and wine bottles of red, yellow, and white grape. So far no one was about to make the truce by breaking the bread that rested by that wine.

"Evening, Lestrade," Gregson grinned, and he thought Lestrade was annoying? Lestrade simply wasn't in it when Gregson got into the contest.

"Evening yourself," Lestrade whuffed as he was thrust into a chair identical to Gregson's. *Ah, well . . . at least there's something to look at besides these fellows . . . nothing like a grey sheet of ocean against a blackening coast pounded by deadly surf to lift one's spirits.*

"You may take these gemstones and buy an orphanage with them for all that it matters to me." Clay was still using that soft, even and unsettling voice even as his glittering eyes flitted mothlike across face to face in the room. "We must come to an agreement on other things . . . more important things if we are to accomplish anything out of this meeting."

"What's up?" Lestrade whispered.

"Not much. Seems they've been trying to decide who's going to rule without the Professor – The Colonel, or some other fellow they call "The Tiger". – Clay's speaking for him, and Quimper follows Clay."

"So Sir Niles follows Moriarty?"

"Up to a point. He's the money holder for the gang, and as the Treasurer, he has his own control over things. He agrees that Moriarty should be the leader, but the gang's almost broke. So he has to be persuaded that Moriarty has what it takes to bring the gang back to its old glory."

"No wonder he wants those gems."

Both men were silent a moment – the argument appeared to be circling like vultures . . .

They stopped talking just in time. Sir Niles turned and leveled a finger straight at Gregson. "You, sir! How did you know the gems were being robbed out of Afghanistan graves?"

Gregson blinked as if startled to be the topic of conversation. "Wasn't *difficult*," he protested.

Oh, I can't wait to hear this, Lestrade thought. On the other side of his bland expression, he was hanging on every word. Gregson bragged about how smart he was . . . but he rarely demonstrated it. It looked like they were all about to be treated to a show.

Chapter XXXII – Target Practice

"We shall be the judge of how smart you are," Clay's voice channeled three generations of skepticism. "Pray continue."

Gregson shrugged as if he had to prove his brain was a working three times a day. "Because they were stolen out of a cave." He pointed it out as if it was such an obvious thing, it embarrassed him. "The Arabs of today, they only bury a fellow in a cave unless that's exactly where they dropped dead." He smiled in that smug way of his that had probably led to his blackening left eye and openly missing first molar.

John Clay folded his arms over his chest as neatly as a book. "So far you've explained nothing."

"Oh, I'm afraid I did, lad. Would you like me to explain it with smaller words?"

Lestrade winced. "Gregson, mind you that I'm the uncontested expert in irritating fools, but this isn't the way to go about it."

Gregson gave him a good-natured face pulling. "The Arabs tend to leave the bodies of the dead alone. Even the bodies of their ancestors who never saw the Prophet. I'm surprised you didn't know that, Mr. Clay. You made such a point out of being a gentleman . . . Didn't you get a gentleman's education?"

Clay's face slowly sifted into a colour more known for the lobster as it slowly boils.

Gregson didn't give him a chance. "It was obvious Lestrade pulled the gems out of a cave to begin with . . . the cave where Hamish Watson hid them."

"This solves nothing," Jethro Quimper cut in as mannerly as possible, but it was rather obvious to the Yarders that he disliked Clay. "You can't prove it."

"Lestrade came back with a carnelian carving of Qwan Yin, the Chinese Goddess. You see her a lot when you work on the docks. She's sympathetic to the poor and downtrodden. Thing is, a live Arab wouldn't have been carrying something like that around with him . . . Are you familiar with the laws of the Koran? No images . . . and no images of heathen gods especially."

Lestrade kept the bland look on his face while he catalogued the way the thugs about them were staring at Gregson. *No wonder Mr. Holmes was like to hold off until the last minute. It's like throwing nuts to monkeys.*

As a professional, Lestrade couldn't approve. As someone who dearly wanted to get some of his own back after a campaign of harassment and misery . . . Well, he was only human.

Gregson had paused to let it soak in . . . and also to be insulting. "The cache then had to be part of a burial back before the Prophet. That's not so long ago, far as the calendar goes . . . but the Ayub Khan wouldn't have cared for despoiling. Nor would any of the puppets the Army instated as fake rulers. On the other hand, we're talking about quite a lot of money, aren't we? And here it was, gathering dust in an old burial cave. Is that what gave you the idea of smuggling the pieces out, one bit at a time, inside the bodies of our own dead soldiers?" His voice dropped. "And then, if that wasn't bad enough, you kept on with it . . . *robbing the bodies of the enemy for the wealth they had?* There's a limit even to ghoulishness, but you gave yourself away on that one . . . There were emblems of the Faithful squirreled into that box of loot along with the older stuff."

Lestrade tried not to jump at Gregson's other sound and startling deduction. He was right. *There were Fatima Hands sprinkled all through that box . . . Moriarty had the perfect smuggling ring going on . . . Why would he stop at just a dead noble's grave?*

Moriarty was still livid, but he was beginning to calm down. "You haven't explained how you know it was in a *cave*. It could have been buried in the desert somewhere."

"Unlikely, that," Gregson sniffed. "It was part of a dead man's goods . . . a man dead before the land saw the Prophet. The locals didn't want to muck about in those places, but you did, and you found the plum!" He grinned at Lestrade, who was trying not to sweat at some of the expressions he was facing. "Clever men . . . they just can't help but be clever. Trips 'em up every time with the patterns."

"I'll try to remember that, Gregson."

"But drawing inspiration from history . . . I'm not certain that was so clever. You had a treasure you couldn't really spend, even once you got it out Afghanistan. People talk, and you needed someone who could be really trusted . . . not your average banking problem, especially with the British a little sensitive on the whole subject of Maiwand. You had to let it keep a bit . . . at least, that was the plan, until Hamish Watson came about and alleviated the problem from you."

"And you found out just like that?" Jethro Quimper had seated himself on one of the ornate chairs, and he had at least accepted a wineglass, but so far no one else was offering the olive branch. "That's quite a lot of reasoning in a short period of time."

226

Gregson sighed through his nose, a model of patience. "There's only one reason why you people can operate. You keep us ignorant. You ought to see what we can do when we have a lot to work with."

"Hamish Watson wasn't long for the world." Lestrade figured Gregson had been the centre of attention long enough – time to take some of those glares off. "It probably gave him the push he needed to stick one last rock in your eye, Colonel . . . He passed on the message of where the stones were kept to his brother . . . and then he died. John Watson knew the dangers, but he's not the kind of man his brother was. For him, he only wanted to spare the widows and orphans and grieving parents the truth of what had happened to their beloved sons – used as a means to smuggle foreign wealth in their very bodies. He had no moral solution to the filthy lucre, so he let it sit where it was. It was safe enough. But you got tired of waiting, didn't you? Mr. Holmes utterly wrecked the gang and you're all that's left, save a few scattered players here and there."

"I'm thinking whoever takes over the remnants of this pathetic little tea party is going to be the one with the biggest bank account," Gregson mused. "Is the competition a bit of a big spender, Colonel?"

"Would have to be," Lestrade chipped in. "But a box of gold, silver, gems, and whatnot would put a stop to that."

John Clay and Quimper were clearly amused at the reactions of Moriarty and Sir Niles. They were trying to be gentlemen about it, but there was a betraying twitch to their lips and Clay was beginning to find great interest in his portion of bread.

"It wasn't all gemstones." Lestrade had caught on to Sir Niles' expression at *gold* and *silver*. "Would you like a listing? Let's see . . . there were twenty-four solid silver Fatima's Hands . . . two silver chains studded with turquoise and pearls . . . *freshwater pearls*, normally low value, I know, but they had a rather an interesting pink tint that would be hard to peddle on the market . . . ."

For a wild moment, Gregson thought Lestrade had lost his sodding mind, giving out each item with careful descriptions . . .

"Thirty-six opals set in mixed gold filigree . . . ."

Sir Niles had yanked a little book out of his jacket with almost enough force to break the spine.

"Forty-four gold coins of various sizes . . . about half were Greek. The rest were Egyptian . . . early mamlukes . . . ."

The baronet was writing as fast as his fingers could allow.

Oh, A-ha, and Eureka! Gregson caught on. *Someone as powerful as Sir Niles – and as barmy – wouldn't be happy at being shown a pile of rocks now! He would have to look up each dratted piece and line it up.*

And mentioning the pieces makes it more real, too . . . Gregson tried to ignore the way they were being watched *now*.

"Twelve rubies, rather an unusual cut . . . almost like a rose cut . . . of a uniform size just smaller than the dimensions of my little fingernail . . . Those were pigeon bloods, but there were seven spinels too – one was cracked, I'm afraid." Lestrade acted like he was completely unaware that a ruby larger than ten carats was considered a good sight more valuable than a diamond of the same size.

"There weren't that many emeralds, but they were all four flat-cut . . . about the same number of diamonds, unset, and thirty-six pieces of carved carnelians, jades, and white ambers. They were all of a set of some sort . . . little gods and goddesses, I'd say. Looked awfully dignified with long robes . . . The amber was unusual . . . ." Lestrade suddenly shrugged. "Not a bad little haul," he concluded.

"Where are the pieces now?" The Colonel was so quietly spoken, yet his voice seemed to thunder in the room's hush.

Lestrade let the silence hang out, just a bit.

"Gave them to Patterson. Like I told you the first time."

A muscle spasmed like a stabbed spider all over the left side of the Colonel's face.

"He's got to be lying," Quimper threw in harshly. "Perhaps he gave them to Patterson – but what did he tell Patterson to do with them?"

"Hardly counts, Mr. Quimper, as I can't say for sure what he did with them once he got them." He grinned. "I'm sure it will be a simple matter to track them down."

"Simple, right," Gregson sniffed. "Mr. Sherlock Holmes sort of simple."

"Speaking of," Clay cleared his throat. Of the four, he was showing a startling presence of mind. "Mr. Holmes has been spotted on this isle, if we are to believe rumors."

"Bosh!" Moriarty shot back. "The man's dead. How could he be alive?"

"Alive or dead, no one has seen the body." Clay faced the bigger man with a startling show of courage – genuine courage. "But my men have sworn they have seen Mr. Holmes alive and walking about the island, causing calculated damage to the telegraph station and the docks."

"Sir Niles," Quimper donned an entreaty for the first time. "We need Dr. Watson if this is honestly Mr. Holmes. He will come to Watson's side."

"I am the one to say what is to be done with Watson," Moriarty growled. "I am the one who brought him here to settle our business."

"After you killed some of my best men, you mean. We had him first." Clay's voice had turned sharp as reef rock.

"Enough, all of you!"

Silence held in the room as the baronet made his way to the board, and stabbed a slice of bread all the way to the table.

"Watson is not to be found by the likes of any of you." Sir Niles lifted his head proudly. In the gaslights, his shadow wobbled behind him like a dark, living thing. A familiar out of the old fairy tales against the stone walls and time-bleached tapestries. "When the Colonel entrusted him to my care, I made *certain* it would be in a way that prevented misunderstandings." He calmly poured himself a glass of wine and held it to his lips as the atmosphere about the room grew charged. "As treasurer, I decide the state of our finances. As the owner of this house and keeper of this island, I decide what is to be done with my guests." He paused to glare at the Yarders. "*All of them.* I took precautions instantly. You may search the entire isle, but without me you won't find him. That I guarantee you."

"And you find no pertinence in rooting out the man who killed the Professor?" Clay demanded. "The very cause of our dissent?"

"None whatsoever in the scheme of things. My instructions were clear." Sir Niles sipped his wine and ignored how the air grew even heavier. "The Professor's logic would scorn revenge for its own sake. He would, I confess, admit to the usefulness of revenge when it finished up a business, but this is bipartisan squabbling and gentlemen, we can do better than that."

He crossed over the carpet and put his back to the ocean. Lestrade could see something happening at the beach below . . . dark shapes flitting out of the stones and moving with the swirl of the high tide. Sir Niles ignored it and faced his audience like a grand lord out of the past.

"Someone is wrecking havoc on my island, but whether or not it is Sherlock Holmes is immaterial. They won't be capable of eluding my men forever."

"Sherlock Holmes is alive," John Clay repeated flatly. "We have proof."

"Proof I'll not believe in unless the man is in the room!" Colonel Moriarty sniffed.

Sir Niles had a low sound in his throat. He gathered all eyes before him. "You may have that moment soon enough," he said carefully, and his eyes were slitted beneath the thick black brows. "I sent my best men on a hunt for any strangers, and they ought to have results quite soon." He lifted his glass to his lips just as Lestrade saw someone break apart from the knot of seamen.

Wine splashed through the air along with Sir Niles' blood. Lestrade threw himself to the carpet as well, grimacing at the fine spray of blood lighting on his face like already-cold mist. Behind him Gregson was doing the same. The baronet fell across the carpet, his left eye a black hole where the bullet had come out and struck the wall just above Gregson's chair.

Moriarty was screaming. Clay and Quimper got the bloody blazes out of the way of the window just as a second bullet sent an afterthought into the ceiling. Glass bits fractured down. *All right, we heard you the first time!* Lestrade thought ridiculously.

"Lestrade, get your fool self against the sideboard!" Gregson panted.

"I'm not moving an inch or an ell!" Lestrade shot back. "Did you see him? Did you see who that was?"

"Yes." Gregson was quite pale – and rightfully so. "I mean . . . I know who it looked like."

Lestrade swallowed hard. "Me too."

Gregson struggled for something to say, to show he wasn't defeated or cowed while chaos ran rampant. "Still shooting into the bloody walls, I see."

It was awful, but a bit of hysteria rose up in Lestrade because he understood the joke. "I suppose all of that was target practice . . . ."

Chapter XXXIII – Truth in Plain Sight

"**B**loody Tinkers . . . ." Gregson subsided to a mercifully inaudible tirade into his battered collar.

Lestrade sighed. Other than the resounding slam of the door locking them into the Murder Room with the corpse, events (from their side at least) had diluted.

He wished he hadn't such a sterling view of Sir Niles. "All right. I'm going to move now."

"Good for you," Gregson grunted. "See if you can get to his pockets. Man keeps bloody notebooks about him. He has to be just as batty with a ring of keys."

"Sound reasoning . . . ." Lestrade grimaced and, slowly as possible, managed to pull his hands down behind his back and legs to get his cuffed hands out in the front. He paused to wipe the baronet's blood off his cheek. (God be thanked he'd shut his eyes in time.)

Gregson waited with as much patience as he could bear while Lestrade struggled with the unenviable task of going through a dead man's clothing whilst done up in bracelets.

"If it's not Mr. Holmes, who is it?"

"Gregson, I haven't a blessed clue, and a part of me almost doesn't care . . . ." *If it is Mr. Holmes, then we're going to have to arrest him for murder or as an accessory to same, and I'm not certain our own families wouldn't exile us for it . . . . .* "We have *so many* different things to worry about right now . . . ." *Getting out alive, without any further injury . . . finding Watson . . . .*

"Just trying to think ahead and prepare for whatever will happen."

"Think ahead to Patterson. He survived, if you can believe it. Hopkins and Bradstreet fished him out of the drink but the wound isn't doing well, and they're trying to fashion up the colloidal with some seawater and batteries."

"Good luck to them," Gregson sighed. Lestrade was scowling and trying to pull an assortment of oddments out of the baronet's pockets.

"*How* did you know all that, Gregson?" he asked. "You knew I was lying to you the whole time? That I really did find the jewels when I found the chest?"

Gregson cleared his throat. "Not at first. Normally, it isn't like you to fabricate. You simply don't tell someone more than you have to. You were convincing enough when you showed me the Chinese goddess . . . but I started to think about a few things."

"Like how clever men can't resist being clever?"

"On the nose. He was so successful getting those antiques out of Afghanistan, why wouldn't he keep at it? Bottom line is that he did. He'd just keep on."

"Oh, good – Oh, damn." Lestrade's fingers had found a key. But when he managed to pull it out, he could see it was attached to twenty just like it. "We could be here just a few minutes longer."

"No time like the present," Gregson grunted as he eased his big body up. "Your turn . . . how'd you find the cave?"

"Everything kept coming back to the bloody sabre that caused the mess!" Lestrade confessed. "Dr. Watson showed me one sabre . . . but not the other. I went to check out the other sabre and there was writing scratched over it. It referenced a – *Oof!* – cave in Northern Scotland and a local hero – named Hamish – who sent some greedy treasure-robbing Vikings to their deaths."

"Clever men again," Gregson shrugged. "But I think we can say that Hamish really was clever. He found a hiding place that left gaping chunks of circumstantial evidence all over the bloody place. I wonder why that was so important to him?"

Lestrade was suspiciously silent.

"Lestrade? Just because we're getting along today doesn't really mean we're at The End Times."

Lestrade snorted, but he relented. "As you said, Hamish Watson was clever. I think he set it up so *someone* would eventually learn the truth. But why make it so hard for his only brother? You have to wonder if there was some resentment."

Translation: *Lestrade* had to wonder. Not surprising, considering how his older brothers treated him. Gregson chose to ignore it. "Maybe he didn't trust his own brother to follow his trail on his own brains."

"Yes . . . that does no credit to the Watson we know."

Definitely speaking on a personal level. "No . . . that's an *intellectual* decision . . . not a human one. That's the real problem with smart men, y'know," Gregson sighed. Lestrade was fast running out of keys. "They can measure anything but what a man is capable of. Too many shadows and shifts, and they like the world black or white without any greys."

"Ha!" Lestrade breathed as a *snick* released his cuffs. "Roll over, Euclid. Let's see if we have a Universal here."

Gregson rubbed at his sore wrists. *Why hasn't help come by now . . . ?*

. . . Unless something happened to Hopkins and Bradstreet. As badly as they were prepared for that level of ambush . . . he couldn't outlaw that cold possibility.

"First thing's first. We find Watson – while avoiding any trouble. If we can get to Watson, Patterson has a chance, am I right?"

"You are." Lestrade's dark eyes had narrowed in concentration. He stuffed the derbies in his pocket – no doubt thinking of how he might need that later. "Hopkins actually looked frightened when he spoke of Patterson."

"Hopkins? *Frightened*? Things *are* bad."

"Ha." Lestrade was disgusted. "No iron . . . you'd think he'd carry *something* with the sort he hosted."

"For all the good it would have done him anyway," Gregson pointed out. "Let's get out of here."

"Someone's coming."

Bradstreet didn't look up at the sound of Hopkins' voice. He was focused on recleaning the wound in Patterson's flesh. Did it look better or worse? He wasn't certain. While the man was out, Bradstreet had gone ahead and poked around for more threads and foreign material, but he wasn't a doctor. Holding a man down while his shattered leg was set was his usual trick, thanks for his strong upper arms.

Lestrade would have been a bit better with this . . . he'd had far, *far* more experience with dead and injured bodies. Cut his teeth on the wreck of the *Alice* where the corpses were stacked like sea coal behind the gasworks.

He finished covering the dressing before rolling to the side in the soft sand. (Of all the places to hide, and the entire isle either boggy or rocky, they had to pick the one loose sandy spot.)

"It's Loseth." Hopkins tried to lisp a bit, making the sound less carrying.

Bradstreet grunted. He didn't fully trust the man – not just yet – but he was a friendlier face than most here.

Loseth was dragging his heels as he lugged a large canvas sack over his back. He was not exactly easy on the nose. His shattered mien of the night had settled to a dull, slightly lost look, and he cleared his throat often when he spoke. It was apparent the younger brother had been the speaker and motivator for the two.

"Not safe here now," he said carefully, mindful of his accent. "The men at the Big House are searching . . . they won't stay away from th'shack."

"Why is that?" Hopkins asked. "For that matter, Loseth, why have we been left alone here?"

"Because of the murder." Loseth explained with a slightly puzzled air. "Patterson said you gentlemen weren't afraid of th'ghosts."

233

"He did, did he?" Bradstreet didn't blink. "Good man. He was right, you know."

Hopkins kept his mouth shut, thinking of several grisly anecdotes Bradstreet liked to tell after the sun went down. He sighed and accepted Loseth's offer of a meat pasty with relief.

Bradstreet pulled out Patterson's gun and gave it to the younger policeman. "I think I spared it from the salt, but I fear the rust will come on it soon."

Loseth shook his head. "Should have washed it in tea."

"Good God."

Gregson's horror justified speaking.

The room was done up like an underground pit. He could see dried mud and mortar mixed with grass and roots and peat and, when he backed away, he brushed against the outcropping wall. Dust and grass trickled down. He backed away from that with a baleful look.

His nerves were not suited for this horror. They had been running for what felt like hours through the confusing maze of the manor, and the entire time recapture or a final bullet had never been more than a step away.

"Dr. Watson mentioned this," Lestrade whispered. His eyes were large. A waxwork barbarian king marked with woad reposed on a wooden barrow, its wax hands folded neatly over a gleaming weapon. It was far too realistic, even for men who were so inured they could face a museum chamber of horrors with polite boredom.

"Diseased brain," Gregson decided. He checked the door to make certain it was still shut. "Keep your ears sharp," he whispered. "There's got to be some sort of weapon we can nick out of here . . . something that won't be as bloomin' obvious as that sword."

Lestrade nodded his agreement and gingerly rested his back against the door – while Sir Niles had stopped short of putting up the door in daub and clay, he had painted it dull and black to resemble a lightless tunnel.

Diseased, indeed.

Gregson puttered about coolly and calmly, his big form soundless. Lestrade watched, aware of the way time slipped through their fingers with each passing minute.

"Hst!" Lestrade pushed backwards, blocking Gregson with his body. "Hide!"

It was an easy enough matter to plaster under the heavy wooden barrow. Lestrade joined him a breath later.

They made it just in time.

Footsteps clicked on the stone floor, patient and deliberate. A tipped walking stick patted out every third measure.

"No sign."

"*Why* did he do it?" Jethro Quimper's low voice was harsh with intensity. "That puffed-up fool!"

"First we have to prove the Colonel *did* have him killed." John Clay's cool, controlled voice was like meltwater running slowly over smooth stones.

"Is our word not good enough?"

"It is our word against his. To do that, we need to find his assassin."

"You saw him. You saw him as well as I did. How *could* that be Sherlock Holmes?"

"I thought you were a skeptic, Mr. Quimper."

"I am a businessman. And if it is Holmes . . . then what the devil is he doing here? How could he have learned of Dr. Watson so quickly?"

"That I do not know . . . but if we find Watson before the Colonel, we can ask questions of our own. Where are the men?"

"I told them to pretend to go along with the others and help search the proper estate."

Silence.

Lestrade tried to breathe as lightly as possible. In his own ears, he sounded like a wheezing elephant.

Someone was pulling out a cigarette case. A gun clicked as it was inspected.

Gregson could barely move. Every nerve thrummed. His world was dusty plankwood above his head, shrouded in funeral cloth like a morbid curtain, and the floor was freezing. Lestrade's quiet breathing was reassuring in the darkness.

"The question is where would he hide Watson so no one else could find him."

"Charter would know. He was the penultimate butler . . . and you know what else he did for Sir Niles."

"Ugh! You needn't remind me."

A match was struck. Smoke slowly wafted down to the stone floor where it curled around polished shoes like milk poured into a clear water glass.

"This isn't the place or the time, but I'm not upset he's dead. What a ghoulish businessman. I can't look at this waxwork without thinking of Madame Tussaud's. He probably even commissioned the modelers to make this chieftain."

"Hmm. I daresay you're right. We ought to find Charter . . . and I should wager Sir Niles left him instructions on the worst case scenarios . .

. If things went to hell like they are now, sir, then Charter is probably right on his way to wherever Watson is . . . and he's liable to kill him to minimize the damage."

"Then we need to think of where he would be."

"We've been through most of the manor as it is . . . and not to mention most of the secret passages. What's left?"

"What about the dig sites? That old barrow is solid enough, and if a man were kept there with the entrance blocked up, there'd be no hearing him at all."

Lestrade soundlessly turned his head to stare at Gregson.

"You're right . . . it would be a logical place to hide someone . . . ."

Ash dropped to the floor and burst like a snowflake not six inches from Lestrade's wrist. The little professional's heart nearly stopped.

The expensive boots clicked down the stone hall.

Gregson swore violently without making a single sound. In the damp chill of the stone, his hands were aching ferociously.

"Time to get out of this snakepit and find the others," he announced firmly – and still very quietly. "Once we have Bradstreet and Hopkins with us, we'll be as good as an army – " He stopped. Lestrade wasn't behind him, wasn't moving to join him by the door.

Gregson turned reluctantly. Lestrade had come to the point where he'd risen to his feet after crawling out from under the table. No further. He was standing by the ghoulish waxwork king with a face almost as colourless as the dummy Celt stretched out on the barrow.

"What is it?" Gregson hissed.

"Tobias . . . ." Lestrade felt the floor beneath his feet wobble under his shock. "I've found Watson . . . ."

Gregson went numb.

He felt his blood congeal within his veins.

Lestrade grabbed up a small bronze cup sitting against the sacrificial exhibit – a drinking vessel for the afterlife. He pressed the cool metal surface to the face of what Gregson had thought was a dressed-up waxwork.

It wasn't a waxwork.

Chapter XXXIV – Arise

Gregson wasn't convinced Watson was even alive.

The doctor was lying as if dead, gussied up in handwoven linens and leather like some sort of Celtic barbarian. Gregson paused to wonder several things all at the same time: Was that beard and moustache real? What was Lestrade doing with the cup? Could that great big sword be used as a real weapon in the fight about to happen? Why wasn't Watson moving?

Lestrade lifted the metal cup up and held it out for Gregson to see. A faint mist dulled the shine of the brass.

Gregson realised what Lestrade had been doing. "Well, he's breathing," he whispered.

"He's drugged with something . . . ."

Gregson glanced about nervously and went to Lestrade's side. Watson's chest rose and fell with silent efficiency.

"Hidden in plain sight," the big man breathed. "They walked past him and never knew it."

"Good thing we're not smart enough to take things at face value," Lestrade said darkly. "Now what, Euclid? They'll find us any minute, and we can't help him."

"A moment here . . . ." Gregson joined him and a quiet search commenced.

"Phew!" Lestrade took a large step backward. He'd put his face too close to Watson's face. "The false beard . . . ." He turned his head and gagged into his palm.

"And that's why we keep you around, Ratty." Gregson pulled off the woven net. Beneath the stitching that held the false beard was a small pad of dope. Despite the jab, he was glad that Lestrade's reaction to most known sedatives was so strong. He flipped the tiny wad into his sleeve, far out of range of any nose. "They're going to catch up with us any moment. What say we do it far from here?"

Lestrade nodded. At this moment, the odds were against them, but getting Watson to wake up would be on their favour without question.

"Hold on." Gregson suddenly stopped in his tracks at the sight of another door set into the side wall. Lestrade promptly collided, and gave him an ugly look.

"Not meant to be seen," Gregson explained. "Still got those keys?"

"Wouldn't be without them." Lestrade held up the ring in a way that demonstrated its use as a handguard in battle. He promptly moved forward, eyed the lock, and found three contestants. Gregson glanced behind them to the black-painted doorway as he worked.

The door opened, but Lestrade grabbed it with lightning speed to keep it from swinging on its hinge. "Might need oil," he explained hoarsely, and pushed up, taking gravity off the mechanism. Gregson waited until he was fully inside before following.

"Good Heavens," Lestrade said without thinking. "Gregson, I don't care if I sound like a Hanging Judge. There are some forms of insanity that ought to be outlawed."

Gregson needed a moment to swallow before he agreed.

It was a library . . . or had been at one time. Shelves lined the walls from ceiling to the tip of the wainscot.

Over the books were photographs of the archarological digs. And what was being dug up.

Gregson felt nauseated, and told himself it was the lack of anything to eat and drink for too long. He took a step backwards just as Lestrade was turning back to look at him. The instant he caught Lestrade's expression he tried to move out of the way but it was too late. Iron-hard arms had come up and a knife was digging into his throat.

Lestrade took a step to the side – neither forward nor backward – and lifted his hands up (right still holding the keys) in a cautionary fashion.

"Charter . . . you're only making this more difficult for yourself."

"I am willing to accept that," the butler said coolly. He smelled like bay rum this close to Gregson, and something else . . . a lingering of bitter opiate.

"What are you bothering for?" Lestrade asked softly. "Your master is dead."

"He left me with instructions. Sir Niles planned for every outcome."

"Except discovery," Lestrade sniffed. He sounded and looked like he was already growing bored with this conversation. "Drop it, Charter. Gregson talks quite enough without you giving him another mouth."

Gregson bared his teeth at the runt. "You'd best hide behind your wrestling wife, Ratty, because when I – "

Charter squeezed the knife closer to his throat, cutting off his voice. Gregson coughed from the pressure and a sudden sting of sweat bloomed out of his skin.

Lestrade sighed. "You're mad," he told the butler. "Mad as your pathetic master. You kill him, you'll leave yourself open to me." He lifted one eyebrow.

"If you don't want him dead, then you will not interfere." Charter's hateful voice shivered Gregson's exposed flesh worse than the knife. "It is a very simple thing, to slice open a man's throat."

238

"And you know about that, do you?" Lestrade glowered.

"Lestrade – " Gregson hissed. "Would you mind – ?"

Lestrade shrugged. "We appear to be at a standstill, gentlemen. If I try anything, Charter kills Gregson . . . but if Charter kills Gregson, I'll have an open field." His dark eyes glittered in the gaslight. "I know my Euclid."

Charter frowned, but Gregson went still as a snail inside. He knew a code when he heard it. *Trust me. Play along.*

Clink.

It was a strange sound, like a tiny piece of heavy iron falling to concrete and rolling. In the pounding silence the three of them hesitated. Lestrade tilted his head to one side, listening. Something had just shifted in the air. They heard it through their heavy breathing.

Nothing happened. With their nerves stretched taut, the only conclusion was a false alarm.

The butler grinned at them both, and slowly dropped his arm from around Gregson's ribs. It was back again before Gregson could formulate a plan of defense: A second blade was now digging into the soft spot that was an easy upward stroke into the heart.

Lestrade paled, and his eyes went from one blade to another.

Charter's grin grew. Gregson didn't need to see it. He could feel it. If a shark could grin in anticipation of a meal, he was doing that right now.

"I don't think you're quick enough, Inspector," he said to Lestrade.

But like sand drizzling out of a punching bag, the strength slipped out of his grip. Gregson twisted out, moving backwards with his arms up for protection.

Charter was dead. A small slit was in the back of his swallowtail coat, and surprisingly little blood shone in the white cloths underneath.

Over him stood an absolutely furious John Watson, the dead king's arms gleaming in his hands.

"Watson – !" Gregson strangled.

Lestrade couldn't even say that much. He'd seen Watson wake up and had done his best to keep Charter's eyes – and ears – facing forward.

The doctor was so angry they could see it come off him like the rays of the sun coming back on a hot road. His face was set and dark beneath the woad stripes. He suddenly reached up and yanked his hand through his hair. It was missing its circlet. That must have been the ring on the stone.

"I," he said coldly, "will wring the neck of the jester who did this." He tugged at the sleeve of the saffron shirt. "Now how do we get out of here?"

Gregson recovered. "Easy, man, we're not in a safe place right now . . ."

"I gathered that." Watson carefully stepped over the fallen butler. With movement, flakes of thin wax cracked and fell to the floor like the peelings off a sunburn. Lestrade was relieved beyond words to see that with the wax came the woad. Marking the man in such a way would have been personal torture.

My God . . . How long had he been in such a state, knowing what they were doing to him and what they were planning to do when the time was ripe?

Lestrade didn't believe in personal justice, but the thought of Watson having to explain in court before strangers what these animals did to him . . . He didn't think he could bear to witness such a humiliation for the proud man. Proud and proud twice. His pride was one of the few things he had left to hold on to.

"And I apologize for what I was forced to do. I would have preferred to send him to legal justice." Brown eyes flashed like fireworks inside a cognac bottle.

"You did fine, Doctor." Lestrade barely spoke above a whisper, but it was reassuring all the same. "You did what we couldn't do."

A soldier knows when he must kill in order to preserve life.

A doctor knows how to kill painlessly, and in a way that a man wouldn't even know he was dying.

Lestrade certainly didn't know the trick, and didn't care to.

Two serpents on the staff, he reminded himself. One poison, one not. Both needed.

Gregson was coming to the same conclusion. He gave a short, crisp nod and pulled the knives out of the dead man's hands. "He seemed to be an expert."

"He was!" Watson said harshly. "He worked for Colonel Moriarty before he came here. We'd heard rumors he took trophies off the men he'd killed."

"Moriarty just can't resist looting," Gregson said in disgust.

"I wasn't talking about that sort of trophy . . . ." Watson spoke as gently as possible. Even here, he was mindful of another man's precious morals.

Gregson looked blank for a moment, then sick. Watson nodded to confirm the silent question in the Yarder's eyes. "Noses and ears . . . ." He whispered softly. "And . . . tattoos."

Lestrade avoided witnessing the loss of his comrade's innocence by kneeling and going through Charter's pockets.

"Damn, that's almost no good at all." He held up a tiny pea shooter. "Lady's weapon." He passed it to Gregson.

"They're careless over here," Gregson realised. "I imagine they aren't accustomed to opposition. Bloody toy derringers. Good for women in an alleyway, or a gambler shooting a man from across the table."

"Just make your two shots count," Lestrade rasped. His voice came out wrong. Watson's eyes shot to him sharply, openly concerned. "I'll be . . . fine, Watson. We all need to get out of here though! Patterson is slowly dying of a bullet hole and we need to get him *off* this evil-infested isle!"

And for that matter, they all needed to get off before it crashed down about their ears . . . .

Watson's gaze turned sharp as fresh needles. "Agreed. Behind the bookshelf is another passage. Sir Niles opened it by lifting a loose stone in the corner and stepping on a trigger beneath."

"I'm glad you said that . . . Sir Niles is dead now. Someone shot him through the window."

Gregson glanced at Lestrade first. "There was a man in the group . . . it looked a lot like Mr. Holmes."

Yes, quite a lot, Lestrade thought.

Watson frowned. "Holmes is dead." He spoke with more than needed firmness. "Is this another of Moriarty's tricks?"

"We don't know. All we know for a fact is, Moriarty was in some way responsible for Sir Niles' assassination."

Watson pondered that carefully, his face set and cautious.

"If we don't get out of here and bring help to Patterson, there will be another death in this circus," Lestrade said to Gregson. "Hopkins said they couldn't voltage the sea water for the silver."

"I'll see to that," Watson promised. Intentional or not, Lestrade had galvanized the doctor to his chosen profession. "There's half-a-hundred batteries in here . . . Sir Niles' paranoia extended to all things it would appear." He scowled as a thought struck him. "Give me a moment, and I should think of where he'd hide a medical bag."

A whuff of compression struck the air, weak and spent, but there had to have been something momentous going on outside. With a single glare to Lestrade that dared anyone stop him, Gregson stalked straight out into the hallway.

"What do we do?" Watson was shocked.

"Nothing," Lestrade sighed. "It works for him more often than not . . . I can't explain it."

Watson had found the loose stone and stepped down into the floor. Something creaked oddly and the bookshelf opened.

"Strange sound."

"The hinges are made of wood. He was worried about rust."

"What didn't he worry about?" Lestrade marveled.

"The condition of his soul, I would venture."

Gregson's heavy tread came back to them in record speed. Lestrade held the shelf open, and waved him in. Watson lifted a lantern burning on the nook and they shut it after themselves.

"What the devil is it?"

"There's been a firefight, and we aren't going to get anywhere near it!" Gregson exclaimed. "I just saw three men cut down like sheep!" He wiped at his neck. "And there was screaming in the back. John Clay and Quimper have fled the isle."

Lestrade's mouth dropped open. "What do they know that we don't?"

"Ratty, I couldn't say. But I hope when we find out, it won't affect us the same way." Gregson cleared his throat. "Where does this lead, Doctor?"

"Upstairs to the solarium," Watson explained. "There's ground cover, of a sort outside. It is a decent enough place to start looking for our allies."

"Lead the way, MacDuff."

Chapter XXXV – Struggle

Patterson revived as they moved to shelter. Between Loseth and Bradstreet, the gangly CID Inspector was light as a scarecrow. For long minutes he kept his head down, watching where his foot slowly placed itself after the other. He had to have been in severe pain, but the stoicism that Hopkins was beginning to recognize as part of his survival undercover asserted itself. Bradstreet kept up a murmuring soft commentary as they moved across the coastal rocks, far too close to the angry-looking surf. Hopkins followed behind, his sharper eyes much better with for spotting any trouble.

For someone who had no better claim to water than the boating of Cambridgeshire, Hopkins was eerily at home at this rough coast where the sun shone against the flying clouds with all the success of a housewife sweeping mice with a broom. Bradstreet promised to follow up on this promising insight into the man's talents. The fens were very different from cold sea surf and rocks. This Crane [1] was suited for more work with the CID.

"*Sae deeskit,*" Loseth said sadly. Under the strain of the situation, his verbal skills wobbled and wavered between slow and painfully deliberate English, and his more natural tongue. The poor man was almost a monoglot.

Bradstreet found it surprisingly easy to understand the man – he hadn't heard Orkney jar [2] of this thickness in years. "'s weary work recovering from a bullet," he agreed.

"He's ahl heuved up, tho' . . . ." Loseth was doubtful of Patterson's survival. "But nae beerin' at all."

"He's not the complaining sort," Bradstreet pointed out. "Is it much further?"

"Neracaboots," Loseth assured him. "We're t'gae in ahead o' the gouster."

Hopkins cleared his throat, moved where Bradstreet could see him, and threw a helpless look.

"Gust," Bradstreet translated.

"That place there?" Hopkins guessed.

"Th'same." Loseth tightened his grip as Patterson's strength began to ebb. His next words were drowned from Hopkins' ears as they stepped around a lying boulder and found themselves against the sea.

"He said we have to be careful, because a few people still know about the secret passage," Bradstreet repeated.

243

"Bloody . . . ." Hopkins felt free to curse under the circumstances. The two older men tried not to smile at him.

Hopkins suddenly hissed and dropped down. They were wise to follow suit.

"What is it?" Bradstreet hissed.

"I heard a shot!"

"I heard noth – " Bradstreet clammed his mouth up as a distant *pop-pop* rattled off. "Damn. That was a rifle of some sort!"

"Common men don't have rifles," Hopkins whispered. "That's a gentleman's weapon."

"Or a soldier's . . . ."

"The Big House." Loseth lost what little colour he had left.

"If Lestrade and Gregson aren't a part of it, you can at least bet – " Hopkins breathed. " – that they aren't far."

The passage was primordially cold and thick with must. The lantern caught the clouds of their breath against the flying motes of dust that settled on their sweating flesh. Steam rose from Lestrade's body almost instantly. Watson caught Gregson giving the little man a baleful look.

"Man's a furnace," he growled. "Guess that's why he's so little. No chance for meat to settle on his bones."

"I'm afraid you're not the type of beauty that improves with jealousy," Lestrade panted. Neither of them looked like beauties at that moment . . . and it would take weeks for the bruises to fade off Gregson.

"You're just glad you won't be anywhere near me when the wife sees what happened to my new necktie."

Lestrade looked upwards, askance as he realised the extent of the passage. "Mac would be praying to St. Barbara about now," he stared. "This must be like one of those underground mazes the pagans buried their royalty in."

"I thought you *liked* caves, Ratty."

"This is a cave?" Lestrade whispered his worst possible contempt. "Looks to me like someone's breeding tent spiders."

"There must be quite a lot of them," Watson mused, unconscious of the fact that his comrades were trying to squabble to keep their spirits up. "Sir Niles had Charter sweep it all out only a few days ago."

The policemen fell silent as they appraised the spinning abilities of insects that had only a few days to line the tunnel with sticky crepe. It was an effective dampening effect.

"Where to?" Gregson swallowed thickly. His throat clicked in the sudden silence.

"Straight ahead, and when the passage forks, we turn *right*," Watson pointed discreetly but nodding in the correct direction, rather being gauche and pointing. Behind them a bullet slammed into the thick wood from the other side, and he winced as deeply as the others. "*Always* turn right when we're in this place, gentlemen . . . !"

"And that'll get us out of here?" Gregson wanted to know, but to do him credit, he was calm as a boulder. *Thup-thup-thup.* A trio of missiles hammered into the wood not far from Lestrade's left arm. A man screamed out, barely perceptible in the layers of wood and books.

"No," Watson said grimly. "But it will get us away from *this*."

"Good idea," Lestrade voted fervently.

"Martini Rifles," Watson lectured coolly as if in a meeting hall as he led their tread through the black, "are not to be trusted at close length with such enthusiasm. Their accuracy pales after they reach a certain age."

Lestrade shivered slightly at a breeze. He didn't doubt the soldier could identify a rifle by just the sound. "How far are we from the open air?" he wondered. "If the spiders can come back this quickly, and the dust . . . ."

"There are several passages that lead outside, but I'm not certain of how safe they are." Watson held the lamp up high, and brightened at the sight of a loaded sconce in the stone wall. "And with the tide shift, the air whistled about us like a very demon . . . Here we are," he paused to light the torch and passed it to Gregson who was taking up the rear. Gregson narrowly avoided setting fire to a long curtain of webs a moment later. He yanked it away just in time, and manfully ignored Lestrade's glare.

Watson either ignored the silent conversation, or politely pretended he never saw a thing. "This is like one of the barrow mazes, actually." The doctor's demeanor had calmed somewhat, but he was more than ready to act. Once in a while he absently brushed more wax off his exposed skin as he walked. It was quite the trail of breadcrumbs if they ever had to retrace their steps.

Lestrade didn't want to think about that.

"What do you make of Quimper and Clay running off?" Gregson finally asked in the shifting dark.

Lestrade was grateful for the distraction. "They're smart, and they're less powerful. I'd say whoever is giving Clay orders would tell him to pull out if it looked hopeless. And if Moriarty is killing the opposition . . . well . . . ."

"It would be stupid to hang about," Gregson agreed. "Quite stupid."

"I'm wondering why Moriarty had Sir Niles killed," Watson murmured. "Was it because Sir Niles ultimately controlled the purse strings of the Empire?"

245

"It's an explanation I'll take," Gregson nodded. "Sir Niles isn't – wasn't – the sort who would just let someone run roughshod over the late Professor's plans. I'd say that as famous as he was for keeping notes, the Colonel'd figured on finding the passwords, ciphers, and keys soon enough."

"The search for power will disrupt any coalition." Lestrade batted angrily at a scarf of misty webs. "Seems to me Quimper was the smartest of any of them – galls me as it does to say it. He prefers to govern from the background . . . in secret."

Watson came to a stop by degrees. They stopped as well. Here the passage forked in the shape of a T lying on its left side.

"If that is so, Lestrade, then we should be keeping a very close eye on his whereabouts. Very close."

Lestrade cocked his head to one side, impressed at the way Watson was staring off into the darkness as he thought.

"Why so, Doctor?"

"That was how Moriarty rose to power in the first place . . . never overtly governing . . . but working from within . . . and behind the curtain while all eyes were on the stage."

Watson turned his head slowly, and the full force of his gaze struck the little professional.

"If anyone will become the next Moriarty after this, I would stake my reputation on Jethro Quimper *right now*."

Lestrade shuddered at Watson's finality. His nose and cheeks felt burnt in the cold air and he concentrated on rubbing warmth into the skin.

"You aren't afraid of him," Watson noted softly.

"No . . . of course not." Lestrade blinked, not comprehending what Watson was getting at.

"Understand the history," Gregson came up behind Lestrade, his usual irreverence low and serious. "Lestrade's never known a day in his life where Jethro Quimper *wasn't* the man holding all the cards. He's always been the . . . royalty. The master of the house. The one you aren't supposed to stand up against."

Watson nodded, and something like a smile flickered in his tired eyes. "Commendable," was all he said, "If anything else, Mr. Lestrade, you have a commendable taste in enemies."

"I'd rather not have any, if there was a choice in the matter," Lestrade grumbled.

For some reason that brought a wide smile to Watson's face. "Enemies often choose themselves, Mr. Lestrade."

"Dear God," Hopkins had time to say before he was diving back behind a sea-wracked boulder that stank of things that were far worse than vegetation.

"Whu – ?" Patterson asked in slurred confusion. He didn't know enough to protest as he was bundled willy nilly behind a part of an ancient rock wall set against the sea. Behind them, a small army of furious waterfowl took to wing, their throats shrieking outrage.

Lovely, and if anyone wondered where they were . . . Hopkins sewed his lips shut. Fresh bullets sprayed the pitted rock over his shoulder. His ears rang from the compression. *"Where the Bloody Hell are they?"* he shouted and didn't care who heard him shout.

Bradstreet lunged forward and nearly threw the young man to the stinking sands with his hand over the recalcitrant mouth. "Shut your gob!" He gasped. "These loonies might know how to shoot th' ricochet!"

Hopkins felt his skin pale to the point of coldness, and he nodded. Bradstreet released him, clearly relieved.

"What do we do, Roger?"

Bradstreet didn't seem to realise he'd been addressed by an inferior and with his baptismal name. He only burrowed himself deeper into his dirty muffler and watched as Loseth bundled the much-weakened Patterson into a patch of sand that was at least sun-warmed.

"We do nothing for now," he said. "We just wait."

"Wait for what?" Hopkins demanded.

"Wait for them to lose what patience they've pretended to," Bradstreet muttered. "Might as well. We're stuck here until we get a bit of assistance."

Hopkins reluctantly looked past the sheltering boulder to the buried secret doorway. One step to that safeway would expose them to the assassins waiting on the beach.

"Damn." He struggled with restraint.

NOTES

1. Hopkins' Cambridge roots are my own invention. He came across as being well-educated and clever, and natives from the area were called "Cranes", possibly from the marshy watersheds.
2. The Orkney dialect. The English is a rich stew salted with Gaelic and Nordic – its trademark words are usually Nordic.

Chapter XXXVI – Betrayal of Dust

Inspector Patterson reclined like a poorly stuffed pillow onto the shingle of Streat and wondered just *how* close to death he truly was.

Sand grains dug into the thinness of his cheek, and his eyes slitted half-closed of their own volition against the fine grains that blew up at the faintest puff. It wasn't normal to feel this detached from his surroundings . . . and being fired at with companions who were in great danger was not the sort of thing to be detached from.

He could no longer tell where he'd been shot. The pain had dulled at the epicenter but spread outward, sharing its agony with every bone, nerve, muscle, and cell. Half his body felt as though it were slowly splitting down the middle.

Fever rose within him, and came and went . . . chills passed with the sensation of lying inside a bake oven. Bradstreet continued to dose him with contents out of various flasks . . . he could feel lassitude crawling in. It was dangerous.

Sheer exhaustion could kill a man quite easily.

They lowered him to the sands when it was clear his strength was at an ebb. *Ebb.* He was waning like the tide. He knew this was a poor sign of his future. Death came slowly, one inch at a time until it seemed such a good idea to just give in and close one's eyes against the mortal pains.

When the shooting started up, a part of his brain was sensible enough to be grateful for being out of the worst risk. The rest regretted that they were putting their own lives on the line to protect him. *He*, who was the weakest one of the group and the most likely to die.

A bullet kicked dust and powdered salt not far from his face. He closed his eyes and held his breath for it to settle. A sense of surrealism had become a part of him. The rocky earth had lost its hard texture and was starting to feel soft . . . yielding . . .

. . . comfortable.

Comforting as the last bed on earth . . .

Something shifted beneath him, like the beginning of a delusion. He knew that sensation well. Unsure if he should miss it (real or imagined) the inspector forced his heavy eyes to open, inch by inch.

Sand shifted, hissed as it sank downward into a trench shaped like a perfect square. *A door,* he realised even as the shooting from across the stones reached a frentic pitch. Behind him, Hopkins was cursing with new words, and Loseth had melted to an unintelligible shuffle of Orkneyjar, while Bradstreet scolded like a bearded fishwife. Patterson ignored them easily. He was frozen with cold, pain, weariness, and yes, surprise.

A door in the sands . . . someone found the tunnels from the old settlement . . .

Watson rounded the turn first and paused, lantern high to show the tunnel gone. It went up and layered with concrete-set steps like a fruit cellar. At the top rested an oak door, black with age and water. It was probably hard as the iron bands holding the hinges in. Sand tried to collect, but someone was scrupulously sweeping it away. There was even a broom propped in a corner for the duty. A web was forming on its tip.

Lestrade glared at something small as it scurried on many legs to dark places, and slapped another flag of web off his shoulder. "I haven't been this filthy since I was in the Cornish stanneries," he said under his breath.

Watson paused to look at him. "What were you *doing* in the stanneries?" It was the sort of voice one might use in saying, *"Why were you vacationing on the Isle of Dogs?"*

"Tin mines. Someone was helping themselves to a portion of the Prince of Wales' rightful tax."

"Hmph. It's not a tin mine unless there's a Cornishman in the bottom of it." Gregson held back on a resounding sneeze as the dust in the air was replaced with minute grains of sand. He could make out thin strips of light – brilliant as mercury after their long walk – and took a step backwards with the rest just in time.

The wind gusted through those narrow windows of light around the heavy oaken doors, kicking up more powdery sand like ground glass against their eyelids. They covered their lower faces with their sleeves and put their backs to the damp walls until the dust storm passed.

"That's not right," Gregson said when they could speak again. "There has to be something to release the air pressure or the wind *wouldn't* be coming in like that."

"I think they have this part of the isle riddled with passages." Watson put the lantern down for a moment to flex his stiff fingers. He looked almost himself with the last of the painted wax off his face. "It couldn't be as such on the other side with the bogs . . . that wouldn't be practical at all . . . not to mention it would be dangerous."

Now that they'd stopped, Lestrade was starting to feel the past two days catching up to him. He tucked his hands inside his sleeves and wished for a cup of something hot. Hot enough to scald the stomach on its way down.

They didn't smell sweet, he noted. Blood, sweat, and the reek of the rough men who'd put their hands on them was overlain with the cold, damp must of the tunnel.

When he thought about it, Sir Niles' *entire* manor had something of that musty, mushroom smell in it.

What a dreadful place to live. Ancestral titles be damned, I shall take the first street off the Neckinger as healthier.

"Watson, I can't help but notice you aren't just rushing outside into the open air." Gregson cleared his throat.

"I'm not certain what would be out there," was the doctor's quietly disturbing response. "I was brought in at night, but I could discern a low sweep of the coast, a few rough boulders and a path that winds along the pattern of the island rock. It leads to the Hall in a very indirect fashion . . . but if we're to just come outside, we could be exposed to something worse."

"Strange to put a secret hatch this close to the sea," Lestrade pointed out, and then abruptly frowned, dark and brooding.

"Easy there, Lestrade. That glare you're putting out is enough to snuff my torch."

Lestrade spared only one second for a pointed look at Gregson. "This manor of Sir Niles . . . how long has it been here?"

"I could not say . . . Why?" Watson wondered.

"Well . . . ." Lestrade flushed slightly. "What if the manor was *here* . . . originally? What else would explain a hatch this close to the water? Water lines change. The coast sinks, and the water moves in. And if that's the case, a man as . . . well . . . *mentally ill* as Sir Niles would be keeping track of all the underground passages . . . what if one of them led to a ship or a boat in case of emergencies? Charter did say his master was prepared . . . Moriarty seems to know a lot about what Sir Niles knew . . . What if he wasn't far from this place?"

Watson blinked as Gregson grinned.

"It's so gratifying to see my own smarts finally rubbing off on you, Lestrade." He smirked in a way that made Watson think he would have challenged the man to a duel years ago. "Does this mean you'll finally be my apprentice?"

Lestrade didn't kill Gregson on the spot – thus earning at that moment Watson's eternal respect – but he glared at him with such ferocity it was a wonder the other Yarder didn't expire. "I declare to you, I will eat a *raw* eel before that happens!" he vowed. [1]

"You'll not while I am here to stop you," Watson said firmly. "I've seen what happens to people who do such a thing on a dare."

250

"Lestrade's stubborn enough that it wouldn't affect him," Gregson sniffed. He pushed aside and began to make his way up the steps.

"Gregson! Watch what you're – "

Gregson's hand had been about to touch the heavy metal bar on the door when a piece of the thick wood burst into splinters. Something small and deadly passed the air over their heads and smashed into the cut stone behind.

"I swear I'll kill you myself," Lestrade cursed. "Get your barmy head down, Gregson! There's another tea party out there!"

"If that's your idea of a tea party, this tunnel must connect to Boston!" Gregson would never let Lestrade get the last word.

"What the blazes are you doing, you sot?"

"Huh . . . ." Gregson had leaned down on his belly and, faster than seemed possible for such a big man, reached up from the steps and flipped the iron bar off its support.

And looked straight into the equally surprised face of Inspector Patterson.

Gregson was never a slow thinker. Looking at Patterson (who looked like he was already dead), lying on the sands not three yards from his own face, while Bradstreet, Hopkins and – *Loseth?* – fumbled and tried to avoid the bullets peppering the air . . .

Well, Gregson didn't need to be a deep philosopher to accurately assess the situation.

"One more moment, and I'll pull you back in here!" Lestrade was shouting over the bullets' ring.

"Hold on . . . ." Gregson hastily let the hatch drop and blinked sand-smoke out of his eyes. "I think we're in a crossroads," he gasped. "The others are out there, and they're huddled up like chickens behind the rocks that are ringing this door! They can't get a clear shot from the other side!"

Watson's face cleared as he understood what Gregson was saying. "Do they have weapons?"

"For all the good it's doing them," Gregson complained. "They'd have a chance on the angles if they were as far back as we are, but they'd be too exposed for that sort of maneouvre."

"Then we are saved, Gentlemen . . . ."

Patterson watched the hatch lift up again. This time the heavy wood lifted up a good sight higher than six inches. Dr. Watson's grim face looked back at him. Wisps of pale blue paint mottled his face in the grey sea light. He looked like some sort of barrow-wight rising to wreck vengeance on foolish invaders.

"*Throw us a gun!*" he commanded.

251

There was no disagreeing with that voice. Patterson rolled over while the bullet spray grew thicker, and tugged at Hopkins' trouser cuff. The young man glanced down, his mouth parting to say something . . . and then he took in what was happening just behind him. His mouth finished dropping.

"*Gun!*" Watson barked.

Hopkins flipped the catch and threw without a second's hesitation. *Smart man.*

The small handgun flew end over end into the air and went down with a splash of sand. Watson grabbed, as quick as a man who must seize a poisonous serpent before he himself is bitten. A stray bullet slapped a coral past his arm and sprayed the air with black grit. Watson already had the gun in his hand.

"There's one fifteen degrees to the left of the centre," Lestrade snapped. "But there's two twenty degrees to the right."

"Hopkins!" Gregson signaled frantically. "Tell them to toss their guns here!"

Watson didn't wait for that to happen. He aimed and fired.

"Good Lord." Bradstreet hunched into the smallest possible space over Patterson. "Loseth, do get down. You're too big to be an inconvenient target."

Loseth obeyed without a peep. He'd thrown his iron to Gregson, who'd promptly passed it on to Lestrade. Bradstreet was grateful. Lestrade was the better shot. Gregson used a different form of force when he was on a case.

Watson only fired thrice.

It was enough.

Watson led the way out in the stillness of the surf. About them there was a conspicuous absence of any sort of noise.

The three men employed to kill Bradstreet, Hopkins, Patterson and Loseth were dead instead. Lestrade found himself staring at one of the hooligans, whose brains leaked into the dark grey sands less than a yard from the lacework of salt foam.

They would have killed them if given the chance. That was the whole point, wasn't it?

And yet he was trying to keep his feelings to himself. He wasn't trained for this sort of battle. Nor was Gregson, to go by the way the big man was paler than usual and his chill blue eyes lingered slowly over the dark forms.

Most good Britishmen never used a gun. Especially for murder. It was an expensive thing . . . bulky . . . cumbersome . . . hard to conceal and prone to its own troubles. Even with his long history in the CID, Lestrade couldn't think of more than twenty cases that involved this particular sort of gun death. A fight of this nature touched upon a cold, distant form of mayhem that somehow was more terrible than the personal depravity of knives or clubs, garrote wires, or even poison.

Watson had been prepared and capable of the worst, able to strike like a single man Army into this pack of poor fools.

"Lestrade," Gregson's thick, white hand descended on his shoulder. "Sit you down and take a breath. You're fagged out."

Lestrade complied only because he promised to take it up with his rival later.

Later. Need to make certain there is a later.

About him, Watson was bending over Patterson and asking questions in a low, crisp voice that said he at least knew what he was doing. He chose Loseth as his assistant as he tore cloth into strips.

Gregson was talking to Bradstreet and Hopkins.

" . . . He said it!" Gregson was insisting to an incredulous audience. *"I didn't! I wouldn't make such a thing up, gentlemen! For whatever reason, John Clay and Jethro Quimper believe Colonel Moriarty had Sir Niles shot!"*

Good luck explaining that, Lestrade thought wearily. His head ached. When he stared at the sands beyond his hand, the subtle pattern shifted and blurred before his eyes and became something . . . something else.

It's cold, he thought.

"You did well." Watson nodded his approval. "But we need to double the amount of colloidal silver."

"How am I?" Patterson rasped. He was clearly prepared for the worst.

Watson looked at him kindly, from beneath ghostly blue marks of woad and wax. "You shall live, Inspector. You are merely very tired. I don't recommend a night about after being shot."

"What about Lestrade?" Hopkins whispered. "He looks like death on rarebit."

"He's worn out, Hopkins," Gregson said gruffly. "Had a lot less sleep than I did, and a bit more banging about."

"We can't rest just yet," Patterson whispered. "Not safe out here."

"I'll get him up," Bradstreet promised. He took firm, long-legged strides around Loseth and knelt by the Yarder.

"Geoffrey, you look tired out, but we need to all be on our feet. We've got to get going to some place safe."

"It's cold . . . ." Geoffrey mumbled.

"Yes, it'll be even colder, Geoffrey . . . come on, now . . . ."

Lestrade shook him off halfway through the assistance. "We've got to get out of here!" He yelped. "Or close the hatch! Where's a rock?" He looked wildly back and forth. "Somebody find a bloody rock!"

"What?" Gregson exclaimed.

"The sand!" Lestrade gasped in shock. "It wasn't being *blown in*, Gregson. *It was being sucked in!*"

"Bloody Hell!" Gregson turned as white as the cliffs of Dover. *"Someone's in the tunnel behind us!"*

Chapter XXXVII – The Calm
in the Eye of the Storm

"**B**loody Hell!" Gregson turned white as a Dover cliff. The roar in his ears was scarce louder than the tumult of the sea behind his back. *"Someone's behind us in the tunnel!"*

"Whoever they are, I'm sure we needn't stand about for formal introductions," Bradstreet snapped. "Unless they're the Bloody Red Cross, that is – and I doubt it."

"Later," Gregson answered absently. He spared a moment to take in the hard fact that Lestrade was also right about the original manor. What he'd taken for sea-roughened boulders were once-squared foundation pillars. Whoever was looking for them . . . they knew quite a lot about secret passages.

"You, Mr. Loseth – where does this tunnel go to besides here?"

Loseth shook his head. "Never used it, sir," he explained. "Only the baronet and his people."

"You knew about it, but you never used it?" Gregson started to rant but caught himself just in time. Sir Niles was no ordinary villainous mind. He couldn't blame Loseth for wanting to live as quietly as possible, but if only they'd known of his shenanigans years ago!

"Now that's just lovely," Bradstreet muttered to Hopkins behind Gregson.

"We need to get out of here, and we need to get off this island and back to the mainland." Hopkins reminded them. "Patterson is doing poorly, and I'm frightened of what may happen to Dr. Watson if we've overpowered again."

"You needn't concern yourselves over *me*, Inspector." Watson was tying strips of cloth about Patterson's arm to bind it from moving and stressing his muscles further. The gun had been almost casually returned to Hopkins once he was done with it. "Patterson is stable for now, but we need to get him on a boat as soon as possible." His face abruptly twisted. "While I would welcome the chance to assist you bringing these . . . ." The doctor's wordsmithing skills failed him for perhaps the first time in the Yard's memory. " . . . these criminals," he decided, "As a physician, I cannot part with Mr. Patterson."

"Gouster coming bad," Loseth worried to Bradstreet. "Could spin to a skreevar easy."

Bradstreet blinked as a thought came to him, and he groaned. "You're right. We need to get out of here and soon." He looked at Hopkins. "Hopkins, I am sorry. I was wrong . . . I forgot there's another meaning to gouster. Loseth was trying to warn us. The wind's going to go badly."

"We need to at least find decent coats for everyone." Lestrade butted into the conversation with some of his old arrogance. *Clunk.* A heavy chunk of reef rock rolled to the top of the hatch under his hands. "The wind I'm feeling *right now* will wipe out half of us the way we're dressed once we get to the water, and if the fishermen see Dr. Watson the way he is, there could very well be sudden panic about avenging Chieftains come to seek their stolen treasure!"

Watson straightened up to reveal the most disconcerting grin the policeman had yet seen on his face. "I confess, I rather *like* that idea." He continued to smile in a very unpleasant way as he wiped his hands clean with a rag. "At the very least can you imagine the distraction I could cause?"

"And not a few heart attacks," Hopkins muttered. He had joined Lestrade and Bradstreet in the pirating of a few stray stones of distinguished weight, and was piling them upon the top of the hatch. "This is the best we can do. It will slow them down, but it might not stop them."

"We can't stay here. Loseth, where can we get to a boat?"

Loseth shrugged in a way that only an islander could. "There cargo boats . . . steamers. Kept 'em off the line of the rest . . . kept 'em with the divers' gear."

"Divers' gear?" Gregson's swift mind pounced on the implications. "Who owns the gear, Loseth?"

Loseth looked at him as if he were mad. "Th'baronet, o'courst."

"Why am I not surprised," Gregson growled. "I wonder what the coastal police would think of that . . . Well, later. We're getting to the cargo boats, Loseth. Lead the way."

The path was narrow and the sun dipped below the sea too swiftly for their comfort. There were no streetlamps on Streat. No gaslights that spoke of the niceties of civilisation. They came to the shattered telegraph station, and they paused for something of use for poor Patterson. The lean man was shuddering as if wrapped in the deepest cold though the weather was only uncomfortable for the others. A rough carpet was their only haul until Hopkins yelped the discovery of a box of buried batteries.

"We'll take that for certain." Watson remembered again there were no pockets in his garb and paused to give the woven cloth a scathing glare. "But if we can find a supply of colloidal or similar, we can toss them as superfluous."

256

"We need to add nicking you a suit to the list of things to do," Gregson commented. "You look far too natural in those threads, and I'm starting to feel sympathy for Scrooge, escorted by all those ghosts."

Watson grinned at him again. There was little more than the flash of teeth and eyes as the clouds slipped across the moon, but the homespun was pale and reflected strange markings. Gregson was justified in his feelings.

Out of the shack things grew risky. They paused and hid behind boulders as they went along, hearing or glimpsing distant shouts.

"More shots," Hopkins whispered.

"Good ears," Lestrade grunted. Watson thought the little professional looked terrible. He moved like a much older man and paused often to look about him as if specifically looking for something or someone. Whatever fueled his personal actions, he did not know. Lestrade was keeping something to himself.

"We need to get over there," Loseth whispered harshly. He then gave up under the stress and fired off cylinders of syllables to Bradstreet.

The Bow Street Runner made a strange grunt beneath his mustaches, and translated. "We'll be passing behind the warehouse that Lestrade and Gregson were caught in. Nothing for it. There's nearly always someone in there, but if we walk quiet and act like we know what we're doing, we might be able to get through without questions."

"I'll take a look first." Lestrade got to his feet. "Give me a moment and we'll find out if there's anything going on."

He was gone before Gregson could tell him not to be a fool.

"Damn that little goose, I swear . . . ." Gregson gnawed on his knuckle as they waited.

A few minutes later, Hopkins made a soft whistling sound. They peered as well as they were able. Lestrade was making his way back to them quietly. He was making no particular effort to hide himself.

"Ought to flog you for that one." Gregson hid his relief the old-fashioned way.

"If you think it'll do any good," Lestrade shot back as he lifted his recovered gun. "I'm not leaving without this, Gregson. It has my name on it."

"Put it that way . . . ." Gregson was glad Lestrade had added to the armoury. It was going to be hard enough to explain their presence to the Home Office when they got back. "See anything?"

"Lots," Lestrade answered coldly. "Those shots Hopkins heard? There must have been a tear-down. I counted eight bodies. Lined up and shot down like so many sheep."

Hopkins shuddered, but Lestrade wasn't finished.

"And gentlemen . . . I think we need to see what's in there. And so . . . and so does Dr. Watson." Lestrade hesitated openly. His silhouette shifted in the dark. "If you're willing, that is."

This sudden reticence was not like him, and Watson felt a prickle sit upon his skin.

"There's all sorts of bits lying about," Lestrade continued, still in that awkward voice as the wind picked up strength about them. Sand swirled about their ankles. A Glouster indeed . . . "Surely there's some sort of kit for Patterson in there . . . and a change of clothing."

"Watson, you stand out a bit in this light with those – with that . . . ."

"Tabard?" Watson suggested.

"Right. Stay in the middle of us with Patterson. We can at least block your outline."

Watson merely nodded once to show his understanding and went to Patterson's side. After seeing him in a combat environment, his return to the calm surgeon they knew was swift enough to make the head spin.

Gregson sweated to suddenly put them all out in the open like this – even for a few moments – but Lestrade's natural distrust was good to rely on. If something was wrong, the smuggler's blood would warn him.

Gregson just hated to give up his authority on something.

Lestrade nipped ahead and held the cargo door open with his back, hand resting on the hilt of his reclaimed gun. He paid Gregson a long look as the man brought up the rear.

"Trouble, eh?" Gregson guessed. "Hopefully you won't have to use your old friend tonight."

"Huh," Lestrade scorned. "I need light. I'm not using this until I take it apart and put it back together."

"Isn't that a little worrisome? Even for you?"

"Quimper was on this island," Lestrade snapped. "I won't trust my own shoelaces until I've inspected them."

Gregson thought that was overreaching just a bit, but he allowed the man his anger.

"Inside," Lestrade urged. "We need to make a decision about this."

With that note, he slipped back inside. Gregson followed. He breathed relief to shut – and lock – the door after him.

Hopkins was lifting a vesta to a safety lantern hanging on the wall by its bail. He blew out the wax and traded Gregson a look over the smoke and flame. Every line and beard growth was illuminated, and Gregson saw the older, seasoned man waiting to come out.

The warehouse was painted with horror.

Gregson took in the chilling lack of blood – only bodies, neatly shot and lying on their backs or sides where the punch of the bullets had cast them like so many sand-filled dolls. The men closest to the door were lying on their shirt fronts, face-down into the filthy planks with small holes in their skulls.

Lestrade had managed to count eight in the poor light. With the lantern, there were at least four more.

"I've seen this before," Patterson whispered. The tall man stopped to clear his throat. Watson was lowering Patterson to a long crate for a table. His dark brown eyes were black.

"Where did you ever see something like this?" Lestrade whispered back. By consent, they were affording some sort of respect to the dead.

"Ah, Lord . . . it was years ago . . . a man paid his most trusted gang leaders to shoot down anyone who would squeal . . . He stood behind them while it was done . . . and when it was finished . . . he shot his loyal sergeants. It was then he fled."

"Just like here," Bradstreet said hoarsely. "But who was it? Clay? Quimper?"

"Neither," Watson whispered.

They watched as the doctor slowly rose up and walked with shaking legs to where Gregson was standing. He knelt and picked something off the floor by his shoe. Gregson stepped backwards violently, realizing he was next to evidence.

It was a thin paper band off a cigar.

"The Colonel has a preference," Watson said hoarsely, "for Moroccan, Cuban, and Iberian cigars."

Gregson stared at the tiny ring. "I've never seen an Iberian cigar in my life," he admitted.

"Nor have I," Lestrade murmured.

"I have," Bradstreet growled. "They're expensive enough to be obscene. Just one would keep my coke stove going for a week."

Lestrade saw Watson's stiffen as he took in a long form tumbled up and face-down. He opened his mouth, thinking to warn him. "Doctor, just a –"

Watson saw.

He made a single sound – inarticulate, a briefly helpless sound that had nothing to do with the strong, capable soldier of his nature.

They all followed Watson's horror-struck eyes to the long, lean form in black. The dead man was built much like Patterson. Skeletal and spare, with oiled black hair raked brutally to the back. A receding hairline was glimpsed over the top of the sleeved arm.

The cuff about the arm was pushed up to expose the bare skin. There were needle marks.

The doctor shambled slowly to the corpse, and just as slowly turned it over. Dust had settled over the lean face, stuck in the dulled grey eyes.

It wasn't Holmes.

But it looked so much like him that Lestrade felt ill beneath his heart to see it. And Watson's expression was enough to crack anyone's fortitude.

The dead man stared upward into the trembling lamplight, his grey eyes flat.

Ridiculously, Lestrade thought of the great eyes of the amateur . . . Would this imitation's gaze have approximated such quick thought and action? How would it have been possible?

"He . . . that's why he laughed when John Clay said Holmes was alive . . . He hired a double . . . a double to fool us . . . to fool Mycroft . . . ." Watson whispered. "And when everything started to go wrong for him . . . He . . . ."

The doctor started breathing hard and fast. He couldn't seem to stop.

"He shot his own men."

Lestrade had seen the signs of shock before – and many times – but it never occurred to him that Watson would be its victim. Watson was a soldier.

No . . . that *was* it. Watson was a soldier . . . and a superior officer – corrupted though he was – had done the unthinkable *by killing his own men*.

Watson was a strong man, but that sort of betrayal went beyond the depth of depravity. His men had been loyal to him . . . and they had been in the way.

Lestrade tried to imagine how he would feel if C.I. Miller (cankerous as the old man was) would blatantly sacrifice some of his own policemen. He couldn't. Even Miller, much as he hated Lestrade, tried to get rid of Lestrade honourably, by practically forcing him to take trainings and classes that would qualify him for some sort of survival wages if he wanted or needed to retire.

"That son of . . . ." Hopkins' words failed him. He let his hands fall to his sides. "We're in a crime and we can't do anything."

"What? Of course we can!" Patterson rasped. He tried to get up but Loseth gently prevented him.

"We can't now," Bradstreet said heavily. "Hopkins is right to the centre. We have to have some of these Bludgers [1] set to rights before we report what's going on."

"How?"

"The Queen's too close to Streat. We daren't report a half-started job. Streat's partially underneath Scots law. English law when it supplanted the old Viking laws." Bradstreet clasped his hands together. "And when

260

something like this . . . something big happens . . . it all goes straight to the Home Office, and sometimes the Foreign Office."

"Foreign Office my eye," Gregson grunted. "More like paranoids. They'll use this as an excuse to move in and take over. Just watch. Mycroft Holmes won't be the least bit happy to find someone was out using the likeness of his brother for their own purposes."

A howl of wind suddenly cut the conversation off. It rattled against the loose planks. Hopkins quickly grabbed the lantern down from its nail with a breath.

"There we are then," Loseth whispered. "No getting off the Isle until it stops, or you'll be reaching the Mainland floating face down."

"We'll make wise use of our time." Gregson spoke coldly and quietly. "Everyone pick a man. We need to find clues for identity . . . any little thing that can prove Moriarty will be another nail in his own coffin."

It was revolting work. The wind gained teeth in the space of a quarter-hour, and sand kicked through the cracks. Patterson dozed under the discovery of a field medical kit – Watson had judged the morphine safe enough – and had him drink up the colloidal silver found inside. While the Yarders searched the dead, he wired Hopkins' batteries to Lestrade's watch and lowered the lot into an empty tin filled with seawater. With the extra voltage the silver came off like a cloud in the water.

"I've never understood how that works," Hopkins confessed.

"Silver is anathema to most forms of harmful bacteria," Watson explained. "Especially the ones that encourage infection. It also appears to help the body fight off invaders." He shrugged lightly. "In the desert, we would put a silver coin in our canteens. One never knew if the water we drank was clean." He had recovered from his initial shock and was back to his familiar duties as a doctor. "Or if the natives had poisoned the wells."

Few of the men were unscathed – even Hopkins had his own collection of once-broken bones from the past. These old offenses were alive and well as the storm's pressure rose and fell. Watson began limping noticeably, and twice reached up to hold his bad shoulder. Lestrade was limping as well, and Gregson saw he was rubbing at his head as if the pain had returned.

Gregson's once-broken ribs gave him a twinge now and then, which worried him without cause. It was the fear of the brittle bone disease. So far there were no signs of it in him, but he also paid attention to his diet and did what he could to take care of himself.

They each selected their man, wrote down what they could find of them by simple observation and the contents of each man's pockets, and then let the men have the last dignity of putting them out on their backs in the coolest corner, covering their faces with a tarpaulin.

261

And the work was grueling. They were obvious criminals. Their pockets contained the tools of their trade: weapons, lengths of garroting wire, a packet of poison here and there . . . thin shanks for silent assassinations . . . but there were also signs of human beings: Wedding rings. An engagement token. A dried tussy-mussy . . . a handkerchief neatly embroidered with the hair of a murdered assassin's wife. Hopkins found a plain farmer's turnip and snapped the lid open, hoping to find engraved initials. What he found were the chromolithographs of two little boys.

He choked out something – or choked it down.

Lestrade sighed and rubbed at his head again. "For what it's worth, Hopkins, I doubt their families knew what they did."

"That helps some." Hopkins forced himself to pry the paper off the back. The names of the children were written in grease pencil. "I'm sorry for my weakness."

"You shouldn't be," Lestrade said at last, because he felt something should be said. "This is revolting work. I've worked amongst corpses stacked to my collar bone, and this is . . . this is not something I could get used to."

Bradstreet had taken time off to examine the crates. His reward was a cache of foodstuffs. "Here. We need to get something to eat – especially you three." He managed to glare at Patterson, Gregson, and Lestrade all at the same time despite their being far apart. "Hopkins, that looks like a lamp brazier in the corner . . . ."

Supper did not lighten the gloom. The single lantern doubled as a cook stove, its tiny flame catching the heat off the small iron frame where a pot of water boiled. Bradstreet's discovery of a jerrycan full of drinking water had been the highlight of the evening. They put up a makeshift broth using the water and a handful of dried beef that Lestrade grumbled looked to have been the same rubbish the Rockefellers sold to the Union Army during the Civil War.

"How would you know about that?" Watson asked in surprise.

Gregson snorted around a handful of raw bacon with his hardtack cracker. "He used to work the ports . . . You'd be surprised at what the Confederates and Yankees were trying to do to each other in the name of Patriotism."

"The worst part of it was *after* the war, actually . . . ." Lestrade grimly set his teeth into a hard cracker. "The market was flooded with this cheap dreck. There weren't any more gullible soldiers to take advantage of."

"I learn something new every day," Watson decided.

Bradstreet suddenly lowered his portion. "I don't want to say this, but we need to get you gents into coats . . . and we need to find a suit for the

262

doctor. He really *is* going to frighten the good people of this isle into conniptions if they see him."

Loseth looked openly puzzled at the last part. "There aren't many good people here, Mr. Bradstreet."

"There's one." Bradstreet didn't blink, which flustered the grizzled sailor all the more.

"There's still some men in the corner that need to be tended to." Lestrade paused to glare at Gregson's exaggerated offer of the tea can. "One looks to be about your size, Doctor."

Watson set his lips in displeasure. "I would refuse if I could," he said firmly.

"So would any of us," Bradstreet assured him.

The hour grew late. It was hard to appoint sleeping shifts. No one wanted to talk about it, but they were all thinking of who it might have been in the tunnel behind them. Finally, Gregson lowered the flame to conserve the oil and bade himself, Lestrade, and Patterson the first sleep.

"Half-hour," he dictated. "Or I'll know the reason why."

Bradstreet grinned.

NOTE

1.   Violent criminals. Bludgeoners

Chapter XXXVIII – Traps Sprung

Lestrade woke up barely ten minutes later.

Bradstreet frowned. "Back to the Sandman with you, Geoffrey. Gregson will murther us both."

"Gregson's catching up on his beauty sleep." Lestrade sat up with a faint groan. "For God's sake, don't disturb him . . . I rested some earlier, Roger. I promise you."

He leaned his head against the makeshift headboard of a crate marked in sigils. About them, the sound of the storm howled about the small cushion of silence.

Hopkins and Loseth were asleep together, sharing the warmth of one of the larger carpets. Bradstreet had been trying not to look at the Islander too closely. He cried in his sleep every so often.

Bow Street Runner and Whitehall Yarder regarded each other in the pale yellow flame.

"I need to go over my iron," Lestrade said at last. He pulled the weapon out and stiffly walked over to the spool table Bradstreet had set up. Two crates made passable chairs. As Bradstreet watched, he broke open the handgun and let the bullets spill upon the rough wood surface. They pattered and rolled to the edge. He stopped them with the flat of his hand absently, and wordlessly took the tiny cleaning kit Bradstreet kept in his inside coat pocket.

Long moments passed as Lestrade scrubbed out, examined, and frowned his way through every detachable and workable part of his Bulldog. [1] Neither man needed to hold conversation with the other . . . they'd known each other too long for that sort of nonsense.

Until Lestrade grew more and more dissatisfied with the gun.

"I don't understand this . . ." he muttered as he rolled each bullet off the table and back into the chamber. "The weight's off . . . but everything's as it should be . . . ." He ejected the bullets out again and swept them up in his hands. He froze just before he could return one into the chamber.

Bradstreet saw his friend's face grow light and sick. "Geoffrey?"

Lestrade wordlessly held out the handful of bullets.

Bradstreet frowned, thinking they looked like ordinary .44's and picked them up. His eyebrows shot to his hairline at their weight.

"This – "

"Fake," Lestrade said hoarsely. He stared aghast at his once-loyal weapon. "He . . . he found my gun . . . and he knew I would try to get it back . . . ."

"And the next time you'd pulled the trigger . . . you'd . . . ." Bradstreet took a deep breath and held it. "I suppose it isn't paranoia when you know a man is out to get you."

"Roger, this is why Hazel won't let you visit people in hospitals." Lestrade shook his head and transferred the dummy bullets into his coat pocket. Bradstreet fished out his bullet box and they divvied up what he had between them. "Let's keep this to ourselves for now. Gregson will have a seizure if he finds out someone accosted a man on his team without his knowing about it."

"He's just practicing for the day when he replaces Miller," Bradstreet comforted Lestrade as the wind kicked stormy heels against the planks.

Lestrade snorted delicately. "I hope to God that day isn't long in coming," he said with feeling. "Miller should have retired years ago . . . Still . . . ." He rubbed at his eyes. Dried blood itched at his neck and he scrubbed at it angrily. "I don't know," he said. "What's left for an old man when he does retire? Not much."

"Not much for any of us when you think about it," Bradstreet said with the sad, gentle bluntness no one else could emulate. "Can't blame him for not retiring . . . I don't think he could do anything else."

"No . . . you're right there."

"S'odd." Bradstreet laughed self-consciously. "This wasn't what I wanted to show you of Scotland."

"Going to sugarcoat it, were you?"

"Not even that . . . I wanted you to see what I loved about these wild lands." Roger sighed, his large hand sweeping invisible cobwebs through the air. "The crofts . . . the farms . . . there's even some of the old Highlanders over among Hazel's family. You'd like them. Hell, you might even understand them when they start cursing the goats . . . The winters can be harsh, but it would be a good place to . . . to rest, Geoffrey. You understand?"

Lestrade was quiet for a long time. The wind spoke for him, battering patiently against the thin skin of wood shielding them from the sand and what sounded like pebbles, cobbles, and chaff.

"I don't want to be like Miller," the small man said at last. "I should have a plan for my retirement . . . It's just . . . I don't know if I'll ever live long enough for it . . . and what would I do, Roger? Shouldn't my pay be going into something more realistic . . . such as school for the boys?"

"I can't tell you that . . . but if you ever decide to do something . . . plan for one of the inevitables . . . let me know. Roane Cove is a good place to live, Geoffrey. A good place to rest."

"I'll . . . I'll think about it."

The moment chilled slightly between them.

Bradstreet slowly withdrew from his side of the table and pulled out his flask.

Lestrade grimaced. "If my grandfather had allowed himself a true retirement . . . Roger, I wouldn't be alive now. I don't know what to do yet . . . perhaps I never will. But I know that the Met is within some of the deepest troubles of its history. And we've lost too many of our allies."

"You mean Mr. Holmes."

"Especially him. Insufferable pill," Lestrade grumbled under his breath. "Still, there must have been something to the man for Dr. Watson to be loyal to him. He's not a fool by a longshot. Probably one of the smartest people you or I will ever meet – "

"I would have agreed with you as far back as 1885, Geoffrey. Before we caught your Martin trying to make his own version of the alphabet."

Geoffrey groaned faintly. "*Must* you remind me?"

Bradstreet chuckled softly. "No, I know what you mean. He was a pill. A royal one. But he could get things done, and the gentlemen respected him. At least, they did what he commanded. They wouldn't have listened to us, would they?"

"No. We aren't gentlemen." Lestrade stated the fact without rancor. It was a fact of life, and there was no sense in resenting it. "We're workmen, and I'd rather be a workman, where your honesty is measured in what you do, and not the size of the house you live in . . . But we've chosen this profession, and we have to be doing something right with it." His lip crooked up in faint humour, and not-so-faint pride. Bradstreet watched it fade. "Nicholas is talking about joining the Met."

"Ah." Bradstreet knew the peculiar pain and pride that signified. "He's young yet."

"What about your Garrett? We all thought he'd become a book-binder or something. He'll be testing soon . . . don't tell me it can't happen with Nicholas."

"It could . . . it very likely will. But Nicholas has time to change his mind. You'd rather he not follow his father. I know what that feels like. And . . . you'd like him to find his profession away from your shadow where someone will pass judgment on him for something you did in the past. He's smart enough when he applies himself . . . and he's stubborn enough to get the marks he wants to get in school." Bradstreet took the flask and spun its corner like a top on the table, giving his fingers something to do. "Every thought you've had about your Nick, I've had with my Garrett."

"No doubt," Lestrade grunted. They passed the flask back and forth for a moment. Someone rolled over with a weary sigh.

266

"Patterson's already looking better," Bradstreet admired. "Wonder why Watson put iodine on his *feet?* "

"I'm sure if you asked him, he'd tell you."

"I'll try to figure it out first."

"Luck to you there."

"I know. I haven't a prayer."

Lestrade lifted his eyes and met Bradstreet's across the table.

Bradstreet sighed through his nose, which brushed his mustaches. "Yes, I'm worried about Garrett. He's smarter than his old gaffer . . . I thought . . . I thought it meant he'd take a career where he'd be using his brains . . . not wearing himself down as a policeman. I want better for them, Geoff."

Lestrade lowered his eyes to the table. He didn't trust himself to speak. He could see part of Bradstreet's arm. The lower arm, with its once-clean cuff and the cufflink holding it together. Unlike the usual metal or gem, Roger's was made of petrified wood and gleamed like honey-dipped wood in the tiny flame.

A gift from Hazel. It was supposed to be from the Holy Land. Lestrade didn't know exactly what that meant, save that Christ was supposed to have walked there. He was a bad Christian and a terrible, utterly terrible, pretend-Catholic. His views of God were immature and half-baked, reflecting the flaws in his education. He approached the Bible like a book of law: By memorizing as much as possible.

Only in London could a man make his way without revealing his complete ignorance. He wouldn't survive a week among Roger's kin.

Something hit the wall by their heads and they both jumped. The spell was broken and they were glad of it.

Lestrade got to his feet, taking one last nip before handing the flask back.

"I know that look." Bradstreet cocked an eyebrow.

"I want to look at him again."

They'd closed those grey eyes out of respect. The bones beneath that pale skin were long and hard, like the man they remembered. Lestrade stared, sinking his gaze into every inch of the dead man. The hands were so much like what he remembered, and the nails were trimmed a little long . . . like a gentleman's.

Sherlock Holmes had the nails of a gentleman, and the long, fine fingers of a man who was born to better, but Lestrade remembered the man as having the least gentlemanly hands in London. They were scarred – atrociously so – with tiny plasters, bruises, scratches, cuts and scrapes – of self-inflicted chemical experiments and the hazards of his work.

Of all the things Mr. Holmes had done to convince Lestrade that he was serious about working as a detective . . . it had been his hands that did the trick – not any arrogance or foreign quote or sleight of mind.

Mr. Holmes *used* his hands, and that confused Lestrade to this day, for it made no sense.

Gentlemen didn't lower themselves down to the level of a workman. After all, their ancestors had sacrificed to better their children . . . Why would anyone want to regress? Mr. Holmes's genius – and his hands – should have been cultivated with his violin before the halls of music, or seeking answers in dusty old books.

For some reason, Mr. Holmes had chosen to work in a way that incorporated the police into his field. He could have done so much better . . . He could have taken a post with his brother in the Foreign Office. But instead, he had stubbornly chosen to carve his own way through the world . . . and small surprise that he'd made such a unique path for himself. Lestrade wasn't certain Mr. Holmes could walk across a street without calling attention to how well he did it. But credit to the man (God rest his soul) for wanting to make a difference in the world . . .

Morbid thought, Geoffrey. Time to stop it.

"The dead are different from the living," he muttered. "As soon as they stop being alive . . . they don't look the same."

"Makes me pity the fools who don't believe in the soul," Bradstreet agreed.

"It looks so much like him." Lestrade shuddered. "But there's little things. I don't think Mr. Holmes had that – " he pointed to a tiny mole at the wrist. "And the nose is just a bit off . . . ." He sighed. "I don't know what I'm looking for . . . except . . . something that would show who he really was. A name."

"There's no way of knowing, unless we find a record somewhere," Bradstreet said softly. "A Potter's Field for him, once the coroner is finished."

"God help us. I thought the Professor was bad enough, but . . . from what Patterson told me, he wasn't *personal*. This brother the Colonel is so much worse. He's as personal as war can get."

"He did his share on the doctor," Bradstreet agreed thoughtfully, his voice low as the lamp flame. "All because he thought he had something he wanted."

"People murder each other for less," Lestrade reminded him grimly. "Which makes me wonder: What next, now that the trap's been sprung?"

Watson blinked lead out of his eyes to find the Yarders in various stages of waking up. Hopkins was groaning as he kinked out his back, and

Bradstreet was complaining about the inability to make a decent cup of tea in the savage wilderness.

"There's some bee balm in that chest full of dry stuff," Gregson mumbled. "Throw some of that in and call it Earl Grey."

"You are a Philistine. As if I'd trust your advice on a decent cup."

"He's right." Watson yawned behind his hand. "It does make Earl Grey." In the suit of one of the dead men, he looked far more like he ought to. The fact that he was wearing a dead man's clothes was a protest under record. Gregson promised to give him a blank complaint form as soon as they reached safety. "Did we miss anything, gentlemen?"

"A male alligator will charge if it hears a tuba in *B-flat*."

Watson gulped down his yawn to stare at Bradstreet incredulously.

The Runner held up a slim volume. "We found this in one of the crates," he explained. "It seems to be some sort of half-baked advice on how to survive a visit to the Colonies."

Watson continued to stare, utterly flabbergasted.

Gregson rolled his eyes. "The man who taught you to read should be excavated and shot," he grumbled. "Don't mind him, Dr. Watson. He's like this. Give him a book and he gets a bit dangerous."

Hopkins grinned at Watson. "Welcome to Scotland Yard, Doctor."

Paddington Street:

Martin Lestrade tapped on the bedroom door as quietly as possible. After a moment he pushed it in. The hallway lamps let him see well enough into the darkened room.

Nicholas was sound asleep – finally. His face was still red and moist, and *Mamm* was resting her hand on his forehead as she looked at him.

Martin thought she looked very tired.

"Will he be all right, *Mamm*?"

"He'll be fine, sweetheart." *Mamm* stood, gently as possible so as not to wake him up. "He needs to rest." She shut the door after them with a click and took a deep breath. He saw her looking at him and smiled. She smiled back and ruffled his hair.

"I'm afraid your brother takes after his uncles, dear. This is something Cheathams are famous for. They pay a price for growing so big, you know."

"Did I ever have growing pains like that?" Martin knew he didn't. He couldn't. He would have remembered.

"No, Love. You grow very slowly. You take after your Papa. Nick takes after the Cheatham side . . . and they grow big and fast. Sometimes it hurts them. They need to eat more when that happens . . . and they need

269

to sleep more." She hugged him with one arm. "It hurts. I remember seeing your Uncle Bartram going through this. I was just a tot, but even that big lug was sniffing a tear back now and then."

Martin struggled to see that in his mind, and failed.

Mamm chuckled, bending and kissing the top of his head. "You'll be taller than your mother in a few years," she noted. "What will you do with all those extra inches?"

"I don't know." Martin was suddenly bashful. "*Mamm* . . . can I sleep in the living room tonight?"

"I don't see why not. You might wake your brother up if you crawl in bed with him . . . and he does need his rest." *Mamm* sighed. "If I don't know the feeling." She squeezed his shoulder. "Let's head off then. Going to bed early one night never hurt anyone. Who knows what the morrow will bring, hmm?"

"I should feed all the animals first," Martin worried. "Nick's going to fret if I don't."

"Get you going, then." His mother laughed. "See to the poor dumb beasts, and hie yourself to bed. You may be growing slower than your brother, but you are growing . . . and growing boys need their rest!"

Streat:

Watson watched the seawater cream in the wake of the steamship. He could feel the thrum of the large motor beneath his skin, vibrating against his very bones. It was not completely pleasant, but he tolerated it. Streat was vanishing into the horizon line. It was a fair trade.

"Doctor?"

Watson pulled out of his heavy thoughts. He looked up. Lestrade was watching him with an expression that might have rubbed him the wrong way not so long ago: Watson had never bourne solicitations for his welfare with grace.

"I wanted it to be Holmes."

So much raw honesty within six words.

Lestrade answered back with seven.

"So did I, Doctor . . . So did I."

They watched the swirl of water pass by without saying anything for a good long time.

Limousin:

Starlight poorly lit the oak orchards of France. Within the patternless tangle of briar and thorn, shrub and canopy, something was moving.

270

Holmes knew better than to be too obvious in his steps. There were many hunters who thought nothing of pulling the trigger of their gun at whatever they thought might be a game target.

He hoped no one here would link his exhausted shamble with that of a four-footed deer or wild boar.

The forest broke its fringe and he sank down into the open grassland, the stars above him like mute lanterns.

Long minutes passed as he knelt on the damp earth, trying to breathe while clutching at his arm hard enough to constrict his own chest.

He should feel something . . . some sort of triumph at besting Moran at his own game . . . but he did not.

I did not truly best him. If I had, he would be in the hands of the authorities, and I would be free to walk in London again.

The bitterness of his play threatened to choke him, and for a moment he fell heedless upon the damp orchardgrass.

Moran had missed killing him by a hair.

He had missed foiling *Moran* by the same dimension.

A hollow victory, for it meant he had created two outcomes: The first was that he and Moran were both free to play games with each other.

The second was the worst: Moran would not be snared unless he was proven guilty of a crime serious enough to keep him behind bars.

In other words . . . he would have to wait for Moran to do what came naturally to him. The man could not resist killing, no more than he could resist breathing.

Another life before the tiger.

Watson mentioned being on a tiger hunt in India once. His respect could only grow in hindsight, for Moran appeared to have absorbed too many of the maneater's traits. Every fruitless hunt was a failure.

And I failed. I thought I was hunting a man, not an animal.

He slumped forward, almost too tired to think.

And yet, he did. He would never be permitted the luxury of thoughtlessness. No matter how weary his mind was, it would never allow him peace.

Moran would recover from his loss . . . .

And like any hunter, he would re-bait his trap.

Patience had never come so painfully.

NOTE

1. British Bulldog was an 1878 short-barreled (2½") five-shot Webley revolver designed to be kept in a coat pocket for self-defense. President Garfield was assassinated by an American copy of this gun. Effective for fifteen to twenty yards, it was extremely popular for its time and had various calibres . . . In this case, we'll say it was a .44.

Chapter XXXIX –Particular Tension

London was never completely *dry* save on the rarest of occasions. The fog saw to that. This example was spectacular: A London Particular had descended not an hour after the heavy rains brought up from the Continent, and the oily fog saturated the entire city, afflicting even the respectful buildings on Pall Mall.

Mycroft Holmes sat in his usual chair, ignoring the missives collecting on the table. He would place them in the drawer when he next rose, but he would not stand just to put them aside.

Before him the imperfect light of day had long passed to an equally imperfect night: Lamps burned fitfully against the swirling miasma like lit chains before the single, large window of his sitting room. Traffic slowed, started up as fitfully as a stop-and-go engine, and continued on. It would be a terrible night for travel. The fog was only building. In a few hours, one wouldn't be able to see the hand before the face.

The big man sat, and waited.

Corpulent and staid his body was, but the body was only the frame. What existed was the *mind*, and his was ever-active. He could ponder more than a few thoughts simultaneously, and had confidence in his ability to come to the correct conclusions. But to prove he was right would be to step backwards – and that was unbearable.

Under periods of intuition, a person may painstakingly trace their steps from that flash of genius to prove they had in truth operated under logic – but the flash had performed so swiftly that the brain could not consciously track its own paths.

Mycroft could no more go backwards, even to prove himself right, than he could physically fly. The few times he had been forced into the action, he had felt as though he were wading in deep glue. Every individual observation had been presented to the Foreign Office and examined. The next observation following after that. The experience invariably left him drained and weary.

Sherlock had been a great convenience, for not only could he lower himself to explain his thoughts, but he did actually enjoy the explaining. Granted, Sherlock's mind did not have to lower itself as steeply as Mycroft, but Sherlock rather enjoyed showing others how he thought – no doubt in the hopes it would also show others how to think.

And so, Mycroft pondered the thin collection of letters, two wires, and a dryly agonising cipher of a report – agonising in its simplicity, and transparent to anyone with a basic education in astronomical physics.

1) Moran had failed his attempts to kill Sherlock in the depths of Limousin – Why had Sherlock not hied to Montpellier? A premature arrival was better than never arriving at all . . . No doubt he would have some glib excuse or an interesting fact "accidentally" hidden away to justify his action. The fact was, Moran's hunt had not ended according to the old *shikari*'s expectations.

2) Moran's failure was no doubt influenced by his method of hunting. He preferred to hunt the unwary. Sherlock was anything but unwary – hyper-vigilant would put it better. When Mycroft thought of the thick oak forests of that part of France, and the herds of cattle, he could not imagine Moran there for long. He would have tried to lure Sherlock out on some pretext . . . as if Sherlock would fall for the same trick twice!

And he didn't even fall gull to it the first time, when Watson was lured away from his side . . . He knew and was going to meet his end anyway . . . perhaps by now he has learned a bit of caution . . . .

3) Sherlock had failed as well. Mycroft had entertained the hopes that as far as Moran went with Moriarty, what was good for the goose would suffice for the gander . . . but Sherlock was unable to dispose of Moran as neatly as he had Moran's master.

4) Moran had the untenable advantage of being nowhere near the debacle of Moriarty's generals as they subsided to their inevitable anarchy. By focusing on Sherlock, he had ironically *protected* himself from being part of the sweeping-up of the Family.

5) The Foreign Office was still refusing to believe Moran had anything to do with something as revolting as Moriarty's Empire of Crime. Moran's birth really was an inconvenience at times.

6) Sir Niles' murder in a room full of witnesses had been interesting. The baronet had been the perfect purse-holder for the late Professor. Mycroft could only hope they would listen to him now and search the man's records with great aggression.

7) Colonel Moriarty had been shrewd indeed to arrange the man's death while he stood in the same room. Mycroft

had needed no more than a few seconds to sift through the possible candidates. John Clay was against Moriarty, but he would not have acted without Moran's authority. Nor would he have sullied himself with murder. Mr. Quimper would have been capable, but not willing to act alone. Ergo, it had been Moriarty who saw to Sir Niles' murder . . .

Quimper would have been ideal in inheriting Sir Niles' role of office.

8) And Moriarty had created a most convincing double of his brother . . . *That* had been a moment's worth of disconcertion. It explained the strange reports and rumours filtering in at odd places. Mycroft had wondered if it had been common hysteria and wish fulfillment, for his brother had not been anywhere near the countries in question when those rumours were flying about . . . Moriarty was a clever man, and successful because he could easily walk the line between civilisation and savagery. Moran shared that ability . . . They were both dangerous, but Moriarty currently had the greatest potential for causing harm.

9) The oldest Loseth had been the exception to the calculations. His persona had emerged in the absence of his overbearing brothers. Mycroft was glad the man had a moral compass after all. He did wish he knew better how *that* steamer had been finagled. Inspector Gregson's brief ciphered wire to Whitehall had not given details. *"Cousin to the captain"* would have to suffice for now.

10) Dr. Watson was none the worse for his enforced adventure, and he had been able to save the life of Inspector Patterson. Doubtless he was furious over Moriarty's creation of Sherlock's double – more furious than he would be over his own treatment.

11) The bog bodies were being quietly removed from the Museum. Mycroft did not care what pretext was being used. They were not artifacts, and in his own opinion it ought to inspire a bit more research and ethical caution in the future.

12) Clay and Quimper had been the first to flee the island – their combined intelligence had been enough to show them the folly of staying anywhere close to the Colonel.

Mycroft did wonder about the storm that had followed on their heels. So far there was no word, no sighting of their ship, but Quimper was a fox renowned, and capable of changing the identity of even a large craft on short notice.

That left Colonel Moriarty.

Mycroft was positive the Colonel had been the one in the tunnel coming after Watson – and indeed, it was Watson he was after. Watson and Inspector Lestrade.

And there it came down to it.

Mycroft remembered there was a glass of wine in his hand. He sipped it lightly.

Mycroft did not share Sherlock's impatience with lesser intellects, for there were ways – interesting ways – in which the human brain compensated for its shortcomings. Mycroft rather enjoyed the company of men more than his brother, for it gave him the opportunity to see how men could solve problems within their own abilities.

Dr. Watson's willful, stubborn, and silent war against the Colonel had frankly been a surprise to Mycroft, and it had lifted his estimation of the man. He knew better than to battle the more powerful and ruthless Colonel on his own terms, so he had simply created his own. The Watsons had worked well together, and finished their duties despite the distractions of tragic love, blindness, and the horrors of war.

There must have been a pact sworn for secrecy, for Watson had to figure out a way to quietly alert Lestrade. Lestrade was not intelligent the way Sherlock understood intelligence, but he was refreshingly undistracted from superstition and class intricacies. And he took his time in drawing to his conclusions *if he was suspicious.* Mycroft understood both from reports and statements that if Lestrade had no doubts in a case, then no doubts existed. But let *one* thought to the contrary occur to him, and he would hammer the issue to death until some sort of conclusion was reached.

Watson had deliberately timed a mustard seed of doubt into Lestrade from the very beginning. And it had been beautifully done. Lestrade had found Moriarty's graverobbing . . . and quietly taken the matter out of Watson's hands. Watson's sense of honour was kept intact. Lestrade had dealt with the case as he saw fit.

The question is: *What did Lestrade do with the treasure?*

It all led to Patterson.

Patterson had met with Lestrade, then taken his inexplicable departure from the Yard, only to return to help dismiss the remnants of the

Moriarty Empire . . . Lestrade had told them Patterson had been the man to take the stones . . . Mycroft believed that.

Even for a man of intellect, there were plenty of ways for an unintellectual man to cause confusion, obfuscation, and defeat.

Inspector Gregson knew more than he was saying in his reports. Very well. Mycroft expected nothing less. Gregson was not on his par, but he was creative. Creative in a way few men were.

Watson, Gregson, Lestrade, and Patterson. Four men bound by the same threads to solve a burden they would not have chosen for themselves. They were all men of honour, fixed in their moral codes and determined not to pass on any responsibility they could not shulder for themselves.

He would be most interested to see what the future would hold.

"I cannot believe they let us on the train looking like this."

Gregson blinked bleary eyes at Lestrade. "No train on the Western Line will refuse a coal miner, Lestrade."

"Do we look like coal miners?" Lestrade wanted to know, his voice just a touch shrill. It made Watson blink in confusion.

"Don't talk about coal miners around him," Gregson explained. "Bad history."

"Oh," Watson said without understanding.

"Bad history, my twisted left foot!" Lestrade barked. He reached up and tried again to fruitlessly wipe soot off his neck. "For five years, the Met was farming me out to every bit of CID work that involved coal, tin, or Cornwall."

"Drama doesn't become you," Gregson sniffed – but without his usual force. He was dog-tired as the other two. "We stuck you in Devon twice."

"Why Devon?" Watson wondered.

"Tin smuggling." Gregson paused to yawn. His jaw cracked like a party snapper. "He's perfect for the jobs – short, dark, weasely . . . everything you'd expect with a stubby little Celt."

"Normans." Lestrade did not quite growl low enough to be ignored.

Watson was just relieved things were back to normal – but they wouldn't be safe yet if the two Yarders were back to normal – at each other's throat. He sank into the window corner and closed his eyes for a long moment. They did look filthy. Rumpled, unwashed, smeared with dirt, soot, reeking with the worst aspects of the sea and no recent baths . . . Well, Lestrade had drawn a bucket and scrubbed the worst of the grime off his neck and face with icy seawater. Gregson had tried to pull Watson into the argument that Lestrade was going to kill himself with a fatal chill, but Bradstreet pointed out (rightfully so, in Watson's mind) that if

Lestrade wasn't allowed to get himself clean somehow, the fatality would be Gregson's for tipping Lestrade over the edge of sanity.

"And since we're on the subject of medicine . . . ." Bradstreet had cleared his throat as they waited for the train to depart, taking Watson, Gregson, and Lestrade back to London, "might I ask you something?"

"Ask away."

"Why did you paint the iodine on the soles of Patterson's feet?"

"So he could draw the iodine into his blood without drawing notice." Watson said it as if that explained everything. "We're obvious enough to the eye without adding something that looks like blood to the mess."

"Wouldn't have guessed that," Hopkins admitted. His honesty was bald and unapologetic. It caught Watson's attention because Lestrade tended to admit to his failings in a similar way.

It caught Gregson's ear too. "Hopkins, never admit to anything unless you have to," he grunted in a friendly manner. The steamship slowed, and they all adjusted their balance as the port loomed. "You and Bradstreet ready?"

"The hospital should take care of Patterson good enough." Bradstreet was already shouldering his small bag up. "I think it would be a good idea to post a guard until he finishes recovering."

"You're certain the staff is discreet?"

"I'd say ten percent of my family works in it . . . They're discreet all right. I just tell them the Luddites tried to kill the poor fellow and he'll be as safe as a night in the vaults of Cox."

Gregson snorted. "We need to remember that tactic."

"Never admit to ignorance, but a white lie is fine?" Hopkins muttered, and Watson was hard pressed to keep from smiling.

Leaving the other three – Bradstreet, Hopkins, and Loseth – had been the easy part. Loseth had quietly refused to accompany them south, saying his cousin had offered him a berth for now, and the sea was safer than the land. Bradstreet and Hopkins had stayed to start cleaning things up.

Lestrade, Gregson, and Watson watched the battered tug head to the northeast.

"We'll never see Loseth again." Lestrade was final. "But I can't say I'm sorry. He would have been put to trial for what his family pulled him into."

"His stripe is better off on a boat," Gregson agreed soberly. "Well, we just mark him under the anonymous file as an 'informant' . . . Bloody Hell, I still need to write up tripe to the Office. What say you we all grab

278

something to eat before we find a train?" He didn't wait for a response. "Lestrade, you're the cleanest . . . You find a pasty shop or somesuch."

Lestrade muttered further under his breath but did not argue. Watson found a place to sit in what passed for the train station, and dozed by the low heat of the stove.

The next six hours were grueling. The two Yarders were frankly worried about Moriarty's absence, and Gregson selected a circuitous route that kept them hopping from line to line. They ate and rested when they could. Watson was restless and pensive. He frequently caught himself out of the start of a doze and stared wildly about.

"I must appear to be utterly shot with nerve," he said the third time it happened. "I still feel as though we're being watched . . . and followed."

"You aren't the only one." Lestrade rubbed at his eyes. He had aged another five years in the past few days. "Quimper's at large . . . I'm more worried about him than I am the Colonel."

"That's because Quimper's a snake in the marsh," Gregson pointed out with harsh honesty. "The man's cold enough and bold enough to hide right in the heart of London while we comb the ports all over again!"

"Don't remind me," Lestrade groaned pitifully. "I don't . . . I just do not want to think of that. Moriarty will run to his foreign landholdings . . . much as I want him to come to justice, I don't want to think about him running at large in this country right now."

"You aren't the only one," Watson assured him.

Lestrade agreed that Watson could still be in danger.

"You too, Lestrade," Gregson finally pointed out. "Moriarty wants to know where 'his' treasure is."

"I don't have it," Lestrade shot back. Regional variations had affected their meal, so he was concentrating on a skewer of what the vendor *said* was mutton but was obviously goat or poached venison. He held the quiet peace a man has upon knowing he is too small to deal with the problem before him.

"Dare I ask what you did with it?" Watson asked uneasily.

Lestrade slipped him a look. "It's out of our hands . . . all of us. I made certain of that." He lifted his cheap cup of tea (tepid brown water) in a salute.

Gregson finished thumbing through a grudgingly purchased *Bradshaw*. "We'll be stuck at Abingdon for a good three-quarters-of-an-hour," he announced. "Time enough to send our wires home."

Lestrade groaned. "So near and yet so far."

"I'm just worried we'll be still long enough to go to sleep," Gregson confessed. "But first Abingdon, then the Great Western Railway, and straight on to home."

It must have been the right thing to say. Watson nodded off before the train even reached Abingdon.

"Thank God," Lestrade commented.

"You think he's caught on we really are being followed?" Gregson gnawed on a cigar.

"I'd say so," Lestrade confessed. "I can't wait to get to London . . . and stick him in a safehouse."

Paddington Street:

"You're supposed to drink this."

Nicholas Lestrade glared wearily at his older brother and for once in his life, faced the prospect of food without enthusiasm. "You drink it, Martin. I don't feel like it."

"I'm not telling *Mamm* you didn't drink this," Martin said seriously. "She made it just for you."

Nicholas sighed loudly and sat up. His hair was ruffled in all directions. With an air, he took the mug of yellow split pea soup and toasted bread.

"*Tad* coming back soon?"

"Supposed to be." Martin assured him.

Nicholas accepted that, ate, and threw himself back under the covers without a thank you. Martin snickered and took the empty tray back down the hall.

Mamm was just coming up the stair, with a wire in her hand. "That was your father, Love." She held up the little square. "He'll be home sometime tonight, probably late, but he lost his key."

"Do you want me to hide the spare under the flowerpot?" Martin asked as she took the tray.

"Best not. It's against safety . . . I'll stay up tonight and listen for his step."

"I can help, *Mamm*," Martin was quick to offer. "There's been nothing to do all day . . . Please?"

"You think it will be exciting waiting up for your father?" Clea brushed his thick hair with her fingers. "All right, you imp. Though I just think you want an excuse to play camping out! You're lucky I'm at my strength's end tending after your brother."

Watson opened his eyes to Abingdon . . . and an outlying district of Hell.

The fog swirled about them like a living thing – a malevolent living thing. He blinked as he rubbed at his eyes and saw how the yellow smoke from the coal-fired stacks coiled downward and rolled along the streets. The night was still young, but the glass against the streetlamps were already greasy and streaked.

"Almost home," Lestrade smiled wryly at him. "Home, foggy home."

"I'm *particularly* attached to it," Watson punned, and they shuffled off the train to the thick bank of atmosphere.

"Ye Gods, it's quiet," Gregson said out loud. His breath – cleaner by far – mixed with the coils of fog and he waited for them to catch up. "Look at that," he marveled. "Can't even see half-across the road. Been a while since we had one of these."

"Bet it was pushed down from that storm on the coast," Lestrade grumbled. He pulled off his confiscated bowler and stuffed it back on with relief. The Thames lapped behind them, a soothing sound for such a darkly historic river.

Watson looked about him from side to side, and his expressive face was pensive.

"Problem, Doctor?" Gregson asked.

"Just remembering . . . ." Watson let his voice trail off. He did not feel comfortable with expressing his worries – too often he thought a worry would become a fear.

But Holmes always swore a criminal could do his worst on a night like this . . . under a fog just like this one.

Just that quickly, Watson felt his hackles lift as several thoughts came together:

Lestrade and Gregson are as edgy as I am.

We are being followed.

They aren't talking about it where I can hear, so they must think I am the target . . . .

Watson would have done the same thing, but that sense of wrongness was now rising with the fog, and threatening to spill out of his very psyche.

"I think we need to leave this place, gentlemen."

They looked at him, and silently accepted what he was saying beneath the shallow words. As one they nodded. They felt it too.

281

Chapter XL – Fixation

"Someone's out there."

Lestrade's voice was barely a whisper, and his hand slipped deep inside his coat to rest where he could get to his revolver.

"I hear it too," Gregson whispered in the same voice.

Watson said nothing. His eyes were not the sharpest in such lighting conditions, but nothing was wrong with his ears – and he could detect a most unsettling, soft scuffle of wooden soles against the rough cobbles of the street. It was like listening to large rats . . . and he could not help but think of rats in the motive.

"They're between us and the train station," he muttered into his mustache.

"Where's the nearest tavern?" Gregson cleared his throat loudly, shuffling his feet in a show of idleness, and looked about. "Can't see a blessed thing in this fog. What timing."

"Perhaps if we keep moving . . . ."

"We're going to have to." Gregson wiped his mouth. "A bobby walks by four times an hour . . . We need to find one. Where's the railyard copper?" He worked his lip in scorn. "Off drinking a pint, I'll wager! Quarter-hour until the next train . . . that's long enough to get shot."

"Then we move," Watson pointed out with cool military calm. "We cannot see them. We are exposed in the pitiful light of the lamps. One misstep and we could be pushed in front of the 3:15 as it comes in."

"Aren't you cheerful," Lestrade said without heat. Watson was right. They couldn't see, and they were against opponents who knew the lay of the land. And the rail station's lamps let those scurrying, furtive shadows see them far better than they could see out.

"We start walking," Gregson whispered. "Keep your hands close to your weapons, gentlemen."

But it was easier said than done. Abingdon was smaller than London Proper, and carried the illusion of being flatter along the canals. The fog rolled constantly before them, clinging to their faces and clothing until they felt a part of the clammy, chilly night. It reeked of rotting matter – a sign of the warming weather.

The footsteps followed – shy and furtive, never a whisper from a human mouth catching on their ears. A heel scraped from within an alleyway just after they crossed it. In the distance, a horse was rattling a dogcart with misbalanced wheels. It was the only sound for the city.

The scuffing whispers tripped delicately behind them – sometimes almost side by side, and twice they heard a firm click of footfalls directly across the road. Steps raced ahead and vanished, only to start up again behind them.

They knew how far to stay away. They knew how to hide in the swirling fog.

Nine hundred seconds never felt so long and infinite.

Lestrade decided to take a risk, and quietly eased his revolver closer out of his pocket. He alternated between bringing up the back and walking with Watson between his right side and the walls of the buildings. It made him nervous to think of the dark, narrow caverns of the alleys, and he stepped to Watson's right whenever they grew close to them.

It would be a perfect place to grab him, Lestrade grimly considered as the lap of the canal fluttered to their left. No sounds there – yet. The lock couldn't be far up ahead – they were getting to the point where they had to turn around . . . And if they didn't work quickly enough . . .

And then Gregson, who was in the lead, made a mistake.

He stopped so quickly the other two crashed into his back.

"What?" Lestrade hissed.

"They're driving us!" Gregson didn't bother with being quiet. "Get across the lock – it's our only chance!"

They ran then, with Gregson forcing the lead and blocking Watson when it looked like the doctor might be able to get in front. Lestrade had no difficulties with staying behind Watson – he was not a fleet runner. Their hearts pounded in their ears. Watson's breath rasped painfully against Gregson's heavy puffing. The bridge across the lock was small, and arched, and they might be exposed, but so would anyone who tried to approach them.

Gregson cleared the apex of the road and grabbed the rough matrix of the rail to stop running – his arm shot out like an iron bar and caught Watson across the chest, stopping his progress almost hard enough to lift the man's feet off the ground. Lestrade whirled behind and saw pieces of the shadows breaking off and slowly flitting beneath the low ground broken up by hedge and shrub and the uneven sward guarding the hard-packed road.

"Watson, stay between us." Gregson stared, transfixed with loathing at the same sight on the other side of the lock.

The train whistle blew.

They would never make it in time. Even if they ran unimpeded through the shadowy dangers.

Something whistled past Gregson's ear and he quickly ducked, but the stone continued to its target. The single lamp on his side of the water.

Half the world was plunged in darkness.

"Too smart for guns." Gregson cursed.

"That was a sling," Watson growled. "Mind you don't stop a missile with your head."

The lamp behind Lestrade burst. A single spark fluttered to the ground.

They were now in complete gloom.

Lestrade put his back to Watson, his revolver tight in his hand. He waited for the betrayal of a footstep.

They all waited.

Watson hoped no one could hear their frantic breath. It sounded like the ocean in his own ears. But try as he might, there was nothing that would reveal someone coming up. Either the gang was being very quiet, or they were being very careful.

Or they aren't moving at all.

The thought perturbed him, for he couldn't divine the motive for stasis.

Yet I cannot hear anything . . . If they moved we would hear them . . . All I hear is the water under the canal . . .

The water . . . .

Watson shouted something incoherent. Lestrade felt a powerful arm lock into him from the other side of the rail. The other arm clutched at his gun hand. He caught the odor of sweet violets. On reflex born of hate he threw his body into a mindless attack and grappled with his attacker – *Not Quimper, too big to be Quimper* – while the blood roared in his ears, too loudly to hear Watson and Gregson running for them. Lestrade pulled the trigger and the burst of flame caught Gregson's pale face . . . then something happened and they tumbled over into the dark water of the Thames.

"Lestrade!"

Watson lunged for the water's edge, but Gregson held him back with his sheer mass.

"Don't you even think it!" the big man roared. *"Not in your shape!"*

"We have to do something!" Watson pointed out at the top of his lungs. The footfalls were scurrying away from them, mission completed. A police whistle was sounding – a more welcome note he'd never heard.

"We will!" Gregson stabbed at his collar. "Stay close to me, Doctor, no matter what!"

Watson flinched as Gregson bellowed into the fog.

Gregson puffed between bursts of curses. His normally pasty-white face was flushed like a coronary. "Fool twice and thrice," he kept saying over and over.

"I don't understand," Watson said hurriedly as the heavy clop of constable clamshells pounded up the cobblestones. "I thought they would be after me."

"They are! We didn't think – you *are* the target, Doctor," Gregson spat. "Promise me you won't be going anywhere out of my sight – promise me!"

"I promise," Watson assured him, taken aback by the hard lapis glitter in Gregson's eyes. He didn't fully understand what it was that Gregson understood . . . but it was enough to upset him.

Gregson accepted that – for now. He turned his face to the knot of uniformed men – constables on the beat, railway policemen . . . even a waterman was staggering up with his laces half-done. Before this immeasurably tiny army, he barked his orders.

The next two hours of Lestrade's life felt as though each minute would be his last. The gun had at least hit its target – the big man who grabbed him was badly wounded and soon disappeared in the flurry of trading him back and forth (after saying goodbye with a stunning blow to the chin with his good arm). After that he was tossed into a drugget that not only kept him from moving, it made every breath a conscious effort.

Leave it to Jethro Quimper to stick to the Classics. Lestrade kept his body tight as possible to keep the yards of heavy weave from slowly suffocating him. He *knew* Quimper was behind this as sure as anything. *Never could resist showing off how much he read . . . and does he love to play Caesar.*

By the time they unrolled him, he didn't even care he was just being freed to face something worse. He just wanted out.

Dank concrete walls and pillars dripped over their heads and the concrete floor was disturbingly painted with fine river silt. The entire levels flooded with the tide and had only just receded. Damp pools lingered. Small animals still struggled, but rats ran out of the dark corners like their attackers had, and fed without fear. Their sleek, wet fur gleamed like oil in the lantern spills, and small black eyes threw back lights as red as a bull's-cyc.

And because the confusing rabble of hoodlums that would be scorned by the Crawlers weren't satisfied with their job, they threw him with all their might against the concrete steps. He slipped badly on the silty floor and went down – catching himself from the worst of it, but his ribs protested another mistreatment.

The tip of a walking stick pushed like a bullet below his ribs as he gasped for air.

And here we are . . . mistreatment three.

Lestrade couldn't believe Quimper looked so well after what had happened on the Isle. The agent had found time to rest, redress himself in good clothes, and – of course – found a new walking stick. He withdrew his stick for now, and leaned on it as the detective was more or less picked back up, shoved, carried, and dragged to the bottom of an underground pier.

God forbid he miss a chance to gloat, Lestrade thought. *I'll know then the Devil's sleeping in late.*

"Got the wrong man, didn't you?" he panted. Someone – a gorilla reeking of the Jago – holding his head in a vise – tightened like pincers around a walnut.

"No." Quimper lifted his trimmed eyebrows. "I sent them out shopping for *you*, and *you* they brought back."

"Where's your immediate supervisor, Mr. Quimper?"

"I have no idea." Quimper seemed unperturbed. "Wherever the currents took him. I thought it best to . . . part ways." A quick glimmer of sadism displayed itself. "You have your orders, gentlemen." He lifted his voice.

The men, who no doubt thought it corking to be called "gentlemen", threw their charge down and vanished like cockroaches. Two remained, and they were more than enough for Lestrade in the condition he was in. In fact, they were so adequate for the job of protecting their master, Lestrade wondered if he was supposed to feel flattered.

Lestrade had time to get his breath. He was used to some of the underground passages of the Thames, but not wherever they were. The river sounded louder than before. More powerful. And if they were back in London . . . ?

"Don't worry, I'm not going to kill you just yet." Quimper made a show of patting the small revolver-shaped bulge that was disfiguring his coat pocket and coolly went to a tiny gas jet set into the concrete wall. As Lestrade watched, he lit himself a long, slender cigarette wrapped in delicate blond paper.

How did a gas jet get in here?

"I figured you would get around to it sooner or later," Lestrade rasped. "But what's the point of all *this*?"

"If I were foolish enough to take your doctor friend, all of London would rise up in the search." Quimper sniffed. "I daresay he's popular even with the street urchins . . . and there's no telling if my men would feel a pang of conscience . . . He patronises the free clinics where they go to for help, or for the hundreds of times their wives welp out . . . ." He sniffed again, as if something foul rested in the air.

"But a policeman? You won't be *nearly* as popular, L'estrade."

286

Lestrade had to admit that was true. If there was a more-liked man than John Watson, he'd yet to meet him outside of Parliament.

"So why settle for second best?" he grimaced as he managed to heave up out of the silt. "Or have you finally come to the point where you can admit you made a mistake?"

"Oh, I've thought this out very carefully." The agent paused for his tobacco, and pale, expensive smoke slipped through his lips. "Dr. Watson is even more stubborn than his brother – all my sources are clear on that regard. He'd die rather than compromise his personal honour in giving in to the criminal element such as myself." He grinned like a shark. "But a sense of honour can work both ways, can't it?"

"Even more than usual, you're not making sense," Lestrade spat.

"It all comes down to those wretched gemstones – no wonder the superstitious attach nonsense about curses. That much money is bound to make no friends." Quimper muttered and blew another smoke ring. "Small wonder the Colonel wanted to keep them to himself. Whoever has that much wealth would *have* to take the reins in the Organisation."

"So you've joined the hunt? Good luck to you. You're going to need it."

"I don't need luck, L'estrade," Quimper spoke patiently. "You see, even if your confession under duress is true, the Colonel isn't liable to believe it. That's the difference between myself and the Colonel. He can't fathom another's point of view . . . or their morals. He still believes Watson has the stones . . . or he knows their location. If I give him Dr. Watson, he'll be forced to accept my bid in this play."

"Watson isn't going to come to you, even if you gave him an engraved invitation!"

Even as he said it, Lestrade knew the words weren't true.

Quimper grinned. "That's the worst lie I think I've heard this week. *He will.* As a man of honour, he can't be easy with saddling you with this mess . . . and now that you're imperiled, his sense of honour won't allow him to let you and the Yard do your jobs." He paused to inhale, exhale another lung of smoke. The scent of sweet violets trickled down after him – Lord, but Lestrade had learnt to hate that smell.

"Dr. Watson will go against his sternest oath to obey Scotland Yard's attempts to protect him, and come right here. He'll trade himself for you in a heartbeat."

"There won't be a trade!" Lestrade spat. "You'll make off with Watson, and you won't possibly let me go."

"No . . . no I won't." Quimper agreed lightly. "It is as you said, L'estrade . . . It's time we settled this once and for all." Blue eyes sparkled. "And I could have taken Mr. Gregson. I'll admit it would have been amusing to watch you try to recover the situation . . . but you were my first choice." The smile crept down like wax to pull up the corners of the man's mouth. "I rather like you sitting here, dependent on Gregson's attempt at a rescue."

"Gregson, talk to me right now, I insist!" Watson exploded at the big man. His nerves were frayed to the woof at Gregson's curt organization of the troops. "Why are you wanting me to remain so close to you, when they've taken Lestrade!"

"Pretty soon, a ransom note will come along, and you're going to feel obligated to do what it says." Gregson spoke so coldly it was like listening to a stone. He pulled out what remained of his purchased cigar and puffed softly into the air while Watson waited in a ferment. "And you are not going to do such a thing if I can help it, Dr. Watson. Lestrade's only the bait to get at you."

"That's absurd!" Watson knew he was shouting, but he could not have cared less. "Gregson, have a moment's pity and think! Lestrade has a wife and two children! I have nothing, no one! I would quickly take his place!"

"Dr. Watson, you'd best get this through your altruistic head *and you do it right now*," Gregson snapped in bitter contempt. "Lestrade is no one's husband . . . no one's father. *He is an Inspector of Scotland Yard*." About them, Gregson's words were congealing all movement to watch the tableau.

"It is not his duty to allow a citizen of the England to fall victim to the clutches of anarchy, terror, or self-imposed lawbreakers who flout their contempt for the precepts we hold dear."

Watson stared at Gregson as though he had never seen him before . . . Perhaps he hadn't. The big man was breathing so hard his chest heaved within his coat. His eyes gave off light from the force of his tightly controlled anger.

"If you have some understanding on what it means to be a soldier, then give us the credit for knowing where our own duty lies. Lestrade will not thank you, nor respect you for interfering. Should he live at your expense, it will be a betrayal of everything we in the Yard stand for."

The tension knotted, drew tight, and snapped between the two men. Gregson could see that Watson dearly wanted to take up his gun and rush through the crowd in a fruitless pursuit of Lestrade's attackers.

Just as quickly, calm sense reluctantly filled in those deep brown eyes.

"They'll kill him," he said for the record.

"Perhaps. But as long as Quimper is being Quimper, we've got a decent chance against him. And he won't kill Lestrade just yet. Not while there's the hope he can get to you."

"You sound certain of that . . . when Lestrade himself swore Quimper would kill him at the first chance. Wouldn't he know the man better?"

"Lestrade's too caught up in Quimper to see what's right in front of him," Gregson gnashed through his teeth.

"See what?" Watson demanded.

"That Quimper *has lost his mind*." Gregson stabbed the air with his finger, his rage sending the tension forward like a shot. "He's not sane, can't even *pretend* to be sane . . . and he's got some sort of . . . I don't know, a *focus* on him. Like he's the reason for everything wrong in his world." Gregson stabbed the air again. "Lunatic," he emphasized. "He'll kill him, but that's only *after* he makes Geoff pay for everything he's wronged Quimper for first. *Lestrade's his only outlet for that madness.* Like he's also the only reason for it."

Watson groaned under his breath. "A fixation," he spat. "But you need to understand this, Gregson: If Quimper manages to kill Lestrade, he'll be much worse than he ever was."

"Eh?"

"He'll be without his chosen target. What do you think will happen then?"

Gregson whitened at the thought. *"Clea."*

Chapter XLI – Past Time

*P*ast time to get out of here.

Lestrade waited while Quimper's footsteps melted to the distance. His two hired thugee went with him, but there was hardly a need to guard him, was there? He was cuffed by his right hand straight to an iron bolt set into the wall not far from the gas jet.

Damn that gas jet anyway. What was the use for it here?

Possibly important – but for now it was a trifle, and trifles weren't for him. He gritted his teeth together and started working the metal circle back and forth around his wrist.

If he doesn't come back and I'm here, I might drown.

He wasn't certain what was happening in these murky rooms with only a blue flame to see by – the doors were obviously designed to be shut, but were any in the back open? That they were designed for Quimper's smuggling empire . . . well, that was an inevitable conclusion there. The question was, what the devil was the man dealing with?

The Thames was faint in his ears. The Old Man must be in a mood today. He seemed louder, and in the concrete corridors the water carried an eerie sound, like heavy sighs and wails.

The derbies were too tightly shut.

He gave up for a moment, breathing hard from his own frustration.

Have to get out of here before he snares Clea . . . and Dr. Watson . . . . What else?

Tired, he leaned on his knees in the silt, and had another reason for frustration as he promptly began to slide. The silt was full of charming stuff today! He leaned down with his freed left hand to brace his balance, and blinked.

Charming stuff indeed.

Lestrade scooped up a jot on his fingertips and held it under his nose. His eyebrows shot up.

Well, well. Someone must have lost some oil out of their cargo today . . . unless the oil is something Quimper does smuggle out . . . It isn't cheap, but it would be waterproof if the drums were large enough . . .

It was a good thing Clea preferred a grimy and living husband to a clean and dead one. *Not that she won't take it out of me later . . .* Lestrade spread the oily clay on his chained wrist.

Paddington Street:

Martin grunted slightly as he used his body for leverage in getting the water bucket to the floor. He was getting stronger. A year ago he knew he couldn't bear that sort of weight.

"A pint is a pound, the world around," his mother would say, *before* reminding him it was a rough rule not a constant, but a five-gallon bucket meant at least forty pounds' weight for his arms and back.

Martin smiled and lifted the bucket a few times, just to test himself.

The last one of the morning. It was hard to believe they had so many animals in the building – and Mrs. Collins was a saint to put up with half of them – at least, to hear their mother and Aunt Elizabeth talk. He went to the top of the building first, where Mr. Dooley's pigeons rested. Martin so far had his doubts about this, especially since Nicholas insisted on getting the most drab-dreary birds in the entire flock. They were the same shade of blue clay the grey London brick was spawned from, and when they roosted there was no picking them out with the eye.

Nick had his reasons . . . but Martin couldn't figure them out yet and that halfway bothered him.

He was trying to think of a few reasons that would fit when he reached the little foyer out of the kitchen. It was then he caught the rattle of a key in the front door lock.

Tad didn't have his key.

In that moment, Martin Lestrade froze to stone. He couldn't move. The water bucket rested useless at his feet. All he could do was watch as the lock snapped and the brass doorknob turned.

The door turned inward from the press of a cane tip against the wood.

Martin took a single step backwards before he caught himself. His mother was upstairs. *Nick. Mrs. Collins was somewhere.*

The stick dropped behind the door. A shoe clicked on the polished wood. And the owner stepped inside the house.

He was very tall.

He smiled as he shut the door after him.

"Good morning, young sir. Is this the Lestrade residence?"

"Sir?" Martin asked quietly.

The man stared at him with a strange expression. "You're just like him," he accused the boy. "And they say you're the *smart* one." He shook his head dismissively. "Clearly your mother's brains."

"My father says that," Martin answered. "But Nick is smart too. With animals and machines."

A low chuckle was his answer. "Do you know who I am?"

Martin looked him up and down. "Sir?" He put his hands behind his back so he could grip them tightly without being seen.

His father didn't know he'd seen the photographs under the bed. His father probably didn't know the stories his uncles told the boys – he wouldn't have liked it at all.

Martin was certain he knew who the man was, and he was beginning to feel quite afraid.

"Are you here to hurt my mother?" he asked. A straightforward question was the best one. *Tad* was strict about that. *"Cut through the fine words, ignore manners if you have to, since too many people use manners to be cruel. But don't forget to be civil. You can always be civil."*

The tall man tilted his head to one side, like he was seeing him again for the first time. "You're a bright little boy, aren't you?" He leveled the question gently, like Uncle Cutler's wife when she was about to say something that would hurt someone else. "He used to talk to me like that. Your father."

Martin said nothing. He didn't know what to say.

"Would you like to talk to your father right now?" The man smiled. "I know where he is."

Martin felt his throat turn to dust. "I'm not allowed outside without a coat." He instantly hated himself for sounding so silly.

The man laughed. "We can get you a coat. You can even leave a message for your mother. Wouldn't you like that? It would be polite and keep her from worrying."

Martin bit his lip. "What should I say?"

"Just tell her the truth . . . that you went to see your father . . . and that her old friend from Lord Beckett's escorted you."

"Martin."

The sound of his mother's voice washed the fear out of Martin's mind. He looked up the steps. She was standing at the top, her hands clenched into her apron.

"Martin, why don't you go back upstairs now, Love?"

Martin was too afraid to move.

She walked slowly down the steps, one hand at her skirt like a lady ought, and her eyes never left him.

He edged to her side, afraid to look away from the smiling man at the door.

"It's all right, Love." She rested her hand on his shoulder. "You forgot to feed your puppies, dear. Why don't you go do that now?"

"But . . . *Mamm* . . . ."

"Go feed your puppies, dear," she repeated firmly.

"Yes, *Mamm*." His throat squeezed up and he slowly made his way up the steps.

The adults sank into each other's eyes when they were alone.

292

"You are staring at me, Mr. Quimper."

"Am I?" He shook himself slightly. "I'm merely . . . surprised." Still rude, he examined her up and down, and she could only let him. "The years have treated you well, Miss Clea."

"That is Mrs. Lestrade to you, sir. You have my husband's key. Where is he?"

He shook his head, smiling without an answer.

Clea clawed down the walnut that was rising in her throat. "You were going to take my son away from me. I'll not have it. What did you do with his father, Mr. Quimper?"

"Normally," was her slow answer, "I would be the one asking the questions in this situation. You still manage to surprise me, dear lady." He touched his hatbrim. "Our last meeting hardly went well, did it?"

"Fair is far," Clea said hoarsely. "You still have not answered my question."

"Then I shall answer you." Mr. Quimper rested both hands on the head of his walking stick. "Someone must come with me and see for themselves how your husband is. Oh, it needn't be you – !" He lifted one hand swiftly. "It could be your son . . . one of your sons."

"If you've killed him there's no need for me to come." Clea spoke sharp as a needle, and she saw how his eyes widened. Good. She'd shocked him. This was hardly any different than brokering a contract with the calico pressers who wanted a hundred pounds for a single print-block. The men had been as cold and ruthless as this one, and for all she knew there were deaths on their hands as well. *Never inch down, never show fear . . . never think of how they could hurt you until the deal is done.* "I'll not risk my sons for your pleasure, Mr. Quimper. If Geoffrey is dead, I cannot bring him back."

"You're quite the fighter, aren't you?" He tipped his head in admiration. "I always knew you were full of starch . . . as stubborn in your own way as your foolish husband." He lifted one hand. "I vow to you, your husband is still alive."

"And why would I believe your word, sir?"

"You doubt me?"

"I doubt a man who promised to take me home safely one evening and so quickly forgot his promise."

He grinned. "I was merely stretching the boundaries of my promise . . . I hadn't broken it . . . but to give you reassurance . . . ." His smile froze. "It suits me not to kill him yet. I enjoy my amusements, my good woman."

Clea wished for breath beneath her corsets. "I have no desire to go with you," she forced out. "Nor will my sons."

"You or your sons – the choice is yours." He responded as soft as a snake's tongue. "And I won't be gulled by that little knife you keep under your apron this time."

"Martin!" The agent lifted his head with a smile. His bark sounded up the steps. "Come down here, would you, please? Your mother has something to say to you!"

There was a terrified silence from upstairs . . . and Quimper smiled as the door creaked slowly open.

Soon enough, his smile became a scream.

Irish wolfhounds are among the most intelligent dog in the world. And Phorp and Luath remembered the voice of the man who had lamed Phorp last year . . . .

When the Black Maria pulled up, it was to a madhouse: Half the street was lumbering about, with all the sense of ants at a picnic. The police were moving the crowd back and along, trying in vain to get them to ignore two sheet-wrapped forms lying on the sidewalk in front of Lestrade's house.

"What in God's name is happening?"

Gregson beat Watson to the question. As one they jumped out of the Maria and nearly collided into Inspector Morton.

"They're fine, sirs!" Morton lifted his hands and shouted to the crowd: "Off with you! There's nothing to see here!" He looked back at them, pale and grim.

"We did what you said, Tobias. Staked-out his building for must've been two hours before a knot of 'em showed up." He lifted a piece of telegraph paper out for the world to see. "How did you know?" he breathed.

"Later," Gregson promised. "Who are they?"

"I've no idea."

Watson had knelt and was pulling a sheet off a face. "One of Mr. Quimper's men," he announced. "I remember him from the isle." He repeated himself at the second face. "What happened?" he demanded. "Their throats are gone!"

"Those dogs the damn Gipsy dropped off to Lestrade while he was gone." Morton shuddered. "Seems wolfhounds are a bit protective when someone they don't like comes along. Mrs. Lestrade says she signaled Martin to open the door to the room where they were kept, and they went down for Quimper, but he got away."

Watson was so white he trembled as he got to his feet again. "Please tell me how Quimper managed to escape *that*!" He pointed behind his back to the corpses on the concrete. "Sir Hugo Baskerville's Hound couldn't have done worse!"

294

"Mr. Quimper wasn't far from the door, Dr. Watson."

Everyone turned to look at a pale but composed Clea Lestrade as she took a step out the door. A tray of food was in her hands. "His men were just on the other side . . . I suppose to keep me or the boys from escaping. When he saw the dogs coming for him . . . he took a step outside and threw his own men to their jaws." She shuddered slightly, but did not seem completely horrified. "I'm afraid the dogs are in a terrible mood. They really wanted to have him."

Gregson swallowed so loudly his throat clicked.

"Would you like some tea, gentlemen?"

"Ah . . . no . . . no . . . thank you . . . ."

"Rubbish!" Clea snapped. "You're both dead on your own two feet. If you're to rescue my Geoffrey, you need to be stronger than that. I brewed up some good black tea, and it won't be going to waste!"

"W-well . . . ."

"Do it!" Morton hissed under his breath. "Treasure said no and she hit him with that tray!" The man's eyes were wild. "Some womens, they cook to settle the nerves, and I think Mrs. Lestrade is very, very nervous right now!"

"You're a great blooming babby, Inspector!" Clea barked. "I made sure I got his helmet!" Her eyes flashed. "Yes, I am feeling nervous, and yes I do cook and brew when I am upset, but if that's a matter of record, why are you all gawping about it? Tha' two barmpots look to be dead on tha' feet, and you don't look as though you could fight a Prussian right now, much less *Jethro Bloody Quimper*!"

Three constables and half the crowd shied backwards.

"I'll take a cup, if you please," Watson said hastily. He wasted no time getting to the steps.

"Good 'un." A voice deep as a well rumbled just behind his shoulder. Watson started to see Andrew Cheatham just behind him.

The most foppish and expensively dressed member of the infamous Cheathams was not unlike Jethro Quimper in his taste and choice of suitcloths, but Andrew carried a confident, raw power about him that Quimper would have never donned. A neatly trimmed spade beard swept down his strong, pale face.

"She'll hang you on some antlers if you don't mind. My sister was born a clocker." [1]

"Don't be getten a cob on," Clea exclaimed. "Tell me where he went!"

"Back under the city, little sister." Andrew blithely grabbed up the nearest teacup and washed his throat out with its contents. "PC Brown ax me to tell you and the inspectors that the only place he could be headed now is the Limehouse."

"And what are you doing here?" Gregson snarled with no discernible grace.

Andrew grinned at him, displaying a fine set of teeth. "Still sore about those keelboats, Inspector?"

"I'll arrest you for forgery *later*, my young fellow. Right now my comrade and your brother-in-law come first."

Andrew sobered quickly. "Clea took the wire you sent her and sent one of her own to us. The problem was, she was so tired staying up with Nick she fell asleep without meaning to, and Martin was in the downstairs when Quimper walked in bold as brass. She sent him upstairs with a word to take care of their puppies, and Martin took that to mean let the dogs loose." She slurped the last of his tea down, forbearing against manners just this once.

"No one was home to read the wire she sent – so *Feyther* sent for me, but I didn't get his message until late. I was on my way down here when one of those little street Arabs caught sight of me an' flagged me down – he'd seen Mr. Quimper heading to the water. So I took him with me to the river – "

"Where you lost him," Clea said sharply.

"He's run out of places, little sister." Andrew told her calmly. "Some place close to the water, and Inspector Jonesi has all his men in the boats."

"Then that is where we're going."

"Not without me, Inspector Gregson," Watson cut in sharply. "I promise you I will not leave your side . . . but nor will I leave Lestrade's."

"If I had the time, I'd argue, but I don't," Gregson grumbled. "Put that tea in you, and we'll go."

NOTE

1.   Broody hen. "Clucker"

Chapter XLII – Profit a Man

The tiny gas jet was worthless in the rising dark. The Old Man sang in his ears,

The door was locked.

Lestrade wasted too many seconds in pounding on the wooden frame . . . He stopped when his hands left streaks on the splinters and stared at the marks in his flesh.

Freed . . . but trapped unless he found a way out.

He set his lips. If he thought of these strange rooms as a cavern, he would be all right. At the least, he would have a fighting chance.

Cold, soaked, and bone-weary, he turned his back to the door and plunged into the slowly rising water of the Thames. There were corridors upon corridors in this maze. He might not find the one that led out . . . but if he stayed meekly by the door as the river rose . . . well, that outcome was a certainty.

Watson wished he had taken more of Clea Lestrade's good black tea. The offerings in PC Murcher's battered tin were clearly from a leaf that had been used two or three times already. Still, the man's earnest face poked out from between his helmet brim and his chin strap.

"Good for what ails ye," the big man said, "And better for you than the strong stuff people buy in the shop."

Watson remembered that used tea leaves were part of the pay with the higher-ranking hired servants. He didn't often think of the people who took home the diluted tea-leaves to brew for their own family. Did Murcher have a female relative who was cook or maid in a fine household?

"It's quite good, thank you, Constable."

Murcher smiled, showing three lost teeth since the first time Watson met him, back in 1881. He looked a good deal older now. A scar decorated his withering face. Some men only weaken with age, but Murcher was metamorphosing into the old Police Constable that was invulnerable, as how a soft seabed can turn into hard limestone with time.

Watson rarely had the opportunity to see how Scotland Yard worked. He had learned from Holmes to prefer the swifter routes of individual hunting and tracking, and a man was welcome to such work if they had the initiative.

Here . . . individual freedom was a *handicap*.

One earned a degree of independence upon the rank of Detective-Sergeant. They could pursue cases "individually" but a constable was never far from their sides, and to a great extent, the inspectors were dependent on the constables for information, as the constables were dependent on the inspectors for their conference of authority.

London was alive with Water Police, dockyard workers, and the handful of constables that counted the wharfs on their duty shifts. Watson thought it all looked like a spilled ant nest.

But no, ants have pattern and order to their movement . . . .

Encouraged, the doctor tried to pay attention. He was tired, but also exhilarated. They had all gone beyond the moment where simple exhaustion could have stopped them. It was the old battle *persona*, and within it, Watson remembered those moments when being tested created a sensation of life that was rarely equaled.

He seized the moment within himself while Gregson barked orders and sent men from lowly constable to his own peers and superiors across specific points on the river.

Each man here knows their route by heart. They know what belongs and what doesn't.

Watson pulled his breath in. He could finally "see" in his mind what was before his eyes. The Metropolitan Police were creating a living gridwork, a chessboard of the city, and there was at least one policeman on each square.

A chessboard. Ironic that Colonel Moriarty loved chess so well. They've created a game board of the entire city where it rings the Thames . . . They'll find out where Lestrade was . . . and where he wasn't . . . .

It was slow. It was stupid in places were they all *knew* Quimper and Lestrade couldn't possibly be – but they had to find out for themselves in case they were wrong.

It was like a controlled casting of the nets. And like any day of fishing . . . the results could not be predetermined.

"Sirs?"

Inspector Jonesi paused to pull off his seaman's cap. His thick skin was beefy from the winds and water off the Thames. "Nothing at all at Hammersmith Bridge. Some unaccounted for boats moored up, but they've been vouched for. Matthews and the Irish Twins covered the Thames downstream to Battersea Bridges, and there was nothing of note."

Gregson looked over his watch and snapped it with a displeased air. "Nothing for all the hours of searching?"

"We know where they *aren't*," Jonesi answered. "And they won't be able to cross back through our territory."

"Has to be the West India Docks . . ." Gregson said at last, as if agreeing most reluctantly to Jonesi.

Jonesi nodded. "I know how you hate that place . . . but a man like Quimper has to have a dozen bolt holes, starting with the Isle of Dogs."

"Who's been on the search over there?"

"I sent Lords to control those sheep. He'll be wiring a report any moment now."

"He'd best be careful," Gregson worried. "We're not very popular with the dock workers right now."

"They've been in a much, much better mood since the Labor got their sixpence-an-hour." Jonesi assured him.

"Islanders are close-knit and suspicious," Gregson pointed out.

"True."

Watson cleared his throat. "If we're talking about the docks . . . and Quimper would like to secrete himself there . . . ."

"He's been hiding his ill-traded goods in places like that for years. We find one place and shut it down, but we miss three more." Jonesi sighed. "As bad as his father . . . We were lucky to even learn who he was."

"I am thinking: Which part of the isle would he be the most likely to hide in?" Watson pulled out his ever-present little notebook – he must have grabbed a new one at the stationery's when Gregson wasn't looking – and sketched the isle with a pencil: It was almost exactly like an uvula, and the docks striped across the uvula from one side to the other. "The Import Docks provide quick access from either side . . . ."

"He exported too, so he wouldn't be spending all his time in just the Import Dock." Gregson gnawed on the tip of a battered cigarette. A moment later he brightened. "The Limehouse bit . . . it connects both of the docks at that one spot!"

"We've already been there," Jonesi protested kindly. "There's so far . . . nothing."

"We're talking about Quimper. He would have to be at the Limehouse."

"Gregson . . . ." Jonesi was shaking his head, "we've already been there."

"Do it, sir," Watson snapped. "Mr. Quimper is a clever man – he would have to be stationed *somewhere* about the Limehouse."

"I don't follow you, Doctor."

"Limehouse is the connection point between two of the three docks, and it is connected to all three basins on the eastern part of the Isle . . . but Quimper would be attracted to the Limehouse. He would have secured the best bolt holes at that part of the isle – so look for hidden passages, smuggler's coves, whatever seems amiss!"

Jonesi looked skeptical. "It's a hunch, is it? With all do respect, sir, we professionals are not victim to hunches."

Gregson opened his mouth to tell Jonesi what a load of rubbish *that* was when Watson turned to cold fire.

"You'll find Quimper's people have been part of that section of the Isle for generations. You will also find he helped *develop* it! The name itself ought to give it away!" The doctor put his hands on his hips in exasperation. "Mr. Quimper is from the part of France that is famous for its pottery . . . He built up a good deal of his respectable fortune in pottery . . . and the *Limehouse* was so named for the number of *lime kilns* built in the area . . . *for the express purpose of the potteries!*"

"That's good enough for me," Gregson cut in. "We're missing something over there. Something probably small but important."

Jonesi wordlessly nodded, and turned his back to give more orders.

"Nice, that," Gregson said when they were alone. "How'd you know?"

"I was interested enough in the subject of Mr. Quimper to read up a bit on him . . . ." Watson did not mention the experience of reading Holmes's copious notes. It had been painful.

He chose another way to answer, also the truth. "On our honeymoon, Mary fell in love with the potteries of Kemper. She became most interested in the subject."

He was shocked to feel something tremble behind his eyes.

By God, it was cold.

Lestrade reminded himself that being cold was better than being cold for real, and stroked on. At least this wasn't the middle of winter!

But the tide kept rising, and it wanted to push him back.

He was spending too much of his time in just holding his own against the current. He wasn't certain how badly he was failing, because of the lack of light. But something was shining deep flickers against the waves, something casting light from below.

Lestrade stroked his way to the nearest pillar, and clutched it with all his might. He was still breathing hard when the light on the prow of the fishing batteau sent a sleek trail across the briny Thames.

Quimper.

Hard as it was to move to a less-safe spot, Lestrade let the current carry him to the side and ducked below. The lantern's flame caught an eerie paint, like luminescent oil upon the surface. Behind it slid the almond shape of the wooden boat.

Quimper was high and dry . . . and coming back for him.

Alone.

300

Lestrade surfaced behind the agent, his hand clutching silently to the flat edge of the boat. It was a logging batteau – hard, light, sturdy. Quimper must have chosen it for its swift maneouvers.

One tiny fluke was all Quimper needed. He whirled at the faint sound, stick in hand, and it cracked down. Lestrade grunted and nearly fell back. He grabbed up, caught the polished blackthorn with his hand, and pulled Quimper to the edge of the boat for a good strike. A moment later, the empty boat bobbed upon the silent caverns like a seashell.

"You were too stupid to be grateful!" Quimper swam closer and pushed Lestrade deeper into the water with a splash. Stunned, the detective sank without moving, not knowing up from down.

"*Everything!* You owe everything to me and my father!" Quimper ranted when he surfaced. *"Everything you are, you owe to us!"*

"And what do *you* owe to my family, Quimper?" Lestrade shouted back as brine stuck to his face and eyes. "You and I share the same blood – or have you forgotten?"

Quimper snarled, lunged, and pushed him again back under the water. Lestrade found his purchase weak and twisted up.

"Your hour has come, L'estrade. At long last."

The hour has come . . . .

Quimper grinned at him. They treaded water in the night. His eyes were white balls of light. Behind him, a dark swell of water was coming up. The latest increment of the Thames, slow and gentle. Lestrade's heart sank even as he watched it, for it wasn't nearly powerful enough to distract the madman.

The hour has come, and here is the man . . . .

"If I have to use my last breath to kill you, *kenderv*, I will – " Quimper's hand lifted up for the killing blow –

The hour has come . . . .

And then . . .

Quimper was . . .

. . . *gone.*

The hour has come, and here is the man.

Lestrade was alone in the rising river.

"There!" Gregson barked. "Watson! Hold the lamp!"

Watson couldn't see a thing at first, but Gregson's eyes were obviously the sharper in this rising subterranean hell. Their boat lapped closer to the pillars. A huddled shape was pressed against the heavy wood.

Gregson had his coat and shoes off before Watson could protest the folly of the action. He sewed his lips shut as the big man tied a length of the rope around his waist and launched into the Thames, the force of his spring pushing the craft backwards. Watson hadn't the time to curse, so he just dropped the anchor. The rowboat bobbed like a shell against the waves.

We should have brought a constable, he criticized, even though he knew the folly of that action. A constable was up for drowning in this clime, with his heavy wool coat, leather collar, thick shoes and metal helmet.

The doctor had shared many of Holmes's derogatory opinions about Scotland Yard, but they had never once criticized the bravery of the men who made the law their profession. Gregson swam with strong, angry strokes against the pull of the mighty river, to save the life of his rival.

Some things needed no words. Some things would be diminished by words.

"Lestrade," Gregson was talking loudly against the water. "*Let go, man!* I have to get you to the boat!" There was no answer of sound or movement. The waves slapped against the two forms as they blended together.

"Watson!" Gregson puffed. "Can you haul us in? I don't think he can swim!"

"Can you get him to let go?" Watson tugged experimentally, but Gregson couldn't leave without Lestrade.

"He's stuck like a limpet. I think he's shocky!"

"Hold on!" Watson snapped firmly. "I have to makeshift with what I've got here . . . ." He knelt, and the boat rocked from side to side. "Just stay with him . . . tie him to your rope if you can . . . ."

Gregson struggled to comply, his teeth chattering like rattles. His fingers were growing numb. "Try to hurry," he gasped.

He risked looking up to Watson (getting Thames water in his eyes). Watson was taking up the spare coil and tying it to something – a stone fishing weight? With a grunt, he tossed it as close as he could to the Yarders. The weight splashed and went straight to the bottom.

Gregson clung to Lestrade without having the slightest clue as to Watson's reasons.

The doctor straightened in the spider-work of London's starlight mixes with pale gaslamps. He had his hands around the anchor rope. As Gregson watched, he slowly pulled the anchor back up, but the stone weight held – barely – the weight of the boat against the pull of the river.

And Watson threw the anchor at him.

Gregson nearly let go of the pillar in shock. A moment later he caught on: When Ships were becalmed, they forced slow travel by throwing anchors out, and pulled the ship to the anchors. Watson was doing the same thing on a single-person level.

302

Never let it be said the doctor was short on his smarts.

"Hold on, Lestrade." He could feel his lips growing stiff in the cold.

They had to pull Lestrade on board like a stiff plank. He could barely move, and it didn't seem to just be from the effect of the chill water. Gregson waited until he had Watson's word they were both settled before he asked for a hand up. The big man was beginning to lose his grip. His hands were bloodless and blue as his cold allergy sank through his limbs into his nervous system. Watson forced himself to find the strength to pull, and finally both inspectors were gasping in the bottom of the watery boat.

"No sign of him," Gregson panted loudly, shuddering in the cool air against his wet clothing. "He must have found another place to shore up."

"No . . . ." Lestrade's teeth chattered. Watson quickly pulled his coverings tighter, his dark brown eyes black with worry. "I don't think he made it, Gregson . . . ."

In fact, he was certain of it.

There was little more to say after that. One by one the three fell silent, resting their backs against the wood as the boat took them with the current. The sun lightened the dark sky about them. Birds were already out and singing, discordant against the silent quality of the dark.

Watson suddenly sighed. The tips of the dawn curled silvery stripes into his face and hair. He might have been a man carved of metal.

"Are you . . . all right?" Lestrade barely trusted himself to speak.

"Yes." Watson answered slowly, almost in wonder. "I believe I am, Lestrade. Thank you." He looked at his hands and turned them over as if to memorize their patterns.

"My word," he said as if to himself. "I don't understand any of it . . . and yet I could summarize it for you."

"We do that all the time at the Yard," Lestrade's voice cracked on the briny water. "What's . . . what's your summary?"

"*'What doth it profit a man, if he shall gain the whole world . . . .'*" Watson stared into the slip of firmament where the water met the sky.

"*'. . . And lose his own immortal soul,'*" Gregson finished.

They were quiet for a long time. In the distance, men were scrambling for the rescue boats.

"What about you, Lestrade?" Gregson twisted in his seat to look down upon his much-smaller rival. "Got anything similar to say in that tongue of yours?"

Lestrade didn't answer at first. They could see him sifting through possibilities in his mind, patiently seeking one that fit.

"It doesn't make much sense to English ears," he said, "but there is one thing they say."

303

"Well, let's hear it."

"Pelloc'h e vimp marw eged paour."

"What does it mean?"

"'*We will stay longer dead than poor.*'" The small man finally smiled. "You might call it a caution against material profit."

Gregson stuck his bottom lip out slightly as he pondered it. "I think I understand it," he said. "Your people aren't much on padding out the comfort, are you?"

"There's little point," Lestrade admitted wearily. "Comfort's for the end of the day, when the work is done. For the Graveyard Judgment. For the eyes of the world." He was asleep as soon as the sentence finished.

"Hmmph." Gregson tried to sound like he disapproved. "I wish I could fall asleep that easy."

"He is exhausted." Watson smiled. "Best we conserve our strength. Rescue is coming."

Chapter XLIII – Eulogy

"You know, we still need to find the Colonel."

Watson stirred himself to look at Gregson. The man looked dreadful, he thought. But to be fair, he probably didn't look much better. His borrowed clothes weren't a match, and the seams rubbed and chafed against his old wounds.

"And John Clay," Watson added.

"And John Clay."

"I don't know about that."

Gregson looked down at Lestrade. "I thought you were taking a nap."

"Quimper said something . . . I didn't . . . well . . . I had things on my mind. Something about parting ways and not knowing where he was." Lestrade rubbed at his aching head. "There was something about the way he said that . . . ."

"You think Clay is dead?" Watson guessed.

"He smiled when he spoke of Mr. Clay. He doesn't always smile like . . . that."

Gregson mercifully changed the subject. "Here comes our rescue."

Lestrade waited in silence. The London Particular was slowly dissipating against the cool sea air. Sunlight was actually trying to break through. A good omen. Watson was relieved the men had no need to speak. His head rustled with thoughts, most of them in the nature of worrisome questions.

Colonel Moriarty was different from what he understood of his brother the Professor.

It still shook him to think of how he had been so ignorant of that spidery, tall, dangerous, and cold man that had taken Holmes from the world. Perhaps if he had been more vigilant . . . .

But he had put that world behind him – to protect not just himself, but others. Holmes had done the same thing many times – countless times, for the man's energy had created scores of opportunities to mix Law with Justice, and to place them both into his own hands.

The Professor had turned his enmity into a war to the death. Holmes had accepted the unspoken terms of the challenge.

The Colonel was a different man.

Professor Moriarty had to fight to the death because it had taken him too long to conceive of a worthy opponent, capable of bringing him down. Perhaps it was arrogance. Watson suspected the man was unused to failure.

Colonel Moriarty would be prepared for failure . . . he was smarter than his brother in that way . . . He will flee to his own bolt hole . . . one that is out of British Law.

Watson tried, but had no room in his heart for bitterness. For all his corruption, Colonel Moriarty had been the most paranoid man possible for his family's name and reputation. He liked to perform his foul deeds in the darkness, never letting them come to light.

He could not – yet – prove the Colonel's actions in Afghanistan in a way that would not punish the victims' survivors.

But he had won something from Moriarty that the Colonel could never recoup.

After "The Naval Treaty" saw print, "The Final Problem" would follow.

And the world would know.

Colonel Moriarty could flee British Law, but he could not flee British Justice. And he could hide, but he could not live outside the bailiwicks of his own language.

Where men spoke, read, and wrote English, there were copies of *The Strand* to read.

Jonesi and Lords led the way to wool blankets and gallons of hot tea with brandy. Watson smiled to see Lestrade gamely struggle to accept the sweetened brew, but he shuddered as he did so. The three of them resembled rats accidentally washed under the piers.

Small figures were breaking out of the crowd and running to the dock. "*Tad!*" Nicholas, as always, spoke first, even if his brother was the faster. Their mother followed with quite a bit more dignity, but her eyes were shining.

"Stand back, Doctor." Gregson pulled the other man away. "That lot'll trample you like miniature buffalo."

Lestrade was already dropping off the still-settling boat. In seconds he was deluged. Watson felt tears sting his eyes at the sight of inspector's family huddled together, and a ridiculous smile had nailed itself to his face, impossible to remove.

Gregson regarded him silently, perhaps with a little concern for his own loss.

"Thank God." Watson's voice was choked. He yanked his handkerchief out for his eyes and looked away for a moment, wholly overcome. "For a while there, I wondered if *any* of us would make it back." He swallowed hard. "I kept wondering what I would tell his wife . . . or *your* wife . . . if . . . ."

"It's something we do, sir." Gregson gave the other a steadying hand as they left the craft. In the rush of police, well-wishers, and parasitic newspaper reporters, they were easily ignored. "Part of the job. It's one reason why Lestrade avoided marriage as long as he did. But during all that wait, the right woman was waiting for *him*." He grinned suddenly. "Now, as for me, I was *smart*. I married my childhood sweetheart. She knew what I was on about from the beginning. Since I couldn't scare her off, I bought the rings."

Watson heard himself laughing. It felt good. It felt very good. Clea Lestrade was holding on to her husband for all they were both worth, and to hell with what the polite and censorious public said and thought. The foggy lamplight caught the pink glow of her face. Only love could bring that look to a woman's face . . . .

Watson felt his jaw drop. He *recognized* that look.

"Doctor?" Gregson asked. He sounded worried.

"Ah . . . trying to think of too many things at once, Inspector." Watson shook himself.

"John!"

Watson spun in his shock on his bad leg. He would have fallen without Gregson's hand. Colonel Hayter was stamping across the platform, his blackberry eyes gleaming. "John, my boy, d'you have any idea how intolerable these train lines are? I've been waiting *fifteen minutes!*"

"Colonel?" John strangled.

"And then I had to up and follow you – one train line and I suppose three to four streets behind as you went off on another jaunt – all the while wiring Mrs Forrester to let her know what was going on, and that took time as well as a few pence!"

Gregson had heard of the man's exuberance, but never had its pleasure. He instantly saw why Lestrade had difficulties in describing it. He moved away just in time. Hayter looked as though he was about to incorporate him in his embrace as well. Watson gasped as his lungs were compressed inside a band of iron-strong arms.

"I came as soon as I heard," Hayter announced.

"Who . . . who told you?" Watson stared.

"Oh. Inspector Lestrade . . . George? Gasper?"

"Geoffrey." Gregson was enjoying himself muchly. "But you can call him 'Ratty' or 'Ferret'. He doesn't mind."

"Ah, yes. Geoffrey. Like Geoffrey of Monmouth. Geoffrey Chaucer. Don't know why I keep forgetting. He said he thought I might find it interesting that Colonel Moriarty's gang is being destroyed." Despite his ale-flip attitude, the old soldier had tears in his eyes. "By *God*, it's good to see you, son. Come home with me and get your sea legs again."

"Oh, but I couldn't," Watson began.

"Go on." Gregson deliberately clapped him on the back hard enough to propel him deeper into Hayter's clutches. "Reports can wait. Peace of mind can't. We have rank here at the Yard too, you know. A Colonel isn't a man to be ignored."

"Nor is a Major." Lestrade had come up from behind, Martin still hanging off his neck. He was enjoying the sight of Hayter as much as Gregson was. Watson tried to give him a scolding look, but his smile got in the way. "Go on, Doctor. If you stay here, you'll be eaten alive by the reporters."

"Well, we can't have that." Watson laughed. "I am outnumbered, and so I must accept."

Two hours later, John Watson slept.

And he dreamed, for the first time in years, of his days in India.

Because it was a dream, he did not think it strange that Mary would be with him . . . .

It was she, and three of his old friends from the Fusiliers – Wyatt being stationed the longest, and taking the duties of escort seriously. For hours in the dream they wended through the open markets, catching the endless variation of sights, and sounds, and scents. Wyatt was insistent that they not fall victim to the tantalizing odours rising from the vendor stalls, telling them there was "something better" on the other side of the market against the temple.

It was difficult to believe anything could be better than the roasting cashews over the slow flames, or the bright colours of mangoes pressed into juice. But they trusted him on his word, and followed across the living maze despite the rising growl of their stomachs.

At last, while Rogers complained he was about to faint, Wyatt stopped at a large canvas tent painted up to look like something that resembled peacocks, and held open the flap. In the dream, John partially remembered the moment, even though Mary had never been here with him.

But we talked of our days in India, and she said so many times she wished to have known the India I had known . . . .

"Are you hungry now?" Wyatt teased – always a great teaser . . . even when he was about to die from dysentery, he still managed to smile and show fun at something. Where was he now? Do dreams borrow the dead for the sake of the living?

"Come along, then! Feast your eyes on the finest cooking a man can imagine!"

And inside the tent was cool and dim. Plants John did not know – and to this day there were still some he did not know – hung from above and to the sides, discouraging the repellant insects.

308

A tiny charcoal fire burned hot in the corner where the tent brushed into the trunk of a banyan tree. "What will it be, sirs – and gentle lady?"

"We would like your roast lamb, sir!" Wyatt put down the money and pressed it forward on the wooden counter. "Don't spare your tarka!"

"Of course . . . ."

And Watson woke up to find Hayter guiding his old butler into lining up dishes against the wall.

Colonel Hayter was a man of surprises, and it was easy to forget how wily the man could be.

The old man smiled from curled mustache-tip to tip, all dignity and mischief at the same time as he lifted covers off the steaming dishes – confirming that John hadn't lost his mind.

"I thought I was dreaming when I smelled the ajwain," he breathed. "It is so hard to get sometimes . . . we've had to make do with thyme . . . but it isn't the same . . . ."

"You need to eat more," Hayter scolded as he dished out piling portions of green beans spiced with ajwain and ginger. "My new cook has lived throughout most of India . . . What do you think? Shall we see if he can muster up?"

His guest took in the smoking tureen of cauliflower soup, the roast lamb, and broccoli with garlic and mustard. He closed his eyes for a moment, remembering that first meal in India. The cooks made *tarka* by throwing garlic into the oil and browning it. The oil took on the flavour of its spice and married to the meat and vegetables.

There are no words to describe the feeling when a man abruptly discovers he is suddenly living within a hitherto fore unknown dimension. At the first bite of the sabzi and the texture of the flour-fine rice, he'd realised he had stepped inside another realm of experience . . . one whose existence he had barely known.

Holmes had laughed at his dependence on food, but Watson could not attempt to describe that it was the *experience* of food he treasured. But then, Holmes was an aesthetic gourmet, who would go without rather than go down, and Watson was a gourmand, who read countries, climates, crops and even religion into every mouthful.

Mary, Colonial Child, had shared with him the joy of the unexplainable, and with her death he hadn't the desire to eat alone.

"I'd forgotten," he said. "I actually forgot the meals we had in the subcontinent."

But Hayter hadn't. Hayter had kept those memories some place where they hadn't hurt him, and waited for the right moment to bring them out.

"When a memory is painful, John, sometimes the brain takes the whole thing out." Hayter spoke in a self-accusing way, and continued to serve his dishes. "I enjoyed those evenings . . . as I know you did."

"Thank you." John barely spoke above a whisper. It was all he could manage.

"No." Hayter passed a cup of steaming tea rich with cloves. "Thank you."

Morning in London

The Isle of Dogs rested quietly along the Thames' meander, wrapped in a soft mist that easily deceived the eye into peace and calm. Lestrade tugged his muffler closer about his throat and eyed a swoop of gulls balefully as they taunted their wingtips against the water. Rats on the ground and gulls in the air, and here was the Londoner in the middle.

"D'you see anything yet?"

Lestrade did not answer Inspector Youghal just yet. His dark eyes were piercing something very far away, deep into the cloudy water of the receding Thames.

"I'm not certain," he said. "But it won't take long, will it?"

"No. No, that it won't."

The two men stood side by side while the Water Police continued their sharp organisation of the Dredgers and Hookmen.

Youghal saw it. A flutter in the smooth texture of the water. He opened his mouth to say something . . . but something held him back.

It was like walking into a house and finding yourself interrupting a funeral, he thought. Lestrade hadn't slept a wink to judge by his face, and his wife had let him leave the house as soon as he was clean. She was an understanding woman, and that was the truth.

But this . . . Youghal could understand it.

Lestrade was keeping vigil.

The waves lapped, and gently rolled. Something rocked beneath the surface of the water. About them, the rivermen were signaling to the hooks to come.

"Hold it!" Lestrade barked for the first time, and everyone within a quarter-mile seemed to halt at that voice.

"Let it stay there for now," he said in a quieter voice. "I want to see how it happened."

The nodded, and pulled back. The Dredgers were paid the same no matter what.

The rocking form grew in definition. It was dark brown, and the clothing rippled with the water, like seaweed caught on a stick. The feet

310

were hanging down, just like the head and its fading blond hair. The arms were spread gently out from the torso.

"I'm ready," he said.

Youghal nodded and signaled.

The bateau brought them down from the edge to the water itself, and two of Jonesi's men rowed them alongside the body. By this time they could see something of the cause of death.

Lestrade suddenly hopped out of the boat and into the water, giving Youghal a start and making every man present stare without apology. If anyone ought to know by now what was in that river, it would be Lamps.

"Youhgal, where's your pocket knife?"

"Right here . . . you should remember." Youghal joked lightly. "You keep wanting to borrow mine . . . I'll remember that if I get your name on the Christmas List."

"Well, I lost mine on the Isle of Streat a few days ago," Lestrade snapped. He took the proffered blade and leaned into the water almost up to his ear. Youghal grimaced. Lestrade grabbed the floating body with the other hand and made a wrenching tug from somewhere deep. Silt bloomed upward like a flower. The body floated free. Sergeant Lords grabbed the other end and kept it from moving. Youghal gave Lestrade a hand back up and they both made a face at the way the riverbottom plastered at the bottoms of his trousers and shoes.

Youghal knew what Lestrade was about to do, but he had to keep from glancing away as the small man turned the corpse over.

Lestrade never blinked. He was far too used to what the fish did to the drowned . . . starting with the lips and eyelids.

"It's him, surely." Jonesi protested.

"Oh, I never doubted that." Lestrade spoke absently, detached and calm. He turned the floating corpse around like a disk and showed them the leg. "I wanted to find out what killed him."

Jonesi only shook his head, but Youhgal's usual high spirits were dampened. "A branch like that . . . caught in his cuff?"

"He must have panicked," Lestrade mused. "If he'd just . . . leant down and felt with his hands, he would have known it was just a branch . . . he could have ripped himself free."

"But I suppose he just lost his head and kicked."

"I suppose," Lestrade agreed.

"For everyone comes the hour, and the hour comes for the man." Jonesi pulled his cap off for a moment's respect, and just as quickly re-donned it. The wind was fierce against the island.

Lestrade said nothing.

"Well, Lestrade?" Youghal greatly dared. "It's over now . . . isn't it?"

311

"Over?" Lestrade echoed, and looked at Youghal as if he'd quite forgotten about him. "I suppose it is over. For *him*."

Early 1894 – Somewhere in France:

The wooden ox cart ground slowly to a stop, the wheels sinking just a bit further into the fine layer of soft loam over the Roman Road. Too much rain, too much *weather*. The salt panners would have a poor year if this kept up . . . but at least the oyster parks were thriving. The old drover had relatives in both trades.

He waited as the traveller picked his way across the less-soupy parts of the grasslands, and his smiled around the stem of his old pipe. Young people were so impatient, and young men the most of all.

"Where to, young fellow?"

Sherlock Holmes smiled to be called a young fellow. This was his fortieth year on earth. "Montpellier, *mon ami* . . . ."

MX Publishing

MX Publishing is the world's largest specialist Sherlock Holmes publisher, with over six-hundred titles and over two-hundred authors creating the latest in Sherlock Holmes fiction and non-fiction

The catalogue includes several award winning books, and over four-hundred-and-fifty have been converted into audio.

MX Publishing also has one of the largest communities of Holmes fans on Facebook, with regular contributions from dozens of authors.

www.mxpublishing.com

@mxpublishing on Facebook, Twitter, and Instagram

314

www.ingramcontent.com/pod-product-compliance
Lightning Source LLC
Chambersburg PA
CBHW072100020726
47501CB00003B/660